D1050913

Life in Reverse

BETH MICHELE

LIFE IN REVERSE
Copyright @ 2016 by Beth Michele

Cover Design by Sommer Stein, Perfect Pear Creative

Editing by Lea Burn & Dawn McIntyre

Interior Design by Angela McLaurin, Fictional Formats

ISBN-13: 978-1530643622
ISBN-10: 1530643627

No part of this book may be reproduced or transmitted in any form or by any means, electronic or mechanical, including photocopying, recording, or by any information storage and retrieval system, without permission in writing by Beth Michele. Warning: The unauthorized reproduction or distribution of this copyrighted work is illegal. Criminal copyright infringement, including infringement without monetary gain, is investigated by the FBI and is punishable by up to 5 years in federal prison and a fine of $250,000. Please purchase only authorized electronic or print editions and do not participate in or encourage the electronic piracy of copyrighted material. Your support is appreciated.

This is a work of fiction. Names, characters, places and incidents are the product of the author's imagination or are used fictitiously, and any resemblance to any actual persons, living or dead, events, or locales is entirely coincidental.

The author acknowledges the trademarked status and trademark owners of various products referenced in this work of fiction, which have been used without permission. The publication/use of these trademarks is not authorized, associated with, or sponsored by the trademark owner.

All rights reserved.

dedication

For Sherri, Mona, Philly, & Leigh

For summers that are so much a part of who I am

And for both Lenny's

The one I knew well, and the one I never got a chance to know.

And for Erika G.

Happy Birthday.

"She wasn't doing a thing that I could see, except standing there leaning on the balcony railing, holding the universe together."
J.D. Salinger

Life in Reverse

prologue
Vance
One year before...

TO ANYONE ELSE, this day would have looked like absolute perfection. The sun poured down from a sky that was so blue it could have been packaged by freaking Crayola. Tips of lush green trees glistened gold in the light as if they had been touched by the heavens. No denying it made for a pretty picture.

Too bad it was a fucking illusion.

All around me people were smiling, practically skipping into that place like they couldn't wait to get inside. Like there was something wonderful waiting for them beyond that door.

What a *joke*.

Me, I hated coming here—but I wouldn't stop. Yet in that moment, I wished for something—anything that could numb the nagging anxiety that crept into my vital organs. The kind that made my feet stall inches from the door. The desire to flee that...that place was overwhelming. I wouldn't though. Not as long as she was there.

I steeled myself with a big breath that felt stale rising up my throat. My hands were clammy and I shook them out before my fingers curled around the door handle. But then I hesitated—again—like I always did. Another lungful of fresh air, and still it did nothing to push down the knot twisting like a fucking knife in my stomach.

1

Reaching into my pocket with desperation, my thumb found the smooth surface of the stone. Somehow when it touched my skin, a calm entered my veins. It gave me the courage to swallow down that grating of raw emotion and push open the door. Immediately, I was suffocated by the stiff scent with a vengeance.

I'd never been able to describe it accurately. It smelled like my grandmother's house used to at our Sunday dinners. The scent of mothballs, bacteria particles and old blankets invaded the air and I winced, quickly clearing it before someone caught my expression. After all, this was their home. For some of these people, this was the last place they would see before they were buried six feet in the ground. The thought instantly made me sick to my stomach and I grabbed onto the corner of a weathered blue and white plaid sofa to steady myself.

"Hello there, Vance," Mr. Hinkle called out, lowering his newspaper and giving me a flash of salt 'n' pepper hair and a grin. I wondered to myself how he could be so happy—here. I didn't think I could do it. No. I knew for sure I couldn't fucking do it. I'd rather have someone put a bullet to my head than be in a place like this.

I forced a smile so fake it actually hurt. "Hey, Mr. Hinkle, how's it hanging?"

He made a rough sound in his throat. "I'm afraid, son, it's hanging a little lower than I'd like." A chuckle escaped his wrinkled lips and I laughed. As shitty as this place was, he was always in a good mood when I visited and it eased the dull ache in my chest. "One of the nurses just brought your mom back in from physical therapy."

"Thanks Mr. Hinkle."

"Anytime, son. Enjoy your visit," he told me. Again, with that same happiness I couldn't quite wrap my head around. It made me wonder what his drug of choice was. There had to be something. Otherwise how could he stand it?

My shoes walked the walk, heading down the hall and to my left. A path I was so familiar with I could find my way blindfolded. The entire sprint only took a minute but my feet were sluggish in their efforts and it seemed to drag on.

Before I entered Mom's room, I felt around in my pocket for the smooth stone again, clasping it as if it were a lifeline. Prior to her illness, she used to take me to the river frequently and we'd skip stones. It was one of my favorite memories and I would hold onto it as long as I could.

With a shaky breath, I turned the handle and stepped inside, only to be blasted by bright rays of sunshine exploding into the room. The curtains were drawn and she was sitting by the window. Glare from the sunlight casted a warm glow on her wavy brown hair.

"Hey Mom," I greeted. Her head swiveled, the lack of recognition in her gaze coupled with her stoic expression made my heart wither.

"Charles? Is that you?" The corners of her eyes crinkled as she squinted, but then a smile overtook her features. "Charles, where on earth have you been?"

Sadness exited my chest on a ragged exhale. I gave her a kiss on the cheek then pulled up a chair beside her. "No, Mom. It's Vance."

She glared at me with deep blue eyes that resembled mine. "Charles, stop trying to play tricks on me. I'm already mad enough that you didn't come by last night to pick me up for the movie. I got all dressed up and waited by the door." My heart sunk in my chest. Charles is my father but I have no idea what she was referring to—and if this was a real memory or not. "Charles, I'm talking to you. Did you hear me?" She scooped her dark hair over her shoulder and waved a trembling hand, fanning it in front of her face. "Boy, it's awfully warm in here. Would you mind letting some air in, honey?"

"Sure." I leaned forward and cranked the window open. The slight breeze wafted in, carrying with it the smell of freshly cut grass and flowers in bloom. Sitting back down, I fiddled with the rock in my jacket as my teeth gripped my lip repeatedly. "Mom," I said again. My voice cracked as I took her hand in mine. "It's Vance, your son."

"Vance," she whispered as I searched for a flicker of clarity in her eyes. The same one I prayed for every time I came here. The force of my stare willed her to remember the countless times I asked her to read *Where the Wild Things Are*. The secret Saturday trips to get ice cream for breakfast. Sunday morning cinnamon rolls. But all that was gone. When I glanced at her now, there was an emptiness that made my heart crack open. It made me want to crawl onto her lap and shake her until all the memories came spilling out. But then she shook her head as she spoke and all the hope melted in my chest. "Charles. You know we don't have children."

I painted on a smile and took her hand. "Would you like me to read you some poetry?"

"Yes," she replied, her eyes glittering.

I stood up to retrieve a book from the overstuffed shelf next to the small television. My gaze wandered to the various paintings on the walls. Paintings she put her entire soul into, but now had no recollection she was the genius who created them.

Something inside me that was already broken managed to shatter even more. I wondered how God could be so fucking cruel—giving us beautiful memories only to take them away. After all, what are we without them?

Then I glanced up at the ceiling, praying to that same God I cursed that I never had to find out.

chapter one
Ember
Present Day

THE CURRENT IS rough, splashing over the side of the raft. The sheer force of it makes my heart pound as I watch from the edge of the river. It looks like it could toss bodies around as if stirring a soup. Zack is smiling, though. He loves the danger, always has. I glance over at him from a distance. He flashes me one of his goofy grins, sticking his tongue out as if we're twelve years old again. I reach out my hand to him. Though he's too far away, he does the same. We're not touching, but I can somehow feel the small callous on the base of his thumb, the jagged scar along his knuckle from an old scissor cut.

The sound of rustling in the tall trees nearby pulls my gaze away. I blink a few times then return my focus to the river—only to find that the raft is overturned. My eyes frantically scan the water, but there is no sign of Zack and his friends.

And then I scream.

Skin slick with sweat and heart hammering, I bolt up, thrashing around the room as I desperately search for him. When I'm greeted with nothing but the sound of my own heavy breaths, my eyelids flutter open and I become aware that it was a nightmare.

I try to calm my breathing as I sink my head down into the pillow. Maybe it can swallow me up so I can forget. It's been two years and I'm doing better—most of the time. But every now and then it returns when the darkness settles in, bringing that feeling of sheer helplessness right along with it.

One glance at the time tells me I forgot to set my alarm. It's already after nine. Part of me wants to pretend I have a sore throat or a stomach ache to avoid class. But that's not me. That's something Avery would do.

A tap on the shoulder startles me and I nearly jump out of my skin. My mother looks equally startled when I spring up to a sitting position. "Sweetie, I thought I'd better wake you. It's nine fifteen." Her brows pull forward, deep set green eyes holding concern. "Are you okay? You're pale."

I make a lame attempt at a smile. "I'm fine, Mom. Just nervous about my presentation this week." I don't want to tell her about my nightmare because she'll start to worry again. She's doing pretty well and thinks that I've recovered. And I have...I'm pretty sure I have. It's just that every now and then I wake up in a cold sweat, the smell of the river and pine trees sticking to my skin and I can't seem to shake it. But I refuse to burden her with this. I don't want to make her heart any heavier.

She tilts her head and surveys me, pressing her hand to my forehead. "Well, you don't feel as though you have a fever. But maybe you should stay home and rest." Her stare goes to the window for a moment before returning to me. "You haven't been yourself for the last few days. Are you sure everything is okay?"

"I'm good, Mom. Really." Another lie. Another fake smile. "I'll take a quick shower then come down for breakfast."

"Okay, sweetie." Her tone indicates she doesn't necessarily believe me, but she doesn't push the issue as she backs toward the door. "See you downstairs."

I let out a relieved breath then kick off my Mickey Mouse blanket. My gaze flickers around the room to dove grey walls that hold my childhood secrets, not to mention memories and art. The first sculpture I ever attempted, a distorted blue jay, makes me grin. I've come a long way since then. Hanging beneath that is a poster of the Foo Fighters beside a framed picture of Zack and me, and I couldn't possibly be smiling any bigger. Sighing, I look up at the puffy white clouds painted on my faded blue ceiling. For the briefest moment, I feel like I'm floating. My eyes travel back down, falling to my favorite red velvet chair stained with marker. All pointing to my failed childhood attempts at drawing the tree outside my window.

When I was little, I'd come up here and pretend I was going to some far-off land—like in Peter Pan. I'd disappear for hours at a time with my Play-Doh, making imaginary characters in every color of the rainbow. My dad always said I had a brilliant imagination. That he could tell I was going to '*create*' when I was older. I remember asking him what I would create and he'd say '*anything you want.*' Funny how in vagueness there can be so much certainty. My dad is like that a lot.

"You haven't even taken a shower yet!" Avery's voice bursts through my thoughts. "I'm setting the timer! Hurry the hell up. I need you to drop me off at work."

"I heard that," my mother calls up the stairs. "Avery. Mouth."

I smirk and she sticks her tongue out at me. Yup. That's my twin sister, Avery. Twenty-two going on twelve. The only similarity is our green eyes. But that's as far as it goes.

"Be careful, sis, or Mom's going to wash your mouth out with soap."

"Better than winning the goody-goody award," she counters, but her smile is warm. She loves me to pieces, even though she's cornered the market in the obnoxious department. "I'll save you a seat at the table." She winks, then flicks her long blonde hair and saunters off.

I hop off the bed and cross the room to gather up a towel. My mind tries to erase any earlier thoughts and replace them with my upcoming presentation for sculpture class. Being a summer course, I'm not worried about the grade. It's the standing up in front of the class that makes my hands clammy and my pulse race erratically. It's just not my thing and never has been. I'd much rather sit in the back and quietly go unnoticed.

My feet drag as I head down the hall, simply wanting to make it to the bathroom. It doesn't seem like a lot to ask, but inside, it's too much. I pause outside of Zack's room and tell myself I'll go in for a minute—

just enough time for me to feel like I can breathe again. I need this today. I need to be close to him.

I suck in a lungful of air and twist the knob, stepping inside and quickly closing the door behind me. Once I know I'm alone, I let my head loll back against it and release the breath stuck in my chest.

When my nerves calm, I allow my head to drop and my gaze to move around the room. As strange as it sounds, I can still feel him here. I can still see him sitting in the middle of the bed with his eyes closed, earbuds in, listening to Kings of Leon. The way he would pat the spot next to him, then put one of the earbuds in my ears so we could listen together. My eyes land on the worn Portland Trail Blazers hat hanging off a silver hook above his bed. His hair always poked out from the side of that darn cap, and he was forever tugging at it.

Scrawled pencil marks etched into the wall from his growth chart sit untouched beside the closet. The amusement in his expression every time he reached a new height clear in my mind. His laugh settles around me and I close my eyes, wanting to remember all the tiny details. Like how we would hide from Mom in that closet when she was calling us to do chores. All we wanted was to steal a few more minutes. God, what I'd give to have those minutes back.

His room is still filled with life—a life way too short. His adventures line the walls and I shake my head. He may have been tall and skinny, but he was a force to be reckoned with. And he was crazy—in all the best ways. I miss that crazy.

I miss my brother.

Death confuses me. I don't understand why it comes too soon sometimes—why some people live to be ninety while others don't live past twenty. It doesn't seem fair. A tear tumbles down my cheek, but I'm safe here to let it out where no one can know how much it still hurts. I wonder when that hurt will go away—if it will ever go away.

The last photograph ever taken of us still sits on Zack's bedside table. I dragged him to one of those make your own pottery places. He told me he didn't want to go in his dramatic fashion, but in the end, had a great time. I lift the picture, my finger tracing the freckles on his face, the smile curving his mouth. Mom's voice calling me breaks into my memory and I set the photo down and hurry out of the room. I don't want her to know I'm in here, to worry about me. Because I'm fine.

"I'll be down in a sec," I yell out, speeding to the bathroom in hopes of washing everything away. I need a do-over this morning.

Typically, I'd linger in the shower. In fact, Avery's comment is not unwarranted. I'm known for spending an exorbitant amount of time in here. Today, though, I can't afford it. I scrub myself clean as quickly as possible before tossing on a pair of jeans and one of my favorite Mickey Mouse t-shirts. I leave my hair down in loose waves.

I'm just about to head downstairs when I double back and grab the Mickey Mouse charm from my dresser. My father gave it to me for my tenth birthday. I stare at the inscription on the back—*my little creator,* and my chest fills with warmth. My fingers rub over the words before I place it in the zippered pocket of my purse.

"Emberrrrrrrrrr," Avery screams, and I bolt down the stairs.

"I'm here, I'm here. Geez Louise." I loop my purse over the back of the chair and sit down next to Avery. Fabric swatches cover the table and Mom collects them, dropping them in a nearby wicker basket. "Whoa, what is all this?"

She places two glasses of orange juice in front of us. "Those are the colors I'm deciding on for the Kensington remodel. She said she wanted Pottery Barn colors so I'm looking at greens, burgundies, and golds."

"That's so boring, Mom," Avery scoffs, stuffing a piece of bagel into her mouth. "How about black on black?"

"That's called goth, Ave." I snort. "Highly doubt the Kensington's are into that."

She leans closer and cups a hand over my ear. "I'd like to find out what Scott Kensington is into. I can tell you that."

"I heard that, Avery." Mom's tone is stern as she peeks over her shoulder and raises a sharp, black brow. "I'd like you to stay away from those Kensington boys. I hear them all the time when their mother and I are discussing design ideas."

"*Mom*," Avery sneers, because she can't help adding fuel to the fire.

"I'm twenty-two, not fifteen. You kind of don't have a say anymore."

My mother's full body emerges, her arms poised across the jacket of her black suit. Her oval-shaped face set in a scowl. "You're still living in this house for a few more months, so I still have say. And what I say is they have quite the mouths on them." She spins on her heel, wielding what little control she thinks she has left over my sister and disappears into the living room. Avery and I look at each other and bite back a laugh.

"I hope so." Avery mouths with an exaggerated expression.

"Speaking of which...," Mom pops back in and takes a seat across from us at the table, "Mrs. Kensington told me the house down the street and the colonial around the corner sold. I guess she saw moving trucks this morning. Perhaps they might be able to use some of my design magic once they get settled."

"Yes. Maybe you can give them tips on shaping their bushes, too." It takes a second for me to absorb Avery's words, and then I practically spit juice into my cereal bowl. Our mother gives her a one-eyed glare.

"Avery, sometimes I wonder." She smiles, tossing a dishtowel at her face. "I really do."

"So how was work today?"

"Work was...whoa." Avery cocks her head, straight blonde hair hanging over one shoulder as she tries to get a good view of whoever is standing beside the moving truck.

"Avery. You crack me up. You can't see anything from here."

She pinches my arm and snorts. "You know I've got bionic vision when it comes to guys. I can certainly see that whoever that is...has a great ass."

"I'm going to pretend I didn't hear you say that Avery Bennett," our mother chimes in from behind. "I've got a wonderful idea though." She steps in front of us and hands Avery a broom and a smile. "Why don't you finish sweeping the kitchen floor and then you two can make some brownies and bring them over to our new neighbors."

Avery takes the broom, a frown pulling down her lips. "Brownies? Mom, we're not nine years old."

Mom holds the door open, waving a path with her hand. "There's no age limit on welcoming someone to the neighborhood. Let's go smarty pants."

"I can't wait to get out of here," Avery grumbles. "Let me loose in New York City."

"I'll be right in," I call after them, hoping Mom didn't hear her comment. "I'm going to clean up some of this stuff." I bend down to scoop up Mom's gardening tools from the grass, but not before I catch Avery's waggling brows as she disappears into the house.

Navigating my way around the garage is a bit of a challenge. Piles of fabric and design books lay on the floor while Dad's tools litter a countertop covered in sawdust. Bundles of wood from a new project he's working on scatter the ground and it makes me smile. Dad is always dabbling in new ideas, but never manages to finish one thing before he moves on to the next. This last notion shouldn't make me laugh, however, it does. My parents divorced five years ago but remain the best of friends. Because of that, evidence of Dad is still everywhere. Today is Wednesday, and every Wednesday he comes over and has dinner with us. This is aside from the rest of the time we spend with him. I'll admit that it's a strange setup. But it works for them and Avery and I couldn't be happier they've remained close. It used to give us false hope. Now we understand and have settled with it.

I set the pruning tools down on the wooden counter. A picturesque rendering of a new design for our backyard snags my attention. We live in a craftsman-style home in Eastmoreland that, as far as I'm concerned, is already fairly picturesque. My mother, being a visual person, has bushes trimmed to perfect ovals and tulips in every color dotting the brick path surrounding the house. I told her I'd much prefer Mickey Mouse-shaped bushes but she didn't go for it.

Sifting through the dusty maze, I find my way back outside. It really is a beautiful day. The sun shines bright in a cloudless blue sky. It makes me want to get in the car and drive, the wind on my face and freedom within my grasp. I really do know how Avery feels. Still, I worry about Mom.

I lift my arms above my head in a catlike stretch and make my way to the front door, stopping only when I see someone in black running shorts on the sidewalk. He's bent over at the waist and I try not to stare, but muscular calves and a flattering behind give me pause. Asses aren't really my thing, though. That's Avery's department. I much prefer eyes.

Take Exhibit A—the eyes that catch me gawking from a distance. Mortified, my cheeks flame but luckily he's too far away to notice. He waves and I lift my hand to return it, fleeing into the house like Cinderella leaving the ball, sans the glass slippers.

Avery has her ear buds in and she's humming along to, I'm guessing Taylor Swift, as she sweeps the floor and attempts to dance at the same time. I sidle up next to her and pull the white cord from her ear. "You might want to get started on those brownies right away."

"What are you two whispering about?" Mom shuffles into the kitchen carrying a new batch of fabrics. She drops them on the table and tilts her head with interest. "It looks very *conspiratorial*."

"Here are my three favorite girls," Dad calls out as he enters the room, holding a slab of wood and a piece of paper. He's wearing his favorite jean overalls and his dirty blond hair sticks out in all directions. "Who wants to help me build a birdhouse?"

Avery and I burst into laughter and she reads my thoughts when she says, "Dad, you've already got three unfinished ones in the garage."

"*Ahhh*," he lifts a finger in the air, "but this one is very special. It looks like a Chinese pagoda. Lots of areas for the birds to feed. This is the winner right here." He crinkles the paper and his thick sandy eyebrows rise with his smile. "Any takers?"

"Actually," Avery pipes up, "we were just getting ready to make some of those Ghirardelli fudge brownies to take to our new neighbors down the street." She nods her chin at Mom. "Upon Mom's insistence, of course."

Mom returns a knowing smirk and narrows her soft green eyes. "Of course."

"Right. Okay," he answers absentmindedly, reminding me of the nutty professor with his black-rimmed glasses and quirky smile. "Well, maybe I can double back when it's time to paint it, huh Em?"

"Sure, Dad." I give him a thumbs-up. "Hit us up then."

"Whaddya say, Dolores?" He sets the wood down on the center island and plucks a stale doughnut from the box.

"I can't," she responds, distracted by colors and texture. "I have to get these fabrics in order for my client tomorrow."

"All right." Dad sighs dramatically around a cloud of sugar. "I'll just go it alone." He lets out a chuckle and rubs his small potbelly. "See you pretty ladies later." He shoves the rest of the doughnut in his mouth, white powder sticking to his lips. "Oh, and save some brownies for me," he calls over his shoulder on his way to the garage.

I walk to the counter and pour myself a cup of coffee from the Bonavita coffee maker Avery and I bought Mom for her birthday. She had been eyeing it during one of our trips to Williams-Sonoma. It was kind of a win-win for all of us. Both Avery and I are coffee fanatics, except she takes hers black while I like mine with cream, heavy on the sugar. Mom loves making iced coffee while Dad is the odd man out. He is fanatical about tea.

"Anyone for coffee?" I sing out, and Avery peeks over my shoulder as I'm spooning the sweetness into my favorite mug.

"Coffee, yes. I wouldn't call what you're drinking, coffee. Why don't you just eat a pound of sugar and get it over with?" Even though she's correct, it doesn't stop me from flicking her shoulder and sticking my tongue out. I can't be the mature one all the time.

She reaches over my head, pulling ingredients down from the cabinet. "Now let's get started on those brownies. I'm hankering to get a better look at that...," her chin subtly scrapes her shoulder to check for Mom, "ass."

chapter two
Vance

I'M IN A hole. I'm not sure whether I fell in or crawled in at this point. But it doesn't fucking matter. I'm being suffocated by my memory. However, as my lungs tighten and my breathing stalls, I welcome it. Because it terrifies me to forget.

The sound of Dad whistling from the living room makes my jaw stiffen. Of course he's happy. He got a huge finance promotion and a transfer to the Portland office; a perfect location for a short commute and more distance between us and Mom. Then again, maybe that was the whole idea. The thought makes me clench my fists at my sides, gearing up for yet another stand-off with my father.

"Hey, Vance, can you get the rest of the boxes from the lawn?" he calls up the stairs. "I have to run out for a bit."

Not a good time to ask me since I'm seething with hatred for him. I'm not interested in lifting a fucking hand to help. Why should I? I don't understand how he can be so cheerful when Mom is wasting away in that place, her life no longer her own.

I know it doesn't sound like I'm a good person. But when it comes to Mom, all bets are off. I won't tolerate bullshit. Excuses. Tossing the word love around. It may not mean anything to him, but it means everything to me where she's concerned.

"Can't right now, *Dad*. I'm a bit busy." I know he can hear the sarcasm dripping from my voice when I catch his frustrated sigh. Oh well. The door slams and I breathe out my relief as I continue to paint on the wall above my bed. Exhaustion sticks to my limbs when I scan the cardboard boxes filled with books that still need to be shelved. I'm tired as fuck and want to collapse on my bed and sleep it off.

The doorbell rings and Julian yells out, "Hey, Vance. Get that, will ya?"

Paint splatters on my bed frame and I mutter a curse before shouting back. "I'm not living to serve today, get it yourself."

"I like it better when your head is in those books of yours. At least you keep quiet," he utters as he walks by, and I chuckle. As much as we rib each other, Julian is by far my favorite person in this world aside from our mother. Strange as it may seem, I've always looked out for him, though he's a year older than me. He's kind of an easy target. He's just too—nice.

I'm just about done with the last letter when I hear muffled female voices from downstairs. Considering we know absolutely no one here, I have to wonder who it is. Since they're of the female persuasion, I owe it to myself to at least scope out the premises.

I drop the paintbrush in the bucket on my desk and wipe my hands on a nearby towel before hopping off the bed. As I draw closer to the hallway, the smell of chocolate finds its way to my nose and I realize I'm pretty fucking hungry.

The voices are light and airy, friendly, though I'm not interested in making any friends here. This was never my idea to begin with, and the fact that I'm forced to be here pisses me off. Okay, maybe forced is too strong of a word. No one forced me. I'm a big boy. But no one told me it would be this hard to find a job after I graduated college either—especially in technology. It makes no fucking sense after sending out a shitload of resumes and several interviews. Now I wish I'd listened to Julian when he told me to get a part-time job in college to save money—among other things. Why the hell did I assume this whole thing would be easy? I need something to be easy right now.

As I get closer to the stairs, I remain hidden but catch a glimpse of the girls standing next to Julian. One of them is, holy shit, pretty hot; all long legs and big tits, with straight blonde hair and from what I can see, a pretty nice ass. And she seems to know it, too. But it's the Mickey Mouse t-shirt and red Converse sneakers on the girl standing next to her that catch my attention. I almost laugh because it's so ridiculous. But she's cute. Rosy cheeks, wavy brown hair cut to her shoulders, lots of gentle curves—sexy, in a girl next door, unassuming way. She doesn't appear as happy as the other one to be here. Whoever they are, they look like total opposites.

"So you brought brownies," Julian's tone carries, "*and* you're sisters. I like it here already." He chuckles and the blonde laughs. The other one stands there with a half-smile fiddling with what looks like a hair tie between her fingers. Of course they're charmed. Because Julian has been known to charm a girl—or fifty. He's charismatic, and from what I hear girls say, pretty good-looking. I'm his brother so I don't pay much attention to that shit.

He's definitely imposing though. At nearly six one, he has a solid build from all the sports he plays and one of those toothpaste commercial smiles. I watch him drag a hand through his short brown hair as he eyes the quiet one, gunning for some kind of reaction. She's not biting, though.

He turns his head and spots me. I'm about to duck around the corner when he calls my name. "Vance, get down here. We have company."

Shit.

I hesitate a beat, tugging on the hoop in my ear. But his insistent stare causes me to take my ass downstairs even though I'm not in the mood to socialize. "Hey." I nod my chin at the girls. Again, the blonde chick is all smiles and the other one hardly looks at me—until I get closer. Then her gaze does a quick scan of my face, landing on my eyes—and she appears dazed. She snaps out of it quickly when her sister elbows her. Weird.

Julian clears his throat. "I'm Julian...Davenport, that is. And this is my brother, Vance."

The blonde is the one who speaks. No surprise there. "I'm Avery

16

Bennett, and this is Ember. We live at the end of the road on the cul-de-sac." She points out the window. "The blue house with the white shutters and the bushes trimmed in *perfect* circles." Her sister giggles and I don't get the joke, but I do realize it's the first loud sound out of her since she's been here.

Let's see what else I can get out of her. Because I'm in a poking mood.

"Ember? What kind of a name is *that*?" My brother knocks his shoulder against mine but it doesn't dissuade me from my line of questioning.

Bubbly laughter is cut short as she raises a brow and deadpans, "Same kind of a name as Vance, I suppose. But then again," she adds with a flagrant flick of her wrist, "what's in a name?"

I'm not usually at a loss for words, but that gives me pause. She's donned in Mickey Mouse attire and quoting Shakespeare. That's fucking strange.

"Touché," I counter, for lack of anything snarky as her deep green eyes bore into mine and we have some kind of odd, mental standoff. I don't know this freaking girl but I find myself becoming increasingly pissed off for no apparent reason. Then again, it doesn't take much to piss me off these days.

My brother coughs as if he can sense my heightened aggravation. "So who wants a brownie? These smell amazing."

"This is the best time to eat them. They just came out of the oven a few minutes ago," Avery offers as they follow Julian into the kitchen. I stay behind Ember and cackle to myself when I notice the embroidered Mickey Mouse on the back pocket of her jeans. She must've heard me because I'm on the receiving end of a one-eyed glare over her shoulder.

"What?"

"I didn't say anything." Her expression suggests she doesn't believe me but I really don't give a shit. I don't have time for this. "Listen, I need to get back to unpacking. See you guys around."

"Welcome to the neighborhood," Avery yells out as I walk up the stairs, and Ember laughs.

I don't like her.

chapter three
Ember

AVERY LINKS HER elbow with mine and gives me a tug as we make our way back to the house. "Holy shit, those guys are hot. They'll definitely raise the property value around here, don't cha think?" I swear my sister has a one-track mind. It's a wonder she can focus on anything else.

"I guess so. The shorter one seems a bit cocky. Oh, and broody."

"The shorter one?" She teases. "They were both giants." She purposefully bumps into my shoulder. "Anyway, I saw you checking him out."

"No." I shake my head in protest. "He had nice eyes. That's all. Besides, any good looks he had disappeared the moment he opened his mouth. He seems like kind of a jerk."

"A sexy jerk with an earring," she throws in. "Not to mention a great bod." She huffs out a sigh, the heaviness of it hitting me in the stomach as I mentally prepare for what she'll say next. "You have to get back in the game sometime, Em. It's been...a long time since you dated anyone."

"Whatever." I wave her away with my hand, quickly dropping the subject she knows I have no desire to entertain, much less discuss. "I have more important things to think about. Like my presentation for sculpture class. I need to put together the rest of my research and finish writing it."

"Seriously. We're out of college and you still study way too much." We walk up the driveway, greeted by the sound of Dad's drill and the smell of freshly sanded wood.

"And you never studied nearly enough," I counter, extracting my arm from hers to check the mailbox. I flip open the top, then pull out a stack of envelopes and sort through them one at a time.

"Whatcha looking for?" I can feel her taunting eyes on me as I thumb through the letters. "Something from that gallery in New York, perhaps? About that job?"

"No." I glance up and give her a light slap with an envelope. "Well," I smile, "maybe."

"I'm all-knowing, remember? Oh, that reminds me. Dad said he's going to come with us next month to Manhattan when I have my third interview for that Assistant job. He wants to help us look around for places to live," she informs me as we walk inside. "So get ready, because New York City here we come." She gives me her trademark Avery wink then bounds up the stairs, stopping when she reaches the landing. "I'm going to change and help Dad make *another* birdhouse." The sound of her laugh lingers in the air until her door closes.

"Hey, sweetie. How are the new neighbors?" Mom emerges from the dining room with a large portfolio under her arm, wearing another new outfit. This time it's blue dress pants and a crisp white blouse. Her ash brown hair is twisted up in a bun.

"They're interesting." I drop the mail on the side table next to the door. "Not too much else to report."

"Okay. Well, perhaps we can invite them for dinner at some point." She grabs her keys off the hook beside the hall mirror, taking a quick glance at her appearance. "How do I look?"

"Fantastic, Mom. Where are you going?"

"Meeting a potential client. I told your Dad already so you guys go ahead and start dinner without me." Her jacket is lying on the sofa and I pick it up and lay it over her arm.

"Sounds good. See ya later, Mom."

I putter around in the kitchen after she leaves, opening the fridge to check on preparations for tonight's dinner. We're making chicken piccata, and it was my choice because it happens to be my favorite. Mom is an excellent cook and it's one of the things we've inherited from her. Well, more so the baking, but still an *"imperative life skill"* as she often calls it.

With my notebook and index cards in hand, I pour some fresh coffee into my Mickey Mouse mug and dump in a couple of sugars. My iPod is on the kitchen counter and I snag that too along with my ear buds, doing a bit of a juggle until I reach the front porch. I drop everything on the bench swing and take a few sips of coffee before setting my mug down on the ground.

Lost in sculpture terminology, I don't realize someone is standing in front of me until a throat clears. My gaze travels up from a pair of chucks and faded jeans to a face that I'm very surprised to see.

"Hey." Vance leans against the porch railing, one hand stuffed in his pocket, the other holding the brownie pan. "I thought you might want this back."

"Did you now, *Vance*?"

"Okay." The corner of his mouth lifts in a smirk. "I deserve that. I was kind of being a dick before and...I'm...sorry." His distressed attitude coupled with his hesitance tells me he must not apologize often.

I peer around his body before returning to his mildly interesting, and I'll admit, somewhat attractive face. "Did someone put you up to it? Or did you come here of your own volition?"

"Why would you think that?"

"Well...." I tap the pencil against my lips as I survey him. "You don't seem like the apologetic type."

His eyes grow wide in disbelief and I take a moment to study them. I'm trying to determine what color they are—definitely blue, tinged with maybe gray when he snaps. "Seriously? You don't even know me."

"Just a perception." I shrug, then bend down and latch onto the handle of my mug before bringing it to my mouth for a sip.

He eyes the mug and his expression shifts to one of amusement.

"What's with the Mickey Mouse theme?"

"Oh." I smile over the rim of Mickey's head. "I have an unhealthy obsession with Mickey Mouse."

"I didn't know there was such a thing."

"Yeah. It started when I was five and it's gotten progressively worse. Even at twenty-two, I can't seem to shake it. I've tried everything but...." I stop myself when I realize I sound like a babbling idiot. Because that's just something I don't do. He crosses his arms over his chest and my body heats from the conviction in his stare. I brush the feeling off. "Anyway, thanks for bringing the pan but if there isn't anything else, I really need to get back to work."

"What?" He blinks twice and strokes his thumb over his lower lip as if he's having difficulty comprehending my words. "Are you dismissing me?"

"Pretty much," I retort, glancing down at my notes then back to him.

"Well, *shit*." He places the pan down on the bench and scratches his head. Covertly, I watch him walk down the steps, quickly moving my eyes back to the paper when he stops on the sidewalk. "By the way, the answer is my brother."

"The answer?" I drop the card on my lap, racking my brain for whatever question I might have asked. "The answer to what?"

The sarcasm when he speaks is unmistakable. "Who put me up to this." Then he walks away with too much swagger for his own good.

I really don't like him.

chapter four
Vance

"SHE FUCKING DISMISSED me. Can you believe that shit?" I collapse onto the couch, tossing my keys on the coffee table.

Julian rifles through a cardboard box but pauses to meet my annoyed stare. "What do you mean, she dismissed you?"

"I mean exactly that. She *dismissed* me. Told me she was busy." And that's a first. I've never been let go by a girl. If anything, it's always the other way around. Who the fuck does she think she is anyway? "Plus, that whole Mickey Mouse thing. She's twenty-two for fuck's sake." My lips curl into a sneer. "Anyway, she's weird."

"I happen to think she's cute," Julian remarks with a gleam in his eye, and I glare at him. "Actually, they're both cute."

"Whatever."

"She bruise your ego a bit, little brother? Not falling at your feet fast enough?" He chuckles and I lob a pillow at his smug face but he blocks it with his elbow.

"That's rich coming from the Pied Piper of chicks."

He nods his head and smirks as his eyes roll upward in thought. "Pied Piper. I like it."

I grab another pillow and bunch it under my chin. "So...I'm going to head over to see Mom tomorrow after I make those changes to my resume you recommended and apply to a fuckload of jobs. You gonna come with me?"

He drops some pictures in the box, tugging on his lip a few times. "I don't think so. I've only got a few days off from work and I want to make a dent in the unpacking and get my room together. I'll go...another time."

I lean forward, elbows on my knees. "Julian, she wants to see you."

He blows out a weighted breath, frowning. "She doesn't even know who I am, Vance."

"So what does that mean? That's it. You won't even go on the off chance that something might trigger her memory?" I flop back against the couch, tossing the pillow to the side. "Sounds to me like you're running away."

"*You're* talking to *me* about running away? There are a lot of different ways to run, Vance."

My spine stiffens as tension rolls through my shoulders. "Oh yeah, and what does that mean?"

"It means...." He rises from the floor, brushing dust off his knees. "Sticking your head in books and refusing to engage, that's not exactly meeting life head on."

The anger brewing inside of me dictates that I'm done with this conversation, and I push up from the couch. "I need a cigarette."

"You don't smoke."

I push open the screen door with more force than I intended and let it bang shut behind me. "Why not start? There's no time like the present," I mumble under my breath.

It's the only thing I have anyway.

chapter five
Ember

MY LEGS FEEL sluggish today, uncertain. Or maybe I'm the uncertain one. So much change is happening in the next few months; our move to Manhattan, a job, grad school—a whole new life. I'm excited, but also apprehensive, unsure what this next chapter will bring. Knowing that Avery will be by my side, though, gives me that extra boost. It certainly won't be boring. That's for sure.

Every other store I pass in the mall reminds me of how much I dislike shopping, until the scent of warm bread fresh out of the oven fills my nose and distracts me. I turn around to find two girls eating those giant salted pretzels from The Pretzel Shack. Immediately, I'm thrown back to the day I got my driver's license. The first thing I wanted to do was pick up my best friend Troy Buchanan and drive to the mall to get one of those pretzels. I smile a little at that. Freedom is a funny thing.

I walk past a few more shops trying to find this new restaurant that Troy bragged about, stopping to drool over the different types of clay at The Perfect Sculpture. I'm not sure where this new 'Serve Yourself' place is located. I'm also not big on the whole buffet thing. But I am big on seeing Troy, and this is what he wanted to do.

My phone pings and I pull it from the zippered pocket of my purse, grinning when I see a text from him.

Troy: *Hey, Love, be there in 10. Grab some grub and a seat. Oh, Avery is with me.*

I swipe my thumb over the screen and type back.

Me: *Hurry up. I'm hungry.*

Troy: *xo*

Tucking my phone back in my purse, I round the corner. Sure enough, there's a sign pointing to the restaurant followed by an orange awning with the words 'Serve Yourself' in bright green letters. The place is nothing like I expected. Rows of neon picnic tables fill one side, while on the other, various types of food and desserts are shielded behind a half sheet of glass. It reminds me of our dorm cafeteria at Oregon State University, only much cooler.

Slabs of chocolate fudge cake make me reconsider my original thoughts about this place. Nothing like chocolate to lift the spirits. I immediately pick up a tray then fly over and nab the biggest piece with the most frosting. The pasta doesn't look half bad either and I scoop some on my plate before grabbing a drink. Out of nowhere, a long finger makes a mad swipe for the top of my cake and I yank it to the far end of the tray.

"Whoa, Ems. Now *that* is a serious piece of cake," Troy remarks. He's almost as enthusiastic about chocolate as I am. Almost.

"Hands off. Get your own." I smirk and cup my hand around the cake, guarding it with my life.

He bats his long, blond eyelashes and gives me his best lopsided smile. "Not even for me?"

"No." My tone is firm but playful. "Not even for you." He kisses my cheek and I laugh. Sensing a moment of weakness on my part, he reaches for the cake again. "Stop trying to distract me. The answer is still no," I repeat, and he sighs. "So...how was your date with Nick last night?"

He rakes a hand through his straw-colored hair. "That's something we need to discuss over food. The jury's still out. He's hung like there's no tomorrow, but something just wasn't right."

"Oh My God," I shriek. "That is wayyyy too much information."

He winks and traipses off toward the hot dishes, throwing me a glance over his shoulder. "See you at the table, and plan on telling me what's wrong. You can either tell me now or at work later. Your choice."

Crap.

Troy and I have been friends since the first day of second grade when he practically accosted me for my Mickey Mouse pencil. He was adorable with his missing teeth and his big grin that I had no choice but to give it to him—and the rest is history. He lives for making other people smile. Something I can't help doing right now as he balances a tray with one hand and tosses an apple in the air with the other, not a care in the world.

I felt like that, too—before.

I shake my head to try to empty out my thoughts as I wander between the aisles of tables. Avery and Troy wave their arms in the air, gesturing for me to come over when I spot something out of the corner of my eye. Someone sitting alone at the far end of the restaurant.

Vance.

My feet propel me in his direction, almost as if there's an invisible hand on my back guiding me. Troy and Avery yell my name but I ignore them until I find myself standing next to Vance. Heavily engrossed in a book, he shovels spaghetti into his mouth like a caveman, hand gripping the fork while spaghetti hangs from his lips. I clear my throat to announce my presence and it takes him several seconds to realize I'm there. He gives me a sideways glance, flipping the book over on the table to wipe sauce from his mouth with the back of his hand. I peer over his shoulder at the novel but he slides his free arm across the cover.

"What are you reading?"

"What do *you* care?" He spits the words out before returning to his plate of spaghetti. It's actually a very good question. I have no idea.

"Just curious."

He drops the fork onto his plate with a clatter and side eyes me again. "Curiosity kills. Didn't you know that? Besides," he adds, those blue-gray eyes drilling holes through my skull, "how do you even have time to talk to me? One would assume you're too fucking busy. So if you don't mind," he continues after a pause, "I'd actually like to get back to my book."

I glare at him with the same intensity he's giving me. "You know, I don't know you that well and already I don't really like you."

He exhales a laugh, uncaring and bitter. "Well, I guess we're even. Because I don't like you much either. And don't worry about the knowing me part...because you won't." He rattles the words off with such venom I have to wonder where the anger is coming from. But I'm certainly not sticking around and subjecting myself to it.

"Arrgg." I huff out my frustration and stalk over to Troy and Avery.

"Wasn't that a great little lunchtime show," Avery muses with too much enjoyment as I drop my tray on the table.

"He is so annoying." I hook a leg over the bench seat and twist the cap off my Snapple Iced Tea, chugging down my aggravation.

"Yes," Avery replies with a smug grin, talking around a mouthful of apple. "I can see just how annoying he is."

"Okay." Troy steals a look at Vance then leans into the table. "Will someone please tell me what's going on? Because that dude is hot, and annoying turns me on."

"Oh my God." I playfully smack his shoulder then twirl spaghetti onto my fork. "Trust me on this, Troy. That one is hostile. I'd stay as far away as possible."

"Just like you're doing?" Avery counters, and I give her a dirty look as I bring the pasta to my mouth.

"Wait. I'm totally confused. Are you into this guy, Ems? And how do you even know him?" Before I have a chance to answer, Troy stabs at my cake adding, "Because you've gone through quite a dry spell and if you are, I fully support it." The humor in his words is muted by the concern in his eyes. I know he worries about me. But the truth is, I'm okay. The last thing I need in my life right now is a guy. I've got work, my sculpting, Troy, and Avery. That's enough for me.

"No." I drag my cake to the far end of the tray. "I'm not. He and his brother moved in down the street so they're our neighbors now. I was just," I shrug, "Well, I don't know what I was doing."

"That's okay, love." Troy puts a hand on my shoulder. "You don't have to know."

"Well this is a surprise, neighbor." I look up as Julian plops down next to Avery. He has a huge smile on his face and an enthusiastic spark in his hazel eyes. "What's up?"

"And who might you be?" Troy brushes his hair away from his forehead and studies Julian.

Julian sticks his hand out in the middle of the table. "I'm Julian. And you are?"

"Entranced."

Avery and I snort a laugh and Julian's straight nose crinkles in the center. "I don't get the joke."

Troy shakes his offered hand then pulls it away as he finally puts the pieces together. "*Ohhhh*, you're the new neighbor."

"Talking about me already, huh?" Julian winks and a huge grin splits his face. He really is quite charming.

"I'm Troy," he presses his palms together and makes a swinging motion with his arms. "I bat for the other team. It's nice to meet you."

"Yeah. Good to meet you too," Julian responds.

"How come your brother is sitting all by himself?" Avery blurts out, fluttering her eyelashes at Julian. I want to roll my eyes and laugh at the same time. She's so obvious.

The smile disintegrates from his lips almost as quickly as it appeared and he lets out a long sigh. "Vance is, well, kind of a loner." He glances over at his brother. "Hey, Vance," he yells out, gesturing to our table. I turn my head in time to catch Vance smirking and flipping his brother the bird. Julian shakes it off and returns his attention to us. "He's got a lot going on."

I want to ask him what. But I don't. It's obvious that Vance wants to be left alone, and the fact that I'm even analyzing this to begin with is enough to make me push the spaghetti away and go right for the chocolate cake.

"Hey." Troy tries to insert his fork into the fortress I've built around my cake. "I thought you were sharing with me."

I glare at him, a playful narrowing of my eyes. "I don't think so. I need it more than you do."

His chin skims his shoulder as he takes another look at Vance. "Yeah, I kind of think you do."

AVERY AND TROY take off after lunch to peruse the stores. They tried every which way to persuade me to join them, but shopping doesn't hold my interest. I need to be at Anna's for work at three anyway. What I should probably do is dive into my presentation or finish the sculpture I started over the weekend.

Emptying my tray at the far end of the restaurant, I stack it on top of the others when I notice a book left on one of the benches. It doesn't matter that it happens to be close to where Vance was eating his lunch. I look around first as if someone is watching me, before I walk over to check it out. The moment I see the title—*The Sun Also Rises* by Ernest Hemingway—I decide it doesn't belong to Vance. Still, I pick the book up to bring it to the register in case someone comes back for it.

The spine on the novel is cracked and worn, the back cover nearly torn off. In the bottom right hand corner is a name scrawled in barely legible pen. I have to examine it pretty closely before I can make it out. When I do, it surprises me to find that it does, in fact, belong to Vance. He doesn't seem to be the kind of person who would read books like this. I feel awful thinking that, but he doesn't strike me as the literary type. I brush off the thought and stuff the book in my bag, figuring I can drop it off on my way to work.

When I arrive at Vance's house an hour later, the door is wide open. I peer in then knock on the screen a few times. A man who I assume is Vance's Dad, with whiskey-colored hair and a sharp black suit, addresses me.

"Oh, hello...who might you be?"

"I'm Ember. A friend of Vance's?"

Friend is definitely too strong of a word.

I sound as unsure as he appears, standing there as if my words stunned him before he snaps out of it. "Sure, sure. Come on in for a sec." I step inside as he hurries around the living room, scooping up paperwork and his briefcase. Once again I notice the house is incredibly neat; not a pillow out of place nor a speck of dust to be found. It's comfortable, but it doesn't appear lived in, not like our house. There are no pictures on the stark white walls. No indication of their past or who they are. Then again, they did just move in. "Vance isn't here," he supplies. He pulls on the lapels of his suit jacket then straightens his tie in the mirror.

I retrieve the weathered book from my purse and hold it up. "That's okay. He left this at the mall so I only wanted to drop it off."

"Yes." He pauses with a strange expression before heading to the door in a rush. "Would you mind leaving it in his room?" I hesitate and he adds, "Up the stairs. Second door on the right. Just lock up when you leave."

Then he's out the door. Well, that was perfectly odd. It's almost as if he didn't want me to dirty up the room with this book. Plus, he left me standing alone in his house and he doesn't know me. I shrug it off and make my way up the stairs.

Upon reaching Vance's room, the door is partially closed and I suddenly feel as though I'm trespassing—which I guess I am. But I can't deny I'm curious. Vance Davenport peaks my curiosity. Still, I stand in the hall for a full minute before deciding to push the door open and walk through it.

I blink twice, taking in his room and thinking this can't possibly be the same house. Another galaxy, maybe. Walls painted in a serene ocean blue and, unlike the rest of the home, covered in photographs. Not an empty space to be found. On an adjoining wall is a plain oak bed frame and a bed that's clearly been slept in. Above the bed is a quote in white brushstrokes—"*I read like the flame reads the wood.*" It stop me momentarily, because it seems...deep, and unexpected. My eyes move to the third wall where two wooden shelves are crammed with books. Another shelf is stuffed with computer equipment. My mouth falls open. Unable to decide where to go first, the pictures win out.

As I get closer, I discover that many of them are of Vance as a little boy. I only know this because he has that same mussed dark hair and penetrating blue eyes. A woman with those same eyes is crouched next to him—his mother I presume. With flowing dark hair, high cheekbones, and a wide smile, she is the mirror image of her son. There are also several photos of Vance and Julian, the four of them, and many with just his mom. I can't stop staring at the pictures because the resemblance is striking.

While I know I should leave, I bite my lip and glance over my shoulder at the books. There must be hundreds. I walk backwards then turn around until I'm standing in front of them. My fingertip rolls over the spines; Hemingway, F. Scott Fitzgerald, George Orwell, J.R.R. Tolkien, John Steinbeck, Tolstoy, and so on. And on the bottom shelf— Dr. Seuss. I smile when I see *Oh, The Places You'll Go!* My father used to read that to me before bed in his animated fashion.

"What the hell are you doing in here?"

I freeze at the sound of Vance's voice, gnawing on my lip as I slowly turn around with my palms up and an apologetic smile on my face. "Um." I point to the book on his desk. "You left that at the restaurant and I was dropping it off."

He leans against the doorframe, arms crossed over his chest in a defensive posture. "It looks like you were doing a lot more than that."

"I was...." I pause, staring at the carpet before meeting his eyes. "I was admiring your books actually. You read." *Oh my God.* I meant to say it as a statement but it came out like a question. My cheeks warm and I avert my gaze again.

"Yes. You sound surprised." His tone is accusatory, hard. "Did you think I was illiterate?"

"No, not illiterate." I let my eyes reach his face again. "Just not this well-read."

"Judgmental much?" He pushes off the wall and brushes past me to drop a bag on his desk.

"I wasn't trying to judge you," I quickly counter, attempting to deflate the tension flying around us. "I was just being honest."

He puts his hands together in a slow clap and couples it with a bland expression. "Good for fucking you."

"Okaaaay." I huff out a breath and make a beeline for the door. "I'll be going now." His room may be comfortable but nothing about him makes me feel that way.

He mutters a curse before his voice finds me. "Hey."

I look back over my shoulder, one foot out the door. "Yeah?"

He holds the book up, mouth sealed in a flat line. "Thanks," he utters, the word appearing unwelcome on his lips. Unable to reply to his feigned endearment, I focus my gaze straight ahead and bound for the front door.

My mother always says that one of the many things she loves about me is my curious nature. My most popular question growing up was *Why?* followed by fifty questions to explain the why. I know it drove Mom crazy. To her credit, she always took time to answer them, though she probably wanted to pull her hair out.

Right now, that curiosity is making me mad. Or maybe it's Vance's attitude that is making me mad. I can't be sure. But as I push open the door to Anna's pastry shop, all thoughts of Vance evaporate, replaced by the aroma of warm cinnamon sugar and hazelnut espresso. Anna's is known around town for her gooey cinnamon rolls and her coffee, which are to die for.

I started working for Anna about seven years ago. She and my parents are longtime friends from their high school days. When I was younger, I'd hang out here and inhale cinnamon rolls while I watched Anna work. As I got older, I'd assist with clean-up and actually get paid. Plus, she allowed me to help her bake in the kitchen which was by far my favorite part.

"Hey, Ems." Troy greets me as I stow my purse behind the counter. Automatically, my lips lift high onto my cheeks. We've been working together for a couple of years now, since the day I roped him in when he needed extra money and one of our employees quit. He makes me laugh on an almost daily basis, and he's good for my soul. Tugging on the black and white polka-dotted bow tie around his neck, his soft brown eyes blaze with excitement. "So, what do you think?"

"I think...," I angle my head to the side, lips tilting in thought, "it's adorable, but it's not you."

"Agreed." He yanks on one end with his fingers until it loosens, tossing it into a nearby trash can. "I knew I could count on you to tell me the truth. Thanks, love."

"Wait." My head spins around. "What just happened?"

"Your sister happened, that's what." He chuckles, touching his neck like he can breathe again. "You know how pushy she can be. Not to mention the fact that I had to drag her away from those stores so I could get here on time."

"Yeah, I have no idea how anyone can shop that much. But you already know how I feel about *that* topic." I lower an apron down from the hook and tie it around my waist. When I look up at Troy, he's leaning against the register, studying me.

"Spit it out already."

"Okay, okay." I take in a much needed breath. "I dreamt about Zack the other night," I confess, frowning.

"Oh, Ems." He steps closer and wraps his long arms around me. "You miss him, I know. I miss him, too," he whispers, squeezing me tight. His words grow quieter. "It's okay."

"I don't know what brought it on. It's been a while since I've had one." I pull back from his hold and give him a weak smile. "I'm fine, though. Really I am."

He grasps my hand in his, a softness in his eyes. "You don't have to be strong all the time. The world isn't going to think any less of you." He lifts his hand from mine and taps a single finger against my nose. "Not that you care what the world thinks."

We both laugh, right when the doorbell jingles and in walks Vance Davenport. That makes three times I'm surprised today. What is *he* doing here? I duck behind the counter like I'm ten years old and tug on Troy's jean-clad leg.

"Can you handle him?" I whisper. "I'm going to see if Anna needs help."

Troy stares down at me, a gleam in his dark eyes. "That depends. What's in it for me?"

"Troy!" I whisper-shout.

"Okay, okay. Run along. I'll handle the angry man."

With my back to the counter, I casually stand up and walk through the swinging doors that lead to the pastry area. Once they close, I slump against them and let out a sigh that earns me a chuckle from Anna.

"Afternoon, doll. You okay?" she asks over her shoulder as she opens the oven to take out a fresh batch of cinnamon rolls. My stomach rumbles in response, it doesn't care that I had chocolate cake earlier. Anna sets the pan down on the center workspace and shoots me a knowing grin. "Come on over here. You can have a hot cinnamon roll and tell Auntie Anna what's going on."

I slink past the oven and grab a chair. "There's nothing going on and absolutely nothing to talk about. Can I still have the cinnamon roll? Because—"

"Ember," Troy peeks his head in, "that guy you were hiding from, Mr. Hot and Severely Angry, he asked for you."

"Since when do you hide from anyone, Ember?" Anna chimes in, glaring at me. "Nothing to talk about, huh?" She blows her strawberry blonde bangs away from her eyes as I reluctantly yield and hop off the chair, replacing my awkwardness with a metal suit of armor.

I have a feeling I'm going to need it.

chapter six
Vance

IT FUCKING PISSES me off that I'm sitting here. But the reality is, I acted like an asshole earlier and I do have a conscience.

The smell of this place jogs my memory; Sunday mornings and homemade cinnamon rolls, fights between me and Julian over which ones had more icing while driving Mom crazy. Now she doesn't remember it and that makes my heart fucking shrivel inside my chest.

The sound of a plate laid on the table drags me back to the now. I stare up at Ember who doesn't look all that happy to see me. Not that I can fault her for that.

"One cinnamon roll and one hazelnut coffee." Her words are clipped as is her tone. "You asked for me?" A lightbulb goes off in her eyes. "How did you know I was here? Did you follow me?"

"Follow you? No." I pick up the cup, pausing before it reaches my lips. "You didn't spit in this, did you?"

Her nose wrinkles but she's still not smiling. "No. Why would I do that?"

I take a sip then set it down on the table. "Wow. That's really fucking good."

"Anna's is the best." She fists a hand on her hip, still staring me down with those penetrating green eyes. "You didn't answer my question."

"Oh yeah, right." I point around toward the back of her shirt with my index finger. "It says Anna's Pastry so I just used some deductive reasoning and took a shot. Plus," I add, unable to prevent my lips from twitching. "No Mickey Mouse."

Ember lets out a strained laugh. It's obvious she can't tell if I'm being playful or mocking her. I think I'm teasing, but I'm so out of practice from having any normal interaction that it comes out uncertain. The sound of my own chuckle is entirely foreign that for a second I look around nervously and wonder where it's coming from. I don't want to laugh, because I don't want to allow myself that simple pleasure.

"Anna is pretty strict about work attire," she explains. She glances over her shoulder at the line forming in front of the counter, then at the dude behind the register who is watching her like a hawk. "Anyway, I need to get back to work."

"Wait."

She's about three steps away when my voice stops her and she turns around. "Yeah?"

"I wanted to...apologize for earlier."

She cocks her head to the side, eyes probing as if I'm under a microscope. The way she studies me makes me shift in my seat. "Is this an apology of your own volition?" Again, her words make my lips want to crack into a grin. But this time I hold steady.

"Yes."

With a brisk nod of her head, she retorts. "Okay then. Apology for acting like an asshole accepted. See ya." She's nearly to the counter when she pivots on her heel and I end up staring at the side of her face. "I'm sorry, too." Then she spins around and saunters off, reminiscent of a tornado. The way she whirls in and causes all sorts of commotion, then walks away, not realizing the damage she's left behind.

Or maybe that's me.

chapter seven
Ember

I LEFT WORK in a hurry. It was a long day and I'm anxious to take a hot shower and wash the remnants of it from my skin. As I steer Zack's silver Honda into the driveway, I shift the car into park and close my eyes. Fingers curled tightly around the wheel, I drop my head against it, a mountain of exhaustion releasing on a heavy sigh.

Gathering strength to lift myself up, my eyes wander to Dad in the garage and I wonder what he's doing here. He's sitting on the workbench amidst the tools, his shoulders hunched over. My father is rarely in a bad mood and warning bells go off. My stomach drops to the ground as I worry my lip between my teeth.

I leave the bag of cinnamon rolls on the passenger seat and exit the car, heading straight for the garage. "Dad?" He doesn't respond, so I walk over and lay a hand on his shoulder. He startles and practically falls off the bench, his hand going to his chest.

"Oh, honey, I didn't hear you."

Dad rights himself and I take a seat next to him. "What's going on? What's wrong? You're not supposed to be here today."

He places a hand over mine and pats it a few times, giving me a weak smile. "Okay, first of all calm down. Everything's fine." The strain in his voice doesn't reassure me. He exhales and the air around us grows heavy. "Your mom had a difficult day and she needed me." My jaw tenses as my free hand grips the bench, nails digging into the wood. "There was a letter today in the mail addressed to your brother. It was from an old friend of his from high school. Someone...who didn't know he, well," he pauses, tempering the emotion in his throat. "That he'd passed away."

"Oh, *Dad*."

"It hit her particularly hard and we talked about it for a while, but she ended up with a migraine and she's lying down now."

Until my brother died, I didn't know that longing could hurt so much. That it was a physical ache you feel in your bones; the kind of ache that nothing can tranquilize. People used to tell me it would "diminish" over time, but I don't believe that's true. How can losing a piece of yourself be repaired over weeks, months, years? I'll never stop seeing his reflection when I stare at my own. I'll never stop expecting to find him in all the subtle intricacies that made up his life.

"He's been on my mind a lot lately." I wipe the pain that's found its way from my eyes and lay my head on Dad's shoulder. "I wonder...if I make it harder for her sometimes...because I look just like him. Do you find it hard to look at me, Dad?"

"Oh, honey, *no, no, no*." He turns his entire body to face me, his palm coming up to stroke my hair. "Don't ever think that. If anything, you keep him alive." The expression around his mouth softens. "When I see you smile, I see him smile. And when you get those sun freckles on your cheeks it reminds me of how he used to complain about the ones he had," he admits, and relief whooshes out of me over words I didn't realize I needed to hear.

"I loved his freckles."

"Me too. But he hated them. Remember how he always thought it would drive the girls away, because '*who the heck likes freckles?*'" Dad shakes his head then bops my nose. "My son, all right. Thirteen going on seventeen." His laughter lightens the mood and he pats his belly. "What do you think he'd say about this thing I'm sporting now?"

I glance down at his round stomach, my lips quirking up at the corners. "He'd probably say to have another cinnamon roll. You know food was his patronus."

"Ah, yes." A tiny noise sounds from his throat. "And I think patronus was his favorite word." He places his hands on my shoulders, eyes burrowing into mine. "I don't want you to worry about your mother, okay? She's going to be fine. We're going to take a drive by the coast later and maybe grab some dinner. I think the air will do her some good. Do you want to come with?"

"Nah." I kiss my dad then hop off the bench. "I think I'm going to do some sculpting actually."

"Okay, honey. Enjoy." I'm on my way to the side door when he calls my name. I pause with my hand on the knob, darting a glance over my shoulder.

"Yeah?"

The wrinkle in his cheek deepens. "I love you."

"I love you too, Dad."

Inside the house, I don't waste any time. I drop my purse on the kitchen table and open the basement door, taking the stairs down two at a time. The automatic sensor for the lights kicks on as my foot hits the last step.

And then I breathe.

This is my sanctuary. This is where I create. And this is where I escape. I love this space. Many years ago, my dad had the basement finished as a hangout spot for our family and friends. The room is warmed by soft track lighting overhead and plush carpeting below, and divided into two sections. One side boasts a generous L-shaped chocolate brown sofa with pillows in various patterns—matching of course. Pressed cushions where we spent hours lying about listening to music or watching movies. The distressed coffee table in the center holds evidence of spilled drinks and shoe scuffs, the warm tan walls memories of laughter and whispered conversation. Avery's weathered mustard-yellow beanbag chair still sits propped in the corner. It messes up Mom's design scheme but Avery refused to part with it. I think she does it on purpose.

My favorite area though, is the one on the opposite side. A long, rectangular table sits in front of a window looking out at the backyard. To the right of my work area are six shelves Dad built for me, lined with sculptures. A metal closet with sliding doors stands beside them and houses all of my clay—my lifeline. Some people do yoga. Some exercise. This is what I do. It's the only thing that frees me.

I cross to the cabinet and secure a hunk of clay, setting it on the table before swiping the remote for the CD player. The one built into the wall—again, courtesy of Dad. Pressing play, Aerosmith's "Dream On" fills the room, as does Zack lip-syncing it over a hundred times with his fake microphone and lopsided smile. That chestnut brown hair, same as mine, gelled up as he pretended to be some sort of rock God.

I'm glad I have these memories. As much as it hurts sometimes, it's the one thing that still allows me to hold onto pieces of him—to bring him back whenever I want to—even if it's only in my head.

My body won't let me sit. Too much energy flows through my veins. Electricity buzzes its way around my insides, zapping me every time a thought takes shape.

I lean over the table and my fingers curl into the smooth clay, cool to the touch. As I sink my nails deep, I exhale, my feelings already beginning to leave their imprint. Somehow as I pinch and poke this incredible substance, it silences me, allowing me to exist in another world—one where my brother is still by my side.

My fingers continue to find purchase, molding and shaping, and the piece begins to take form. The music is everywhere and it overwhelms me, pounding in my ears, but still unable to block out the intensity of my own heartbeat.

Both hands start to shake. Grief comes out of nowhere and tramples my cheeks. I close my eyes, my vision too blurry to enable me to see. Pretty soon, the tremble in my hands won't allow me to sculpt. I collapse onto the chair, putting my head down between my folded arms.

"Em?"

A hand on my shoulder makes me lift my head, but not before I pat my cheeks and not so gracefully wipe my runny nose.

"Oh, Em." Avery pulls up a seat beside me and draws me in for a hug. She strokes her hand up and down my back, whispering calming words that get lost amidst the noise in my brain.

A few minutes pass before she lets me go but gathers both my hands in hers. Her eyes radiate her love for me and some of her own grief.

"I miss him so much. I can hardly stand it sometimes." My breath gives way to a tiny hiccup. "I want him to mess up my hair in the morning again, or hear him singing at the top of his lungs in the shower. I...." Salt trails over my mouth and I lick the corner of my lips. "I want to look out the window and see him and Dad playing basketball together."

"I know, Em. I miss him, too." She tucks a wayward strand of hair behind my ear. "I also know it's been harder for you because you guys were so close, while he and I...well, we just weren't. I don't know, we always seemed to rub each other the wrong way. Plus, I...," she stares down at the floor, "I wanted that with you. That connection the two of you had." Her gaze climbs to mine. "There were times when I felt like an outsider, when all I wanted was to be on the inside. But...I did love him. I really did." She tries to shrug it off, as always, but I won't have it.

"Oh, Avery. I wish you had told me sooner. And I'm sorry you felt that way. But you have to know he loved you, very much." I put all my energy into a smile that I hope will comfort her. "And *I* love you very much."

She nods her head. That rare display of emotion fading away with her stoic expression, and I find it difficult to say anything else. She gestures with her chin toward my slab of clay. "What was that going to be?"

I lift my shoulders in a shrug. "I have no idea. I've lost my mojo."

A mischievous sparkle lights her eyes. "I know a way you can get it back. Let's do some baking. We'll go shopping and get some ice cream and ingredients to make chocolate chip cookies. Dad is taking Mom out for a while so it'll just be us for dinner anyway."

"Because she had a hard day." I sigh. "I'm worried about her, Ave. She's still so upset and I know she tries to keep herself busy to get through it." I tug at the corner of my lip. "You know how difficult graduation was for her, and now this. Do you think we should wait longer before we move to New York? I don't know." I let out another anxious breath. "Maybe we can suggest she start going to her group again?"

"I hear what you're saying, Em. I do. But...." She places her hand on top of mine, attempting to reassure me with a soft smile. "I don't think us staying longer is going to help her. We've done that and I think for all of our sakes we need to go. She'll find her way just like we need to find ours." I nod, though her words don't comfort me. She bobs her head from side to side and perks up. "So whaddya say? Shall we shop? Actually, let me rephrase that." Pushing her chair back, she pulls me to my feet. "I'm not giving you a choice. We're going."

I heave out my exhaustion with another sigh. "I'm kind of tired, Ave."

"No rest for the wicked." Avery tugs on my arm giving me no choice but to follow her. Especially when she adds, "I'll throw in a box of Bubble Gum Cigarettes if you don't fight me."

She doesn't play fair.

chapter eight
Vance

JULIAN PUSHES THE cart down the aisle as I toss in random shit—Cocoa Puffs, Lucky Charms, microwaveable brownies. From the way he glares at me, apparently he's met his limit. "*No, no,* and *no.* He reaches in and pulls out the brownies and the Lucky Charms. "Microwaveable brownies, Vance? Seriously? And Lucky Charms? *All* sugar."

"And the problem is?"

"I'm not eating that crap. That's the problem." He turns around and grabs a box of Special K cereal from the shelf.

"And I'm not eating *that* crap." I brush past him to nab a box of Frosted Flakes. Holding it up with my brightest smile, I ask him. "Better?"

Julian chuckles, but it's nothing short of sarcastic. "Whatever, Vance. How about you go grab some olive oil so I can sauté some chicken tonight?"

My jaw tightens and I pop the knuckles on my fist. "Where's Dad? Did he go see...Mom?"

"No." He throws three boxes of plain corn flakes into the cart and I cringe. "Dad's got a lot on his plate right now with the promotion. He has to work late this week."

"Of course he does," I mumble as I stalk off.

After searching three aisles for olive oil and still coming up short, I'm about to ask a store clerk for help when I spot Ember and Avery heading toward me. Avery sees me first and gives me a small wave coupled with a huge smile. Ember's attention is elsewhere.

"Hey, Vance. Fancy meeting you here."

Ember glances up when her sister speaks. Her eyes are red-rimmed, cheeks puffy. She doesn't look like herself and something about that doesn't sit right with me. Strangely, I don't like seeing her sad.

"What's up?" I'm staring at Ember when I ask the question, but her posture is slumped and she won't make eye contact with me. Internally, I'm chastising myself. I don't typically want people noticing me, but right now all I want is for her to give me the time of day.

"Not much." My attention goes back to Avery when she responds, "We're just picking up some things for dinner." She angles her head, staring down the aisle. "Be right back. I need to find the basil." Avery walks away and Ember finally gives me her eyes. And, fuck, there is so much sorrow in them. It hits me square in the chest. I've seen that same look in my mother's eyes and it shatters me. I want to do anything to make it disappear.

I hold up my hands, trying to lighten the moment. "I know what you're thinking. But I swear I'm not stalking you."

Her words are empty as is her expression. "I wasn't thinking anything." Then she stares off into space and I've lost her again.

"Hey." I bend down a smidge as she's pretty tall, and try to catch her gaze. "You okay?" I realize how idiotic it sounds the moment the question leaves my mouth. It's obvious she's not even close to being okay.

Her eyes climb to mine, lacking any of the spark I'm accustomed to in the few interactions we've had. "I've had better days."

I'm at a loss of how to respond. I'm used to people trying to pretend they're fine. So while her honesty is refreshing, it throws me off and I say the first thing that pops into my head. "So, uh, I can do a pretty fucking amazing headstand, wanna see?"

A puzzled expression crosses her face as if she doesn't quite understand me. "*What?*"

I shove my left hand in my pocket while my right fiddles with the hoop in my ear. "I don't know, I...I'd do anything to see you smile right now." She glares at me like another life force has taken over my body and I can't say I blame her. I've been nothing short of hostile since we met. But then she surprises the hell out of me.

"Okay. Let's see it."

"Huh?"

"The headstand." Her face is stone cold serious and once again, I'm at a loss. Luckily, Julian and Avery appear and save me from acting like an idiot—having to do a fucking headstand in the middle of the grocery aisle.

"Look who I found roaming the organic chicken section," Avery teases, and Julian chuckles. He's such a sucker for a pretty face it makes me laugh. "I offered up my expertise on free range chicken. So your dinner," she backhands me playfully across the shoulder, "is not only going to be delicious, but very healthy."

Julian points to the Frosted Flakes on top of his healthy food pyramid with a snicker. "That's not really an incentive for Vance."

"My brother's quite the comedian," I offer up, eyeballing Julian while having little effect.

"Hey." Julian snaps his fingers in front of *my* face. "Why don't you both join us for dinner? Vance can vouch that I'm a pretty good cook and it'll give us a chance to get to know each other."

"Maybe some other time."

"That sounds great."

Ember and Avery reply at the same time.

Avery nudges Ember's arm and whispers loud enough for me to hear. "Come on, Em. It'll be good for you to get out."

I'm kind of hoping she says yes. But I certainly won't voice that out loud. At least it would give me a chance to maybe cheer her up and find out why she's so upset. Not that it's any of my business, I remind myself.

"Sure." Ember finally speaks up with the lowest amount of

enthusiasm to a dinner invitation I've ever heard. But my brother makes up for it tenfold.

"Great!"

Julian coerces Avery into helping him get the rest of the ingredients for dinner, and the four of us walk up and down the aisles for a good twenty minutes before we're ready to check out. Periodically, I glance over at Ember, still stoic, looking around at everything yet nothing in particular. I feel the need to give her some sort of an out because this is obviously the last thing she wants to do tonight.

I sidle up next to her and clear my throat. "So...if you're not up for coming over it's totally cool."

She turns her head in my direction, the red around her eyes beginning to fade. "No, it's fine. I mean, all that excitement over free range chicken." She shrugs her shoulders and I think I see a padded smile. "I kind of couldn't pass it up."

"What the fuck is free range chicken anyway?" The answer to my question is a small giggle that bubbles up from her throat, and I catch myself laughing too. Laughter is as alien to me as civil conversation these days. But somehow I find myself doing both with this girl.

WHEN I ENTER the kitchen, an array of vegetables is laid out on the cutting board and Julian stands at the sink filling a large pot with water. He places it on the stove and shoots me a grin over his shoulder. "So you were getting kind of chummy with Ember, huh?"

I hop onto a stool at the center island, snagging a cookie from an open box. "Even your vegetables are organized. Do you realize you have them sectioned off by color?"

"Do *you* realize you're evading my question?" Julian reaches up to the cabinet beside the fridge and takes out a package of pasta. He tears it open then sets it on the counter.

"Actually, I'm not." I smirk before taking a bite of the cookie. "It's just that I'm both fascinated and distracted by your mad skills." After I finish chewing, I add, "For the record, she seemed upset and I just wanted to make sure she was okay."

He's facing the sink and I can't see his expression when he counters with "Hmph."

"What's hmph?"

He spins around, holding a red pepper in one hand and a sharp knife in the other. "Since when do you step outside of your little anger bubble to make sure anyone other than me or Mom is okay?"

"Since...." I hear Jeopardy music playing in my head as I try to think of the answer to his question.

"Exactly. Since never." He waves the knife at me. "So this is a good thing. You're making a friend."

"Next thing I know you'll be filling my Scooby lunchbox with free range chicken." My smug grin disappears behind another bite as the doorbell rings.

"Hey, sue me. I worry about you, little brother." He crosses the kitchen, lobbing a dishtowel at my face that I dodge quite effectively. While I'm not the sports-minded guy that Julian is, I did spend several years in martial arts. I have a black belt to show for it and can block a punch like it's nobody's business. This definitely came in handy when anyone was messing with us. More often than not, it was because some asswipe was making comments about Mom. Anger grazes my chest as I jump down from the stool. I take a minute to shake it off before making my way into the living room. I'm just in time to catch the tail end of Avery's words.

"Yeah, we did. We brought dessert again. It's kind of our thing. Actually," she hikes a thumb toward her sister, "Ember's a bit better at it than I am, but who's comparing?"

"Excellent." Julian holds his arm out to Avery and she links her elbow through his. "This way, lovely. I could use some help in the kitchen." I wait for them to walk away then turn back to Ember.

"Your brother is quite the charmer," Ember remarks, and she looks so much better. Her green eyes are brighter and that frown has disappeared.

"Yes, he is." The sound of Avery's laughter makes me glance toward the kitchen before returning to Ember. "He's been known to attract a girl or two. Julian is...." I twist the hoop in my ear. "You won't find a better person."

Ember studies my face, paying special attention to my eyes. It unsettles me and I clutch the back of my neck. "That's really nice."

"Yeah, well. Just don't tell anyone." I jerk my head toward the sofa. "Have a seat. Do you want a soda or something? I think we've also got lemonade."

"I'm good for now, thanks." She plops down on the couch and I barge into the kitchen to grab a soda from the fridge. Avery is chopping vegetables next to Julian, her shoulders shaking so hard I'm afraid she's going to lop a finger off.

"You guys are a regular comedy show in here." I twist the cap off the Coke, knocking the fridge door closed with my hip. "What gives?"

Avery puts the knife down and uses her sleeve to wipe her eyes. "Julian was telling me about the time you guys went fishing. That you got so mad that nothing was biting, you dove into the water and tried to catch one by hand."

I glare at his back, loading daggers I'm prepared to shoot if he doesn't keep his mouth shut. "Nice. Thanks for that bro. Just remember, payback's a bitch."

"I've heard that," he mumbles without turning to meet my wrath. "Just remember who's feeding you," he reminds me a bit louder this time.

"What's going on in there?" Ember questions as I take a seat across from her in Dad's overpriced black leather chair.

"Julian has decided to fill your sister in on my childhood." I cross my legs at the ankles and balance the soda bottle in the center of my hand. "She must be easily amused."

A softness touches Ember's cheeks and her mouth curves. "You have no idea. Last year we were at the novelty shop in town and she bought some of those Mad Libs we used to do when we were kids. Do you remember those?" And when I nod she continues. "I swear we were doing those things all night and she couldn't stop laughing. And they had to be Star Wars Mad Libs. Her Han Solo infatuation knows no bounds."

"No shit?"

"Yeah. It doesn't take much, but that's one of the things I love about her honestly. We kind of balance each other out that way. At times I can be a bit too serious and she helps me lighten things up."

I try like hell not to grin but it turns into an epic fail. "No, *really*. I hadn't noticed."

She huffs out a grunt. "Isn't that kind of like the pot calling the kettle black?"

And...she's got a point.

"Touché. So...." This is the longest interaction I've had recently with anyone besides my brother. Anxiety curls in my stomach and I scan the room hoping words fall into my lap. I slide my gaze back to hers, waving my hand from left to right. "So...no Mickey paraphernalia today?"

She sweeps her legs under her knees, leaning back against the sofa. "Paraphernalia. That's quite a word. I haven't heard it in a long time."

I take a swig of soda then place it down on the side table. "Remember? I read. So I use big words."

"Oh, right." Her lips turn down in apology at my sarcastic tone. "Sorry about that." She twirls her ponytail, biting down on her lip. "I have a tendency to say whatever is on my mind." Then she lifts her arm and taps a finger against her wrist. "But, yes. Mickey also helps me keep the time." I shake my head in amusement and am about to reply when Avery struts by me looking like the Cheshire cat.

"I know stuff now. *Very* interesting stuff."

Fucking great.

"*Ooohhh*," Ember pipes up with mock enthusiasm. "I want to know stuff, too."

I jump up from the chair before this gets out of hand. "I'm going to grab some CD's."

Thankfully by the time I come back, the focus is off of me and onto more fascinating subjects. I traipse to the other side of the living room and load the player with several CD's. When the sound of Coldplay's

Shiver pours from the speakers, I close my eyes as the music washes over me. Julian brings me back from the dark place I retreat to when I hear this song.

"Do you think we can hear something a bit more upbeat little brother?"

I twist at the waist to meet his stare. "What would you prefer?" I mock. "Taylor Swift?"

Ember lets out a breathy laugh. "What's wrong with Taylor Swift? I'll have you know we've seen her in concert three times."

"Well, that's three times too many then," I scoff, and she laughs again. But Julian's gaze lacks humor. "Fine. Let me see what I can do." I push the button to mix up the CD's when Ember's words freeze me in my tracks.

"I love that painting. It reminds me a lot of the Impressionist era. Who painted it?"

My eyes move to the painting directly to the left of the staircase—the only picture on the otherwise blank walls of our living room—the one I fought with Dad about for hours because I was determined to hang it there. It depicts a single bench in Central Park surrounded by leaves; reds, yellows, oranges. Dabs of bright color that make it come to life. While it's impossible to see due to the abstract nature of the painting, Mom, Julian, and me are sitting on that bench. She painted that after we returned from a visit there. Our faces are no longer recognizable. Her blend of colors and that "blotting" method as she once called it, make us invisible.

That was a good moment. I remember how happy she was; the way she chased us around the park, her laughter following us. The pit in my stomach becomes a cavern. She doesn't smile much anymore. Nor does she paint.

I fight to take breath into my lungs, never mind form a response. She no longer recalls that day. But I can remember it enough for the both of us.

Julian clears his throat. "Our mom painted it." His voice is hoarse although I seem to be the only one who detects it.

"Really?" Ember's face flashes with enthusiasm. "I'd love to talk with her about it."

Julian lifts his chin to meet my gaze. "You can't, because she's—"

"Away," I cut in. "She travels a lot." My face burns bright red from the lie and from Julian's narrowed glare. Regardless, what's going on with Mom is private and isn't anyone else's business.

An uncomfortable silence follows until Ember breaks it and Julian finally takes his eyes off of me. "She's really talented."

"Yeah. She is." Julian casts me a wicked sideways glance before he rises from the sofa and disappears into the kitchen, leaving a trail of dust in his wake. Remorse wraps itself around my gut and squeezes but I'm powerless to do anything about it—not where Mom is concerned.

"Vance?" Still lost in thought, it takes me a second to refocus. I blink a few times and find Ember studying me again, her lips tugged into a frown. "Everything okay?"

"Yeah, yeah. It's cool."

Julian emerges from the kitchen carrying a tray of puffed pastry. It smells fucking amazing but is no doubt organic. It's probably filled with vegetables. The buttery camouflage draws me in and as he passes by I reach out to grab one. He holds the plate away with lingering attitude. "Ladies first."

Avery and Ember waste no time devouring several in the most unladylike fashion imaginable, finger-licking included. Ember peeks up through her lashes and catches me staring, her cheeks turning a soft pink. She shrugs it off on a cough mixed with a laugh. "What? I haven't eaten since lunch."

"Hey," I lift my palms in surrender, "I didn't say anything. All I care is that there are some left for me." I snatch up the last two as Julian walks past me into the kitchen. You know I must be hungry if I'm eating this crap. Aerosmith's "Walk This Way" starts playing and I grin. "Ah. Finally some real music." Ember's smile falls off her face and I wonder what I said to upset her.

"Oh gosh," Avery remarks. "Zack loved Aerosmith."

"Who's Zack? He obviously has very good taste," I mumble around a mouthful of pastry.

Avery swallows and her eyes dart around the room as if she doesn't know what to do. Her head swivels toward Ember who is now staring at a spot on the carpet.

"Our brother," Avery says, but it comes out as a whisper.

Before I can respond or make sense of what's happening, Ember walks away without another word, the screen door slamming shut behind her.

Julian pokes his head out of the kitchen, lifting his chin toward the door. "Where's she going? Dinner's almost ready."

Maybe this dinner wasn't a good idea after all—for any of us.

chapter nine
Ember

I SHOULDN'T HAVE come here. All I want is for this day to be over so I can crawl into bed and forget. Or maybe I can get lost in a dream; the one where Zack latches onto my hand and I pull him from the water, where I'm crying into his soaked body because he's alive. I'm trying hard to keep it together but it's not working today. While it's been two years since his death, there are times when it feels like yesterday, the hole in my chest an open wound that never heals.

I plant myself on the front step, bringing my knees up and hugging them to my chest. My head falls into my hands and I close my eyes, letting the birdsong carry me away. Memories play in my mind like the reel of a film—Zack's bright green eyes that resembled mine, his shaggy brown hair. The way his mouth curved higher on one side than the other. He always thought he was too tall, too skinny, had too many freckles. But he was perfect. He was the best brother a girl could wish for.

The creak of the door disrupts my thoughts but my head is too heavy to move. Avery lets me sit in the quiet, giving me the space I need. When I'm ready to face her, I breathe out a sigh and look to my left, startled to find it's not Avery beside me, but Vance. Without thinking, I blurt out, "I'm not one of those girls who runs off hoping to be followed. I don't need to be rescued."

His hands come up and he leans away. "Whoa, there. I didn't come out here to rescue you. I thought maybe you needed a friend."

"Is that what we are now?" The harshness of my tone startles me and I wince. My stomach twists with emotion and I can't find the control I desperately need to hold myself together. It's as if pieces of me are falling to the ground and I'm scrambling to pick them up before someone actually sees what a mess I am.

A tiny wrinkle creases the space between his eyes. "No, yeah...I mean, I guess."

"Wow." I heave out a small groan. "I've never had someone show this much enthusiasm about my friendship before."

He chuckles, one of his dark eyebrows disappearing under his hair. "You're just so...."

"So...what?"

"You really do say whatever is on your mind, don't you? Honest to a fault, no filter."

I tuck my fist underneath my chin, contemplating his statement. "Yeah. I just think there's already too much filter in the world as it is, and it leads to too many misunderstandings. If people wouldn't mask their feelings all the time, the world would be a better place. There's something to be said for simple honesty."

His expression falls, seeming to cringe at my world philosophy. His eyes shift away then return to me. He opens his mouth as if to say something, then closes it. And for the first time, I see it. He's all hard angles and rough exterior, but vulnerability resides in those clear blue eyes as if they are an open ocean. I get lost for a minute until he pulls me back.

"That's badass."

I blink out of my trance. "What's badass?"

"Well," he makes a sweeping motion up and down my body, "you wear Mickey Mouse like you just don't care and you say whatever you think. You're badass."

My cheeks warm and my lips curve. "Did you just pay me a compliment?"

He bites then releases his lip, scratching at the light coating of stubble on his chin. "Shit. I think I did."

"So maybe we are kind of like...friends now."

"Shit." He extends his hand out between us, a faint smirk turns up one corner of his mouth. "I think maybe we are."

When my hand settles into his, I don't notice any zing. That zap Avery always talks about when she holds hands with a hot guy. But what I do notice is the easy way we fit together. I find myself staring at our palms and how they wrap around one another. It reminds me of two interconnected puzzle pieces.

"What's so fascinating?" Vance asks as he withdraws his hand from mine.

"I was just thinking about puzzles, actually." I link my fingers together in my lap, suddenly needing something to do with my hands. "I've always loved doing them. When my parents were married, every Sunday morning before breakfast while everyone else was asleep, my dad and I would sit down and do a puzzle together. It was kind of our bonding time, and we'd catch up on stuff from during the week. Anyway," I shrug, "I love puzzles."

I'm glad he doesn't ask what made me think of them because it would have sounded odd to explain the hand thing—and now I don't want to ruin my badass reputation.

"So you don't do puzzles anymore?" He leans back on his hands, pinning me with those charcoal blue eyes.

"We do. But since he doesn't live with us now, we do them less frequently. My parents," I shake my head at the absurdity of it all, "are really close and Dad is over quite a bit. Often he spends more time at our house than he does at his own condo. And they're still best friends."

"Wow. That's pretty fucking rare." His expression softens as his eyes move over my features. "Listen...I'm...sorry about your brother." My face must show my surprise because he goes on. "Avery told us that he passed away." I press my lips together to stop myself from crying, but the sympathy in his gaze makes my eyes water. He edges forward and puts his hand on my arm. "We don't have to talk about it if you don't want to. But...." He hesitates only for a beat, resolve forming behind his eyes. "I understand what it's like to lose someone you love. It's devastating. In fact, there's nothing worse." I nod my head then lower it when I feel the tears spill onto my cheeks.

"Hey," his voice is almost a whisper, "you don't have to hide from me. Hell, you don't hide any other time. Why start now?"

Wordlessly, I nod again. And then for some reason, it's not only the tears that come pouring out—it's the pain. "We were triplets...but Zack and I were identical. As in, I was seriously the female version of him." I pick up a tiny stone from the cement, rolling it around in my hand. "We just...we had this connection and I don't even know how to explain it. He knew me better than anyone else. The same way I knew him. I feel like...."

"You feel like what?"

My gaze climbs to meet his. "I feel like a piece of me died, too."

He swallows roughly, his eyes drifting back and forth between mine. "Tell me about that piece of yourself." His next words come out in a gruff tone. "Tell me some things you remember."

My gaze wanders beyond his shoulder to the giant oak tree on the side of the house. "We used to climb trees and pretend we were Jack & Annie in those Magic Tree House stories. Going on adventures, fighting pirates and looking for buried treasure. Avery never wanted to because, well, she didn't want to mess up her hair or her pretty dresses."

"Not you, huh?" he challenges, drawing my attention back to him.

"No. She was always trying to impress the boys, and I didn't care much for them." I finger away the wetness from my cheek. "Zack had these long legs and watching him climb reminded me of a cheetah. It was like he was made for those trees." I stare down at my feet, the crack in my heart seeming like a vast canyon. "God, he was so...stupid." My eyes sting as I shake my head again and again. "Such a stupid, beautiful boy." I try for a breath. Everything about it feels stale. "I just want him back. I want him to come home."

Vance's posture grows stiff, hard. "I know." He doesn't say anything else as we continue to stare at one another, the air filled with a silent struggle. Me, trying to cope with my brother's loss, and him, with...something I can't put my finger on. He raises his other arm and I think he might reach out for me, but he doesn't. Instead, he holds me with his eyes as they dart back and forth between mine, telling me so many things—that he understands, that he's sorry, that he wishes he could change it for me.

It's too much, and the back of my throat burns. I need to do something—anything—so I keep talking. "Sometimes, it hurts too much to remember. I keep expecting to see him when I pass by his room. Or wake up to him crunching cereal at the table. Or hear him yell '*hurry up, squirt*' when I'm taking too much time in the bathroom. Sometimes, I...I think it would be easier if I could just forget."

"Don't say that. You don't want that, trust me." Something sharp slices through his words and catches me off guard. As if he senses this, his tone warms. "I mean, without our memories, what are we? We have nothing. We are nothing. We're...," his Adam's apple bobs in his neck, "alone." He eases forward and plucks a white dandelion from the grass, twirling it between his hands as if he needs a distraction.

"Zack used to say if you make a wish on one of those and blow the petals in the air, your wish would come true."

"My mom," he admits quietly, "she used to say the same thing. Here." He holds the stem out in front of me and I take it between my fingers. "Make a wish."

His stare is intent on my face as I pucker my lips and blow against the feather-light petals. They disperse in the air, the subtle breeze carrying them away. I want to feel like that—light and airy. Free. I close my eyes and inhale through my nose, breathing in the fragrant scent of lilacs surrounding the porch. When I open them again, Vance is still watching me. And somehow I do feel lighter.

"Thank you," I tell him with a half-smile, my cheeks covered in dried tears.

The lines around his mouth soften. "Don't mention it."

"Oh, but I think I will." That earns me more than a slight curve of his lips, and I'll admit, Vance Davenport smiling is a pretty glorious thing.

I might like to see it happen again.

chapter ten
Vance

"SHE LOOKS SO lost today," Julian whispers as we watch Mom doze by the window. The sun paints her face in shadows, her delicate fingers curved against the armrest of the worn leather chair. Her dress is too big for her frail body. It hangs loose around her neck and the sleeves of her arm.

"She's like this a lot now," I counter with a heaviness in my chest. It kills me to come here, and yet, it keeps me alive. "She's alone, Julian. All alone in her head. She can't remember the important things, and pretty soon she might not remember the little things either."

"Yeah."

We sit in silent contemplation for a long time, both in various places in our heads until Julian barges into mine.

"It's like I'm eight years old when I see her and all I can think is that I want my Mommy." He glances from her to me, his eyes reflecting the same gut-wrenching sadness that tears me up every day. "How messed up is that?"

"It's not messed up at all." I rub my palms back and forth over my jeans like I'm trying to start a fire, garner energy. It's useless, though. I'm depleted. "We were lucky. We had a mom who was always there, present, in all the ways that mattered. It's only natural that we want her back."

"But," he swats away a fallen tear, "she's not coming back."

"Don't say that." Though I do, in fact, know how this works. Anger churns and swirls within me, but this isn't the time or the place to let it out. "I won't give up hope, Julian. I can't."

My eyes wander to my mother's face, peaceful in sleep. Premature creases line the corners of her eyes and mouth. Her dark hair is a messy nest over her shoulder, tiny frame swallowed up by the chair. She's so young, but this fucking disease has aged her well beyond her years.

I need to hit something. To bleed for her, the way she bled for us. Abruptly, I push the chair back against the faded tile floor, the screeching sound harsh and loud. She doesn't wake up. And why would she? What does she have to wake up to?

Julian calls for me as I bolt out of the room, needing to find the nearest exit. Mr. Hinkle also yells out and asks if I'm okay. I pay him no mind. I'm a ticking time bomb, ready to explode—right the fuck now.

The brick wall on the back of the building is ready for me, standing its ground when my fist connects with it. It hurts like a son-of-a-bitch but I welcome it—inviting the numbness into my heart, my chest, and ultimately into my life.

I need more.

The sight of blood dripping down my knuckles gives me that extra incentive. I exhale a heavy breath and draw back to pummel it again when my wrist is grabbed from behind.

"Vance. Stop. You don't want to do this."

"The hell I don't. Let me go," I ground out, attempting to yank my arm from Julian's grasp. He latches on tighter and any additional fight is useless. Involvement in sports has always made him fiercer in the muscle department.

"Mom wouldn't want you to do this to yourself," he pleads, playing dirty and using the only weapon he knows will stop me.

"Let me go." I repeat again through clenched teeth.

"Are you going to stop acting like a crazed lunatic?" I give him a stiff nod and he releases me. "Jesus, Vance. Look at your hand."

Blood trickles down my fingers, skin cut up and hanging off my knuckles. Still, it's not enough. Nothing is enough to anesthetize the torment of watching my mother slowly disappear. Hoping beyond all hope that one day when I walk in, there will be some glimmer of recognition. That she'll remember chasing after me on the beach or teaching me how to drive a stick shift, her patience always conquering my impatience.

I brace my arms against the wall, head hanging low. Sweat pours off my brow, trailing past my temple and mixing with the emotion rolling down my cheek. "I can't fucking stand it, Julian. Seeing her like this...it's...it's...." I let out a shaky breath. "It's fucking killing me."

"I know, Vance. I know." He lays a hand on my back, his forehead coming to rest against his hand.

"I'm scared," I finally admit in a voice that no longer sounds like my own. "I'm so fucking scared. I've...been getting headaches."

He wraps his big arm around my chest from behind, hugging me against his frame. "I didn't know...but it doesn't mean that—"

"I need to get out of here," I cut in before he says the words I don't want to hear. "I'll come back when I can pull myself together."

I'M LEANING AGAINST the car as Julian works on my hand. He cleans it with a cotton ball doused in peroxide then wraps it in gauze, all of which came from a first-aid kit in the glove compartment. "No wonder you were the perfect Boy Scout."

"Lucky for you." He smirks. "There." He snips off the gauze with tiny scissors and seals it with medical tape. "It should hold for now. But that was a stupid thing to do. You could've broken your hand. I'm still tempted to demand you go to the emergency room."

"Nah, I'm good." He rounds the car to the driver's side and I hesitate with one hand on the roof. "Hey."

He lifts his head as he pulls the door open. "Yeah?"

"Thanks."

He jerks his chin by way of acknowledgement. "Just consider it payback."

I duck my head and slide onto the seat at the same time he does, my expression serious. "You don't owe me shit. I love you, man." I focus my attention out the window. "Now let's get the fuck out of here."

Julian chuckles and cranks the engine, making a left out of the parking lot and heading toward the interstate. I turn on the radio to drown out my thoughts and distract from the relentless throbbing of my hand. It's not long until we come to a traffic light. He lowers the music, shifting his body toward me. Both hands rest on the steering wheel, his finger tapping relentlessly against it. "I need to ask you something."

"Okay, shoot."

He breathes out a sigh of what appears to be frustration. "Why did you lie the other night?"

I drag a hand through my hair, brows knitting together. "What are you talking about?"

"To Ember. When she asked about Mom and her painting?"

I squeeze my eyes shut briefly, exhaling my own frustration now. "Because I didn't want her to know. Or Avery for that matter. It's...private and we don't really know them that well."

He glances away then back to me. "I understand that. I do. It's just that I think you're doing a disservice to Mom by being dishonest. I don't think she'd want you to hide her like that."

The light turns green and I chew on his words for a while. Of course, Ember's statement reverberates in my head—*'there's something to be said for simple honesty.'* I feel like a fucking asshole all of a sudden. She pours her heart out to me about her brother. And how do I repay the favor? By lying to her about Mom.

Julian veers off the highway to get gas and I hop out of the car. I need junk food. "How much?"

"Just forty bucks."

"Cool. You want anything?"

He steps out of the car and pops the gas cap. "No, I'm good."

The bell jingles inside the small shop and the golden glow of a

Twinkie package catches my eye immediately. It's the last one, and I nab it before anyone else can, then get in line at the register. While I'm waiting, my gaze snags on a plastic snow globe tucked behind a stand of Blow Pops. Sitting inside of it is Mickey Mouse, his big hand waving hello. I huff out a silent laugh, shaking my head before walking over to pick it up. Tiny white flakes fly around his all too happy face. I shake my head again, this time at myself, and place it down on the counter.

"Forty on pump eight." I hand the attendant two twenties then dig in my pocket for three one dollar bills to pay for the Twinkies.

"What took you so long?" Julian questions when I finally make it to the car.

I almost shake my head again but think better of it. I'm turning into one of those bobbleheads at this point.

"Nothing. Let's go."

Within two seconds he spots my Twinkies and gives me the hard side-eye. "They didn't have any trail mix or anything?"

"Trail mix?" I retort with a sour face. "For who? You know I don't eat that shit." He busts out a laugh as he turns on the air, grabbing a CD from the center console. He pushes the button to slide it into the player and Green Day pumps through the speakers. As he shifts into drive and hits the gas, I plaster my hand on top of his.

"Wait."

His head swings my way, foot jamming on the brake. "Wait for what? What's wrong?"

I lift a finger in the air then push open the door. "Hold up. I'll be right back."

"Okaaaay."

I'm chastising myself the entire short walk back into the shop. I pick up the stupid snow globe from behind the damn Blow Pops and slam it down on the counter. The guy behind the register stares at me with a stupid-ass grin that I want to punch right off of his face.

"Mickey Mouse piss you off?" Then he lifts it and views the price underneath. "Pretty hard to resist though, huh?"

"Something like that," I mumble, dropping cash into his hand.

When I jump back in the car, another smug grin awaits me.

"What's this? I didn't know you had a thing for Mickey Mouse." He taps a finger against the side of his head. "Come to think of it, there's only one person I know of who does."

The smile he's sporting is too big for his face, not to mention disconcerting. I lean my head against the glass in silence all the way home, staring at freaking Mickey Mouse and wondering what the hell is happening to me.

chapter eleven
Vance

I WALK UP the steps to Ember's front door, pacing for a full five minutes before I ring the bell. My palms are sweaty and I'm suddenly regretting yesterday's purchase and questioning what I'm doing here. That is— until she opens the door. Her soft brown hair is tousled from sleep, Mickey Mouse pajamas somehow putting me at ease.

"Oh, hey." She rubs one eye with the back of her hand. She doesn't seem bothered by my presence this early in the morning. Which is good, I guess. What strikes me the most is that she doesn't give two shits about the fact that her hair is sticking up, or that she has a tiny spot of drool on the corner of her lip. Something I probably won't point out.

"Hey." I shove the thumb of my injured hand in my back pocket. "Sorry to come by so early. I, uh, just wanted to see, you know...how you were doing from the other night."

Groggy from sleep, it takes her a second to come up to speed with my question. She blinks a few times, shuffling her bare feet on the carpet just inside the door. "I'm better. Thanks."

"Okay, well...that's good. All right," I look over my shoulder, "I guess I'll be going, then."

"What's in the bag?"

Oh right. The bag.

"It's...nothing much." I stare down at the bag and crinkle it a little. "Just something I happened to see, and...pick up for you. It's stupid, really."

She eyes the bag as if she can see inside it. "How about you stop with the disclaimers and let me decide for myself?"

I gnaw on the corner of my lip before lifting the bag and holding it out in front of her. "Right."

As she takes it from my hand, a weird lump forms in my throat and I swallow it down. Her green eyes widen with excitement and for a second she looks—fucking adorable—like a little girl who races down the stairs at Christmas in her Mickey Mouse slippers. The image makes me chuckle to myself, but then I clear it and have to question what the fuck is wrong with me. She pulls the globe out of the bag. I hold my breath as she examines it, head angled to the side until her cheeks curve and she beams.

"I love these." She shakes it, watching with an amused expression as the little white flecks float around inside the plastic. "Honestly, I can't tell you how many times Avery has dragged me shopping and I stop to admire the snow globes, but never buy one for myself. I've never seen a Mickey Mouse one either." She lifts her eyes to mine. "Thank you. That was really thoughtful."

"Yeah, sure." I lower my eyes to the ground, finding it difficult to hold her gaze. "Okay. Well, I'll see ya." As I turn toward the steps, her voice stops me and I whip my head around.

Ember peeks over at the bench then back to me. "Do you want to sit for a bit?" She lifts one shoulder in a shrug. "Since we're friends and all now."

"Sure." I clear a path with my good hand, gesturing for her to go first. "After you, Mickey."

She cracks up as she takes a seat, though her laughter dissolves when she glares at my other hand, her mouth hanging open. "What happened?"

I flex my fingers a few times and while the pain has lessened some, the skin is still fairly raw. "I ran into a wall."

"Really?" She prompts in complete disbelief, placing the globe down on the bench.

"Really. It wouldn't budge so I fucked it up."

Ember breathes out a small laugh, crossing her arms over her chest. "Gee, I've never heard that one before." Then she adds, her stare burning up my face. "Care to tell me the truth now?"

"Not really." Even as I say it, the words don't sound all that convincing. Part of me does want to tell her what happened to relieve the weight that sits on my chest. And maybe so I can breathe for the first time in days. Something stops me though, and instead, I stare out at the bushes lining her front yard. "Those are some seriously fucking perfectly-trimmed bushes."

"Right. It's none of my business. Sorry I pried."

"No, it's not that. I'd just—"

"Rather talk about my perfectly-trimmed bushes." She taps her forehead with the heel of her hand, her rosy cheeks turning crimson. "I can't believe I just said that." Gesturing toward the trees with her chin, she explains. "My mom is an interior designer so all that visual stuff is really important to her. She's really into the whole balance thing."

"That's cool." I cover my injured hand with my good one so she'll stop glancing at it. "And what about you? What are you into?"

She flattens her palm, making circles as if she's wiping a window. "Sculpting."

"Oh yeah?" I shift my body toward her, resting my elbow on the back of the bench. "What do you sculpt?"

"Whatever comes to mind, really. Sometimes it's people's faces. Other times it might be parts of the body or an object. I typically just sit with the clay and get inspired. It's actually really...," her gaze reaches up to the sky, "therapeutic."

I twist my earring around, studying her face. It's a nervous habit that I've never been able to shake. Being around Ember doesn't necessarily make me nervous. It unsettles me somehow. I'm not sure what to make of her. Though I can't deny there is something about her that makes me want to talk, but also makes me feel inadequate. Perhaps it's her brutal honesty. Guilt fastens itself to my chest and tugs hard. I know I need to tell her the truth about Mom, but the words seem to get lost on the way out. Books however, books I can talk about.

"I kind of feel that way about reading." Her green eyes pop with interest and encourage me to continue. "It's more like an escape for me, I think."

She leans back on the arm of the bench, drawing her knees up to her chest and offering me her full attention. "What are you trying to escape from?"

"Life I suppose." I answer honestly, my mind veering off to Mom and my reality. My shoulders stiffen and I roll my neck from left to right to ease the building tension.

"Ah, the dreaded life escape." She presses her lips together on a half-smile. "So what got you into reading?"

"My mom, actually. I'm pretty sure she started reading to me when I was in the womb. Or at least that's what she used to tell me. I remember she'd always ask me to play and I'd say, 'no, read.'" My heart warms and I crack a smile. "Then when I learned how to read, that's all I wanted to do."

"That's awesome. I'm not much of a reader," she offers, winding her fingers down the weathered link chain holding up the swing. "But I can definitely appreciate why people do it. I think I was too into art so I went that way instead. That reminds me...." She hits the flat of her hand on her thigh. "I'd still really like to talk to your mom about her painting, if that's okay." My stomach sinks to the ground and I want to fucking run. "Whenever I meet another artist, there's just something about it. Like we're kindred spirits."

Emotion balls up in my throat, the need to be alone overwhelming. "I should go." I stand abruptly, the swing rocking back from the force. "I've got...stuff to do."

"O-okay." She's probably got whiplash from my sudden mood swing. Her eyes dart between mine—like if she could bypass me and dive into them—she could find the answers. The truth is, I don't have any answers. I wish I did.

She follows me down the steps and to the sidewalk. I should have known she wouldn't let me make a clean getaway. That's not her style.

She stops, fumbling with the edge of her pajama top, her stare unwavering. "Are you all right? Did I say something to upset you?"

I fist a hand on my hip, my next breath coming out louder than I'd intended. "No. You didn't. It's just that I...," another pause, another big breath, "I've got some things I need to work out. But it's not you," I insist. "I...." My fingernails dig into my palms, the effort to smile exhausting. "I like...talking with you."

"Man, that was hard." She nudges my arm with her elbow. Without realizing it, I back up a step and her expression falters.

"What was?"

"Admitting that you like me." The furrow between her brows indicates I might have offended her and I immediately want to set it right.

"Nah." I gesture toward her pajamas with my chin. "What's not to like? I already told you you're a badass." Her mouth pulls up at the side and she seems pleased with my assessment. Hopefully I've made up for my crappy mood swing. I walk away, shooting her what I hope looks like enthusiasm over my shoulder. "See you around, Mickey."

She gives me a brisk wave of her hand. What a sight she is, standing near the road in her Mickey Mouse pajamas with her matted hair. Damn if an honest grin doesn't spread clear across my face.

chapter twelve
Ember

I'M QUIET AS I enter the house, shaking my new snow globe the entire way to my room. My lips still curled as I flick the light switch on the wall and place the globe on the dresser. Hopping on the bed, I stare at the thoughtful gift and ponder Vance Davenport.

He's hiding something. Or maybe it's not so much hiding as it is reluctance to talk about whatever is eating away at him—because *something* is definitely eating away at him. The fixer in me wants to know what it is because I'd like to help. Plus, he made things better for me the other day and it would be nice to return the favor. But I definitely don't want to push him. If and when he's ready to share, he will.

"Ems."

"Oh my God, Troy." I grab at my chest. "You scared the daylights out of me." It takes a second to catch my breath. "How did you get in?"

He plops down next to me, his weight shifting the mattress. "Your mom let me in." He scoots over until our shoulders are touching. "So what are we doing? We are...staring at your dresser?" I snort, and he touches his head to mine. "Hold up. Is that a new addition I see?"

"Yes. In fact it is," I admit in a happy burst that he examines with his big brown eyes.

69

"It's adorable. It reminds me of the time your parents took us all to Disney and our ears popped on the plane. Remember that? You pulled out those Bubble Gum Cigarettes and the girl sitting next to you tried to take them." One side of his mouth quirks up into a nostalgic grin and I smile. "So where exactly did you get that adorable item?"

"A friend."

"*Really?*" He folds his arms over his chest. "The clock's ticking."

"If you must know," I veer away from his intense stare, "Vance Davenport gave it to me."

"Hellooo." He wiggles his fingers in front of my face to bring me back. "First of all, I'm over here. And second, who the heck is that?"

"Mr. Hot and Angry."

His mouth falls open and he drops his head, his expression shaded. "Really?"

"Yup."

"Wow." He flicks the hair away from his eyes. "I got the impression from the way you were acting that he was a real asshole." He scrutinizes me with a click of his tongue. "I guess you were being too judgmental as usual."

"Yeah. I was and I feel bad about it. I don't know. I get the impression," I twirl an unruly lock of hair, "that he has his reasons." Twisting to my right, I sit cross-legged and face him. "Anyway, enough about me. Tell me about that date you went on, with…," I stare up at the ceiling then back to Troy, "…Sam?" The funny expression on his face throws me off. "What? It wasn't Sam?"

"Not exactly," he admits, his hesitance making me probe further.

"Care to elaborate?"

He scrubs his forefinger over his lip, and I can't figure out for the life of me why he's stalling. "It was…Samantha, actually," he finally squeaks out and I stick a finger in my ear in response.

"Come again?"

Troy lets out a long breath and mutters, "It was a girl, Ems."

"*Ooohh.*" And I know he doesn't miss the way my eyes bulge out of my head. He nods, his lips slanted almost as if he can't believe it himself.

"Yeeeaaah. I'm kind of just as stunned as you are."

"Stunned about what?" Avery pops into the room in a t-shirt and shorts, a towel slung over her arm. Troy glances over to me but I remain quiet. This isn't my story to tell.

"I gotta go," he rattles off, giving me a peck on the cheek and dodging Avery on his way out. Now it's Avery who stares at me with a confused expression. I'm about to comment on his hasty departure when his voice carries up the stairs. "I met a girl." The door slams and Avery's mouth is practically level with the carpet.

"So, wait. Does that mean he's bi—"

"What does it matter?" I cut her off, walking over and placing my hands on her shoulders before turning her around toward the hallway and giving her a push. "He's Troy. That's all I care about."

"You're no fun," she mutters as she skulks off to the bathroom, using the same words she did when we were ten and I refused to run around naked in the sprinkler.

"I am too," I yell back, just to act like a ten year old again.

"You are too, what?" Mom traipses into my room carrying a stack of laundry I forgot to bring upstairs. "Good morning by the way."

"Fun," I pout, pausing in front of my dresser, eyes trained on the carpet. "I am fun. Aren't I?"

"Of course you are, sweetie. Are you seriously listening to your sister?" She lifts my chin with her finger. "You know she likes to get under your skin."

"Yeah."

"Oh." Her eyes move to a spot behind me. "You bought a snow globe. Very cute."

I lean my hip against the dresser, staring down at it. "Actually, I didn't. It was a gift."

"From Troy?"

"No." I don't offer up any other explanation and her bright red lips teeter at the edges.

"No, Mom. It was a gift from...." Her voice is teasing, cheeks now in a full-on smile.

"A friend."

I laugh when her face contorts in disappointment. "In other words...mind your own business, Mom."

"I didn't say that," I retort, and she flips a piece of hair behind my shoulder.

"You didn't have to." She turns to the mirror, patting her skin to dab the blush on her cheeks. "It's a nice gift."

"Yes it is. So where are you off to?"

Fully aware of my subject change, she looks back at me and shakes her head. "I have to go see a client this morning. You headed to Anna's?"

I grab a comb from the dresser, threading it through my tangled hair. "Anna's not feeling well and she needs me to meet with a customer about catering a party." I glance out the window then back to Mom. "I thought I'd get an early start and stop at an art store along the way. It's supposed to be a beautiful day."

"Yes it is." She squeezes my arm. "Okay, have a safe drive and I'll see you later."

"See ya, Mom."

MILES AND MILES of blue sky and bright sunshine stretch out before me. There is something about driving on an open road with the windows down and the breeze blowing through my hair that makes me feel alive. The sweet smell of Ponderosa Pine trees is all around me and I lift my shoulders as I inhale. Snow Patrol blares through the speakers, my fingers tapping out a beat against the steering wheel.

My eyes are drawn to Zack's rabbit's foot hanging from the rearview mirror, swaying to and fro in the wind. He and I used to sit on the bleachers behind the high school and talk about driving cross country when we got older. All those plans we made together. Now, he's wandering the world in a different way—without me.

I'm so lost in my head that I have to swerve to miss the black Mustang pulled over on the side of the highway. But I definitely don't miss the middle finger sticking up from the hood as I pass by. I steady the wheel, trying to calm my racing heart while glaring at the idiot in my rearview mirror. Until he turns around with his hands on his hips to glare back—and I discover the idiot is none other than Vance Davenport.

I check for traffic before I make a U-turn and double back to where his car sits on the side of the road. As I get closer, and he recognizes me, the scowl on his face transforms into a smirk. He stares down at the ground for a moment before his eyes climb to mine, carefully watching me as I exit the car. Sweat drips from his temple down to his neck, soaking the top of his t-shirt. Lifting his arm, he wipes it from one side of his face.

"You've been dying to give me the finger since we met, haven't you?" I tease, tossing a water bottle at him. When I see the glimmer in his eye, I realize my words have a double entendre. I dig my teeth into my lip, hard, as though that can somehow erase the red from my cheeks.

"I'm not touching that one with a ten-foot pole." He twists the cap off the bottle and takes a swig before dumping the rest over his head. His hair and shirt are drenched, droplets of water glistening against his skin. It's not a bad look for him.

"That's Fiji water. It's valuable. And you just wasted it."

"Well it's fucking hot out here, Mickey, and I've been sweltering in this heat for a while."

I jerk my chin toward the Mustang. "What's wrong with your car?"

"If I knew, I wouldn't still be standing here." He shakes his head from side to side, spraying water in every direction. "I'm pretty accustomed to messing around with cars but this has me kind of stumped." I walk past him and over to the car, then stare into the open hood. He comes to stand beside me. "You know anything about cars, Mickey?"

"I know how to change a flat tire."

"That would be cake if that were the problem." His cheeks puff up with air and he blows it out, scratching his head.

"So why didn't you call a tow truck?" I cast a blank look in his direction. "Never mind. I know why. You're a guy and you're stubborn."

"Damn straight."

"Well...." I step around him to the side of the car and notice a bouquet of white lilies on the back seat. I wonder for a split second if they're for a girlfriend but decide to mind my own business. "I could give you a lift to wherever you need to go, and then pick you up after I leave Eugene." He averts his gaze then, staring off into the distance for far too long until something weighs in the air besides the unusual humidity. "Vance?"

"Yeah, uh...if you don't mind I'll just tag along and catch a ride home when you're done. He drops the latch of the hood and it comes down with a hard slam. "Let me call a tow truck. It could be a while."

We sit side by side along the curb as we wait. Vance remains quiet and won't meet my eyes. After too much time passes, I can't take it anymore.

"Vance. What's bothering you? I wasn't snooping or anything, but I saw the flowers in the back seat. Is there someone waiting for you? Because honestly, I don't mind taking you wherever you need to go."

His face is like stone when he decides to let me see it, but again, his eyes hold a truth he's unwilling to share. "No. No one is waiting for me."

"Okay." Refusing to push, I let him have the silence he seems to desperately need. At least until we hear the roar of an engine closing in on us.

The driver jumps down from the tow truck and untangles a cluster of chains, hooking them onto the car when I shout at them. "Wait." Both he and Vance swing their heads my way. "Vance, don't you want to get the flowers from the back?"

He stands there for what seems like an eternity, until the driver spurs him into action when he comments that he doesn't have all day. I watch him drag his feet to the door then open it, hesitating again before he swipes the flowers from the seat.

Vance gives the driver information for the service station as well as his identification number for some auto membership that's going to save him a small fortune. I wait for him in the car, doing a quick check of my cell phone to see if I have any messages. Already, I have three texts from Anna with additional details for the customer meeting. The door opens and I drop the phone in my purse.

"So what do you need to do in Eugene?" Vance slides onto the worn leather, reaching behind him to place the flowers on the seat. His actions are almost mechanical; shoulders stiff, features completely rigid. Even his words seem forced.

"Listen." I insert the key into the ignition then twist around until I'm looking into those eyes I haven't quite figured out the color of. "We don't have to talk. You don't need to feel like you have to make conversation with me."

Vance nods on a loud breath as if I just gave him a 'get out of jail free' card. He turns away and gazes out the side window, hands clasped tightly in front of him. I push the button for the radio, not bothering to search for favorite songs, simply needing something to cut the tension thickening the air between us.

A little while later, I'm humming quietly to Pink and getting lost in the music when I hear "*Shit.*" Not more than two seconds go by and Vance says it again. "*Shit.*"

"Vance?"

His voice comes out in short gasps, thin and hoarse. "Can you pull over?"

I steer the car toward the edge of the road. Vance doesn't wait until I shift into park before he escapes out the door. I watch him pace back and forth, hands firm on his hips. My stomach tightens, mind drifting to Zack's funeral and the sight of my mother and father staring at their only son—my brother—bent over that awful box—clutching onto it as if they wanted to crawl inside too. I wanted to make it better for them. But I couldn't even make it better for me. Seeing Vance like this—I *need* to do something. Determination lights a fire in my belly and I push open the door and round the car. "Vance, I want to—"

The words get stuck in my throat when he doubles over, head bowed, one hand braced on the side of the hood and the other hanging limp at his side as he vomits. I run over to him, resting what I hope is a soothing hand on his back and rub in small circles. "It's okay, Vance.

Whatever it is, it's okay."

"No." He shakes his head over and over, still staring at the ground. "Don't you see? It's not okay." He drags a hand over his mouth and straightens, stepping away from me. "I'm sorry."

I leave him briefly and walk to the rear of the car, popping the trunk. A case of water, boxes of tissue and an old tool box fill the carpeted space. I remove another water bottle from the plastic along with some tissue. When I return, he eyes the items in my hand.

"Are you always this prepared?"

"Yes." I pass both over to him. "Courtesy of Zack and my father."

"Thank you." He uncaps the bottle and chugs, letting the water fill his mouth and swishing it around before he spits. As he allows his eyes to find mine again, the festering pain that has lingered there since we met is overwhelming. It nearly makes me stumble back. "I lied to you," he admits in a small voice. And I know there's more. I stay still, fearing that if I move he'll close up again. He shuffles over to a patch of grass beyond the cement highway and faces the horizon. My heart is already breaking for him, for the devastation and sadness he carries like a quiet badge. "My mother...she...she isn't coming back." He stares up at the sky as if it gives him the strength he needs for his confession. "She has a progressive brain disease that affects her coordination and her...memory. She gets confused and doesn't remember things...." His throat works on a hard swallow. "She doesn't remember *me*."

"Oh, Vance." I move toward him but he holds a hand out to the side, stopping me.

"Please. Don't." He's pensive for a bit, his chest rising and falling on several heavy breaths. "I used to see her every day. Now we're several hours away and it's really hard. This whole fucking thing is so damn hard. We were close, you know? I'm a grown man but I feel like a fucking child who wants their mother back."

I realize he doesn't want me to touch him, but I edge closer as if I'm approaching a skittish animal and speak quietly. "I'm sorry."

If Vance hears me, he doesn't acknowledge it, because he keeps talking. "So you see, you can't talk to her about her painting because she doesn't remember she painted it. She doesn't even know that she could paint at one time."

Wetness builds in the corner of my eyes as something inside of me shatters. I think about sculpting—about not remembering something that is so much a part of me. Most of all, I think about Zack. The thought of not being able to remember him makes me physically ill, as do the words I said to Vance about wishing I didn't remember. Now I understand his intense reaction. Being unable to remember. I'm not sure there is anything worse.

"Vance...I'm so, so, sorry."

His head moves up and down and he sniffs. He's trying hard to hold it together. I wonder if he understands how brave he is. "She doesn't deserve this."

"That's where you were going. Wasn't it?" I step in front of him, blocking his view and forcing him to look at me. "Let me take you to her. *Please*."

Defeat crumples his posture as his weary eyes meet mine. He sighs hard. "You don't have to do that."

"Hey." My tone softens. "I want to. I bet she'd love to have those flowers. They're beautiful."

He glances over his shoulder to the car. "They were her favorite."

"Come on." I offer my hand and he stares at it for several long beats. His struggle is palpable and I can't bear it. I allow my hand to fall, letting him off the hook. The sharing of his pain is probably all he can handle at this point.

He follows behind me to the car and we climb inside. "Hey, Ember."

I check my side mirror, easing onto the highway. "Yeah?"

"Thank you."

chapter thirteen
Vance

EXHAUSTION SETTLES INTO my bones. Saying the words aloud to Ember took everything I had. I've never shared that with anyone before. Still, I didn't feel like I could keep it from her. It felt wrong in some way. Maybe because she's so damn honest. Maybe because of her brother. Whatever the reason, the burden is lighter and I feel less alone.

Several minutes into the ride, her calm voice falls onto my ears. "You okay?" I appreciate that she doesn't harass me for information I'm unwilling or not ready to give. She accepts what I have to offer. I find that to be a rare quality.

"Hanging in."

Eventually, she veers off into a service station. As she pulls up to the pump, I reach for my wallet and take out two twenties. I hold them out to her but she pushes them away. "Nope. Don't think so. I'm good."

"I'd like to help pay for gas."

She pats the dashboard three times. "This old baby is great on gas, so don't worry about it. Pushing the door open, she slides out of the car but hangs her head back in. "You want anything inside?"

"Maybe some mints?"

Fifteen minutes later when there is still no sign of her and I'm ready to call out The National Guard, she finally emerges.

"What the hell, Mickey?" I growl through her window as she lifts the pump. "I was getting ready to call the police."

"If you must know," she smiles, "I was browsing."

I gesture toward the small run-down shop. "Browsing? At a gas station?"

"Yes. And you'll be happy I did. Here." She tosses one of those sample size Crest toothpastes and a travel toothbrush onto the seat along with a roll of mints and a package of Twinkies. "They were the only ones that didn't seem stale and I remember Julian said you're into junk food."

"Thanks," I reply, stunned she picked my favorite. "And toothpaste, too?" I lift the tube near my mouth with a strained grin. "Trying to tell me something?"

"*No*. Actually," she clarifies, her expression awkward, "I thought maybe you'd want to clean your mouth, is all. After, you know...."

"I know." I cringe, realizing she saw me hurl all over the highway. "Thanks."

Nothing else is said the remainder of the trip, but it's not uncomfortable. I've wandered back to the hell that is my mind while Ember hums to herself, the music playing softly in the background.

As we get closer, a storm inside me is brewing. Already, sweat builds on my upper lip and my head begins a slow pound that gets worse as we pass each off-ramp. "It's the Winston exit, one hundred nineteen to highway forty two," I choke out, and Ember proceeds to put her blinker on and get in the right hand lane.

I'm not so sure this was a good idea. At least when I'm by myself and I break down, I can do it without any outside witnesses or judgment. Not that I think she would judge me at this point, because I don't think she would. I just don't want anyone else to see me this vulnerable.

"Take a left at the end of the exit and then a right at the first traffic light." I'm on autopilot now as I square my shoulders and exhale a deep breath as if preparing for battle. The illusion of strength is better than the messy reality of shit living inside of me. Besides, someone has to be strong for my mother. My father barely comes here at all. And Julian, well, it's just too hard for him. I want to scream that this is fucking hard for me, too. But I can't stop—because that means I've given up hope. And once that's gone. What's left?

My fingers grip the door handle, knuckles turning red from the exertion. Suddenly, my skin is too tight for my own body. Everything is coming to a head, like an explosion that can't be contained. "My mother has been here for a few years now. It never gets any easier."

The car slows to a stop and I sense Ember's hand moving toward mine on the seat. It never quite makes it and I let out a ragged breath. I'm not sure it's relief. But I do know it's better for me this way.

"I can't begin to imagine how hard this is for you. Do you...," she starts. A thick pause, then she tries again. "I mean...would you like me to come in with you?"

I'm taken aback, and at the same time, there is nothing I wouldn't fucking do to not have to go in there alone. But I don't want her to see my mother like this. And I'm trying like hell for her not to see me.

I look up to find those big green eyes full of concern, and I want to scream *yes* at the top of my lungs. The one word my lips can't seem to form. Instead, I shake my head as I reach for the door handle, glancing back to give her a half-smile. "I appreciate it, though."

My legs are like lead as I walk toward the building. Putting one foot in front of the other is too much effort. My steps slow and instead of going forward, I end up slouched against the cement wall. Sweat breaks out across my neck and under my arms. Rejection of this whole damn situation crawls along my skin like a rash that never goes away. The clock is ticking though, and I know that. It's been six years and while I fucking hate statistics, I can't ignore them.

I try to catch my breath, but it's choppy and jagged. That fucking meditation shit Julian is into would come in handy about now. Not an ounce of me knows how to be calm about this—how to be 'accepting.' My mind grapples with wanting to kick the crap out of anyone who can't make my mother well again.

"Vance." Ember's voice is soft yet firm. "I'm going to come in with you." Her quiet insistence leaves no room for argument. Frankly, I probably need that right now. I'm in no position to dispute her when my body feels like it could crumple to the ground at any moment. "Come on."

A gentle touch on my lower back propels me forward. She opens the door for me and I walk through as I've done hundreds of times before. My resolve is weakening though. That shell of strength cracking. Maybe it was a façade all along.

I catch a glimpse of Mr. Hinkle out of the corner of my eye, but I don't have the wherewithal to do anything except give him a weak wave of my hand. As usual, he has other plans.

"Vance. Who is this pretty young thing you've brought with you today?"

Risking a look at Ember, I'm not surprised to find her cheeks more rosy than normal. She utters a cheerful hello and without hesitation, reaches out her hand to Mr. Hinkle who is grinning from ear to ear.

"I'm Ember. It's nice to meet you."

"Marty Hinkle," he winks, "and the pleasure is all mine." He turns his attention to me. "I'm not sure where you've been hiding this one, but you've made my day so I thank you." His gaze lands on Ember's feet and he slaps his knee. "I loved that little guy growing up." His stare moves beyond us to the window. "My siblings and I used to sit and watch The Mickey Mouse Club while we waited for dinner." His focus returns to us, eyes crinkling at the corners. "Anyway, any friend of Mickey's is a friend of mine. Enjoy your visit."

"Nice meeting you," Ember calls out as we travel down the hallway. "He's lovely," she remarks once we're out of earshot. "Why is he here?"

"Mr. Hinkle, he's...." I keep talking, my body thankful for something to do or it's going to shut down. "He's the youngest of three but his siblings have passed away as have his parents. Being in the wheelchair, he has no one to look after him."

"That's so sad." Her voice is a compassionate whisper and I try to ignore how it softens me in some way, needing to build up strength for what's to come.

Before we enter Mom's room, Ember hands me the flowers I didn't notice she was holding. I walk in first. The curtains are drawn, bright sunlight bouncing off the yellow walls. My mother sits in her chair by the window, as always, but her eyes are elsewhere. She stares at the painting she did of me and Julian when we were ten. A tiny morsel of hope crops up in my chest. It dies off quickly when she shifts in her chair, startled, and faces me with a blank expression.

"Oh, hello. My, what pretty flowers."

The hole in my stomach grows though I smile wide. "Hi Maggie. It's Vance, and this is—"

"Clara?" My mother squints at Ember then blinks. "I can't believe it. It's been...years." The emptiness in her eyes is replaced by a fondness I haven't seen in a long time. I'm about to say something when my mother speaks again. "Come sit by me, Clara." She pats the bed directly beside her chair and Ember sits down. I set the flowers on the table and lean my hip against the wall. Suddenly, it's like I'm an outsider in my own life.

My mom tilts her head, her recently brushed hair resting against her fuzzy pink robe. With her hands intertwined in her lap, she surveys Ember. Warmth wrinkles the corners of her eyes and mouth. In this moment, she appears so young, so innocent. So...not ill, and warmth spreads through my chest. "The dance, right?" Mom stares at Ember and Ember nods. "I was wearing...." She pauses for several minutes, her cheeks lifting and contorting in thought. But then her smile fades and a tear slips from her eye. "I can't...I don't—"

My jaw ticks and I push off from the wall, wanting nothing more than to wrap my arms around my mother—to take away all her suffering—to bring back her memory. Ember's voice stops me cold.

"I remember." She places her youthful hands over Mom's rapidly aging ones. "You were wearing that blue taffeta dress that crinkled as you walked." Ember lets out a small laugh. "You thought it was so loud." She continues as something jolts my heart and I back up, bumping into the wall. "You had your hair in a twist and you were wearing your favorite bright red lipstick that made your eyes pop." My mother nods, a nostalgic smile curving her mouth as she stares down at her lap. "You looked so beautiful, and when you were dancing, no one could take their eyes off of you." My mother's smile grows as she holds onto Ember's every word. "You're still beautiful, Maggie."

A tear spills from my eye and runs down my cheek. I don't bother trying to push it away. I wonder who this girl is. If somehow she's an angel that's been sent here—which is crazy-thinking for someone like me. Yet a bandage rests over a sliver of my heart, seeing the joy on my mother's face. Even if it is from a made-up memory. It's something she can hold on to. Even though it only brings her joy in this moment, and in the next it's forgotten.

My mother coughs then clears her throat, lifting her gaze to mine. "Would you mind getting me some water?"

"Sure."

I leave for a minute and come back with a cup of water to a room filled with laughter. The kind where old friends share secrets of days gone by. It stops me again, because I can't remember the last time I heard my mom laugh. I wish I could bottle that sound for later, when the silence is too much to bear.

Ember turns her head and our eyes meet. Hers are teeming with a hundred smiles and I only hope mine convey my absolute gratitude for what she's doing for my mother.

When their laughter settles down, I sit on the bed next to Ember. "Would you like me to read you some poetry, Maggie?"

"Yes. That would be wonderful."

For the next hour, I read from one of her favorite poetry books—a collection by E.E. Cummings. When my voice gets hoarse, Ember takes over and reads to Mom until she yawns and her eyelids become heavy. Ember glances over to me as she closes the book. I stand up and she follows suit. "We should probably go and let you get some rest now."

"Yes, I am feeling very tired. I'd like to close my eyes for a bit."

I lean down to kiss her cheek and Ember surprises me when she bends to give my mother a hug.

"It was great to see you, Maggie." She straightens and my mother grabs her hand, embracing it between her own.

"Please come again soon, Clara." She looks from Ember to me. "I'm sorry. What did you say your name was?"

I swallow down the hurt that threatens to surface. "It's Vance."

"So long, Vance."

Every time I leave here, I'm numb. Hollow. Not today. Today, I got to see my mother experience joy. I got to hear her laugh. Ember did that.

As we reach the car, the air around me is suddenly too thick, making it impossible to breathe. I latch onto the door handle for support, fighting tooth and nail against the tear that ultimately tracks down my cheek. Before I realize what's happening, slender arms surround my neck. My hands drop to my sides and I freeze.

"It's okay," Ember whispers, laying her head against my chest. A rush of breath leaves me and I give in, wrapping my arms around her waist. "I'm sorry, Vance," she soothes, and all I can do is nod against her hair. She smells like peaches and feels like the comfort I desperately need right now. I allow myself a minute to get lost before I abruptly pull away.

"We should get going."

Fumbling with her hands in front of her, she gives me a curt reply. "Yeah, sure."

I wait for her to get in and start the car, then angle my entire body to face her. "Listen, what you did in there...thank you."

A lock of hair falls over her shoulder as she turns toward me. "For what?"

"For being her memory."

"It was nothing." Her nonchalant answer infuriates me. She has no idea how much more than '*nothing*' it really was.

"No," I retort, determined. I refuse to let this go. I'm not sure I've felt this strongly about anything in a long time. "It was everything, Ember." I hesitate for a minute and look away. I'm not used to talking about this so earnestly. "I haven't seen her smile or heard her laugh like that in a very long time." I turn back to Ember. "*You* did that."

Her gaze meets mine, and all at once I'm naked to the intensity of her stare. I pull on my earring, desperate to find an escape. "She's wonderful, Vance. And you look just like her. The hair color, the eyes. Even your smile. When you *decide* to smile."

Self-consciousness causes me to rub at my chin. "Well, you definitely made me smile today."

She revs the engine, cutting the wheel to the right and exiting the parking lot. "Maybe I'll see if I can go two for two," she replies, and her belly follows with a loud rumble. One hand on the wheel, she places the other on her stomach. "Wow, um, I guess I'm hungry."

"Good. I know just how I can repay you then. There's a diner only a few blocks from here."

She pauses at a blinking yellow light and lets a car pass. "Ooooh. I love diner food. I hope they have those curled up fries."

Something about the innocence in her phrasing coupled with her excitement makes me laugh. "You mean, curly fries?"

"Yes, those."

I yank the wallet from my back pocket to check for my credit card. "Yup. They've got them." And you'd think someone just handed her the world—her smile is that big.

It reminds me of the sun.

chapter fourteen
Ember

I HOPE MY smile masks the commotion inside my chest. I can't let on how much my heart aches right now. Vance's mom asking his name earlier almost made me break down. He's trying to be strong though, and I want to be strong for him.

The diner is packed when we arrive and I have to make two passes around before we find a space. I unclick my belt and hop out of the car, meeting Vance on the other side. My stomach grumbles in protest about wanting food again and I'm about to comment when I happen to glance up at a nearby tree. I stop walking and unzip my purse to grab my iPhone. Vance turns back when he realizes I'm no longer beside him.

"What are you doing?"

I point a finger toward the highest branch. "Look at that."

"Yes, I see. It's a tree."

I elbow him playfully. "Yes. I *know* it's a tree. But look higher up, almost at the top."

He chuckles. "Those are called branches, Mickey."

I glare at him, still using my arm as a pointer. "There are four blue jays up there. And I love birds so I'm taking a picture."

"Mmkay."

While clicking several pictures from a few different angles, I catch Vance staring at me. "*What?*"

"I didn't say anything. Come on." He teases. "Let's go eat before your stomach embarrasses us." Then I pause again, cognizant of the fact that it's been a while since I've stopped to notice my surroundings. "What now?" he asks, and I brush it off with a shake of my head.

The hostess leads us to the last available booth then drops menus on the table. Being faced with six pages of options, it takes me time to decide. I eye Vance over the page. He's not looking at the choices but fixated on something beyond the window.

"You already know what you want?"

His focus remains elsewhere. "Yeah."

"Are you okay?"

His cloudy blue gaze finally makes contact with mine. "Can I ask you something?"

I put down my menu. "Sure. Anything."

"How did you do that back there?" My face must show my confusion because he immediately clarifies. "With my mother?"

"Oh." I'm about to reply further when the waitress, an older woman with a grey bun and deep red lipstick steps up to the table. She pulls the pencil from behind her ear as she chomps on a piece of gum. "What can I get you two?"

"I'll have a turkey burger with mushrooms and onions, and a side order of curly fries, please."

"Anything to drink sweet young thing?"

I look back at the menu, smiling at the description and her subtle accent. "Just a water with lemon, thanks."

She gestures to Vance with her pencil. "What about you, hon?"

"I'll have a large order of pancakes with extra butter, a side order of bacon and sausage, and one of those glazed doughnuts in the glass case...and a Coke. Please."

"You got it." The waitress picks up the menus, her glance darting between us. "You two are awfully cute together," she comments as she walks off toward the kitchen.

"We're not together," I yell out, and from the way Vance's face twists I think I might have offended him. "No offense," I quickly add. "I just don't like people making incorrect assumptions about me."

He grimaces, heaving his arms over his chest. "You mean much like you did with me?"

"Right." I bow my head, both in apology and to hide my red cheeks. "I'm sorry about that."

"I'm just razzing you. Take it easy there, Mickey."

"Oh." I lift up and he shoots me a half-smile. The waitress shows up with our drinks and I wait until she walks away. "So you were asking about your mom?"

"Yeah." His expression shifts, now stamped with severity and he leans against the booth.

I do the opposite and edge forward, placing my elbows on the table. "I don't know. I reacted, I guess. I saw her struggling with the memory and wanted to take away her pain in that moment. I wanted to make it happy for her."

Vance nods. Of course he understands. "I just...I haven't been able to make her smile like that in so long." His chin lowers. "Sometimes...a lot of times, I don't know what to say or do. It's...I never know what the right thing is...and I used to know. Before she got sick. I always knew."

Something inside of me demands I reach out for him—his hand, his finger, anything. But I know he doesn't want that so I keep my body parts to myself. I won't deny it's a struggle for me, though. I'm an artist and a sculptor. Touch is as natural to me as breathing.

"I understand. But Vance, she's not my mother." I lock my fingers together and squeeze, trying to ease my frustration. "I'm not as close to the situation as you are. It's easier when you're on the outside. I'm not sure I could do it if it was my own mother. I'm not sure I'm strong enough."

"I guess." He pinches a sugar packet, flicking it with his finger while disappearing into his head. I feel the need to find him.

"I loved the poetry. Do you read to her a lot?"

"I do." He lets out a sad laugh. "She was always the one to read to me, and now the roles are reversed."

"It's a beautiful thing."

His eyes flick to mine and linger to the point of making me shift in my seat. "You're right. It is."

The waitress chooses that moment to return to the table with our food, smirking as if she interrupted something. "Okay, loveys. We're a little busy tonight. Food is served and apologies for the delay."

"Thank you," Vance and I utter at the same time.

"Jinx," I hurry and say to him.

"I don't do that shit." He grins, pouring half the maple syrup bottle onto his pancakes.

My mouth gapes open. "Are you kidding me? You could swim in that."

Again he grins, this time around a mouthful of pancake. "Yup."

I cringe as if I'm disgusted, even though I'm smiling. "Yuck."

He stabs a piece of pancake and holds it up, the syrup dripping onto the table. "Don't knock it until you've tried it."

I block him with one hand, lifting my turkey burger with the other. "No thanks."

"You're missing out," he counters, making a big show of swirling his pancake in gobs of butter and syrup.

My face contorts in a crazy way and he chuckles as he continues to eat. Without thinking, I tell him, "I like it when you laugh."

He stops chewing, his grin long gone and I think I might have ruined the rare carefree moment we were having. In fact, I know I did when he replies, "It's not okay for me."

I set my burger down, giving him my full attention. "What do you mean?"

"To be happy. Not when my mother is rotting away in there."

A crushing vulnerability shades his eyes and it resonates in my core. I realize that nobody has ever made it okay for him—to carry on, to live, to breathe. My hand goes to my chest, trying to push back the swell of emotion that wants to escape. For reasons I don't fully understand, I suddenly want to make it okay for him. "Oh, Vance. You've got it all wrong. That woman in there, the one that I saw...she would want you to be happy." I watch him as he tosses my words around in his head, trying to see if they make sense. And then, because

I can't seem to keep my mouth shut, I add, "Well, *I* like your laugh. And your smile, too. If I'm honest. Which," I wink, "I always am."

He attempts to smother a smile, but it's like a beam of light across his face.

"You see. Now I'm two for two."

chapter fifteen
Vance

THIS GIRL. I don't know what to make of her. It's been a long time since I've had a friend—certainly not one that's a girl anyway. She throws me off my game. Not that I have a game. But what I do have is a way I live my life that works for me, and she's chucking a wrench into it simply by existing. And I like that she exists. I also like the way I feel around her. I want to devour her honesty and soak up her sincerity. I'd like to know more about what makes her tick.

"I think I deserve some kind of a medal." Ember and I approach the car after a visit to this woman Kasia's house to discuss topics that put me to sleep. "I just listened to you two talk about cinnamon rolls and bakery shit for over an hour. Not to mention the half-hour conversation about her poodles."

Ember breaks up in a laugh as we both move toward the driver's side. I shoo her away with my hand. "I'll drive there, Mickey. You drove the whole way here. If you don't mind me driving your car, that is."

She stretches her arms above her head and yawns. "Nope. No problem here. I'll handle the music."

"Should I be worried?"

"I don't know," she retorts, plopping down onto the seat. "Should you be?"

I flip her a mock glare then back out of the driveway that looks like it could hold about thirty cars. Once we're on the road and stopped at a red light, I peer over at her. "So Ember Bennett, what makes you tick?"

The air conditioning blows a piece of her hair around as she shifts to face me. "Lots of things, really."

Red changes to green and my eyes return to the road. "Like?"

"Sculpting for one, but you already know that. I also love all kinds of art. I love to bake. And music to me is...everything."

"Oh yeah," I challenge. "Who's your favorite band?"

"The Vines."

Flipping on the blinker, I switch to the left hand lane. "Who?"

She breathes out a frustrated sound. "You don't know who The Vines are?"

"Nope."

Ember pops the glovebox and digs around before removing a CD and inserting it into the player. She places her hand in front of her, palm up, and announces, "I give you...The Vines."

I appease her and listen for a few minutes. My thumb taps against the steering wheel, head bobbing slightly. "They're not bad." They're actually better than not bad, but the smug look on her face makes me not want to give her the satisfaction.

"Not bad?" she huffs, so sure of herself I have to suppress a grin. "You're practically dancing to it."

"I don't dance," I confess, still trying to keep my smile in check.

"Keep telling yourself that." She releases an airy laugh. "Okay, so who's *your* favorite band?"

"Staind."

"They're pretty good."

"Fucking A they are, Mickey." From the side, I catch a glimpse of her smile. "Favorite food?"

"Lobster."

I make a buzzer sound in my throat. "Gross."

"I'll have you know it's quite delicious, especially dipped in butter. I would think you'd appreciate that last part." She huffs again and I like that I'm getting a rise out of her. "Okay, let's have it. What's *your* favorite food?"

"Twinkies," I answer with a huge grin on my face.

"*Twinkies*?" We come to a stop sign right before the entrance to the highway. I look over to find her staring at the package on the console, her nose scrunched up. "That's not a food. That's a chemical."

I try to rile her up with my evil glare but only succeed in making her double over with laughter. "Okay, okay. Favorite color?"

"Red," she replies proudly. "Yours?"

My eyes fall to my black t-shirt and black Chucks and the choice is obvious. "Black."

She rubs her hands up and down her arms on a slight shiver. "Avery likes black, too."

"That's because she's smart." Ember cackles and I press the button to lower the A/C in case she's cold.

She kicks off her sneakers and rests her feet on the dashboard with a contented sigh. The lightness of it travels in the air between us and lands on my chest. It makes me feel a little less empty. As I sit with that, I hear her singing quietly to herself. Her voice is nothing to write home about but she doesn't seem to care. Something else I really appreciate about her.

"So what's your favorite novel?"

Her question drags my attention away from the asshat in the BMW who cut me off. If I was in my own car, I'd give him a run for his money. "Honestly, that's a really tough question. I have a lot of favorites." I pause to think about all the books I've read. I'm inclined toward many different genres which makes it hard to choose. "I can give you a few of them, though. I would say *The Sun Also Rises* by Ernest Hemingway, *The Catcher in the Rye* by J.D. Salinger, *Mansfield Park* by Jane Austen, and *Anna Karenina* by Leo Tolstoy."

"Wait." She drops her feet down on the floor. I can feel her eyes grazing the side of my face. "Isn't Anna Karenina an eight hundred page book or something like that?"

"Yup. Around eight hundred and sixty-four."

"Wow." Fascination fills her voice. "That's crazy long. There's no way I'd have the attention span for that."

Brake lights signal traffic ahead and I change lanes. "I told you. I love to read. In fact, I'd rather read than do anything else. Except maybe play guitar."

"You play guitar?"

I'm trying to discern whether her tone holds shock or awe. I'm also trying to figure out why it matters. "I do."

"Interesting."

"What is?" Traffic slows and I get a chance to view her expression. Her head is angled to the side, fingers outlining a frame through which she appraises me.

"I can totally see that. The hair. The earring. I bet you even have a tattoo."

My head shakes again at her audacity, though it no longer bothers me now that I've gotten to know her better. "You crack me up. Look who's making assumptions again."

"Come on," she coaxes, lifting her chin in the air. "Fess up. I know you have a tattoo."

An obvious sigh of resignation gives her the proof she needs. "Maybe."

"Aha!" She slaps her hand against the leather seat. "I knew it." She looks me up and down before returning to my face. "Can I see it?"

I cock a single brow and smirk. "Are you sure you want to?" That one question is enough to make her cheeks blush pink and her eyes stray from mine.

"Oh. Um. Never mind."

I find her so interesting. In one breath, she's entirely confident. In the next, completely shy. There is an innocence to her I've yet to figure out. It's...dare I say, sweet?

"Ember." Her eyes slowly advance on mine, and again, her reticence makes me check myself and any comments I might have made. "You can totally see it. It's on my upper back. Only not while I'm driving." I hope the smile I put on for both of our benefits washes away her unease.

"What is the tattoo of?"

"It's just three words." I swallow and spit them out. "Lest We Forget."

I don't have to see her face to uncover the empathy I know is there, and when her fingertips lance my arm I do my best not to pull away. She leaves them on my skin and every second I feel them, my heartbeat picks up. A little voice in my head says to keep her at a distance. As it grows louder, I find myself gradually lifting my arm until her fingers fall away. The loss of her touch leaves me cold. But cold I know how to deal with.

"I didn't picture you as a Honda girl," I throw out, attempting to distract from the chill I've created in the air. She doesn't respond right away and I sense she wants to say something. Tension mounts inside of me and I hold my breath as I wait. For some reason, she decides to let me off the hook and I breathe out a quiet sigh of relief.

"It was Zack's car." She clears what I interpret as emotion from her throat. "He worked three jobs one summer to save up for it. My dad wanted to help him out but he was determined to do it on his own...and he did." Traffic comes to a dead stop and I watch her as she brings her knees up to her chest, thumb scraping over a patch of fabric on her jeans. "We had a lot of memories in this car. We made tons of plans for what our futures were going to look like. He...," she glances up as if to gauge my reaction, "showed me how to smoke a joint in this car." My eyes must show my overwhelming surprise because her head springs back. "*What?* I'm not a prude, you know?"

"I didn't say you were." Although I was thinking it. "It's surprising. Sue me, Mickey, but you don't seem like the pot-smoking type."

She quickly corrects me. "I didn't say I was a pot-smoker. I tried it. Just that once, actually. It made me paranoid and I ate a whole bunch of junk food I wouldn't normally eat. So it was basically my first and last time." I chuckle at her reasons for never doing it again and she joins in before she adds, "I ate an entire two bags of Cheetos."

"A whole two bags?" I tease her, and she grabs the Twinkies from the center console and chucks them at me. "That's just...wrong."

Her green eyes thin though her smile shines through. Since she reminded me about the Twinkies, I pick them up and tear open the package, holding one out in front of her. "Twinkie?"

She makes a chopping motion with her hand against her neck, her grin uncontrollable. "Uh, no thanks. I've already had my chemical allowance for the day."

"Suit yourself." I bite into the Twinkie and groan in appreciation. "But you seriously don't know what you're missing."

Her smile dissolves into thoughtfulness and she runs her palm over the dashboard. "I'm going to keep this car until it won't drive anymore. Maybe even longer than that. I don't want to let it go." She exhales a sigh. "It would be like tossing away a piece of him." Then quietly she utters, "And I can't do that."

Finished with the Twinkie, I wipe a hand on my jeans before lifting my ass up to reach into my front pocket. I slide out the smooth black stone with orange and grey flecks and lift it in the air between us. "My mom and I used to skip stones at the river. She's the one who taught me how to do it." I glare at the rock as the memory clogs my chest, making it hard to breathe. "One day we were there and I found this stone. I showed it to her and was getting ready to flip it into the water, but she told me it was too beautiful and I should hold onto it." I smile at the stupid little stone. "So I did. I keep it with me always. I'll never let it go."

She nods in understanding then holds her hand out. I drop the stone into her palm. Her index finger rolls over the surface and she eyes it with admiration. "It is beautiful. I like the little dashes of color. Makes it unique."

The honk of a horn behind us indicates that traffic has started moving again. I bring my attention back to the road. The sun is beginning to set, shades of oranges and pinks skid across the sky— reminiscent of a painting.

"Oh, wow. Vance, can you pull over?" The sound of Ember frantically searching through her purse makes me pause.

"Sure. Is everything okay?" As it seems important, I abruptly check for cars before veering off into the emergency lane. I put the hazards on, venturing a glance her way. "What are you doing?"

She's already out the door when I hear her call back, "I want to get some pictures of the sunset."

I watch her with I don't know what—interest, maybe fascination, as she continues to snap pictures with her iPhone. She holds the phone this way and that, in various angles as she shifts on her feet and changes locations. She's so unlike any of the girls I've known. Then again, I haven't really made an effort to know any in a long time—only in the biblical sense. They're all the same anyway—except Ember. She is...different. I haven't quite figured out if that's a good thing for me or not.

"That sunset is amazing." She bounces into the car with enough fucking enthusiasm to have *me* excited. "Look at these pictures." Lifting the phone, she holds it between us and scrolls through them.

"They're...nice."

She slaps me on the shoulder. "They're fantastic. I'm going to print a few out and get them blown up and framed." I tilt my head, surveying the brightness in her eyes and the way her lips curve higher on one side than the other. "Why are you looking at me like that?"

I rap a finger against my mouth. "I'm just wondering who you are, Ember Bennett?"

She wiggles her dark brows and her eyelashes flutter. If I didn't know better, I'd think she was flirting with me. "Wouldn't you like to know?"

Yeah. I think I would.

chapter sixteen
Ember

WOULDN'T YOU LIKE *to know?* For a split second, I wonder who this carefree person is and where the heck Ember went. I'd almost be mortified by my own words if Vance wasn't looking at me with such interest—as if he wants to know more about me—as if I'm genuinely interesting. I mean, I'm confident with who I am. It's not that. Actually, I don't know what it is.

At a loss of how to follow up that awkward moment, I'm about to say something to detract from it when a yawn escapes. I cover my mouth with my hand. "I guess I'm a little tired."

"Understandable," Vance affirms. "Talking about cinnamon rolls for hours on end can certainly be exhausting." He blows out a breath then winks a ridiculously dazzling blue eye at me. "I know I'm fucking wiped."

"You're a smart-ass is what you are." I motion with my head toward the wheel. "More driving and less talking," I order, and he raises a hand to his forehead in salute.

"You're cute when you're bossy," he mumbles, concentrating on getting us back onto I-5 to head home. It's then that I realize how late it is and decide to check in on Mom. Pulling out my phone, I dial her number. It rings several times before going to voicemail.

"Hey, Mom. Just calling to say hello. I'm on my way back from Eugene now. Hope you've had a good day." After ending the call I notice Troy left me a few voicemails and figure I'll get back to him later. I toss the phone in my purse and lean against the headrest, closing my eyes.

"So you're close with your Mom and Dad?"

"Very. Like I said, it's kind of a weird dynamic. But yes, they're pretty great." It occurs to me that Vance hasn't spoken much about his Dad. As usual, I can't hold back my curiosity. "I haven't heard you talk about your Dad. He seemed nice when I came by the house to drop off your book. Are you close?"

The bitter noise he makes stuns me and I open my eyes. "Uh. No. We were at one point. But, I don't know. He's changed."

I turn my head toward him. "How so?"

His jaw works back and forth, fingers clamped onto the steering wheel. "He's forgotten all about my mother. It's like...he's gone on with his life. He hardly ever goes to see her anymore and it pisses me the fuck off. I realize we're much further from Winston now, but if I can manage it—"

"That's where you moved from?"

"Yeah. And I saw her every day. Sometimes, more than once. We were only a few blocks away from Ridgecrest."

"So why didn't you stay there?"

His loud exhale fills the car. "In a nutshell, I was short on money and didn't anticipate having such a hard time finding a job after I graduated from University of Portland. Especially with a degree in Computer Science."

"I'm sorry." I stuff my hands under my thighs because they want to wander over to his side again. I can't seem to keep them under control around him.

His shoulders wilt and his head dips down. "Yeah. Me too."

"University of Portland is a great school, though. I went to Oregon State and majored in Fine Arts. Still, I don't think anyone really prepares us for how challenging it is once you get into the real world. Of course," I joke, "I haven't quite entered it, since I'm still living at home." I wait for Vance to make a smart comeback but he's almost too quiet. Anxious to shift his mood, I opt for a change of subject. "I like your brother. He seems sweet."

"Yes." He laughs, the sound filled with adoration. "Everyone loves Julian. He spreads charm wherever he goes."

"I think he's already charmed my sister."

"But not you?" He flashes me a sideways glance.

"I'm not easily charmed."

He rubs the stubble on his jaw, appearing to ponder this before he simply asks me. "Why not?"

My answer is a shrug that he can't see. "Just not interested, I guess."

"So." He hedges. "No boyfriend?"

"Nope."

"Are you into girls?" he probes, and I don't know why this topic is important to him. It rates very low on my priority scale.

"Why do I have to be into anything?" I exhale my frustration with a nervous laugh. "If you must know, my last boyfriend was about two years ago," I admit. And instead of dropping it, he digs further.

"What happened?"

"It's simple." I reach out and twirl the rabbit's foot between my fingers. "He ended things because when Zack died...I...I couldn't give him the attention he wanted. I was having a really hard time and needed to focus on me and my family...and that didn't work for him."

"He sounds like an asshole."

Regret over my poor judgment makes me want to shrink into myself and I scoot down on the seat. "He came from a very affluent family and thought he was entitled to the world."

This time, his tone carries more anger. "In other words, he was an asshole."

"Pretty much." I press my lips together, glad he doesn't comment further on my misguided choice. "So what about you? Girlfriend?"

"Nope." He places particular emphasis on the P as if my question amuses him.

"Why not?"

"I like my space and I like distance. Girls always want to ignore that. I've...," he hesitates as if weighing his words carefully, "been with girls. But I don't date." I won't bother asking him how many girls he's been with—one look at him and I'm sure I know the answer to that—dozens.

My phone rings and I lean down to fish it out of my bag. I slide to unlock it and barely get a "hello" out before Avery's voice booms in my ear. It's so blaring, Vance looks over, eyes wide. "Where the hell are you? Do you realize no one has heard from you all day? Did it occur to you that *I* or someone else close to you might be worried? Troy said he left you two voicemails but you didn't call him back, and that you were supposed to meet him for dinner. Did you forget?"

I flinch at the last question because I did forget and that's not like me. "That's four questions. Which one would you like me to answer first?"

"Quit being a smart-ass." She huffs her frustration into my ear. "What's gotten into you anyway?" Then her tone drops significantly. "Are you okay? I was worried."

"Yes, I'm fine. Just so you know, I left Mom a message."

I hear cabinets opening and closing in the background. "Well, she isn't home."

"I'm sorry, Ave. I didn't mean to worry you. Vance ran into some car trouble and—"

"Wait," she interrupts, her pitch suddenly more upbeat. "Vance is with you?"

"Yeah."

"Well, then." She calms down and her tune changes. "As long as I know you're fine. Take your time."

Vance's gaze is heavy on my face and my cheeks warm. "Hold on." I cover the phone while trying to keep my lips from tipping up. "Pay attention to the road so we can get home in one piece."

He grins as if he knows we're talking about him. "Traffic is stopped here, sweetheart. Nowhere to go."

My eyes hone in on the line of cars preceding us. I'm tempted to tell him not to call me sweetheart, but he did it with such a compelling smile that I can only muster one response. "Oh."

He folds his arms over his chest and leans against the door, continuing to stare at me. Flustered, I reach down with my fingers to pick at a crack in the leather. I wish he wouldn't look at me like that because it makes me wonder what he's thinking. All through this, my sister is still talking but I'm no longer paying attention. "All right, Ave. I gotta go. I'll see you later."

"That's it?" she asks, disappointment clear in her voice.

"Yup."

The click of her heels against the wood floor sounds in my ear as she navigates the room. "I hope you've got something better for me when you get home."

"Goodbye, Avery." I end the call before shooting a quick text to Troy. Dropping the cell in my purse, I let out a groan.

Vance's gaze follows my phone, then drifts up to me. "What's wrong?"

"My sister," I explain with another groan and an eye roll. "She has a one-track mind."

"Oh yeah?" His hair tumbles across his cheek as he tilts his head to regard me. "What track is that?"

"The sex track."

"Ah, the dreaded sex track," he muses. "Unfortunately, I know a lot about that." He's not smiling anymore and I have a hard time reading his expression. I think it might be one of regret.

"Maybe it's time to switch tracks," I suggest with humor, trying to keep the conversation light.

"I wish I could," he mumbles under his breath. And I wonder what that means.

NOT LONG AFTER, I take over the wheel and make another pit stop at a gas station. By the time we pull into Vance's driveway, it's late. The streetlights cast a soft glow inside the car, his face in shadows. I can just detect the outline of his smile.

"Well, Mickey, this was...." His eyes seek out mine in the semi-darkness and he pauses as if to chase the words. "An adventure. I had...fun."

"Yeah. Me too."

He averts his gaze as he leans forward, hand poised over the door handle. Then he looks back, his voice quiet. "Thank you for the lift. And...for everything you did today."

I want to tell him I didn't do anything. But the absolute sincerity radiating off of him makes me decide to accept his gratitude without my usual fight. "You're welcome." With a subtle nod of his head, he opens the door and steps out before shutting it behind him.

My fingers gravitate toward the rabbit's foot and I spin it around, mesmerized. I'm about to back out, except something makes me glance up to Vance's front door. When I do, I find him standing there staring my way. I can't make out his face from here because it's too dark. But I can sense he's smiling, and a weird pang erupts in my belly. I don't know what it means. But I know how it feels—

A lot like happiness.

chapter seventeen
Vance

THE PARKING LOT near Anna's pastry shop is pretty empty this morning, but surprisingly, there's a line at the door. I figured I'd come over and buy Ember a coffee, my way of saying thank you for everything she did yesterday. I'm jittery though, hopped up on—I don't know what—and now I'm second-guessing myself. Maybe this wasn't such a hot idea after all.

I cup my hands against the window and peer in. Ember is behind the register alone, whirling around from one side of the counter to the other. Her face is set in determination but she seems...frazzled. Not bothering to be polite, I deal with muttered curses and push my way through the front door. Ember happens to glance up and shoots me a half-smile, continuing to ring up customers. I can't help but wonder where the other employees are. There is no way she can handle all these people by herself.

"Hey, what's going on?" I ask once I weave my way to the counter. She doesn't look over at me when she responds, and I end up speaking to her back.

"I can't talk right now, Vance. Anna and Rosie are both sick, and...." Ember gestures with a hand toward the crowd then spins around. She tries to paste on a smile as she rings up a customer, while waiting on someone else who can't make a decision about pastries to save their freaking life. Grumbles from behind don't make the lady decide any faster, so I give her a subtle shove.

"You might want to choose something. Two minute decisions are key in a coffee shop and," I jerk my head toward the crowd, "you're kind of holding up the line."

The only response I get is an angry brown-eyed glare and a flick of auburn hair over her shoulder as she steps to the side. It's then that I decide to take matters into my own hands. I plow straight back behind the counter. Ember stares at me dumbfounded as I head right for her.

"What are you doing?"

"What does it look like I'm doing, Mickey? You need help, and I'm helping."

She passes coffee to a woman with a huge rack and an amused smile who is watching us like we're some kind of side show.

"If I were you," she reflects, and we both glance at her, "and I wish like hell I was," she winks at me then looks to Ember, "I'd accept his help."

Ember opens her mouth to protest, but all that comes out is a resigned breath as her shoulders sag with relief. "Okay."

"Great." I clap my hands together. "Let's get this party started. Just tell me what you want me to do."

For the rest of the day, since I know fuck-all about making lattes, Ember takes the lead there while I handle ringing up customers and passing out pastries. The morning and afternoon go by pretty smoothly and I'll admit we make a great team. Once we finish cleaning and she locks up, we take a seat at one of the tables. She grabs us a few cinnamon rolls and brings over a hot coffee for me and a fancy whipped cream number for herself.

"So...." She takes a bite of her cinnamon roll with a hesitant smile. "Thanks for swooping in and saving the day."

"Eh." I sip my coffee, so hot I nearly burn the roof of my mouth. "It's what I do."

She leans back, eyeing me above the rim of her cup. "*Is* it now?"

"Not really." I chuckle. "But you looked like you were drowning and

I thought I'd throw you a life preserver." As soon as the words leave my mouth, her smile disintegrates. "What is it? What did I say?"

"Actually, you know what?" She sits up straighter and brushes it off. I wish I knew what that was about. "It's totally fine. You don't have to filter everything you say. After all," her smile returns, "I don't."

Regret and confusion still remain but I nod anyway. "So everyone is out sick?"

"Yup." She brings the cinnamon roll to her mouth and inhales a huge bite. When she places it down on the plate, I notice a spattering of icing settled just below her lips. I tap a finger to my chin.

"You've got some icing...."

Ember lifts her napkin and dabs it against her lips twice, missing the spot. I shake my head and waggle my finger to urge her closer.

"C'mere."

She leans in to the table and I reach out, swiping away the sweet, sticky frosting with the pad of my thumb. Her eyes, so amazingly green from up close, lock on mine. A few seconds pass and I realize my thumb is still moving back and forth over her skin—and it's so damn soft. Abruptly, I draw back and clear my throat.

"So yeah...everyone's sick you were saying?"

Her eyes clear and she blinks. "Yeah. Anna still has a stomach bug and Rosie has strep throat. Troy had already scheduled the day off to spend with his sisters. And I don't know where the heck Peter is. There was also Charlotte, but she quit recently because she moved to Virginia."

"That sucks. But I'm glad I showed up."

Then, as if she realizes she's been meaning to ask me all along. "Why did you show up?"

I fold and refold the napkin in front of me. "I wanted to thank you and buy you a coffee, which I now realize makes no sense." I laugh at my own stupidity. "Because you get it for free. And now I did, too."

"You earned it."

I stare over my shoulder and snicker. "I couldn't believe those people. They kill their own for coffee."

"Yeah, well." She grins, taking a drink then holding up her cup in salute. "I'm one of them."

"Oh no."

"Oh, yes." She sneaks another sip, whipped cream sticking to her upper lip. Her smooth, pink tongue darts out in a half-circle to lick it away. I snag my coffee from the table and gulp some down, not caring that it's still hot. "My mother used to take me with her to Starbucks all the time. She'd order those mocha Frappuccino's and would always let me have some. My father didn't like it and told her she shouldn't be doing it, that it wasn't good for me. But she kept doing it anyway. And I got hooked."

"It's easy to get hooked on things that are bad for you. Especially when they taste so damn good," I agree, trying to ease the burn in my throat.

"Like Twinkies, perhaps."

"Exactly." I grin and peel off a chunk of cinnamon roll, popping it into my mouth. The sweetness lingers on my tongue and I swig more coffee to balance it out. "So what do you do for fun? You the adventurous type?"

She swirls her straw around the layer of whipped cream topping her cup. "Not nearly. My brother was, though. I think the biggest risk I've ever taken was when my friend Troy coerced me into riding the Looping Thunder roller coaster at Oaks Park. I almost had a coronary and didn't speak to him for days after that."

I chuckle at the still terrified expression on her face. "Roller coasters don't bother me. The craziest thing I've ever done is bungee jumping."

Her eyes widen. "Oh my God. I can't even imagine doing that. I'm afraid the cord would snap."

"Nah. It's actually pretty secure." I gesture with my hands, crisscrossing them over my chest. "You're wearing a harness so it's not too bad. Skydiving on the other hand, that might freak me the fuck out."

She stares down at the table then back to me. "Zack was supposed to do his first skydive the weekend after...." Her thoughts taper off, shoulders dropping on a sigh. "He would've done it, too. He was fearless, you know? Whereas me...I'd be afraid to fall." She shakes her head as if she still can't believe he's gone. "He thought he was invincible. I think I did, too."

"He was obviously very brave. Not me, I'll stick to more wimpy things on the ground. Like martial arts."

"What kind?" Another piece of pastry gets shoved in her mouth, her cheek puffing out as she chews.

"Karate." I flex my arms out in front of me. "I actually haven't kept up with it, but I got my Black Belt years ago."

"That's really impressive. I guess I better not do anything to piss you off."

I shoot her a nonchalant grin, shrugging my shoulders for extra effect. "I think at this point you're pretty much exonerated from my wrath."

Her face lights up. "I feel pretty special then, considering...." She circles her hands in the air like she's wiping down a window. "You've got that whole broody thing going on."

For the briefest of moments, I consider telling her that she is special. Because a part of me is whispering *she is*. But it seems too personal, too close to crossing a boundary I have to be sure to stay behind.

"Yoohoo." She wiggles her fingers in front of my face. "Earth to Vance?" I refocus on her, those riveting eyes trying to find me. "Where'd you go?"

"Just zoning out."

High-pitched screams from outside force our attention to the window and the small park across the street. Two little boys are racing from the grass to a low wooden fence overlooking the road.

"Julian and I used to race like that when we were kids, too," I explain, smiling at the memory. "He always used to win. That little fucker." One of the boys punches the air when he makes it to the fence first. "He's always been a lot more athletic than me. His legs are also longer so that helps."

"He sounds competitive like Avery. She was always trying to one-up me. It bothered me when we were kids because I felt like she could master things I couldn't. And that she was doing it to annoy me." She laughs. "Which she probably was."

"So wait," I pick at the crumbs on my napkin, "Are you guys close then?"

Her cheeks hollow as she sucks coffee through the straw, trying not to smile. "We are now. She's like the Yin to my Yang." She rests an elbow on the table, her fist tucked under her chin. "We weren't as close before though. But after Zack died we clung to each other and became inseparable in ways."

Our conversation veers off then into everything from family quirks, to politics, art, and our mutual love for zombie movies and *The Walking Dead*. However, our serious bone of contention arises when she tells me her favorite movie is *Pretty Woman.*

"Pretty Woman?" I hiss out an annoyed laugh. "Come on. That movie is as far from reality as you're ever gonna get."

"And so what?" She throws her hands up in the air. "It's a movie. It's no different from the books you read. Those are *fiction*," she emphasizes, curling her fingers into air quotes.

"Yes," I toss back. "But those aren't fluffy, bullshit, never gonna happen happy endings."

There are no happy endings in the cards for me. But I'm not getting into that with her.

"It could happen," she retorts, her mouth a straight line.

"So you want some rich prince to climb up a fire escape with an umbrella and flowers to save you?"

"Aha!" She jabs her finger in the air at me. "You have seen it. And I already told you I don't need to be saved." She holds her chin high. "I'll save myself, thank you very much."

My grin goes wide at her stubborn and self-assured nature. "I have no doubt you will, Mickey. And FYI, I would never watch that garbage by choice. I was coerced to watch the DVD by Julian and a date." I smirk. "It wasn't a pleasurable experience." Reaching for my cup, I happen to glance at my watch. "Holy shit. Do you realize we've been talking for almost three hours?"

"Not surprising." She lobs her balled-up napkin at me. "You kind of have a big mouth."

"Nice." I push my chair back, the screech echoing in the empty café. "I've got to get back to my job search. You ready?"

"Yeah." She snags our empty cups and the leftover cinnamon rolls and throws them in the garbage. When we reach the door, she unlocks it and flips me a sideways glance. "Thank you for...." Her throat works on a soft swallow and that shy smile of hers is back. "...Saving me. Because today, I really did need saving."

"Don't worry." I wink. "I promise it won't happen again. Besides, it was...you know, fun or whatever...," I half-mumble, my voice trailing off. She twists the knob, but pauses again as I start to speak. "You do realize we keep thanking each other for shit, don't you?"

"I do," she answers with a curious lift of her brow.

"Okay. Just checking."

We step out into what's left of the sunshine and Ember peers up at me, one hand shielding her eyes. "I'm sure there are worse things."

I stare at her lips tipped up into a sweet smile. "Yes, there definitely are."

Her keys jingle in her hand as she turns, heading in the opposite direction. "I'll see ya, Vance."

"Not if I see you first."

I hear her laughter as she rounds the corner and wonder why the hell I'm still standing here, watching her, until she disappears.

chapter eighteen
Ember

I OFFER TROY a contrite smile as he opens the door. "Peace offering?" He barely glances at the giant piece of coconut cake, his favorite, before taking in my appearance. His eyes rove from my hair to the green Michael Kors wrap dress that I borrowed from Avery, to the Louboutin heels—also courtesy of my sister. I don't fill out the dress as well as she does, but the push-up bra I'm wearing certainly helps.

"Number one. You're forgiven. And number two," he whistles a breath through his teeth, "you look smokin' hot." He pulls on my arm and tugs me inside, closing the door behind us. "Sit. I'll be right back." As he walks toward the kitchen, I plant myself on the couch and peel off the container lid. Shredded bits of fresh coconut stick to the sides, the smell heavenly. Troy returns with two forks and passes me one, dropping down on the sofa. "Please tell me you look like this because you had a lunch date?"

"Nope." I stare down at my breasts on display and try to close the fabric tighter around them. Troy slaps my hand away.

"Stop. Honestly, Ems. You look amazing." He brings a bite of cake to his lips with a big smile. "Again I ask, who is he?"

"There is no he," I confess, sweeping cake onto my fork. "I was at that gallery opening in town and it was fantastic."

"You went alone?"

"*Yes.*" My face twists in exaggeration. "I have no problem with my own company. I'm kind of decent sometimes."

Troy bumps my shoulder with his own. "Now *that's* an understatement." He swirls his fork around the frosting while his eyes continue to probe. "So it was good?"

"It was great." As I say the words, electricity flows through me and my limbs tingle. I set my fork down on the table, the cake losing its appeal. "There were quite a few local artists and mostly paintings and photography, but still...."

"But still, what?"

I glance away for a second, staring out the small window to the front yard. "I just got so energized, you know? I'd love to someday be able to have pieces of mine in a gallery. Or—"

"Have your own gallery." My gaze drifts back to Troy as he reads my thoughts, his enthusiasm contagious.

"Yes."

"I see it, Ems. I want that for you. I want *all* good things for you." He covers my small hand with his large one. "You deserve it."

"Thanks." I move closer to kiss his cheek and his smile tickles my chin. "Your turn. Tell me how Samantha is."

His lips tug into a deep frown and he falls back against the sofa. "It didn't work out."

"Why not?"

"Because she doesn't like the fact that I'm also into guys." He sighs, scraping two fingers down the front of his jeans. "She said she wouldn't be able to get past it and doesn't want to start anything."

A fire lights in my belly because Troy is one of the best people I know. I mimic his position on the couch and lay my head on his shoulder. "She's an idiot then and she doesn't deserve you." He places a gentle kiss against my hair. "So let's not waste time talking about her. Did you sign up for those carpentry classes?"

"Yesterday."

"It's about time. And who knows? Pretty soon you might be doing projects with my dad. He'd be happy to have you on board." I snort, and he elbows me in the ribs. "By the way, that sculpture presentation went really well," I mention as I start to squirm, tugging at the belt around my waist.

"What are you doing?"

"This dress." I pull at the fabric, trying to stretch it out. "It's just...I'm not used to wearing stuff like this. It's uncomfortable."

"It looks like it was made for you. In fact, I really think you need to put this dress to good use." He smoothes a hand over my thigh. "You can't let it go to waste."

"We could go to the grocery store." I tease. "Hang out in the produce aisle or something. But Avery will kill me if I get her dress stained."

"You need to go out on a date," he prompts. "It's good for the soul."

"My soul is just fine. Anyway, not to change the subject." Sitting up, I angle my body toward him. "Sorry about missing our dinner the other day."

"Oh yeah, where were you? Your text was kind of vague." He taps my nose. "Avery called me in a panic. And when I told her you hadn't returned my calls, she thought something happened to you."

"Something did. I got sidetracked by an unexpected passenger." When his brows fold together, I go on. "Vance had some car trouble and I ran into him on my way to see a customer. Long story short, we spent the day together." The confusion on his face turns to pleased curiosity.

"And how was that?"

An unexpected smile creeps across my cheeks. "Surprisingly, it was...really nice."

"I can see that." He grins and I flick his arm. "So...do you like him?"

I don't have to think twice before I answer. "Yes, I do."

He continues to cross-examine me in the way that only Troy can. "Do you *like* him, like him?"

I laugh, giving him a deliberate eye roll. "What are you, twelve?"

"Thirteen." He glares at me. "Now answer the question." When I don't respond, he adds in. "I see." Then he nods with conviction as if he knows me better than I know myself. "Do you remember when you were fourteen? You sat in the tree in your yard for three hours with Brian McNulty and had your first kiss?" I start to protest but he puts a single finger to my lips. "When I asked if you had a crush on him, do you remember what you said? And I quote, '*You know I don't crush on boys.*' And that time you were at the college mixer with Connor whatever his name was, who I never liked? You looked all dreamy when you're *never* dreamy. I asked if he was going to be the one you lost your virginity to?" This time, I don't try to offer up anything. "Exactly." He smirks. "Because when a girl who's never had much interest in boys most of her life, takes interest...I rest my case, your honor."

"You might want to stick to carpentry," I joke, and he gives my waist a squeeze. "Okay, I have to get going." I push off the sofa, straightening out my dress as I stand. Troy huffs and follows me to the door.

"Sure, make your escape. It doesn't change the facts," he reaffirms, his head peeking out from the narrow gap of the screen.

Of course I know he's right.

I TAKE MY usual spot in the driveway next to...Dad's car? I'm not sure what he's doing at the house today. While I didn't expect to see him, I'm excited to discuss details of the gallery opening. Dad has always shared my enthusiasm for the arts, encouraging me to pursue my passion.

"Hand me that drill. Will ya, Vance?" Dad calls out, and I scoot higher in my seat to find Vance in the garage. I'm surprised to see him. My eyes drift down to my dress and I bite back a smile. I pinch the sides and front of the fabric with my fingers before stepping out of the car. I want to make sure nothing sticks out where it shouldn't be.

"What's going on?" I yell over the sound of the drill. Vance and Dad notice me at the same time. My father has that familiar jolly expression on his face. Vance, on the other hand, has his mouth hanging open, eyes roaming my body and making my skin flush. Goose bumps parade down my arms and I have to turn away.

Dad switches off the drill, the noise no longer a buffer. "Wow, honey. You look lovely."

My eyes flick to my dad, but the heat of Vance's stare unnerves me and my mouth goes dry. "Thanks."

"This nice young man came by to say hello to you. I needed a hand, and he offered one." Dad winks at Vance then turns his attention to me. "And I find out that he and his family recently moved in down the street, and that he's already had the finest cinnamon rolls around." He pats his belly, his full cheeks bright. "Lord knows I've had one too many of those myself." His amusement dies down with the clearing of his throat. "Anyhoo, how did it go?"

"It was good, Dad. I can't wait to tell you all about it." I sling my purse over my shoulder. "Vance, can I talk to you for a second?" Once more, the buzz of the drill fills the air. Vance walks out on the driveway to meet me, hands stuffed in his pockets, his expression unreadable.

"Hey."

"Hi." I click my tongue against the roof of my mouth. "So '*nice young man*' huh? I guess you've got my dad fooled."

He chuckles. "I can be nice when I want to be." His gaze roves again and I swallow, clutching tighter to my purse strap. "You look beau— great. You look great."

I stare at my shoes to distract from my obvious blush. "Thanks." When I hazard a glance back up, Vance's eyes are zeroed in on a rock. He kicks it around the pavement with the toe of his sneaker.

"So, did you...have a, date or something?"

"No," I reply too quickly. His eyes snap to mine and an undefined emotion flickers over his features. If I didn't know better, I'd swear it was relief. I must be mistaken, though. I have to be. Right? "I was at a gallery opening," I reveal. For some reason it's important to me that he know.

"By yourself?" He continues to scrutinize me, and I laugh because now he sounds like Troy.

"Yes." I place a hand on my hip. "I'm not bad company."

"I know that. It's just," he shrugs, "I would've gone with you. I mean," he clarifies. "If you wanted."

"Oh." I pause, unsure of what to do next. But then my thoughts go to Avery and how she loves to make grand, sweeping exits like in the movies. So I take this as an opportunity of sorts and walk away, calling over my shoulder. "I'll remember that for next time."

The hairs on the back of my neck tingle because I can feel him watching me—and think maybe Avery has the right idea—and that this dress didn't go to waste after all.

chapter nineteen
Vance

THE HOT SUN beats down on my back, sweat building under my arms and around my neck. My legs burn as I push myself hard. The irony— I'm not even a fucking runner. But I had to do something. The vision of Ember in that dress has taken over my brain. All gentle curves and smooth skin, my fingers aching to touch. They curl instinctively into fists at my sides, reminding me that it's a no-go. We're friends. Anything else isn't in the cards for me. If it were, then maybe things would be different. Still, I find myself thinking about her more than I should.

I turn the corner that leads to our house and notice Julian's car in the driveway. It's unusual for him to be home this early. He's been working longer hours since he got the promotion and was transferred to the Errol Heights office. I'm still unclear why he wanted to move back in with us when he's doing well financially. Not that I'm unhappy to have him here. I love having him around. But I question whether his motivation stems from worry about me.

Julian is in the dining room when I walk in, eyeing himself in the mirror. He does a one eighty when he sees me. "Since when do you run?" He laughs at what he perceives to be a joke while I sneer at him. "By the way, the mechanic called about your car and it's ready. He said one of the guys that works for him lives around here, so they're going to drop it by later."

"Did he say what the damage is?" I lumber past him on the way to the kitchen, the heavy scent of cologne hanging in the air.

"Nope. But Dad left some money in an envelope on the table, and I'm sure it's more than enough." He makes a sucking sound with his teeth and glares at me. "How's the job search coming along? Any bites?"

I hesitate. One: Due to my frustration with the job situation. And two: I don't like taking money from my father. It makes me a total fucking hypocrite. "I got a few messages from recruiters about setting up phone screens, so there's that. But I just don't get it. It's *technology*, and we're in Oregon for fuck's sake. Those jobs are everywhere." I dig my fingers into the tense muscles at the back of my neck. "Whatever. I'm on it. And I'm sure the changes on the resume will help so thanks again." Opening the fridge, I take out a bottle of water and twist the top. Sweat continues to drip down my skin making the need for a shower vital.

"You're welcome." Julian crosses the living room and grabs his keys from the coffee table. "Remember what I told you after you graduated college? I know you don't want to hear it again but I'm going to say it. Stop being so stubborn and get something part-time for now, *or* change your attitude and your salary expectations and you'll be surprised how quickly you land a job." I have no smart retort because I chose to ignore his advice the first time around. I won't make the same mistake again. "On to me. I landed another client today. My new boss is over the moon."

"Congrats." I run my palm along my jaw. "Your charm serves you well. So where are you off to?"

"I've got a date." He laughs, correcting himself. "It's not really a date. More like hanging out at that tavern pool bar in town."

"Oh yeah?" I consider plucking an apple from the bowl on the kitchen table, but my mind says *too healthy* and I head for my room instead. "With who?"

"Ember."

My feet halt on the stairs, fingers tightening in a death grip around the banister. Suddenly I'm off-balance. She said she didn't find him charming. My mind becomes hazy, jaw set in a hard line. Somehow my words manage not to betray whatever the hell is going on inside my body.

"Ember? I didn't think she was into the male species that way."

"I ran into her after my meeting in town this afternoon and asked if she—"

"Hey, Julian."

"Oh, hey." His voice sounds off, nervous almost. "I was just coming to get you."

"I had to drop something off at the Lancaster's. Figured I'd walk."

I pin my sights on Ember. That dress she was wearing is gone, back to jeans and a snug t-shirt that encases her small but perfect breasts. Her face is scrubbed free of makeup, save for a bit of lip gloss, hair slicked back in a ponytail. What bothers me the most is she seems excited or something. I can't quite put my finger on it.

She finally glances up, noticing me, and the air shifts. I wonder if she feels it, or if it's just me.

I try to keep my tone light. "Hey, Mickey."

"Hi Vance." Her lips do that half tilt in the corners and she's too fucking cute. Then I inwardly tell myself to shut the fuck up because she's going out with Julian—even if it is just to '*hang out.*'

"Okay. Well, you kids have fun." I rush the words out through gritted teeth and rip my gaze away, climbing the few steps necessary to reach my room. Once I cross the threshold, I slam the water bottle down on my desk and march to the window. My scowl grows as I watch Julian round the car to open her door. Before Ember gets in, she briefly looks up and our eyes lock. I should back away—but I can't. She breaks the stare first, ducking her head and finding a spot on the front seat.

I can't help thinking she's with the wrong guy—wishing that *I* was the right guy.

SURROUNDED BY TWINKIE wrappers, I'm sitting on the carpet strumming my guitar. I've been trying to compose something for over two hours but I can't get the arrangement to work. I'm too distracted. My mind cluttered with shit, wandering to where it shouldn't be. Frustrated, I push to my feet and set the guitar beside the bed. At my desk, I flip the switch on the iPod dock then jump on the mattress, lying back with my hands laced behind my head. The digital clock reads 9:00—too early for them to come home. A peculiar lump settles like a boulder in my stomach. I wish it would go the fuck away.

The book on the side table seems like a good distraction. But when I pick it up, I stare at the same two pages for far too long. As if the world is taunting me, that song Ember liked in the car comes on, the sound of her squeaky voice as she sang along plays in my head—and that's the last straw. I can't sit here twiddling my thumbs anymore.

I slide off the bed and yank the chair back from my desk. It snags on the carpet before my ass lands on the seat and I power up my laptop. My fingers move restlessly over the keys as I wait for it to boot. When it does, I search Google and type in 'Eastmoreland pool bars.' Several are listed, though only one is considered a tavern and located in the center of town—easier than I thought. Of course it takes me another ten minutes to get off the freaking chair, debating whether or not this is a good idea. In the end, I convince myself I'm entitled to show up. He said they were only hanging out. It's not like I'll be a third fucking wheel.

A hot shower invigorates me, as does finally getting my car returned. Back to normal, my Mustang roars to life and I reverse out of the driveway to head into town. Since it's the weekend, I have to circle the block many times before I find a freaking space. Humidity hangs thick in the air as I climb out, bypassing a bunch of dudes lighting up and blowing smoke rings into the black sky.

I push through a vintage wooden door leading to a darkened space packed with people. From what I can see, the front area houses a bar, arranged seating, and a handful of booths near the back. In an adjacent room, pool tables are set up with games already in progress. To my right, couples hang all over each other on a self-made dance floor. I scan the area to find no sign of Julian or Ember. The music is a deafening beat anyway, and would make it difficult to get their attention. For a second, I consider maybe they decided to go elsewhere which means I'm pretty much screwed.

A firm hand squeezes my shoulder and I turn around to discover Julian leering at me. "I was wondering how long it was going to take you to show up."

"Huh?"

"I said," he shouts, cupping a hand over my ear. "I was wondering how long it was going to take you to show up."

I back away with eyes narrowed to mask my grin. "I heard you the first time. And you can wipe that smug expression off your face. You planned this whole fucking thing, didn't you?"

Julian shrugs, playing it off as completely innocent. It might work if I didn't know him so well. "I don't know what you're talking about."

I peer around him but only see heads. None of them resemble Ember. "Where is she?"

He jerks his chin over his shoulder. The music drops down a notch enabling me to hear him better. "She's sitting at a booth and...she hasn't stopped talking about you the entire time," he adds, a little too pleased with himself. "I almost think maybe she came out with me so she could pump me for information. She's curious, that one."

I chuckle while trying not to freak the fuck out about what he told her. "Julian," I warn, resorting to intimidation and not having a chance in hell of being successful. "What did you tell her?"

He whistles, bobbing his head. "Oh, not much. Just about the time we all went camping and you dove in the water and came up without your swim trunks." My threatening glare does nothing to stop his rant. "And I also told her about the time you got caught having sex with that Hooters girl in the bathroom." He taps his forehead and I'm seeing red. "What was her name?"

"The fuck you did."

"I absolutely did. I can't just tell her how remarkable you are, or what a great brother you've been to me. The way you've always had my back and watched out for me. How you read me to sleep every night when I had pneumonia and toted me around when I broke my leg playing football." His expression sobers, the lines around his eyes more pronounced. "Your ability to bypass your own fears and make sure you're there for Mom. Even when I can't be," he admits. "I had to give her the *full* picture."

Any irritation I had dissipates. I wrap an arm around his shoulder, smiling pretty fucking wide and gesturing toward the back. "Let's go. She's been alone too long. Who knows what kinds of assholes are lurking."

By the time we weave through the crowd, Ember is on her way out to dance with some guy—a broad shouldered, blond dude with a smile that's way too fucking big. Of course he's happy. He's about to dance with the prettiest girl here. That lump returns, slowly rising up my throat. I swear if he touches her, I'll pummel his ass.

Julian leaves to get me a beer while I keep my eye on Ember. She doesn't know I'm here yet, giving me an opportunity to sit back and watch. Her arms surround this dude's neck and as of right now, his arms are around her waist—where they better stay.

"Hey, I got you a Corona." Julian sets the beer in front of me and I take a long pull, hoping to wash down this strange discomfort. "Is that steam I see coming out of your ears?" He grins, clicking his bottle against mine. "Cheers." He rests his back against the wall, arm draped over the top of the booth. "This is...different for you. I'm kind of liking it. It's about time you let someone in."

I balk. "I haven't let anyone in."

"I beg to differ on that." He lifts his wrist and glances at his watch. "It only took you two point five hours to show up." He sips his beer then circles the bottle in the air. "Seriously, Vance. She's a great girl."

My eyes seek her out and I tug on my earring. "I know that. But...I also know I'm not good for her and nothing can happen." I flash to Julian's face, a blank slate, as if what I'm about to say is rote. "She'll end up with a broken heart."

"You don't know that. And you can't keep living your life like this. No one can predict the future. Besides, right now," he lifts his head toward the dance floor, "you could be the one dancing with her instead of that asshole. It's one dance." He emphasizes. "What harm could it do?"

That's what I'm afraid of.

I think about it for maybe ten seconds before I submit. "*Shit*. Okay, one dance," I agree, and his lips slide into a grin.

"God, I'm good." He gloats as I stalk off, barreling my way through the crowd.

I know how stupid this is. I keep telling myself this as I dodge drinks being spilled over the rims of glasses, hands slapping together in a series of drunken high-fives. This. Is. Stupid. The words continue to rattle around in my brain until I spot Ember. Her mouth drops open in surprise when her eyes land on me, cheeks lifting in a smile that encompasses her whole face. How could anything about *that* be stupid?

"Can I cut in, Mickey?"

"*Mickey*?" The blond guy's way-too-thick eyebrows edge higher as he steps back. "I thought your name was Ember."

"Private joke," I mutter and he sneers, his beady eyes flicking between us.

"Whatever," he mumbles as he wanders off, and Ember cracks up. My eyes scroll to the Mickey Mouse emblem at the bottom of her t-shirt.

"Not the sharpest tool in the shed, is he?"

"Nope." She places her hands on her narrow hips and stares me down. It makes me want to break into a laugh because she's trying hard not to smile—almost too hard. Her stance and expression are at complete odds with one another. "What are you doing here, Davenport?"

"I was in the neighborhood." I hold out my hand and she doesn't hesitate, curling her fingers around mine. "Now let's dance."

She loops her arms around my neck and mine settle around her waist. I breathe in her peach scent and something that is uniquely Ember, while her green eyes examine my face as if she's searching for evidence. Of what, I don't know. But if anyone can find it, it's definitely her. "I thought you didn't dance."

"I don't...usually," I add, my lips twisting into a grin.

"Wow. I feel special."

"That's because you are." The words slip out, but the way her eyes light up leave me without an ounce of regret.

She draws back further, scrutinizing me. Her gaze is unwavering and the hairs on my arms prickle. I know she can see me and it scares me to death. I swallow, trying to calm the fear rolling around my stomach and hoping to keep it at bay—if only for a little while.

Her gorgeous eyes narrow into fine slits. "What are you up to?"

"You ask too many damn questions, Mickey."

"Well," she scoffs, her ponytail flapping behind her, "maybe I wouldn't ask so many questions, if you'd just answer them the first time."

"Fine," I concede on a giant breath. "I needed to get out of the house and this seemed like a good place to do it. Happy?"

"Very." She rests her cheek on my shoulder. A minute later, her warm breath coasts over my ear. "I'm glad you're here."

I'm unable to reply because my own breath catches in my throat. The feel of her this close to me is pretty fucking amazing. My body wants to gravitate to hers, push closer, but I resist. Straining behind my zipper is a massive hard-on that I'm trying to conceal. I don't want her thinking that's what this is about—because it's not. If it was, I could easily find someone to relieve it. Whatever this is, I don't want to destroy it—because it already means something to me.

Wisps of fine hair brush against my chin as we sway back and forth, our bodies completely in sync. Another slow song plays and we continue to hold each other, neither of us anxious to let go. At one point Ember leans back, her eyes focused on mine. Her full lips too close, but not close enough.

"So, sex in the bathroom, huh? And a Hooters girl no less."

"Jesus." I look up at the grimy ceiling, grasping for a nonexistent defense to the truth. My gaze floats back down. "That was a few years ago."

"Yes. So I've been told." Her cheeks tinge pink and a burst of laughter flies from her mouth. I decide that might be my favorite sound.

"What about you? No sexual escapades of any kind?"

"Not really." Her shoulders stiffen and she loses eye contact, staring at a spot beyond my shoulder. I wonder then if she's a virgin, but decide it's none of my damn business and change the subject.

"Do you play pool?"

Any previous tension dissolves on a quiet breath and she gives me her eyes again.

"I've played. But I'm not that good. Julian and I played two games before you got here. He was trying to give me pointers." She laughs. "But they didn't take."

"That's because you didn't have the right teacher. Come on." She follows me off the dance floor, continuing to clutch my hand as we navigate our way toward the pool tables.

Several heads turn when we walk in the room, though Ember seems oblivious to it. I tamp down the way it makes my chest tighten and focus on her. A game is ending at one of the tables and we hover in the back for a few minutes until they finish up.

"Okay," I begin, picking up two pool sticks and holding one out in front of her. "This is a cue stick."

Amusement erupts from her throat and she points behind me. "And that's a table, right?"

"Yeah." I pin her with a narrowed grin. "Keep laughing, Mickey."

"Okay, okay." She clears the happiness from her face. My heart inflates because it occurs to me that I like her happy—that I like her period. "I'm ready."

"All right. So you're going to break." I grab her gently by the shoulders and move her to the head of the table. "Making sure your body is in line with the ball is key to acing the shot." She bends over to get in position and my eyes fall to her ass. I remove them quickly and remind myself to focus. "Now in order to give you good control, cup your hand on the table and place the top of the cue stick in the groove between your thumb and index finger."

"Vance?" She glances back at me, all rosy cheeks and bright eyes. I don't think she realizes how sexy she looks right now. I'm certainly not going to be the one to tell her.

"Yeah?"

"Um, I kind of already know this part. Can we move along?" She shows her full set of teeth and I fight the urge to smack her across her cute little ass.

"Okay, Miss smart-aleck. What do you do next?"

She refocuses on the solids and stripes, setting up to break. In a flash, the white ball sails into the air before it skips along the table.

I tap my pool cue against the wood floor, smirking. "What was that you were saying?"

"I was saying—"

All traces of her smile disappear, replaced with a tiny furrow between her brows. She rights herself and stands tall, shoulders high, almost as if she's gearing up for a fight. I shift to my right to stare at the person who seems to have riled her—tall, dark, and seriously preppy. Tan khaki pants, a light yellow polo shirt and short, cropped hair. He looks like he stepped out of a catalogue and carries himself with a sense of bullshit entitlement. Something is definitely off about him, making the hairs at the back of my neck stand on end.

"Connor," she greets him, her tone flat. And shit, the name suits him perfectly. It screams asshole.

He walks over to us, ignoring the fact that I'm standing next to her. "Ember, it's good to see you. You look...." His eyes drag down her body then back up and my skin crawls. She crosses one arm over her chest, using the pool cue in her hand to block him from coming any closer. He's already close enough. I can smell the alcohol leaking out from his pores. "...Gorgeous," he finishes. I catch her wince, like if she could wipe the compliment off, she would.

"Thanks," she acknowledges with a nonchalant air. Then she turns to me with a tight smile. "Vance, this is Connor. Connor, Vance."

Connor extends his hand but I refuse to shake it. He snickers as I nod my head, letting his hand drop to his waist. "Would you mind giving us a second, *Vance*?"

The condescending way he says my name makes my pulse throb in my neck. Itchy fingers flex at my sides, aching for just one punch. I look over at Ember to be sure she's all right with this.

"It's okay." Her fake smile returns, and I'm not sure that it is okay. But she's a big girl and can take care of herself.

With a nod, I reluctantly step back. Not far enough away where I can't still pick up bits of their conversation—especially the part where this piece of shit is her ex-boyfriend. That part comes through loud and clear. It ticks me off because I should have pegged him earlier.

My head tilts as I strain to listen. Normally, I might feel bad about eavesdropping. But remorse isn't remotely close to what stirs in my chest.

"Hey." Julian appears beside me. "Who's the douche?"

"Her ex-boyfriend," I ground out, still watching him like a hawk.

"Really? I can't picture that at all."

"Join the club."

My blood boils when I hear him speak. "Still wearing Mickey Mouse, huh? Aren't you a bit old for that?" Ember's lips curl into a sneer and she says something I can't make out. I take a step forward and Julian places a firm hand on my arm.

"Vance," he warns. "Let it be. She can handle herself."

I know she can. And I certainly know she doesn't want to be rescued. But my protection instinct kicks in, and I have to suck in a sharp breath and let it out slow to maintain any sort of composure. All that composure goes to shit when I catch the harsh bite of his next words.

"Maybe things would've worked out with us-s," he slurs, "if you hadn't been pining over your dead brother."

Ember's face pales. Tears spring up in her eyes and I'm fucking done. Even Julian doesn't try to stop me.

My legs carry me over there in two large strides, and before Connor knows what's happening, my fist connects with his face on a loud crack. "What the fuck is wrong with you?" I hiss, spitting the words at him.

He stumbles backwards, blood spurting from his nostrils. "What the hell? I think you b-broke my nose."

"Yeah, and you fucking deserved it." I flex my fist, jonesing for another hit. "You're lucky that's all I'm doing." Sniffling from behind makes me whirl around. Ember's eyes are dimmed with sadness and my insides crumble. I reach out to cup her cheek and wipe away a falling tear. "Let's get out of here."

The crowd that gathered to watch our little sideshow disperses. As we walk past Connor on the ground holding his nose and muttering a string of curses, I wrap a protective arm around Ember's waist and lead her toward the exit. We leave Julian who decides to hang back for a while.

Ember hesitates in front of the bar. "I need a drink," she admits. "Maybe more than one."

"Do you think that's a good idea?"

"I think it's a very good idea." She sidles her way up to the bar, tapping on the counter to attract the bartender's attention. In rapid succession, she sucks down two shots of Tequila and a shot of Vodka. If it were any other time, I'd probably stop her. But I can't imagine what's going through her mind right now other than wanting to numb it.

Dragging her wrist across her mouth, she stares at me over her shoulder. "Okay, I'm good. Actually," she pauses, her lips spiraling upward, "one more."

"Ember—"

"Ah, ah." She lifts her hand. "I think I'm entitled." I don't argue with her but I know she's going to pay for this later. Plus alcohol never solves a damn thing.

The bartender slides one more across the counter and she tosses it back before slamming the tumbler down. She gathers in a deep breath. "I'm ready now." She holds her head high as she dives into the crowd. But she doesn't fool me. My hand rests on her lower back, guiding her. I stay behind, waiting for her to fall apart—and wanting to be there to help pick up the pieces.

The temperature has dropped, a blast of cool air greeting us that I think we both need. Ember is pensive, staring up at the spattering of stars brightening the sky. A streetlamp above casts a glow on her face, highlighting the sadness behind her eyes, in the fold of her lips. My chest hurts for her, and I want to erase that deep frown pulling at the corners of her mouth.

I touch her elbow gently and lead her to the car, directing her toward the passenger side. Opening the door, I bend down to help her in then tug on the seat belt, lifting it up and over her shoulder until it clicks into place. I'm inches from her face but she doesn't see me. Her gaze is clouded, her mind elsewhere. She's lost and I need to bring her back.

But then she laughs.

"You broke his nose."

Pride swells in my chest. "I did." And the son-of-a-bitch deserved it.

"You messed up his face."

"He was too pretty anyway," I counter. He needed life to give him a wake-up call.

Her gaze strays to my red knuckles. "How's your hand?"

I grin. "Never better."

Ember falls quiet again, the air thick with both of our thoughts. The weight forces a necessary breath from my lungs as I close her door and round the car. Once inside, I buckle up and am about to start the engine when her small voice stops me. Gone is the laughter, replaced by something much heavier.

"I wasn't pining away for Zack," she insists, staring out at the dark road. Already, I want another chance at that asshole's face. "It was just...really hard. He was such a big part of who I was, who I *am*, and...I couldn't fathom how to go on without him." Her words hit close to home and a chill slides across my skin. "When all the cakes and casseroles stopped coming and the doorbell stopped ringing, it was just the four of us." She pauses, inhaling a deep breath. "And the silence was deafening. I felt like...everyone else kept living. Going on with their lives as if nothing had happened...and I had this gaping hole in my heart."

Pain rushes from her eyes and my soul feels as if it's being ripped apart. "The only person who could fill it was the one who was never coming back," she whispers, and I reach out to grasp her chin, turning her face to mine. "I miss him so much," she whispers again, tears streaming down, eyes pleading with mine for acknowledgement, understanding. I want to give her whatever she needs—and far beyond that as well.

"Oh, sweetheart." My thumb brushes back and forth over her skin. "I know how much you were hurting. The kind of hurt there's no remedy for." I raise my other hand to cup her cheek, staring hard into her eyes. "It's okay to let yourself feel that." She nods on a short intake of breath. "And I understand," I murmur with a soft smile. "I do."

I draw her to me then and she presses her face into my chest, sobbing loud, painful bursts of emotion. And I let her give it all to me, so I can carry it for her—as long as she'll let me.

She pulls back when her sobs turn to soft cries. The quiver of her lip calms and her warm palm finds my cheek. "Somehow I knew you'd understand."

I cover her hand with my own. "I do understand," I utter quietly and give her a small smile. "Thank you for trusting me enough to share it with me."

She nods, letting her hand slide out from underneath mine. A profound sense of loss comes over me and shakes me up, making me lightheaded.

How can you fear losing something that can never be yours?

THE DRIVE BACK to Ember's house is filled with introspective silence. Though all that changes as I pull into her driveway. The cut of the engine is replaced by muted groans. When I turn to Ember, she has one hand clutched to her belly while the other one holds the side of her head.

"I don't feel so good all of a sudden."

"Hang on, Mickey." I climb out and come around the car, opening her door and leaning inside. "Wrap your arms around my neck," I instruct, and once she manages to anchor her loose limbs around me, I reach under her knees to scoop her up. She continues to moan softly as I ease her out of the car and carry her to the porch. With one arm keeping her body hoisted, my other hand scrounges in her purse for keys while attempting not to drop her to the ground.

"I might throw up on you if this takes too long," she mumbles as I fiddle with the key in the lock. The sound of the loud click makes me exhale with relief.

Except for dim light emanating from the kitchen, the house is dark and quiet.

"Where's the bathroom?" I whisper, not wanting to get caught sneaking around her house. I don't think this would make for a great introduction to her mom.

She lifts a clumsy finger and points toward the staircase. "Up."

Every other step creaks as we climb and I slow down, the noise too loud in the dense quiet. Somehow, I'm able to get us to the bathroom; the last room at the end of what seems like a never ending hallway.

A loud gurgle erupts from Ember's stomach as I push open the door and set her gently on the tile. She springs into action, diving for the toilet bowl and plopping down in front of it. Her limp arms attach to both sides of the cold porcelain, hugging it for dear life. Then she coughs, but it sounds more like gagging. I kneel beside her, holding up her ponytail and soothing her back with my hand.

"I drank too much, t-too quick. I'm drunk."

I chuckle. "You are."

"That was s-stupid." She whines into the toilet.

"Nah. I kind of think it was a human response to a subhuman asshole."

Ember tries to laugh, but throws up instead. "Urggh." She groans, the contents of her stomach emptying two more times before she lies down on the floor and curls up like a snail. Her body starts to shiver as noises of discomfort bubble up from her mouth. Cold races down my throat and I go into panic mode, digging around the bathroom cabinets for a washcloth or anything to help her. I find a small towel underneath the sink and soak it in warm water. Crouching beside her, I lay it across her forehead. Her eyelids flutter and she groans again, arms wrapped around her belly.

"Let me get you into bed." In one motion, I raise her up off the tile, carrying her against my chest. "Which room is yours?" I ask, and she grunts an incoherent response that makes me smile. Basically, I'm on my own.

Through the powers of deduction and the help of Mickey Mouse, I locate her room and navigate my way to her bed. Gently lowering her to the mattress, I keep her head cradled and position her on a pillow. She giggles when I slip her sneakers from her feet.

"Mmm...good."

I have no idea if she needs to get sick again. Just in case, I sprint to the bathroom and grab the small trash can near the toilet. I place it on the floor next to the bed then cover her up to her neck with a blanket. As I sit down beside her, my weight shifts the mattress and she blinks up at me. The scrap of light from the window rests on part of her face. Her eyes are glassy and wide as she stares at me and jabs a sloppy finger into my chest.

"You know, I didn't like you when I first met you. You were kind of a j-jerk. But," she adds, her smile lopsided. "I like you now."

I thread my fingers through the damp hair at her temple as a grin takes over my lips. "I like you too, Mickey."

She lets out a hiccupped sigh then rolls over and snuggles into the pillows. Quietly, I slide off the mattress, glancing around her room but seeing very little in the darkness. "I like you...a l-lot," she mumbles, and I freeze, my heart thrumming to a beat I can't control. With those five words, it's like she's trying to get inside me, push past my skin to a deeper place. I think it might be too late. I already feel her there. I'm scared of that—of her—and what she could do to me. But I let my body ease down the wall where I'll stay to make sure she's all right.

There is no place else I'd rather be, anyway.

chapter twenty
Ember

I DRIVE INTO the entrance of Cannon Beach, the salty ocean air wafting in through the open window. A lightness fills my chest as if a small amount of weight has been lifted. I feel more like myself—my old self that is.

The breathtaking view of the sea makes me pause and my chest flutters. Water may have taken my brother's life, but there is no denying its beauty. The way it glistens and sparkles in invitation, blue-green waves curling before they break against the shore.

It's fairly deserted this time of day. The sun is playing hide and seek with the clouds, doing some sort of indecisive waltz. Four tall white birds perch beside a rock, their noses digging in the sand looking for buried treasures to eat.

It doesn't take me long to spot Vance, though even on a crowded beach he would stand out. I stop to watch him for a minute. His feet are bare, shirt off, the hills and valleys of his back shimmer in the hazy sun. Fine hair dances along his neck, the slight breeze moving it and I shiver, almost as if I can feel the sensation across my own skin.

One arm glides back then forward, a stone leaving his fingers and skipping along the calm surface of the water. The way his body curves inward toward the ocean, giving it his full concentration is truly beautiful.

"You're really good at that." I interrupt his quiet moment, but the way his lips bow as he turns toward me makes me glad I came.

"Heyyy," he chirps, and my eyes move over the ripples of his chest then quickly back up to meet his grin.

"You can stare all you want, Mickey. I don't mind." The ground suddenly grabs my interest. I'm hoping it might suck me in like quicksand, making the warm flush spreading across my face disappear. As if he senses I need an escape, he keeps talking. "How are you feeling?" he asks, and that I can handle.

"Much better." I bypass his chest this time and go right to his face. "Thank you for that hangover cure you left. What was that, anyway?"

"Fresh squeezed orange juice with a hint of Ginger Ale." He chuckles. "The Advil I can't take credit for, though."

"Wait." I edge a few steps closer to him. "How did you make the orange juice?"

"I did it the old-fashioned way." His blue eyes gleam. "You know, I squeezed oranges...with my hands."

"In my kitchen?"

"No. In your front yard." He smirks. "Of course in your kitchen."

"Oh." A tiny flutter pings my belly at his sweet gesture. "Thank—"

His hand comes up between us, cutting my words short. "Don't say it. I think we're good with the thank you's for a while," he explains, and I let out a small laugh.

"Okay."

"So how did you know where I was? Because this is kind of a hike for you." He looks back toward the water as if it's calling him.

"I stopped by your house and caught Julian on his way to a client."

"Ah." He bends down to pluck another rock from the sand and I catch a glimpse of his tattoo. My fingers itch to glide along the curved letters. "You ever skip stones?" When I shake my head no, he motions me closer with a jerk of his chin. "C'mere." As I get near enough to see the beads of sweat dotting his chest, he points to my feet. "Take off your sneakers. You know, to get the full effect," he adds, and I kick them aside. He positions himself behind me, close enough that his breath whispers over my cheek, and places the warm stone in my palm. "It's all in the wrist," he explains, his fingers circling my hand and flicking it a few times. Goose bumps travel up my arms and I'm praying they're invisible. "Okay, on three." We count backwards and release it into the air. The rock plunks into the ocean and sinks to the bottom. "Good try."

Despite two more unsuccessful attempts, Vance remains encouraging while I blow out a frustrated breath. "Do you want to try again? Fourth time's a charm," he teases, and I nod. It isn't a difficult decision because I want him to keep holding my hand. "Okay, same motion. Ready?"

"As I'll ever be," I answer, and together we let go of the stone. It skips once, twice, three times across the water and I squeal. "I did it!" I spin around, still squealing, and nearly fall into him.

"You did at that." He lifts a finger to tuck a wisp of hair behind my ear. His hand lingers and my breaths come faster—too loud now, overshadowing all other sound. But then he blinks out of the moment, as if he realizes what he's doing, and lets his hand drop to his side. He clears something from his throat and turns to face the water. "You did good, Mickey."

Moving to stand beside him, I peer at the ocean, the tide breathing in and out as it reaches then pulls back from the shore. My eyes track a seagull flying overhead as the grey bird swoops down in search of food. "It's so peaceful here."

"It is," he agrees. "And it's a great place to read." He points behind him to two books sitting on a slab of rock. "I saw my mom earlier today." He glances over at me with a smile that reaches his eyes. "She was having an unusually good day."

"Yeah?"

"She knew who I was when I walked in." His happiness is contagious. It blooms inside of me and I rest my hand on his arm. He looks down at it but doesn't pull away. "She told me my hair was too long, but that she liked my earring."

"I'm so thrilled for you." I give his arm a squeeze then let go.

"Thanks. I told her I'd see her tomorrow, and...," he hesitates, his voice littered with emotion, "even though she might not remember me tomorrow, I feel like I can keep today in my pocket for when I need it." He casts an uncertain glance my way. "I know that probably sounds odd."

"Not to me." I flash him a reassuring smile. "It doesn't sound odd at all." His eyes pore over my face before he lowers them to the sand.

Rippled waves cascade under our feet as we continue to gaze at the golden sun, free of the clouds now, reflecting off the water. I chance a glimpse of Vance's profile. His skin misted with a fine sheen of sweat, mouth relaxed and parted slightly. Worry that normally hides in the corner of his eyes is at bay—at least for now.

The strong angle of his jaw and the smooth curve of his nose beckon to me, and I find myself tracing his features as if I was actually touching him. He turns to catch me staring and his lips spread into a wide grin. That's when it strikes me.

"I want to sculpt you."

His eyes sparkle. "It's because I'm devilishly handsome, isn't it?"

I huff out a laugh. "Yes, that's definitely it. Sprinkled with a dash of 'I'm full of myself.'"

A moment goes by and I can tell he's considering my request. He regards me then, his smile transforming into wickedness. "Would I be naked?"

I lift a brow. "Do you want to be?"

"Let's move onto the next question," he answers quickly, and I snort.

"So can I?" Too many seconds pass that I'm sure his answer is going to be no, but he surprises me.

"Okay." My heart does a small leap inside my chest. "When will I be sculpted?"

Lost in my excitement, it takes me a minute to respond. "Huh? Oh, I don't know." I search the sky before meeting his eyes. "How about in the morning? I don't have to work so...."

"I need to send out more resumes, but...." He gestures with his hands as if he's balancing a scale. "Let's see...job hunting, orrrr, being the subject of a work of art? Hmph." He shoots me an uncertain grin.

"Let's do it."

Inside, I'm brimming with enthusiasm but I try to tone it down. "Great."

Vance sweeps his shirt from a nearby rock and tugs it over his head while I try not to stare at his abs, his pecs, his everything really. He grabs his books and we hoist our sneakers from the sand. I swing mine all the way back to the car, unable to keep how thrilled I am under wraps.

"I'll see you in the morning then," he says as we part. The amusement that lights his face isn't lost on me.

"What?"

He walks backwards, mouth curving high on one side. "You're enjoying this a little too much."

"Enjoying what?" I protest with a straight face. "I haven't done anything yet."

"Exactly."

Then he pivots and stalks off, as only Vance Davenport knows how to stalk—sexy and damn near arresting—oozing everything I know I shouldn't want.

But in this moment, I can't think of anything I want more.

chapter twenty-one
Ember

I THROW ON a Mickey Mouse tank with a pair of cutoff jean shorts and stand in front of the full-length mirror, wondering what Vance Davenport thinks about me. I'm not entirely sure why I care. I just know that I do.

Avery's voice startles me from behind. "Well, well. Only ten minutes in the shower. What gives, sister dear?" She's leaning against the doorframe with her arms poised across her chest, one wicked brow scrutinizing me.

"Nothing. I'm just...." I let out a breath and turn around to face her all-knowing smile. "Vance is coming over and I'm going to sculpt him."

Her eyes spring open. "He's letting you do that? Wow."

"I know, right. I'm kind of taken aback myself." I shift to face the mirror again, running a comb through my wet hair.

"I've always been so jealous of you." Avery's gaze meets mine in the glass and I blink. Her comment doesn't quite register. "I've always been jealous of the fact that you're so comfortable in your own skin. That I always felt like I had to try so hard, when you didn't worry about trying at all." Her melancholy expression is as unexpected as her next words. "You always thought you were ordinary. When in fact, you're anything but."

Her gaze drifts to a picture of us on the wall. "You're just so...*you*," she admits, her eyes coming back to mine. "And you're essential to me. Almost like air," she adds. For a second I wonder if she's kidding, but there isn't a hint of teasing in her voice. "I love you. And...I admire you, Ember. I always have. I just wanted you to know that."

Stunned, my hand flies to my chest and I whirl around to reply but she's already gone. I've never seen my sister like that before. Most of the time when she feels something it's concealed, like the world would end if she let someone know there was a thing called emotion.

"Hi, sweetie." My mother walks by as I'm still trying to process Avery's words.

"Hi, Mom. Wait." I step into the hallway to catch her. "Are you all right? What I mean is, I've barely seen you at all. And you haven't been around for our Wednesday dinners."

"Oh." She runs a hand over her hair to smooth it down. "Well, we signed a huge contract for a new residential renovation in Portland so that's underway. Plus, I've received a few referrals as well."

"That's great, then." I think.

She checks her watch and holds her portfolio snug against her chest. "Okay, I have to run." She glances at the time again. "I'll probably be home late tonight, but I'll see you tomorrow."

Frazzled doesn't enter into the equation where Mom is concerned, and something nags at me. "Mom, are you sure everything is okay?"

"Yes, yes. It's great, sweetie. I'm just running behind is all," she calls back as she trots downstairs in her navy blue suit and matching heels. She opens the door and runs right into Vance. "Hello."

"Hi. You must be Mrs. Bennett? I'm Vance, a friend of Ember's."

"It's very nice to meet you, Vance." Mom sends me a rushed smile and then she's gone, leaving my head spinning with questions.

"What's wrong?" Vance asks as I come down the stairs. I wish I had an answer.

I throw my hands up then slap them against the side of my legs. "I have no idea. It's like the twilight zone around here this morning."

"Not to worry. *I'm* here now." He proudly holds up two cups and a bag. The aroma of freshly brewed coffee spills into the air and I smile.

"And I come bearing sustenance."

I sniff a few times and Vance grins. "I smell...blueberries and amazing coffee?"

"Close, Mickey. Very close."

Dipping my nose down, I inhale again. "Boysenberry?"

"Got it on the second try." He passes me a coffee and holds out the open bag. "Not bad."

"I got the coffee right," I tease, desperate for my first sip of the day. As the warm taste of hazelnut floods my mouth, I dig my fingers into the bag to pull out a clump of muffin.

Vance shakes his head in a dramatic fashion, hair flying around his face. "I just figured, to sculpt a work of art of this magnitude, you needed nourishment."

I bark out a laugh and nearly spit coffee in his face. "I might not have enough clay to sculpt that big head of yours. Let's go."

"Cool," Vance muses as we descend the stairs and the basement comes into view. "This is a great space. I could totally read or strum some tunes down here."

"Thanks. I love it, too." Energy buzzes beneath my skin as I look around. I'm not certain if the high is from the room or the person standing in the room. "It's always been a bit of an escape for me."

"What's this?" He points to the small square package on the table. I completely forgot it was there. "It has my name on it."

"That's because it's for you. Just something I thought you might like." He puts his coffee down with the bag and picks up the present to inspect it. Meanwhile, I bite on my lower lip.

"Feels kind of...heavy." He grins up at me, raising and lowering it with his palm. "The Mickey Mouse paper is a nice touch."

"You can open it any day now," I offer and he chuckles, continuing to take his time and prolonging my agony.

As he rips the paper, the smile I was hoping to see appears tenfold. "Holy shit. A hardcover version of *The Sun Also Rises*." His gaze lifts to mine. "My paperback was falling apart."

"I know." I watch the moment his confusion turns to recollection and my lips burst at the corners.

"The trespassing incident." His fingers scroll over the title before he looks up at me. "Thank you. It's great, Mickey. Really."

"Sure." I keep my response casual, trying not to make it as big of a deal on the outside as it feels on the inside.

Vance roams about, book in hand, stopping at various pictures along the wall. "There's a lot of happiness here." Something in his somber tone of voice makes me cross the room to be closer to him. He leans in to examine a photo of Zack and me goofing off in the backyard. I think I was maybe fourteen at the time. "Your brother...that face." He looks back and forth between me and the picture. "It's you."

"I know." I stare at the photo, remembering that day. It was a good one. "Zack used to say that all I had to do was cut my hair short, and I could be him."

Vance smothers my body with his gaze and I suck down coffee to distract from the heat. "Nah. I don't think so."

I swallow hard and way too loud. "Shall we get started?" His chuckle follows me as I make a beeline for the sculpting table. Placing my coffee cup on the metal surface, I busy myself with the task of removing a hunk of clay from the cabinet.

"Where do you want me?" Vance asks, and I have too many answers to that question and no outlet for them, other than trying to hide the blush that refuses to disappear. I point to a nearby stool. "Right there is good."

He places the book on the table then hops up on the stool, stretching his neck from left to right. "Ready when you are."

"I can see that." I smirk, my hands already folding themselves into the clay as if they are one. "I want to ask you a question."

His chin lifts in a subtle tease. "I would expect nothing less."

"Have you ever gotten along with your father?"

At first, he seems taken aback by my question, but then his cheeks soften and a hint of a smile crosses his lips.

"There was a time when I thought he was my hero. He was...well, he was the dad who used to take me to karate tournaments and cheer for me instead of yelling whenever I missed a key move. When I was frustrated with math because I sucked at it, he sat with me patiently to help when all I wanted to do was beat my fucking head against the wall." He laughs, the warm sound filling me up. "My dad used to take me to the library even when he had other things to do. He'd bring his newspaper and stay with me for hours on end because he knew how much I loved being around all those books. I wanted to live there."

I pause with my fingers immersed in the clay. "So what happened?"

"I don't know." He stares past me and I know I'm losing him. "Life I guess." His lips flatten into a line, a hardness forming around his eyes where there was none. "He's not the same person anymore."

Though I know this might upset him, I'm unable to hold back. "Don't you think your mom becoming ill had an effect on him? It has to be really difficult."

"Yes," Vance agrees, his eyes returning to mine. "You'd think it would be, right? But as far as I can see, he's gone on with his life. It's business as usual, while my mother is wasting away in there." He looks away then back to me. "Mind if we change the subject? It's not my favorite one."

"Sure."

"Now I have a question for you. What was up with that dude in the bar? I can't picture it. It's just that you're so...." With my hands firmly planted in the clay, I wait for the words he searches for on the ceiling. But they never come. "How did you guys even hook up?"

The single breath I held tight releases itself and I tell him the not so sordid story. "It's not that deep, really. We met at an art show. His parents were benefactors and...I don't know. He loved art, too, and he knew a lot about it. And we just...clicked."

His gaze beams against my face like bright sunlight. "I don't know shit about art, but I can spot an asshole a mile away."

My laughter echoes throughout the room. "Good to know." Still trying to reconcile it in my own mind, I go on. "I don't know. He fooled me, I suppose. I thought he was something he wasn't. I'm just not that...experienced, I guess. I told you, dating has never been a priority for me."

The words *until now* roll around in my brain. This thing with

Vance. It feels like...*something*. I want to reach for it, like grabbing a star from the sky.

"Why not?" he asks, dragging me from my momentary daze.

The structure of Vance's jaw takes shape and I tilt my head to admire it. "My studies and my art were my focus. Besides," I add, "Avery had enough interest for the both of us. I think she started dating when she was nine." My hands still on the clay as my mind sends me back to fifth grade. "I remember this one time, she had me lure Steven Corbett onto the playground just so she could try to kiss him. She told me he liked those double-stuffed Oreos so she bought a huge pack and I basically bribed him."

"Did it work?"

My answering smile gives me away. "Of course it did. We're talking about Avery now. She gets—"

"Geez, Mickey. Is my head that big?" My eyebrows lift and he gestures with his chin toward the partially formed likeness. "The sculpture?"

"Ohhh. It's a work in progress. And your head isn't big." I smirk. "It's round." He pokes his tongue against his cheek, trying to muffle a grin. "But your hair...." Dried clay sticks between my fingers and I tear a paper towel from the wall dispenser. As I scrape it off, I walk over to him. "I can't see your eyes. Your hair is in the way." I reach out, my hand pausing in mid-air. "May I?"

Wariness flashes in his eyes. He pushes past it and gives me a nod accompanied by a gradual swallow. My only thought—this is my free pass to touch him—and I intend to take full advantage of it.

chapter twenty-two
Vance

GENTLE FINGERTIPS DANCE across my forehead, sweeping the fine hair over my brow. My breathing stutters then halts, her touch like the softest fucking kiss along my skin. "Vance," she whispers. "You can breathe." My shoulders sag as her hand disappears. Heat rises everywhere she touched, electricity crackling in the narrow space between us.

Needing to break the tension, I say whatever words come to mind. "You were just using this as an excuse to touch me."

"Maybe." An absence of teasing in her voice makes my heart thunder inside my chest. It's been a long time since anyone has touched me like this—with something approaching tenderness. And while it's completely foreign to me, with her, it almost feels necessary. *She* feels necessary.

And I'm fucking scared. But I'm *sick* of being scared.

The world I've constructed for myself, for years, is falling apart. My control is slipping. The walls crumbling and I need to scramble to put them back up. Only I can't. Something about Ember makes me helpless to do any of it. I've shut myself down for too long and part of me wonders what it would feel like to let someone in, to share that closeness I've denied myself. Still, fear chokes me until I want to pry its hands from my neck.

"Vance, hey." Her soft tone invades my thoughts and I stare up into the most beautiful pair of eyes I've ever seen. "You disappeared on me."

"Yeah, sorry." I lift my index finger to her skin and gently rub the area below her cheekbone. "You've got a bit of clay here." Her breathing changes and she mashes her lips together, drawing my eyes lower. I wonder what her mouth would feel like pressed against mine. Her tongue comes out to wet her lips and my desire grows.

"Okay, well, I can see your eyes now, so...."

She turns and I grab her wrist. "Ember, wait." The expectant look in her eyes makes me want to be worthy—of what I don't know. But damn it, that little voice in the recesses of my brain won't leave me alone, demanding I pay attention to who I am. "Never mind."

"Okay." She paints on a smile, unable to hide the edge of disappointment in her voice. Little does she know, the disappointment is fucking mutual. Only the person I'm disappointed with...is myself.

"WHEW. I DIDN'T realize how exhausting being a model is." I jump down from the stool, craning my neck in a circular stretch.

"Yes, the energy exertion is over the top." She flings me a grin. "I'm surprised you can walk." She carries the sculpture to a three-tier silver shelf. I can't get over how much it resembles me.

"Holy shit, Ember." I walk closer for a better view. "This is fucking fantastic. You are seriously talented. It actually looks...like me." Yet as I study it more, something is different about my face, my eyes. I'm unable to pinpoint what it is, though.

Pride exudes from her every limb, she glows with it. "I hope so."

"No, I mean it." I hold her gaze. "This is definitely your calling."

"I'd like to have my own gallery someday," she admits. "Maybe even in New York City." Her voice is not as confident as I'd expect it to be. Certainly not after seeing her work.

"It sounds more like a question than a statement. Is that what you really want?"

"Yes," she affirms, insecurity sticking to her tone.

"Then go get it." And I hope my smile conveys how much I believe in her.

Her eyes follow the path of her finger as she trails it over an elaborate sculpture of a bird. "You make it sound so easy."

I bend down until she has no choice but to look at me. "Isn't it?"

"I'm just...," she drops her gaze, "not used to going after what I want."

"Well, get used to it. Because you're going places, Ember Bennett. Trust me on that."

And I wish I could go with you.

"Thanks, Vance." Her eyes come back to mine, alight with happiness, and warmth seeps into my chest.

My focus goes to the shelf and her various pieces of artwork. A sculpture catches my attention; two hands reaching out for one another, their fingers barely touching. I lift it carefully, studying the detail. "I really like this one."

She traces the outline of the hand, a story playing out behind her eyes. "That's me...reaching for Zack." She glances up, allowing me to see her. And *God*, so much is there. Sadness, yes, but mostly sweetness and beauty. Memories of days passed. Suddenly, I'm envious.

Nothing I could say right now would do this piece justice, so I opt for silence. But I do reach for her, stroking the side of her smooth cheek with my fingers. Thick lashes flutter closed and she leans toward my touch, bringing her mouth nearer to mine. It makes me think about how much I want to kiss her. I'm not thinking about a kiss that would lead to me getting into her pants. Maybe it's something I already knew but refused to admit. It isn't the same with Ember as it was with other girls. I only want to put my mouth on hers; a soft brush of lips, one kiss. Except I know with her—one kiss would never be enough.

She opens her eyes and catches me staring. Her chest rises and falls at a steady pace, cheeks hold a pink flush. I'm pretty sure she wouldn't push me away if I tried to kiss her. Apprehension tugs at me like a thread waiting to unravel. I lean forward and press my lips to her forehead. It's not the kiss I want, but it is the one she needs right now.

"This piece is really beautiful," I whisper, her smile touching my chin. I wonder how this could be bad for me. Isn't a short burst of happiness better than none at all? Then again, she'll end up broken—and I'll end up with nothing. But I can't deny that I want to be near her. She zaps me with life in a way that I can't avoid—I'm not sure I want to anymore. I rest my palm against her cheek and pull back to look at her. "Listen, I want to take you somewhere. Are you up for another road trip?"

Mischief lights her smile. "That depends."

"On...."

"Two things," she explains, and my brows lift in anticipation. "One, I pick the music. And two, I want to go in the Mustang."

I tweak her nose and she laughs. "You drive a hard bargain Mickey, but okay."

"Let me get the rest of this clay off my hands and then I'll be ready." She walks off toward the bathroom and I cock my head to the side, staring at the sway of her hips in those cut-off jean shorts. Right before she disappears into the bathroom, she peeks over her shoulder. "Take a picture, it'll last longer."

Jesus, this girl.

She shuts the door and I rock on my feet until my gaze strays to the book. I wander over to swipe it from the table, smiling more than I probably have a right to. Ember emerges after a minute, drying her hands on a towel. "Okay, I'm ready." On the way up the stairs, she gives me a curious sideways glance. "Anything I need to bring on this mystery trip?"

"Nope, just you."

Inquisitive eyes drill into mine as she continues to search for clues. "No hints, huh?"

"Nope."

She's quiet after that, but it's obvious she is chomping at the bit to know where I'm taking her. A pit of nerves grows in the corner of my stomach. I've never shared this part of me with anyone else. While I know it's not crazy fucking exciting, something tells me Ember will appreciate it.

AN HOUR INTO the ride, when we still haven't reached our destination, Ember shifts in her seat. "Okay, where are we going? You're not driving me to Vegas, are you?"

"Vegas?" I tsk, veering over to the left to pass a slow-ass car in the other lane. "I'm not sure I could tolerate your company for fifteen hours."

She flicks my arm while giving me the evil eye. "Have you always been this sarcastic?"

"Only when I like someone," I retort, the words sliding free without reservation—because they're the truth.

That shuts her up for a little while. Actually, that shuts us both up. Me, not knowing what to do with this shitstorm of feeling inside my chest. Like a tsunami I'm not prepared for. My heart doesn't seem big enough for all this emotion. Once again, my head tries to convince my heart that it doesn't matter. But for the first time in my life, my heart says '*fuck you*' and refuses to listen.

A few minutes tick by and I steal a glance at Ember. She ducks her head and peers out the windshield. "Look at that sky, there aren't any clouds. It's like a sheet of blue," she points out, and it strikes me that she has this sense of wonder about the world—almost childlike in ways. Somewhere along the line I've lost that, or maybe I've pushed it away. Because, what's the point? "It's definitely a perfect day for...." She hums to the music. "Where did you say we were going again?"

"I didn't." I grin. "But I'll give you credit for being persistent." With a quick look over at her, I add. "You must've been a real joy on long car trips when you were a kid. Are we *there* yet?" I tease, and she snorts, a smile creeping onto her cheeks.

"Okay, you found me out." She confesses with a spring in her voice. "But I will tell you, my dad was always prepared. He used to buy loads of those word finds and crossword puzzles. Anything he could do to keep us busy, because he knew he was going to have his hands full." She persists, and I find myself hanging onto her every word. I want to learn all there is to know about Ember Bennett. "I always had to sit in the middle because Avery and Zack argued like crazy. So I was kind of the peacekeeper."

"Why didn't they get along?"

"Until recently, I might've said it was because they were too different." She pauses and I can hear the wheels spinning. "But something Avery said...I think she was jealous of his relationship with me. The fact that we were so close."

Our exit approaches and I steer the car into the right hand lane. "Your sister is like a fireball."

"Yeah, she is." Out of the corner of my eye, I see her pull something from her purse. A pack of cigarettes, I think. It makes no sense. I've never seen her smoke before and it seems contrary to her character. "Want one?" she offers, and I shake my head.

"I try to stay away from those things." We reach the red light at the end of the exit ramp and roll to a stop. She stares down at the pack then up to me, frowning, as if she doesn't understand why I don't want to put death into my lungs.

"You don't chew gum?"

"Huh?"

"They're Bubble Gum Cigarettes," she reveals, a smile teasing her lips.

"Are you shitting me?"

"No, why would I be. See...." She unrolls the white wrapper and shoves the pink wad into her mouth. I give her the side eye and her gaze narrows on mine. "Problem?"

"Nope. Just making a mental note." I tap the side of my head. "Mickey Mouse, Bubble Gum Cigarettes. Anything else I should know?" I quickly give the inside of her bag the once over before sliding my eyes back to the road. "Harboring any Red Hots, Doritos maybe?"

"Ew. Those are disgusting, and so bad for you."

I grin wide as the light turns green. "They are."

She makes a clucking sound with her tongue. "I don't know how you stay in such great shape eating all that crap?"

"You checking me out, Mickey?" And I don't need to see her face to know her cheeks are pink.

"You're not exactly hard on the eyes," she blurts, and a surprised laugh lifts itself from my chest. Although I don't know why I'm surprised anymore. She says whatever she thinks, and I love that she doesn't flip her hair over her shoulder or bat her eyelashes to try to get my attention. All she has to do is exist for that to happen.

chapter twenty-three
Ember

I DON'T KNOW what happens to me around Vance Davenport. But I'm starting not to question it anymore. This jittery quivering inside my chest, caught between nervous and excited, doesn't feel bad to me. And truth be told, he really is easy on the eyes. Especially the curve of his overconfident grin. It gets me every time.

I'm busy staring at his lips, the ones that form that irresistible smile when I vaguely hear his words.

"We're here."

I peel my eyes from his mouth to glance out the window. All I can see is a gathering of tall green trees but nothing beyond. As we climb out of the car, I summon a deep breath. "I smell trees...and water."

"Come on. This way." He reaches out to twine his fingers with mine. My gaze drops to our joined hands as I follow behind him, trying not to give my smile away. Butterflies dance in my belly and even break out into song. I know I'm being foolish because it doesn't mean anything. And for someone who always tells the truth, I'm pretty darn good at lying to myself. Because in this moment—it means everything to me. I only hope it means something to him.

We work our way past the opening of trees, stepping over small stones and large rocks until a river comes into full view. The sun casts a bright beam against the mossy green water, and that, coupled with the sound of a rushing waterfall, makes me lose my breath. Suddenly Zack is all around me, and it's overwhelming in a way that's hard to describe. My chest feels heavy, yet light at the same time. Tears well in my eyes but refuse to fall. Somehow as I take in the beauty that surrounds us, it brings me an overall sense of peace. I can see it in Vance, too. The way his shoulders relax, his profile softens. He lets go of my hand and I inwardly sigh at the loss of contact.

"This is my favorite place," he admits, one hand on his waist as he gazes up at the sky. "My mother used to bring me and Julian here. This is where she taught us how to skim rocks. Of course," he lets out a breathy laugh, "Julian sucked at it. It's always been one of the things I was better at than him." Vance points to a nearby segment of rock and we sit down, stretching our legs out on the sun-warmed stone. "I remember this one time," he looks over at me, "I think we were maybe ten or so—" Vance stops mid-sentence, his gaze hard and heavy on my face. "What is it? What's going on in your head?" I want to answer, but I don't want to spoil this for him. "Out with it, Mickey."

Arms crossed over his chest and expectant stare unwavering, he waits for my words to come. I think I need to say them. "That sculpture." I pause to gather a breath. "The one of the hands that you commented on...it's from a recurring dream that I have. The one where I'm reaching out to Zack, where he latches onto my hand and I save him." I blow out my resolve, and along with it, the truth. "He drowned while he was on a white water rafting trip in Colorado," I admit quietly. Vance gasps, but I keep my focus trained on a piece of grass sticking up between two rocks. "My mom didn't want him to go. She told him it was too dangerous and you know what he said?" I continue as if Vance isn't here, as if I'm talking to myself. Words I've replayed over and over in my head for two years. "He said, '*Mom, I'm a daredevil. I've got a zillion lives.*' And that was it. That was one of the last things he ever said to us." I wrap my arms around myself to stave off the sudden emptiness from missing him. "I didn't think twice about it, because it was Zack. And that's just what he did." My eyes travel back to his. "And he always came home...except that day he didn't."

Vance lifts a hand to his forehead, rubbing two fingers against his temple. "Jesus, Ember. I'm sorry. I didn't know. If I had, I wouldn't have taken you here and—"

"*No.*" The last thing I want is for him to feel bad about bringing me here. Especially since he's sharing a part of himself. Head held high, I give him the biggest smile I can muster. The expression catches me unaware. The tingle in my cheeks unexpected as I realize this is not only for his benefit, but coming from a deeper spot in my heart—a place of comfort, not grief. Then my lips spread wide because in some bizarre way this all makes sense to me. Like fitting the final piece into a puzzle. "I'm really glad you brought me here, and I love that this is your favorite place. It's perfect and beautiful, and I want to hear more."

"Are you sure?" he asks, still studying me to make certain I'm okay.

"Yes, I am. Promise." I nudge his foot with my sneaker. "Now finish your story."

He stares at his black Chucks touching my red ones and his mouth relaxes into a smile. "Okay, but no laughing," he orders, and I show him my most serious face. "So I think...we were about ten. Anyway, we came down here with Mom to go swimming." He glances out at the water. "Julian decided he thought it would be funny to put a frog down my shorts and I think I freaked out a bit." He turns to me. "Well," he admits without reservation. "Maybe more than a bit."

"I bet you were cute," I tell him, recalling the pictures on the wall of his room.

He glides a palm over his knee. "I ran out of the water like my fucking shorts were on fire. Plus, I had braces and an early onset of acne so I'd say there was nothing cute about me."

I stare at his face and find that difficult to believe. His eyes probably drew girls in like bees to honey. "I got teased by Martin Fanning in the sixth grade hallway. He used to say, '*How about a little fire, Ember?*'"

"That's original." Vance snorts, shooting me a sympathetic grin.

Heat rushes to my cheeks. "Yeah, it's funny how simple it was though. Troy confronted him in gym and said, '*Really dude, that's getting old.*' Then he just stopped. And I remember wondering, how come I didn't think of that?" Vance gives my foot a playful shove as a comfortable quiet settles between us. Nearby, the sound of birds catches my attention. I close my eyes and lean back against my hands, letting the sun warm my face. "Listen. I think those are Finch. God, it's like a little slice of heaven all tucked away back here." My skin burns, no longer from the sun but from Vance's steady gaze.

"You see everything, don't you?"

I swing my head in his direction, squinting against the bright rays. "Don't you?"

"No." His gaze moves past me toward a steep wall of rock. "I look at things, but I haven't really seen anything for a very long time." I open my eyes fully and his focus is back on me, serious and unrelenting. "Until you," he admits, and my mouth separates but I struggle to form words. I must have heard him wrong. Not that you would know it from my wild heartbeat. "It's impossible not to see you." He laughs, but the sound is strained. "And believe me, I've tried." His fingers crawl over to mine, almost touching. "You embrace life, Ember. Shit, you are life...and I've been avoiding it for so long."

A tear gathers in the corner of my eye, sneaking out and dropping down my cheek. I'm not usually at a loss for words, but all of a sudden my mouth is dry and a nervous tickle resides in my throat—because I want this, whatever *this* is—I want him.

Another tear escapes and he reaches over to brush it away. "Is it because I'm badass?" My voice sounds strange, trying to use humor to calm my racing heart. It's not working.

"Yeah," a grin stretches his mouth, "that's definitely it." He scoots over, sitting in front of me with his long legs crossed. That soap he uses floats in the surrounding air making it impossible to think straight. I watch his hand move closer, then closer still, until his fingertip begins tracing the curve of mine. A slight touch, but it has my pulse unable to slow down. He raises his other hand to cup my cheek and my eyelids flutter closed to the tenderness of it, his thumb trailing back and forth over my skin. Goose bumps dance along my neck as my eyes flicker open to his gaze, fixated on my mouth. Just when I think I might get to feel the press of his lips against mine, he grabs my hand and yanks me up off the ground. "Let's go in the water."

"Ooookay." I exhale a nervous laugh, trying to hide my disappointment as I lean down to remove my Chucks.

Vance toes off his sneakers and rolls the cuffs of his jeans. He glares up at me with a straight face. "Clothes or no clothes?"

"Uh...," I stammer, like a deer caught in headlights.

"Kidding." He lets go of a smile and a chuckle. "Unless you want to."

"You have to kiss me before you can see me with my clothes off," I retort, my annoyance over a missed opportunity shining through. As the reality of how that sounded washes over me, the need to detract from it is overwhelming. However, one glance at the shock overtaking Vance's features makes me change my mind—and glad I said it.

"Duly noted." He smirks. "Now give me your hand."

I slide my palm into his and he folds his fingers around mine. Tiny hairs on my arm tingle and a quiet flush moves across my cheek.

"Holy shit." Vance flinches. "It's freaking cold."

"Really? I don't think it's that bad," I counter, swirling my foot in the murky water.

"No?"

"Nope." I walk in further, smiling, until he lets go of my hand and I catch the mischievous gleam in his eyes. Before I can get away, he leans down with both hands and forces a splash of water up and against my legs.

"Still not too cold?"

"You know?" I bend at the waist, flicking the water back and forth with my finger while keeping my eyes trained on Vance. He braces his body for a rebuttal when he sees the fight on my face. "One of the things you don't know about me is that I took swim lessons for five years. That I can swim underwater the entire length of a pool without taking a breath. That I'm an expert in Marco Polo and water sports...."

He squats down, arms out, knees slightly bent. "You think you can take me, Mickey? Come on. Do your worst."

"Nah. I just wanted to brag," I tease, and he relaxes, standing back up to his full height. Then I pounce, using my leg to kick water all over his t-shirt and jeans. He charges, grabbing me by the waist and throwing me over his shoulder. His hands hold tight to the back of my knees as he trudges through the water, a gushing sound growing louder and louder.

"Put me down," I shout, but I'm laughing so hard I can barely get the words out.

"No can do, sweetheart."

"Vance, do not throw me in that waterfall," I protest, pounding on his lower back. He pays little attention to me, continuing to weave around rocks and stray branches. His fingers are cold and wet against my skin, his grip firm. I decide to stop fighting and take advantage of the closeness, inhaling his clean, soapy scent. God, he smells good.

"You sleeping back there?" he asks after a few minutes of silence. "Because if you are, you might need a blast of say, cold water, to wake you up." He chuckles, pausing to let me down but keeping his hands around my waist until my feet find purchase in the riverbed. "I decided to spare you." He brushes a piece of unruly hair away from my face. "For now," he adds, his fingertip grazing the shell of my ear and making me shiver. His hand slides lower to my short sleeve and gives it a little tug. "So a swimmer, huh?"

"Yeah, but it was just because I had to, that's all," I admit as we lazily wade through the stream. I crouch to pick up a rock beneath the water, rubbing over its rough surface. "My mom always wanted the three of us to do a sport, and it was the only one that interested me. But my real passion was always the arts."

"It's nice how close you are to your mom," Vance says with a hint of melancholy in his tone. He lays his hand on the small of my back to steer us around a group of branches. The light touch sends a prickle up my spine.

"It is. I look up to her. She's...remarkable actually. How she's always worked so hard and stayed so strong despite the circumstances. She definitely has her moments, but I feel like she's the glue that holds everything together. I absolutely love my dad, but he was more laid back. My mom's always been the one to 'wear the pants' so to speak." I toss the rock into the water and it plunks down to the bottom.

"I miss her." His voice goes quiet, eyes distant. "My mom that is." He sighs. "I'd give anything to hear her nag me about eating healthier or remembering to take my shoes off when I get in the house. Stupid stuff, you know?"

"Yeah. I do." Silence wedges its way into our conversation until I ask a question that's been on my mind. "So...what will you do after summer's over?" I know we have two months left, but a heavy lump settles in my throat as the words tumble out.

"I want to move closer to where my mom is. Remember I mentioned that my degree is in Computer Science and that getting a job in IT has taken much longer than I anticipated? Apparently my...expectations are too rigid so it's been a lot tougher than I thought."

"Troy always makes fun of me because I'm so anti-computer. I'm not even into the whole social media thing."

"For me, I just love tinkering around so it was a hobby that turned into something more. Once I can get a job in the field I'll be able to afford a place of my own. I was crap at saving money and that's the only reason I'm still living with my dad." He glances over at me with a shy smile, the first of its kind. "But I'm...you know...glad we came here."

"Me too." I smile back, then point to his ear. "So what's with the earring? When did you get it?"

His hand goes to the small ring and he twirls it between his fingers. "It was about six years ago, after my mom first became ill. I used to have my tongue pierced too, but I took it out." A flash of what that might have felt like in my mouth crosses my mind but I quickly clear it. His mouth curves into a slow grin and I wonder if he can read my mind. "Any piercings for you?"

"Just my ears. I was thirteen when I had them done and it was fairly traumatic. My mom took me and Avery to the mall. I screamed, and that was a small needle. There's no way I would've been able to handle anything else."

He laughs. "I guess it's safe to say you don't have any tattoos, then?"

"Correct. Avery has a small butterfly on her ankle and she tried to convince me to get one too. But that wasn't going to happen."

We reach the waterfall and lean against a wall of rock as the roar of rushing water surrounds us. Vance reclines his head back. "So what are your plans after the summer?"

"Avery and I are moving to New York City." I regret the words the instant they leave my mouth. I've been dreaming about New York for as long as I can remember. Now, the thought of leaving creates this small ache deep in my chest. "We were going to take off right after graduation from Oregon State. But, it was a difficult time for our mom and we made the decision to wait. Anyway...." My thoughts trail off and suddenly I don't want to talk about being anywhere but here.

Vance is quiet for a moment, almost contemplative as he stares out at the stream. "I guess that's life, right. It moves on, whether we want it to or not." Resigned apathy litters his statement and I can't help but question it.

"What's wrong?" I glance down at his hand as he flexes it open then closed. "Vance, what is it?" His cell phone rings but he doesn't make a move to answer it. Until it rings again.

"Shit," he mutters. Then a "Sorry" as he yanks the phone from his back pocket to answer the call. He holds the cell to his ear and his hand quivers. When he catches me staring, he switches hands and shoves that one into his pocket. "Hello. Yes it is." He eyes his watch. "Yes I did. Sorry about that. Uh huh. Yes, I'll give a call back to reschedule. Thanks." Ending the call, he flips the phone in his hand repeatedly, a deep wrinkle creasing his forehead. His chest rises at a rapid pace, breathing heavy and labored.

"Vance?" Before I have a chance to say anything else, he takes his cell phone and lobs it into the air. It drops in the water quite a ways down the river and I glare at him. "Vance, what are you *doing*?"

He releases a single breath as if getting rid of his phone is the answer to whatever plagues him. "You know what, Ember. I don't know what the hell I'm doing anymore. I really don't." He belts out a maniacal laugh. "But that felt really fucking good."

I lift my hands in the air and peer out to the spot where he threw his phone. My head shakes as my gaze returns to his face. "You're crazy."

"I don't know. That felt like the sanest thing I've done in a long time." Mischief returns, brightening his eyes. "This feels pretty sane, too." He walks underneath the waterfall, drops his head back and lets the water pour over his hair, his chest, his legs. If I thought he was magnificent dry, he looks even better wet. He is beautiful. But that's not what draws me to him. Something deeper—a gentleness that hides beneath anger and hurt—a vulnerability that he masks. Maybe the tiny piece of broken inside of him that latches on to my broken piece. Because with him I feel normal again. His head falls and his eyes connect with mine, and he seems—lighter somehow. He crooks a finger at me. "C'mere, you."

This is how Zack must have felt before he climbed a steep mountain or sailed off a cliff. My heart pounds inside my chest and I can't catch my breath. It feels like I'm on the edge of something scary, yet wonderful. And when I finally get my feet to move and Vance sees me coming toward him, rewarding me with fiery eyes and a slight curve of his lips—I'm done for.

He slicks back my drenched hair with his fingers. "I guess you're crazy, too."

"Certifiable," I reply, water trickling past my temple and over the side of my face. His hand slides down and curves around the bend of my neck, thumb stroking along my jaw and I tremble.

"Cold?" he asks, eyes gleaming blue in the sunlight. I shake my head no and let my gaze wander over his face and all its subtle nuances; the single freckle under his eye, the strong angle of his jaw, the lines around his mouth. He pulls me in so my head rests on his chest and drapes himself around me. My arms encircle his waist until every part of him touches every part of me, until no space is left between us. Rivulets of water cascade over our bodies and he holds on tight as if he's running out of air and I'm his last breath. It may be daylight and we may be standing in the middle of a river, but it is by far the most intimate moment I've ever experienced.

We stay like this, connected, until his chest lifts from mine and he draws back to look at me. "What are you doing to me, Ember Bennett?"

My voice shakes as his hand slips into my hair, tilting my head, our mouths merely inches apart. "The same thing you're doing to me." I close my eyes to the lingering scent of mint as his breath brushes against my lips. I'm panting with want, waiting to feel his mouth against mine—but it never comes. After what seems like an eternity, my eyes flutter open to his intense stare. "Aren't you going to kiss me?"

"I don't want to kiss you, Ember," he says softly, and I frown. The words are too loud in my ears and I can't make sense of them. Unsure, I cast my eyes down until I feel his finger under my chin, forcing me to meet his gaze. "Because if I do, I'm afraid I'll never want to stop."

My lips part on a faint gasp, though I still manage to speak. "I'm not sure I'm seeing the problem."

He laughs, the sound mostly air, his accompanying smile taking whatever breath I have left. His hand finds my cheek, his eyes find my mouth. With his fingertip, he reaches out to brush my bottom lip and a ripple of warmth coasts over my skin. My eyes fall closed. "Ember." He whispers my name in a low rumble before his mouth finally lands on mine. The mouth I've been anxious to kiss. And it was so worth the wait. His full upper lip envelops mine, soft, though commanding, and anything that came before this moment is lost to me. I've never been one to believe in fireworks, but this kiss...it does something to me. It overwhelms me, taking possession of my heart—or perhaps he had it all along.

His mouth glides over mine, once, twice, before coaxing my lips apart and slipping his tongue inside. Gentle, teasing licks make me shudder and I moan, pressing against him. Through the wet clothes that cling to our bodies, I can feel every ridge, every curve, every bulge. I latch onto his shirt, my fingers bunching and twisting the fabric to drag him closer as his tongue continues to dip in and out of my mouth. He tastes like mint and coffee, and Vance. I'm just getting used to the feel of him when he breaks the kiss, touching his forehead to mine. Water rushes all around us, but all I hear is the sound of our breaths, all I feel is the swarm of butterflies doing a somersault in my belly.

I'm not sure how much time passes because I couldn't care less about time right now. Vance doesn't seem to either, but I do notice the chill of his fingers against my skin. "Vance, you're getting cold."

"Am I?" He circles my nose with his. "I feel pretty warm, actually."

"We should probably find a way to dry off."

Even though all I want him to do is kiss me again.

He steps back, only enough to see my eyes. His finger skims my bare arm and another shudder moves through me. "I kind of like you wet," he rasps, and my cheeks warm. "You are absolutely adorable when you blush. You know that, Mickey?" He kisses the tip of my nose. "Let's go to the car. I think I've got a blanket in my trunk."

Given the blanket turns out to be wool, it takes extra effort to get ourselves dry. Once we're no longer dripping with water, he folds it back up and throws it in the trunk. "Oh, shit." Vance looks over his shoulder, chewing on the corner of his lip.

I shift around to see what he's staring at, but nothing unusual is there. "What?"

"I guess I need to get another phone."

I snort out a laugh. "Ya think?"

He slings an arm over my shoulder and brings me closer, pressing a kiss to my hair. "Yeah, I do."

I know what I think. I think I'm falling hard for Vance Davenport.

chapter twenty-four
Vance

THE SKY BEGINS to change colors on our drive back; pinks and oranges melting together over the horizon. I half expect Ember to want to pull over and capture it on film. I'm about to ask when I catch a glimpse of her out of the corner of my eye. Thick, dark lashes rest against her cheeks, lips forming a sleepy smile. A loose strand of hair blows in front of her mouth and I reach over with a single finger to push it back behind her ear. She stirs, but doesn't awaken.

This day—I can't decide if it's a gift or a fucking tease. I'd like to believe it's the former. It has to be—given the way Ember makes me feel. The strange ticking inside my chest. How much she makes me want to laugh—want to smile—want to be present in every moment instead of worrying about what tomorrow will bring.

I've tried to stay away from her. To forget the sweet curve of her smile, the simple honesty in her eyes, the funny sound of her laugh. Maybe I need to try harder. Or maybe I should just give up the fight and let the chips fall where they may. Except I'm terrified of hurting her.

"Hey." Her gravelly voice rescues me from my thoughts. "Where are we?"

I stroke my fingers down the side of her cheek. "We're home, Mickey."

She swipes a hand over one of her eyes. "Already?"

"You slept almost the entire way home."

"Oh." She slides her feet into her sneakers and lifts her shoulders in a stretch. "I didn't realize how tired I was." She squints at the clock on the dashboard. "What time is it, anyway?"

"Just after nine thirty." Unlocking the doors, I hop out of the car and meet her on the passenger side. "Let's go, sleepyhead." I reach down, linking our fingers together. She lifts her eyes to mine with a warm smile.

Awkward silence falls over us as we near the porch. The dim light emanating from the lamppost refuses to hide my unease. I glance away and scuff my foot against the ground, stalling to gather my thoughts.

"I had a—"

We both say at the same time.

"You first."

"I...this...oh fuck." I let out a nervous laugh and hope the fucking pavement will swallow me whole. "Considering how many books I read, you'd think I'd be better with words."

"I think you're doing great."

I look up to meet her reassuring smile and it gives me courage. "This was the best day I've had in, well, as long as I can remember."

Her face brightens and she nods. "Me too."

"Yeah?"

"Yeah." She moves closer until she's standing in front of me. I bring her hand up to my chest, my eyes drifting to her lips. Because like I thought, one kiss wasn't enough.

"Good...that's...really fucking good." I fumble, my gaze lingering on the sweet curve of her mouth.

"You love that word, don't you?" she asks, her breath blowing softly against my chin. Her question throws me off and I tear my eyes away from her lips to meet her stare.

"What word?"

Ember's nose wrinkles. "The F word."

Her inability to say it makes me chuckle. "You mean *fuck*?"

"Yeah."

"I do. It's a great word, really. I love how it can be used in so many different ways. Like a noun for example. As in, he doesn't give a fuck. Or an adverb, like, this book is really fucking interesting. Or even as an adjective, like...." Sweeping my fingers through her hair, I let them slide down the side of her face and cradle her jaw. "You are so fucking beautiful. The most beautiful girl I've ever met." Her green eyes glitter with what appear to be equal parts surprise and happiness, and her cheeks stain pink. I glide my thumb over the edge of her lip, anxious to taste her again. "That last one is true—"

She cuts me off with her lips, advancing on mine, soft, seeking. She kisses me slowly. It's the sweetest fucking kiss, sweeter than I've ever been kissed before. Filled with lips and tongue, meaning and desire— and something that makes my pulse rate spike. It makes me hard, too, but I think I could be happy just kissing her like this for a very long time.

She tastes like life.

Like truth.

Like tomorrows.

She makes me believe that maybe these things are possible for me.

A hunger shoots through me and I release her hand to snake my arms around her waist. My palm presses against the small of her back, urging her body closer as her warm tongue tangles with mine. Her peach scent is dizzying and it consumes me as I take control and deepen the kiss, plunging into her mouth. My hand travels up past her spine, her neck, slipping into her hair and tugging at the soft strands. She lets out a breathy moan as her fingers trail over my biceps and come up to frame my face. I shudder, startled by the effect her touch has on me. The way she holds me makes my heart beat way too fast and I don't know if it's fear or something else.

I ease out of her mouth, sucking on her lower lip before dropping my forehead against hers. Heavy breaths fall between us, and I don't have to see her to know she's smiling—I'm smiling too.

"Vance," she breathes. "I should probably go in now, or else...."

I'd like the '*or else*' option. But all that comes out is this one word. "Yeah."

Reluctantly, I drop my arms and she backs away. "My friend Troy wants to hang out tomorrow night. Avery is going to be there, and I was thinking maybe...." She draws her lip between her teeth then lets it go. "Maybe you could come and bring Julian if he wants?"

"Absolutely."

She blasts me with one last smile and I wait until she unlocks the door before heading to my car. I'm about to get in when her voice stops me. "Vance?"

I turn around. "Yeah?"

I hear her grin into the darkness. "That was the best fucking kiss I've ever had."

STILL SMILING, I strut into the house. Julian is sitting on the couch with his feet up on the coffee table reading a sports magazine. Considering we haven't seen each other all day, the scowl surrounding his mouth is unexpected. "Hey, what's up?"

"Where have you been?" A bite threads his tone and I have no clue what I did to deserve it.

"I was with Ember."

His gaze is still fixed on that damn magazine. "Hmph, hmph."

I flip my keys around my finger and rack my brain for what could be eating him. "All right, Julian. What gives?"

He lowers the magazine, eyes boring into mine. "Why don't you tell me?"

"Is that supposed to be fucking code for something? What did I miss?"

"I don't know, Vance. What *did* you miss?" He drops his feet to the floor with a hard thud and when I don't pick up on the hint, he elaborates. "Dr. Sherwood's office called here." He tosses the magazine onto the table. "Twice."

"Oh."

"Yeah, *oh*." He stands up, raking a hand through his unruly hair. "You missed your appointment. Why?"

I feel around for the phone in my back pocket then remember it's gone. "It slipped my mind."

"Bullshit," he spits, and I haven't seen him this angry since...Mom. "The thing that consumes your life slipped your mind. I'm not buying it." He huffs out a breath and some of his irritation along with it. "Listen, just...get in there, okay? So you can know what you're dealing with."

I bite my tongue hard enough to taste blood, but give him the answer he needs to hear. "I will."

"Promise?"

I groan. "Yes, Julian. I promise."

He nods and his features relax. "Okay, good." Then he starts for the kitchen. "I ordered a pizza earlier," he calls back. "You want some?"

"Depends. Is it a real pizza?" I trail behind him as he reaches up to snatch two paper plates from the top of the fridge. He hands me one.

"It's a salad pizza."

My face contorts and I wince, tossing my plate onto the center island. "I'm good, thanks." I open and close a few cabinets to check for SpaghettiOs. "If you want a salad, have a salad. Salad is not meant to be on top of pizza." Finding one can hidden in the back, I slide it out and pop the top.

"And SpaghettiOs are not meant for human consumption."

"Yeah, well, somebody has to keep the health food rebellion going on in this house. Pass me that sauce pan, will ya?" I grin, and he chuckles, stretching to lift the pan from the overhead hook. I flip on the gas and pour the SpaghettiOs in the pot he so graciously handed me. "Mmmm, I can smell them already."

Shaking his head, he grabs a slice of pizza and tosses it on a plate before taking a seat on one of the stools. "You'd think you were deprived as a child."

I open a drawer by the sink, digging around for a wooden spoon. "Aside from our Sunday morning cinnamon rolls and the occasional ice cream for breakfast, Mom did go a bit heavy on the vegetables and that all-natural shit." My fingers rest on the handle of the spoon. "Hey, remember that time Mom made those Brussel sprouts and she was so excited because she thought I ate them?" I laugh. "But when she was cleaning up she found the big clump of green in my napkin."

"I remember." He smiles, warmth filling his tone. "Look at it this way. How many kids can say their mom made homemade bread, peanut butter, and just about everything else?" Emotion lies thick in my throat, preventing me from answering his question. "Vance?"

Little round O's become a blur as I stir them around the pot. "When I saw Mom yesterday, she knew who I was, Julian." I turn around and he stops mid-chew, setting his pizza down on the plate. "I knew it would be fleeting." I touch my head, still feeling the ruffle of her fingers through my hair. "But for those few minutes I had her back."

He stares out the picture window overlooking the backyard. "I miss that excitement she used to get in her eyes when I'd tell her something about my day. It never mattered if it was something I thought was insignificant. She always made me feel like it was the most important thing in the world."

"It was, Julian. To her it was. Because...we were her world."

"I know." His eyes fall in line with mine, the light dimmer than before. I picture him coming home after a baseball game with dirt on his knees, the devastation of missing a fly ball written on his face—and Mom, standing there, with open arms and a huge smile. Always focusing on what he did right, instead of what he could do better.

"What were you doing with Ember today?" he asks, and I swivel around to shut off the flame on the stove.

My spirits lift at the mention of her name, a smile extinguishing any previous sadness. "I took her to Nettle Creek." I chance a look at Julian over my shoulder. His eyes are wide, head tilted with a curious expression.

"Wow." He glances away, blinking a few times as if trying to figure something out. "That's...big."

I shrug, attempting to play it off. "Not really. I just thought she might like it there."

His gaze lands on mine again. "Yeah, okay. That was our special place with Mom, so the *'not really'* isn't believable. Sorry." He takes a bite of pizza, waiting for me to elaborate. My silence only spurs him on. "I guess it's safe to say you've moved past the lunchbox stage?"

To be honest, I'm trying not to think about where we are. We've already bypassed where I know we should have stayed.

In order to avoid his scrutiny, I turn to remove the pot from the stove. "I'm fucked, Julian. That's what stage I'm at." I heave out a sigh, forgoing a bowl and removing a metal spoon from the drawer to eat directly out of the pot. As I swing back, the expression on his face reinforces the knot in my stomach.

"I'm not sure I've seen you like this...." He chews another bite of pizza, talking around a smug grin. "Ever."

"That's because I've never met anyone like Mickey before."

"Mickey?" He clucks his tongue. "Awww, that's so sweet."

"Okay." I grab the dish towel from the counter and toss it at him. "That's enough."

"I'm sorry but you have to give me a little leeway here, or at least some time to digest this new information." He plucks a mushroom off the top of the pizza and pops it into his mouth.

"Whatever. Oh, and by the way, you have plans tomorrow night. You're coming with me to Ember's friend Troy's house. And if you're thinking about saying no," I smirk, taking another spoonful of SpaghettiOs, "Avery will be there."

He matches my grin. "Then I shall be there too. But seriously," he pauses, his expression sobering, "before you try to distract me from the conversation, I'm really happy for you. I like Ember a lot."

A loud sigh escapes as I scrape the bottom of the pot before placing it in the sink. "I know I'm a broken record, but I'm fucking terrified she's going to end up hurt." I grip the counter with both hands, my knuckles turning white. "It will be all my fault...I don't think I can live with that."

Julian's sudden grasp of my shoulder forces a hard breath from my chest. "How about you just try to live for a change, and take it from there."

chapter twenty-five
Ember

"NO WAY, MAN," Troy protests on the verge of losing the third game of Scrabble. "There's no such word as *cambist*." He slams his hand down on the table. "It's time to consult the good old Scrabble dictionary."

"I wouldn't mess with my brother," Julian chimes in. "If he says it's a word, it's a word. He reads books like people breathe air."

Uncertainty passes over Troy's face. "Okay, Vance. Enlighten us. What does it mean, then?"

Vance smirks, reclining back in the chair, arms folded across his chest. "It means...a few things actually. But one of them is...an expert in foreign exchange."

Avery tilts her head, scrutinizing Vance's face. "Hmmm, I believe him. Makes sense. Okay, who wants another beer and one more game?" She pushes away from the table and tosses a flirty glance at Julian. He wastes no time getting up to escort her into the kitchen.

"I've had my fill. Three games is my max." I stand and stretch my arms above my head. "I'm going to get some air."

Troy winks, pinching my arm as I squeeze by him. "You do that, Ems." Vance's eyes follow me while I try to keep my expression neutral.

The chill on the deck brings a wake-up call for my skin. My gaze travels upward to tiny stars filling the night sky. The patio doors open then and automatically my lips twitch. Strong hands come from behind, rubbing up and down my arms.

"You're kind of cold there, Mickey."

"A bit," I reply, Vance's touch adding a second layer of goose bumps along my skin.

"Be right back." The patter of his Converse slapping against the wooden planks breaks the silence. He returns with a soft flannel blanket, wrapping it around my shoulders.

"Thank you."

Vance gestures toward a lounger on the opposite side of the deck. "Let's sit." With a gentle hand supporting my arm, he leads me over to the chair. He positions himself first then tugs me down between his outstretched legs.

"I like this," I admit, my body snug against the inside of his thighs, back resting softly against his chest. "It's like my own personal cave."

"Hmm, well you do fit quite nicely between my legs." My pulse speeds up and I don't need to turn around to know he's grinning.

Extending my own legs, I lean further into him. His arms slip around my waist, fingers clasp over my stomach, cocooning me. "So how come you're not drinking like everyone else?" he questions, and the memory of my night in the bar makes me cringe.

"I'm not really a big drinker. I don't like what it does to people. Case in point, me, the other night. What about you?" I ask, his chin coming to rest on top of my head.

"Alcohol has caused a lot of destruction in my family," he reveals. "Addiction runs rampant. Gambling, but specifically alcoholism on both my mother and father's side. It's part of the reason we're estranged from both of their families." He sighs, his breath fanning my hair. "There's been a lot of damage. Hurtful things said, money borrowed that was supposedly for other things, and instead ended up being used to feed habits and destroy lives." He strokes his thumb over my belly button through my shirt and my insides turn to liquid. "Plus, I don't want to drink when I'm with you. I really enjoy our conversation and...I don't want to miss anything."

My heart skips a million times over. "That's such a sweet thing to say."

He chuckles. "No one has ever called me sweet before."

I tilt my head back to catch his eyes. "Well, you are."

He captures my chin, turning me toward him. His lips melt over mine, soft and warm before he whispers, "I think you're pretty sweet too, Mickey."

My entire body sinks into him, his lean, muscular arms holding me tight. I can't remember the last time I felt this content. "Okay, Vance Davenport, tell me something no one else knows about you."

"Let's see." He entwines his fingers with mine. "I used to be a closet skateboarder."

My nose scrunches though he can't see me. "What do you mean?"

"When I was about, I don't know, maybe thirteen or so, I saved up all my allowance from doing chores to buy this really cool skateboard. I still remember it. It was this deep blue and bright neon green. Anyway, there was a skate park near my house and sometimes I'd sneak off there and hang out with the other kids. They taught me to do these fucking awesome tricks. I never told my mom I bought it because she would've worried and told me it was too dangerous." He breathes out a laugh. "I remember wanting to be an Olympic skateboarder when I grew up, even though there was no such thing in the Olympics." He presses a kiss against my hair. "What about you?"

"I used to be afraid of thunderstorms. When I was little, whenever there was thunder and lightning I would run into Zack's room and huddle under the covers with him. He would tell me the angels were bowling up there to make me feel better. It definitely helped, but for some reason I still don't love them. Oh, and I also have a photographic memory, especially with numbers. Although Avery and my parents know about that."

"That's damn near blackmail material." He chuckles, and I elbow him softly in the ribs. "I like your friend, Troy," he tells me, changing topics and catching me off guard. "He's pretty funny."

"Troy is amazing. I love him to pieces."

"Did the two of you ever—"

"No." I intercept his question. "I was never interested in him like that, and he was always into guys and never looked at me as anything other than a friend."

Vance lets out what seems to be a relieved breath. "Right."

"He's had a hard time and I feel awful for him. When he came out to his parents they couldn't cope with it. They still aren't coping with it. They barely speak to him, except when they absolutely have to." I sigh and Vance squeezes my hand. "From the very beginning they made him feel less than, like he wasn't enough. Sometimes all a person needs to hear is, 'You're enough.' Troy never got that from his parents and I think he needed that. Everyone does."

"That fucking sucks. Is he okay, though? Because he seems happy."

"Yeah, he is. He definitely has his days. But overall he's good. He has two sisters who adore him and have always stood by him, and that makes all the difference."

"That's—"

"Hey, lovebirds." The glass door slides open and Troy peeks his head out. "We're playing Would You Rather, so get the hell in here."

"Here we go," I mumble, swinging my legs over the side of the lounger.

"What's that?" Vance loops his arm around my shoulder as we head back into the house.

"Avery and Troy have a love affair with this game, so brace yourself."

Vance allows me to walk in before him, gliding the door closed. The second I step inside, all eyes are on me.

"Perfect timing, Em," Avery calls out. "It's your turn and you have to play." The three of them are lounging on the living room sofas. Avery clears her throat, trying to intimidate me with a raised eyebrow and an evil smirk. Once Vance and I are seated on the couch, she throws her first dart. "Would you rather kiss Vance or Julian?"

"Both," Troy pipes up. Avery and I laugh, while Julian quickly takes another swig of his beer. Vance's gaze heats the side of my face. "All right." Troy's eyes slide to mine. "Answer the question, Ems."

"Gosh, I...." My face is too hot, glance darting back and forth between Julian and Vance as if actually needing to think about it. The answer is so obvious I might as well have a V carved into my chest—but I suspect my sister knows this. Pushing the blanket away, I flip her a hard stare. "I...have to go to the bathroom." I spring up off the sofa and flee down the hall, laughing as their catcalls follow me. Inches from the door, Vance corners me from behind and spins me around. One arm braced against the wall, he hovers over me, his breath feathering my cheek.

"You didn't answer the question," he murmurs, blue eyes serious and probing. Flames lick up the back of my neck. Not from his proximity, but from something else. Something I don't want to put a name to. The same something that steals my breath and makes my smile endless.

My voice comes out shaky instead of teasing. "I didn't?"

"Nope." His hips press into mine, body trapping me. I can feel his hardness against my thigh, but nothing about this is sexual. An air of desperation in his gaze makes me want to immediately put him at ease.

"Vance," I whisper, skimming my fingertips down his cheek. "All my kisses belong to you." The lines around his mouth relax and he smiles, his eyes flying to my lips.

"Mine?" he questions softly, tongue wetting his mouth, finger tracing the curve of my lower lip until I can hardly breathe. "*Mine*," he repeats again more forcefully before his mouth crashes down against my lips, taking what's his. My pulse accelerates, my heart doing a dance all its own. And I know with utmost certainty—that my kisses are not the only thing that belong to him.

chapter twenty-six
Vance

JULIAN WOULD BE happy to know I listened to his advice—for once. Since the night at Troy's house, I've been trying to put everything out of my head and just enjoy being with Ember. A day hasn't gone by where we haven't seen each other. Between going on interviews, continuing to search for jobs, and her additional shifts at Anna's, it's a juggle. But we make it work. We don't talk much about what happens after the summer ends, though I know it's weighing on both of our minds—for different reasons.

This is all new to me. Being with a girl, not only for this length of time, but without having sex. My body craves Ember in a way I never have before, but fear of the unknown keeps me awake at night and stops me from touching her in the desperate way I want to.

I close my eyes, my thoughts drifting to Ember as I gently pluck the strings of my guitar. Warmth settles around me, flowing in and through my veins. I picture the gentle curl of her lips, the brightness in her gaze. Something has been building inside my chest. It's foreign and fucking uncomfortable, and yet, it makes me unable to control my smile or the beat of my heart.

Lyrics tumble from my mouth, the soft pull of my guitar falls in step with them.

I had no idea
I was walking blindly through my days
Never really seeing
Never really knowing
But along came you
Along came life
Along came life

"Hey."

I'm smiling before I even open my fucking eyes. That's how gone I am for this girl.

"How long have you been standing there?" I ask, taking in the sweet tug of her smile, the confident jut of her hip, the slight tilt of her head as she watches me. Her walnut-colored hair lies below her shoulders now, a bit longer than when we first met. She has a certain glow too, in the pink of her cheeks, the glitter of her eyes. I can't help but wonder if that has something to do with me.

"Long enough to know you've been hiding your voice from me. It's raspy and gorgeous. I'm kind of blown away actually."

"Well," I chuckle, "let's not get carried away."

She struts toward me, a gleam in those green eyes. "I think we should most definitely get carried away." She drops to her knees in front of me, sexy as all get-out and leans in to give me a quick kiss on the lips. "In fact, I think we should get carried away tomorrow night."

"I'm intrigued," I reply, staring at her mouth. "What's tomorrow night?"

She lifts the guitar and places it on my bed, then plops herself into my lap. Draping her arms around my neck, she goes on. "I thought I could make you dinner and...whatever. My mom and Avery won't be around, so...."

"I don't know." I wrap my arms around her waist and edge closer, pressing my lips to the corner of her mouth. Her smile tingles against my skin. "It seems to me you're just trying to get me naked."

Her blush arrives, as usual, but she doesn't back down. "And you would be right." She wiggles her ass against my jeans and I'm instantly hard. "Am I convincing enough?"

"Hmph." My finger brushes down the side of her face, the slope of her neck. "I need a little more convincing, I think."

"Like what?"

"Like this." I grab her cheeks, dragging her mouth closer to suck on the delicate skin of her full bottom lip before finding my way inside. Her tongue reaches for me, warm and wet, and so damn sweet. She tastes of light and joy, and all the things I've missed out on for too long. But I stop thinking and focus on her mouth, her breaths, the tangle of her tongue with mine. Her hands come up to cradle my face, and I never knew that someone's touch—the right person's touch—could make me feel this way. As if anything is possible. And fuck, I want her so much.

Ember's lips leave mine, her expression dazed yet hopeful. "Is that a yes?"

Trailing my hand along her back and slipping underneath her hair, I bring her forehead to my mouth for a kiss. "There's nowhere I'd rather be tomorrow night than with you."

She drops her head against my shoulder, breathing a long sigh into my neck. "Good."

We stay like that for a while. Me stroking her hair, her soft breaths warming my skin. I never realized how peaceful silence can be.

"Can I ask you something?" Her voice is low, words a whisper in the quiet. "Did you ever think about playing in a band or anything? You're *that* good, Vance."

The smell of her peach shampoo relaxes me and I rest my chin against the silky strands, breathing her in. "When I was younger, some friends of mine and I had this garage band. It was just for fun really, but it was pretty cool. My best friend Chris Raven played bass, and two other guys played drums and keyboard. I sang lead vocals and also played guitar."

"I've never heard you talk about Chris before. Do you still see him?" she asks, her finger tracing over my palm. Regret fills the air at the mention of his name and I wonder if she can feel the weight of it. Whenever I'm with her now, vulnerability pours off of me in waves, exposing me. The depth of my feelings for her making it impossible to hide.

I respond with a frustrated growl, not because of her question, but my own actions. "I don't. I kind of...fucked everything up when my mom got sick. I blew him out of my life, pushing him and everyone else away. I couldn't deal. Didn't want to, really."

"He must've understood that though, no?" She smoothes her fingertip along the outline of my hand. "Couldn't you get in touch now?"

"Maybe. But I was a complete asshole to him," I add. "So I don't know."

"We know *that* part's true." She lifts her head, smirking. "That's how you were when we first met." I pinch her ass and she twists in my lap. "Anyway, more people need to hear that voice. It's very swoony."

"Swoony." I laugh. "That's a new one."

A teasing spark flickers in her eyes. "Don't get me wrong, it's not like I want girls throwing their underwear at you. But it could happen."

"Really now?" I kiss the tip of her nose. "Well, news flash, Mickey. There's only one girl I want throwing her underwear at me. The rest of them can go to hell."

An enormous smile makes her entire face beam. "Perhaps I can arrange some underwear throwing for tomorrow night." Her cheeks burn bright red. "They would be sexy underwear of course."

I grin, letting my thumb skim her jaw. "I don't know. I was kind of hoping they'd be Mickey Mouse underwear."

"I'm willing to shed Mickey for special occasions." She twirls a tendril of her hair. "Sometimes, sacrifices must be made."

My hand travels around to the front of her t-shirt, one finger dipping inside the neckline to sweep lightly over her skin and she shivers. "If you must."

"And right now," she pulls my hand from her shirt and wriggles out of my lap, "I have some things I need to do."

"Like what?" I fucking pout because I want her here, with me. "You just got here."

"I'm having dinner with Avery and then she's dragging me

shopping." She rolls her eyes on the last part which I know she finds excruciating. As I stand up, she gives me a kiss way too short and I want more. I try to slide my arms around her but she pulls out of my grasp, flashing me a coy grin. "Until tomorrow."

I flop back onto the bed with a groan, adjusting the crotch of my jeans.

I've never looked forward to tomorrow so much in my life.

"ONE MORE," JULIAN whines after I've already taken his ass in three games of pool.

"Julian. You haven't been able to win the first three." I place the triangle on the table to rack the balls, flipping him a cocky glance over my shoulder. "What makes you think you can win now?"

He props his stick against the table then rubs his hands together. "I was just getting warmed up." Lifting his beer, he raises it in the air. "Cheers. Besides, what else do you have to do anyway? Your girl is busy tonight."

My girl. I like the sound of that.

"Ah, and cue the grin. Come on," he coaxes and I can't help but laugh. "There it is."

I poke him with my stick and he presses a hand to his ribs, feigning injury. "Shut the fuck up and play pool."

"Whatever you say, loverboy." He waggles his brows as he sets the bottle down, grabbing his pool stick and positioning himself for the first shot. "Whatever you say."

"You're just making me more determined to whip your ass...*again*." As I move next to him, he bends at the waist to break, balls flying everywhere except in the pockets. He mutters a curse under his breath and I chuckle. "Would you look at that? You know, the goal is to get the balls *in* the pockets."

"Yeah, yeah. So anyway." He taps the butt of his stick against the floor, hesitating. "Have you...talked to Dad at all?"

"Dad, no why?" I set up for the shot, motioning with my chin toward the table. "Blue stripe in the right corner," I announce, and the ball slides over the green felt and makes a loud crack as it lands in the pocket. "I haven't seen him. He sent me a text saying that he was on a business trip, but nothing else." I walk over to Julian. "What's going on?"

"He got back last night and we grabbed a quick bite. You were with Ember. Anyway, I don't know. He seems...," his voice fades, "off or something."

"Honestly, Julian, I'm not sure I'd know his off from his on at this point," I admit, scraping a hand through my hair. "You know we haven't been on the best of terms."

"So why don't you change that?" He kicks my foot with the toe of his boot. "He loves you, you know."

"What about Mom?" I bite out. "Does he love Mom?"

"Vance." He huffs out a frustrated breath. "Of course he does."

"Funny. He's got a shit way of showing it." Like a knife slashing through my chest, the mere mention of my father rips me open. I march over to the table and drop my stick down. "I'm gonna get some fresh air."

As I pass Julian, I grip him by the back of the neck and squeeze, wanting to make sure he knows this is not about him. He gives me a small smile in acknowledgement, but his eyes betray his worry for me.

Outside, my feet pound the pavement until my chest burns and I have to pause to try to catch my breath. Sweat rushes down my skin and just like me, tries to find an escape. I break into a run, hoping to exhaust myself. Yet when my legs finally give out, that sense of being trapped is still there. Ember's face pops into my head. And suddenly, I want to see her. Lay my head on her shoulder. Breathe her in. I want to touch her in all the ways she touches me. And that's when it hits me.

I'm falling in love with her.

My heart threatens to burst and a laugh tears from my chest. Someone is playing a cruel joke on me, no doubt. But as the clouds open up, rain plummeting from a starless sky, I spread my arms wide to welcome it and for the first time, say—

I'm here life, come and get me.

Maybe I'm crazy, knowing what I do. What my future could possibly hold. But as the cool rain hits my skin, like little pinpricks tapping me and telling me to wake the fuck up, I give in and finally say yes to life. And whatever it has in store for me.

chapter twenty-seven
Ember

CLOTHES ARE BEING ripped from hangers at an unprecedented speed. Not only am I questioning what to wear, now I'm questioning my own sanity. I've never cared much about trying to impress anyone. But tonight is different.

I catch my reflection in the mirror, staring at the black lace bra and panties from Victoria's Secret. Avery kindly emphasized you don't call them *underwear*. And this is one time I'm thankful for Avery's shopping prowess. But then I glance over at the massive stack of outfits in the *no* pile on my mattress. "This is crazy," I say out loud, flinging my arms up and perching on the edge of the bed.

"What's crazy?" Avery asks, strutting into the room and taking a seat next to me.

"I can't find anything to wear tonight." I hike a thumb over my shoulder. "This is my undesirable pile."

She lifts a threadbare t-shirt with two fingers and winces like it has a disease. "I can see why." My eyes narrow on her face. "Kidding. I'm kidding," she adds, tossing the shirt behind her. "Why don't you wear what you always do? Vance wants *you*, not your clothes."

My hands quiver and I hold them out in front of me. "Look at this, I'm a nervous wreck."

Avery takes my hand and tilts her head to meet my eyes. "Hey. You're doing just fine. I'll help you pick something out, okay?" I nod as she studies my face. "What do you know. You really care about him, don't you?"

"Yeah, I do."

"Okay, then." She lets my hand fall and stands up, rubbing her palms together. "Let's find something that's going to knock his socks off. Or," she winks, "some other article of clothing."

For the next half-hour, we dig through every other item of clothing in my closet and still come up short. When we're done, I fall face down on the bed with a groan and Avery laughs.

"This isn't funny," I mumble into my blanket.

"No," she laughs again, "it's kind of adorable actually. Wait here. I'll be right back."

"Where am I going?" I grumble. "It was so much easier when I didn't care." My head sinks further into the mattress as her loud cackle echoes in the hallway.

"Okay, how do you feel about this?" she asks as she strolls back in. "It's simple, but effective I think."

"Do I have to move?" I whine. "I'm comfortable."

She rounds the side of the bed and I drag my head up to stare at a jade green dress displayed on a hanger. "What do you think?"

"It's short and very low cut." My eyes drop to my chest then back to her. "I don't have enough boobs for that dress."

"Nonsense. This will squish them together and make them look fantastic." She tugs on my hand to pull me up. "Come on, try it on."

"Hello? Anyone home?"

My mouth falls open as my eyes widen. "Dad!" I whisper-shout. "What's he doing here?"

"I don't know." Her gaze climbs to the ceiling as if already hatching a plan. "Don't worry, I'll get rid of him."

"Oh my God." I scramble to the dresser to snatch up a tank top before yanking out a pair of shorts. In record time, I slide them both on, nearly falling over in the process. Avery shoves the dress under a pillow on my chair.

"Avery, Em, you decent?" Dad calls out. "I'm coming up."

Avery parks herself in the doorway. Meanwhile, I sit in front of the clothes heap with my arms outstretched like they're actually long enough to conceal my plight.

"Hey, honey." Dad gives Avery a kiss on the cheek then peers around her body. "Hello there, Em."

My smile and wave are a little too enthusiastic and he cocks his head the slightest bit. But I notice. "What's going on? Going somewhere?"

"Yes." Avery raises a pointed finger in the air. "As a matter of fact, we are."

"Oh." Dad frowns. "I called your Mom earlier and she mentioned she was away until tomorrow so I thought I'd take you both out to dinner tonight. It is Wednesday after all."

"Geez Dad," I chime in. "I'm sorry. I forgot."

"Yeah, me too," Avery admits. "But...how about tomorrow?" Her voice has a cheery lift to it and Dad smiles, his earlier disappointment gone.

"Okay, that sounds like a date." He rubs his round belly. "Shall we do Thai?"

"Yes!"

Avery and I respond at the same time.

His eyes grow thin, but his lips remain in a curve. "Gee, that's an awful lot of enthusiasm for Thai food. Anyhow, I...guess I'll be going then. You two enjoy," he pauses, sucking on his cheek, "whatever it is you're doing this evening. Can't wait to hear all about it tomorrow night."

We're quiet until we hear the front door close and then we can't contain our laughter.

"Oh, God, he knows." I flop back on my clothes mountain. "I'm certain of it."

"He knows *something*," she agrees. "He just doesn't know exactly what. Now," she pulls the dress out from underneath its hiding place, "about this dress."

chapter twenty-eight
Vance

My SMILE IS wide as I hike out of the bookstore, pretty fucking pleased with myself. I don't know anything about sculpture, but the girl in the art section was more than helpful. Even if she was trying to shove her tits in my face the entire time.

I wanted to do something nice for Ember to let her know I'm thinking about her—about who she is and what she finds important. Again, I don't understand shit about art but I'm willing to learn.

The parking garage is now packed with cars and it takes some effort to find mine in a sea of black. Once I do, I haul the door open and slide onto the leather seat, setting the wrapped book next to the bouquet of flowers. I'm not really a flowers type of guy, but the pink roses in the shop window made me think of Ember's cheeks when she smiles.

My hands are clammy, sweat forming in the creases of my palms. It sends me back. I'm thirteen years old again, getting ready to kiss a girl for the first time. Everything with Ember feels like a first for me. I suppose that's true in many ways.

The digital clock on the dash tells me I've got at least an hour before I need to be at Ember's house. That gives me just enough time to get home and grab a shower.

When I turn down our street, my father's BMW shines like a

beacon in the driveway and I roll my eyes. Of all nights for him to be home, he had to pick this one. But I refuse to let him ruin my mood. Nor am I interested in having a confrontation. With any luck, he'll be in his office and I can avoid him altogether.

Careful not to make too much noise, I insert the key in the lock then turn the knob with quiet precision. I'm almost to the stairs when I catch a glimpse of Dad slumped back in a chair at the dining room table. He looks like hell. His blue tie is loose around his neck, what appears to be two-day-old stubble sitting on his chin. Eyes that are unfocused stare at a tumbler filled with ice and an amber liquid. A bottle of Johnnie Walker Scotch close by. My father is not a drinker, and while part of me still cares and wants to ensure he's all right, the part of me that would rather avoid him wins out.

I maintain my direction, feet rushing toward the stairs until his strained voice makes me pause.

"I know you don't think I care...but you couldn't be further from the truth."

What the hell does he know about the truth?

Not tonight, please not tonight.

I solidify my stance with a big breath before turning around to face him, preparing for a fight. Three bold strides in his direction, I stop, remembering to keep my distance. Not wanting to get too close to the insanity.

"She was my whole life," he mutters, weary eyes staring at the now empty glass in his hand. "After she first got diagnosed, I used to stay awake every night beside her. I was terrified," he admits, his weakened gaze meeting my hard one. "Terrified of falling asleep and then waking up in the morning to a stranger. Scared to death of the emptiness I might find in her eyes. And then...when it finally did happen and I had to put her in that home, it was worse than I ever could have imagined.

"Your mother and I, we made so many memories...we had a lot of years together before she got sick." He shakes his head, his expression blank. "And all that has been washed away. Almost as if it never happened. But I'm reminded every day that it did happen." He glances down at the ring on his finger. "Because she is the best part of me, and those were some of the best days of my life."

Glazed-over eyes come back to mine. "You see your mother sitting in that facility, on that chair by the window." He pauses to swallow. "But I see my heart." A wretched sound lifts from his throat. "And it's a devastation I can't begin to describe to you. Like a missing piece of me that I will *never* get back."

He pours more scotch into his glass, alcohol spilling over onto the polished wood. "You think you know so much," he spits, his hand coming down on the table with a bang. "But you don't know anything about how I feel or what the past six years have been like for me." The edge in his voice softens. "You're her son, Vance. But damn it, *I'm* her husband."

I look into my father's eyes, uncertain if this is the first time he's showing me, or the first time I'm aware of it. But the sadness and despair that drips from them makes guilt eat away at my chest until I can no longer breathe. My inability to consider what he might be going through—what this has meant for his life and the life he created with my mother. I've been a selfish asshole in more ways than one.

My thoughts roam to Ember. I picture her sitting there with that same expression, that same pain, and it crushes me. Because, although we've just begun, I know what I feel for her and what we could be together. Internally, I berate myself. To think that I actually let it get this far. That I thought...it was even a possibility. I've been fooling myself. And her, too. It's not fair.

The realization makes the bottom drop out of my stomach and my world. My shoulders curl inward and I grab onto the wall for support. But I need to carry myself through this. I refuse to drag anyone else down with me—least of all Ember.

"I'm...sorry, Dad. I know it's not enough. But I'm sorry...for everything."

I turn to leave but my feet are like lead, making it difficult to climb the stairs. My body refuses to cooperate with what my brain knows it has to do. When I reach the top step, my father's words stop me again. "I understand. And I don't blame you, son. It's not your fault."

I only hope Ember feels the same.

chapter twenty-nine
Ember

I'VE BEEN STARING at myself in the full-length mirror since Avery left. The dress she let me borrow was beautiful, sexy even, but it wasn't me. In the end, I peeled it off and opted for a pair of skinny jeans and a Mickey Mouse t-shirt.

Standing in front of the mirror now, I smile. The tee is snug and hugs my breasts. My hair is down in waves, lips stained with a soft pink gloss. Of course I'm wearing the black lace. This is my little bit of sexy while still being me. I've never felt I had to be anything else with Vance, anyway.

The doorbell rings and the grin I've been harboring all day, broadens. I bolt down the stairs, darting to the dining room to light the candles before exhaling a giant breath and opening the door. Flowers and a beautifully wrapped package are what I notice first, and my heart skips. But when my gaze climbs to Vance's face, the grin slips away. His cheeks are pale, mouth pulled tight.

"What is it? Is it your Mom?" I ask, stepping back so he can come inside.

"No, Ember. It's not." Vance holds the roses out in front of me. "I wanted you to have these. They...reminded me of you. And this." He shakes his head and puts the package down on the corner table, releasing a breath filled with too many things I can't identify. I swallow down the nervous ache in my throat, attempt to ignore the little voice telling me something is very wrong, and wait for him to elaborate. He rubs the back of his neck and stares off to the side, eyes glued to a spot on the wall. "I...this...we...we can't do this."

"Vance, look at me." I place the flowers on the coffee table. "What can't we do?"

His desperate gaze flicks to mine. He points a finger back and forth between us. "*This.*"

"I don't understand."

"I know," he whispers, moving closer until he's standing in front of me. "Because I haven't been honest with you. *God*," his palm finds my cheek as his eyes search mine, "you're so beautiful."

The devastation on his face is too much and tears well in my eyes. "Vance, talk to me. What's going on?"

"You have the most genuine heart," his voice softens, "and I refuse to break it." He makes a noise in his throat, engulfing the silence. "There's not much in this world I'm afraid of," he admits. His eyes roam everywhere; my hair, my cheeks, my chin, my lips, as if he's memorizing me. "But what scares the absolute hell out of me, is the thought of not being able to remember your smile. Or your beautiful, beautiful eyes. Or the way your heart calls to me on some level I don't understand. I don't think I could take losing that...losing you."

"Vance," I plead. "Please, you're not making any sense."

He backs away, tugging hard at his hair. A quiet rage rolls off of him. "I'm going to end up like them. It's inevitable."

"Like who?"

"Take your pick, really." He paces the carpet, feet wearing a hole in the small space. "My grandmother, my uncle...my mother." His motion halts and his eyes lock on mine, empty and lost. "It's genetic, Ember, and there's a very high chance I'm going to end up the same way. Julian, he got tested already, but I never did. And now...I don't know if I can handle it."

"I understand." I step closer, needing to be near him. "You have to get tested, though, Vance. I'm su—"

"I already have symptoms."

"Oh, Vance." I don't know anything about this disease but I do know something about fear. I recognize it in his slumped posture, the quiver of his chin, the utter defeat in his gaze. The chill running through my veins. Everything hits me at once and I move to wrap my arms around him like a shield, wanting to protect him from everything bad.

"I...had some tests done and they called to let me know I need to come in to discuss the results, but...." His arms settle around me and he squeezes so hard I can barely breathe. "I'm really scared."

I pull back enough to see his face, bringing my hands up to cradle his jaw. "I know, but Vance, you need to get those results. Knowing has to be better than living in fear, doesn't it?"

He sucks in a breath and closes his eyes as if it hurts too much to look at me. Pressing his forehead to mine, he whispers, "I'm even more afraid now that I met you, now that I know I have something to lose. I couldn't bear it if I broke your heart like that, or if I could no longer remember you...." His words fade as he retreats to a place that is difficult to reach. But I refuse to give up.

"I...I already told you how hard it was for me after my brother died. What I didn't say was that everyone kept telling me what to feel, how I *should* feel. But then...you came along. You stood back and *allowed* me to feel. You gave me room to breathe. And you reminded me of who I am. It was so subtle I almost didn't realize it was happening. And my brother," I smile, "he...taught me about life. Every time he jumped off a cliff or skied off the tallest mountain he took a risk. Because to him, that's what life was all about. I care about you, Vance, and I know you care about me, too. Isn't that worth the risk?"

His eyes snap open and he tilts his head back with fierce determination. "I'm not willing to risk your heart."

"Damn it, Vance." An unexpected passion sweeps over me, making me fight for what I want. "You don't get to decide what happens with my heart. It's *my* heart, *my* decision. I'm a big girl and I can take care of myself. Besides, you can't break my heart," my voice quivers, "it cracked two years ago." I smother any fear of being this bold and say the truest words I've ever spoken. "I want this. I want you here. I want you in my life. I want...I want you to touch me. You're the only person I want to touch me."

"God, Ember." He breathes hard against my cheek. "I want to...how I want to—"

"But you won't."

"No." He closes his eyes on another breath as if trying to gain resolve. A few seconds pass and his gaze is back on mine, forcing me to stare into those tormented eyes. "You have to understand. If I touch you, there won't be any going back for me. Tonight, I...I finally saw the devastation in my father, and it made me realize how selfish I've been. I won't do that to you." His hand lifts but then drops away from my face, the lines around his eyes creased with pain. "I have to go," he whispers, and I bow my head, quietly willing the tears not to fall.

When he reaches the door, he stands there, both of us silent for what feels like forever. I lift my chin as he raises his eyes to mine, and what I find there hurts my heart. I want to beg him to stay, to try to convince him that he could be wrong about everything. But the words don't come.

I watch with eyes that can no longer hold back tears as his fingers curl around the knob, hesitating. His internal struggle showing in the white of his knuckles, the rise of his chest. In the end, we both lose, because he twists the knob and walks out the door.

My limbs are numb, prickly, as if my whole body has fallen asleep. Part of me wants to collapse to the carpet and the other part wants to run after him. But I'm not the kind of girl to chase after a guy, no matter how badly I want this particular one. And this disease. I'm terrified for him. I have no idea what this means for his future but I do know that we're stronger together than apart. How can he not see that? He's so concerned about hurting me later that he doesn't see how much he's hurting me now. Still, I don't know how to save him from this. That all-too-familiar feeling of helplessness creeps over me, circling, making sure I know it's still there. Apparently I'm not very good at saving people. That's why when the door clicks shut, I fall to my knees and let the tears flow.

The clock on the wall ticks too loud, reminding me as the minutes go by that he's not coming back. The smell of the chicken parmesan I couldn't wait to eat, now makes me nauseous. Still trying to soothe myself, I curl my body inward as I stare blankly at the door, trying to process what just happened. I thought.... I guess it doesn't matter what I thought—only it matters too much.

I pick myself up off the carpet, wiping my nose and cheeks against my shirt. Padding over to the table and trying to ignore the roses, I blow out the candles and stack the plates, carrying them back into the kitchen. Since my appetite is shot, I cover the food and store it in the fridge.

An abrupt knock on the door startles me. For a moment, I consider not answering it because I'm kind of a mess right now. But maybe it's Troy, and that would be a good thing.

I leave the plates on the counter and head for the door, doing one more swipe of my face with my short-sleeve. When I open it and see Vance standing there, my pulse races and a tiny seed of hope sprouts in my chest. His expression is completely unreadable and I back up a few paces until he's inside the house.

The door closes and he leans against it, crossing his arms over his chest. More tears spill onto my skin as he mutters to himself, moving his head from left to right. "You and your freaking Mickey Mouse shirts." Another shake. "You're like a fucking light I can't look away from." He takes two steps until he's standing in front of me, warm breath fanning my cheeks, palm reaching out to cup my chin. His eyes land on mine. "What the hell have you done to me? I walked up and down this damn block for thirty fucking minutes, and I realized one thing. It's too late for me to turn away now."

"You came back...," I mumble, stunned, messy tears crawling down my skin. "You chose life." My breathing speeds up as his head dips down until his lips are inches from mine.

"No, Ember." He brushes his fingertips across my cheek. "I chose you. I love—*you.*"

And then he kisses me.

His hands dive into my hair, fingers tangling through the wavy strands. The warm press of his lips, the soft sweep of his tongue, the way he holds me—it's as if there is nothing else that exists beyond right now. The world falls away for me too, save for the sound of our breaths mingling, our hearts beating too hard in our chests.

He eases out of my mouth, his hot breath pouring over my ear and goose bumps prickle my skin. I'm suddenly too warm, my clothes too tight, my skin too wanting—and God, do I want him. His hands slip under my shirt, calloused fingertips brushing over my skin and I shudder.

"Are you...hungry at all? I made food." My voice is unsteady, breath coming in short pants as his tongue slides along my neck.

"I am...." He blows lightly over the wetness left behind and I shiver. "But I have everything I want to eat right here."

"I can't believe you just said that." I moan, his grin soaking into my skin.

"I have a feeling you're going to be thinking that a lot tonight." My pulse skyrockets, the space between my legs growing warm. "I want to do dirty things to you." He nips my ear. "You don't mind dirty. Do you, Mickey?" His voice is a low rasp and everything inside me melts. I'm dying to feel him under my fingers. Sliding my arms around his waist, I wedge my hands under the seam of his shirt, dragging my fingertips up and down, back and forth over the curve of his spine. Ridges of lean muscle contract under my touch. His skin is smooth and I want to feel every inch of him. I let my fingertips drift lower, and he shivers when my hand slips under the waistband of his jeans.

"Let's go upstairs," I murmur, pulling his hips to mine. His lips continue to set fire to my skin.

Without warning, he throws me over his shoulder like I weigh absolutely nothing. "I'm a little anxious now," he admits, and I laugh until his strong hand starts massaging my ass. Then I can't seem to focus on anything but the fact that I want that hand between my legs and our clothes off as soon as is humanly possible.

"You're awfully quiet there, Mickey," he says, and I smile as I hang over his back, breathing in the scent of his soap and admiring his legs as they stride up the stairs.

"Just enjoying the view."

He chuckles, squeezing me harder. "You ain't seen nothin' yet."

Once we make it past my door, Vance sets me down. I walk over to flick on the dim lamp beside my bed, his eyes following me around the room. "So," I glance up at him with a coy smile, "clothes or no clothes."

Vance grins, stalking over to me. His grin alone makes me crazy and my body burns with anticipation. In front of me now, he brushes the backs of his fingers down the front of my t-shirt, grazing the tip of my nipple. That faint touch sends me reeling. "Definitely no clothes." Grasping the hem of my shirt, he lifts it up and over my head. He tosses it behind him and his eyes glaze over when he sees my black lace bra. The two hours I spent agonizing over it seems to have paid off. "*Fuck*." He swallows, raising a finger to toy with the edge of the lace and a slight tremble racks my body. His gaze reaches up to mine. "Nervous?"

"A little," I reply honestly, weaving my fingers through the fine strands of his hair.

His smile holds a sweetness that quiets my nerves. "We've already seen each other naked." He taps a palm over my heart. "In here." Taking hold of my other hand, he says softly, "The rest of it, well, it's just a bonus." My fingers float down from his temple, trailing along his jaw. "Fuck, Ember. If it helps, I'm nervous too. Nothing has ever mattered to me this much and I want to do right by you." With every word that comes out of his mouth, I fall a little bit harder for him.

I pull his face down to mine, my lips sliding over his until he opens and the tips of our tongues touch. It's an explosion of feeling and desire that makes my hand wander to the front of his jeans, rubbing over his erection. He groans, arching into my hand.

"Fuck," he curses again. His fingers fumble with my bra strap and I laugh because it takes him so long I almost offer to do it myself.

"Smooth, Davenport," I tease when he finally flicks it open, easing it down my arms.

"Your tits are perfect." His stare brands my skin, gaze alone making my nipples hard.

"They're small," I counter with a grin.

"Fuck that. They're perfect." He lowers his head to swirl his tongue around the tight peak. The wet warmth makes me moan and my knees go weak. "I want to taste you." His tongue continues to flick across the tip. "I want to know what feels good to you," he murmurs, licking and sucking until my head falls back, giving in to the tingles racing over my skin.

His hands are everywhere, spanning my back, my hip, my waist, as he uses his mouth until I'm barely able to stand up. He bends, his tongue forging a trail along the length of my stomach and my legs quiver. Without realizing it, I find my hands tugging at his hair.

He looks up at me with a knowing smile. "Something you want?"

I smile back but my face is hot, eyes fixed only on him. "Yeah. *You.*"

Evidently, that's all he needs to hear before he rises to his feet and strips off his clothes. Not bothering to wait, I do the same until his eyes blaze, roaming my body like he's lost in the desert and I'm his only hope for survival. In all fairness, my gaze is wandering everywhere, too. From his broad shoulders down to his toned arms, to a wall of rippled muscle. Then lower to his erection, thick and beautiful.

"It's all for you," he grins, and my gaze swoops to his face. "Only for you," he clarifies, eyes holding an intensity that makes heat gather between my legs.

I'm not sure what I expect to happen next, but he tackles me and we fall onto the bed in a tangle of limbs and laughter that is so much like us it makes me glow inside. In an instant though, his body covers mine, the laughter gone. All I hear is the sound of our breathing. All I feel are his lips coasting down my neck, my belly, between my legs.

"Oh, God," I moan, letting my thighs fall open, aware of how wet I am, of how much I want him. His tongue does things to me I never knew were possible, gliding through my folds, back and forth, in slow, lingering circles. "Vance," I whimper, latching onto his bicep and urging him forward.

He slides up my body, face so close to mine I can smell myself on his breath. "I love the way you taste," he whispers, and then he kisses me, begging for entry into my mouth that I readily give him. It's strange at first, but I don't mind it. "I want to be inside you," he rasps when he gently pulls back, and I nod my response because the emotion is too much. He strokes a finger over my chin before disappearing to the floor to find his wallet. My mind catches up with my body that this is really happening. But I'm not scared. I've never wanted anything more.

I watch as he tears open the package and rolls the condom over his erection, returning to me. No words are exchanged between us, and I don't need any. Everything I need is clear in the depths of his eyes and the openness of his smile. I know that I'm the only one he allows to see this side of him. It makes a ball of happiness unfurl in my stomach, warm, like rays of sunshine.

"Ember," he murmurs, breath stuttering in his chest as he guides himself inside of me, easing in slowly. It's a feeling of fullness that already existed in my mind and heart—and now in my body. "Okay?" He studies my face for any signs of hesitation. But he won't find any.

"Yes." I smile, losing focus as he slides in then out, in then out. Long, drawn-out movements that overwhelm me. My hands leave his back and cling to his shoulders, muscles hot and damp under my touch.

"Breathe, Ember."

Emotion gets the best of me and a lone tear comes out of nowhere and rolls down my cheek. Vance kisses it away. "We just fit—"

"I know. I feel it too," he whispers, his expression filled with tenderness. I bring my hand around to caress his jaw and smile up at him. He has so many sides, and I love them all.

The wave hits me then, all at once, a series of small gasps falling into the air between us. "Vance, I'm—"

"Let go," he urges, his body thrusting at a faster pace as he leans down to kiss me. I moan into his mouth, giving him this last piece of myself and waiting for him to do the same.

"*Ember*...." He groans his release as his head drops, hair brushing against my skin, lips pressed to my neck. "I love you."

My words are barely a whisper. "I love you, too."

I feel his smile. "I know."

Neither of us move as our breathing slows then levels out, returning to a steady rhythm. Eventually, Vance rolls away, disposing of the condom before claiming his spot next to me. He tugs my body close, my back to his front, until no space exists between our heartbeats. A contented yawn lifts itself from my throat and Vance chuckles. "Tired already?"

"Yes." I wiggle against him. "And it's all your fault."

"Funny, I don't feel guilty at all." His fingertip skates along the inside of my arm. The tickle brings a smile to my face. "In fact, I was hoping we could go another round." I hear the grin in his voice and I wedge myself closer, if that's possible.

"Just one?" My eyelids feel heavy and although my mind wants to stay awake, my body has other plans. As I drift off, a blissful sigh floats from my lips. "You came back...for me."

"I did," he whispers, mouth resting above my ear. "I didn't have a choice."

"Me either," I admit in a soft murmur, sleep taking over my thoughts. "I really love you."

chapter thirty
Vance

EMBER SAILS OFF into sleep. Her warm, bare skin against mine. As her chest rises and falls, her breathing becomes deep and even. I force my eyes to remain open, wanting to remember this moment. To engrave it in my mind. I wonder if that's possible. If you try hard enough, if you can will your brain to remember something.

But it doesn't matter now. Any apprehension I had is trumped by this crazy love I feel for her. My chest explodes with it. I'll admit, being present in my own life is strange. Not allowing my choices to be derailed by a crippling fear of the future. Because Ember is right. Life doesn't come with guarantees and I'd rather have a shot at happiness with her, than none at all.

I lie awake until the stars disappear and the sky morphs into a black canvas painted in moonlight. The clock beside Ember's bed reads 2:30am. Not wanting to collide with her mother, I sneak out from beside her and tug on my clothes. As I put on my sneakers, I watch her face blanketed in sleep. This girl—she's changed me—and I'll never be the same. That alone makes me smile.

Placing one knee on the bed, I lean close to drop a gentle kiss against her hair. "I love you, Mickey," I whisper, leaving something for her then quietly slipping out the door and into the night.

Cool air brushes across my skin, a peaceful hush settles over the neighborhood. My heart is a complete fucking contradiction, racing to an insane beat inside my chest. Funny how life can be so unexpected, how it manages to put things in your path that forces you to open your eyes.

As I climb the stairs two at a time, a high unlike anything I've ever felt courses through my veins. I can still smell Ember on my clothes, taste her skin on my lips, feel her body moving beneath me. She takes my breath away, and yet, I can finally breathe. For the first time in so damn long, life stirs inside of me, whipping around like a fierce tornado.

A strange noise catches my attention. I continue up the stairs, the sound growing louder the closer my feet get to the landing. I laugh to myself when I realize Julian has a girl over and tiptoe past his room. But I stop short hearing it again—coming from behind my father's closed door. I can identify the sound but it doesn't make sense. Static clouds my thoughts as my legs propel me closer. I should walk away. Pretend I didn't hear anything. But I can't leave it alone. I *refuse* to leave it alone.

My gut twists as my fingers tighten around the knob and squeeze, slowly cracking the door open. The sight of my father's body moving over a woman who sure as fuck isn't my mother makes blood roar in my ears and I lose my shit. "Jesus Christ," I bite out, startled by the fucking display in front of me. The muscle in my jaw throbs and I can't catch my breath. I turn to bolt down the stairs, my head a whirl of confusion. Legs that nearly seize up somehow manage to carry me to the door. My hands shaking, it takes me three tries before the lock clicks and I stumble onto the front lawn, cursing my father to hell and knowing I need to get the fuck out of here. I don't get very far though. I'm inches from my car when his voice calls out to me.

"Vance, wait."

I freeze, but don't turn around. My hands are fisted at my sides, anger coming to a rapid boil. I'm itching to unleash its wrath. "I don't have anything to say to you," I hiss through gritted teeth, still refusing to look at the man who disgusts me now. The man I used to admire.

"Good," he counters. "Because I'm going to do all the talking and you're going to listen. Turn around, son." That word sounds vile in my ears. At this moment I wish I were anyone else's son but his. Still, I spin around to face him, his commanding tone leaving me no other choice. "Let me explain," he continues, standing there in a pair of pants and no shirt. He makes me sick.

"I think what I saw was pretty self-explanatory," I growl. "You're the one who told me about the birds and the bees." Then a thought occurs to me. "What was that earlier anyway?" I snap. "That sad, desperate man with the bottle. Was that all an act? Because from what I can see, it sure as hell was."

"Things are not as they appear, Vance."

"*Obviously.*"

He lets out an uneven breath, hands rigid on his hips. "Do you want to know where I go every Friday night?"

My eyes squeeze shut and I bite my cheek. "I don't want to hear this."

"I go to see your mother," he admits, and my eyes pop open as I glare at him in the darkness.

"Do you want a medal for that?" I snarl, jamming my hands in my pockets. He starts to talk but his words are muffled by the horrific moans that filtered from his room. By his naked form hovering over someone else.

"I bring her a pad and some paints," he adds to whatever I missed. "And I hold my hand over her shaky one, hoping maybe she'll remember something. When we're done, she always tells me it looks like an ugly doodle. But you know what I see?" He pauses, the strain in his tone softening. "I see beauty. Because when she looks up, laughing at herself...I stare into her eyes to find the girl I took on our first date to a painting class, because I knew how much she loved it." He steps toward me and I back away. "I see the only woman I've ever loved. The one that I know," he comes even closer, raw emotion in his voice, "is never coming back to me."

An anguished breath rattles the air between us and my fury wanes. "She may be your mother, Vance. But that's my wife in there. And I miss her. And...I've been so...lonely. It's been a long time since I've been with a woman, and I'm sorry that this hurts you, son. But I won't apologize for being lonely. For needing someone. And if the roles were reversed, I wouldn't want your mother to be lonely either."

His words provoke the crazy in my chest. "But that's the thing, Dad. Isn't it? She's all alone. Without her memory, she has nothing. She has no one."

Thick silence stretches between us until he breaks it. "You have to know, Vance. I'll never love anyone like I love your mother. It's just not possible." The lamppost shines against his face and a tear streaks down his cheek. My heart is in my throat, sympathy for him somehow finding its way inside.

The front door opens then, and my mouth along with it. Any sympathy I had for my father goes right out the fucking window.

Something clicks in my head, as if a light turns on and everything becomes brutally clear. "What the...is *she* the reason we moved here, Dad?"

"Vance—"

I cut him off. "Answer the question. Oh my God, are you fucking in love with her?"

I don't need an answer. It's in his eyes, and on her face. It's swirling in the air around us until it swallows me whole—and I only have one choice.

I should have known better.

Every good thing I felt gets swept away in a matter of seconds. A tidal wave pulls me under and takes it from me, tossing me around until it's gone.

Maybe it wasn't meant for me after all.

My head hurts and I can't think straight. The need to escape before I say or do something I'll regret is overwhelming. My father shouts after me, pleading, as I lunge into the car. But my ears are ringing and my soul is completely shattered.

I shove the key into the ignition then yank the gear lever down, slamming my foot on the gas pedal. Tires screech as I peel out of the driveway and speed off down the street. My hands won't stop trembling and I wrap them tighter around the steering wheel as harsh tears drag across my cheeks.

Everything is fucked now.

With no destination in mind, I keep driving, promising myself that I won't look back—that I can't look back. Because if I do, the only thing I'll see is the one thing I'm leaving behind.

My heart.

chapter thirty-one
Ember

LIGHT BEAMING IN the window startles me awake. The bright moon filters through the curtains and I press my face into the pillow, unable to contain my smile. As I turn over to find the reason for it, he isn't there. Instead, a single pink rose lies in his place. I bring it to my nose, inhaling its sweet scent and remembering every vivid detail of our night—Vance's hands, his lips, his whispered words. My skin tingles everywhere he touched, his smell lingering on my sheets and in the air.

Warmth floods my body as I sit up and swing my legs over the side of the bed, grinning at the clothes scattered about the room. My t-shirt hangs off the other lampshade and I laugh at Vance's perfect aim, even in the near darkness.

Gathering a clean pair of panties from the drawer, I slide them on along with a fresh t-shirt and sleep shorts. The red numbers on the clock blaring 3:00am make me cringe, knowing that my chances of falling back to sleep are nonexistent.

With a sigh, I head downstairs, fumbling for the light switch before padding to the kitchen to pour myself a glass of water. Restless, I putter around, opening and closing cabinets, not looking for anything in particular. I pause to stare out the window and my thoughts go to Vance. As if my whole body is awash with color, the desire to sculpt overwhelms me.

On my way to the basement, the front door opens and I grab my chest, nearly jumping out of my skin. My mom shuffles in the door. She doesn't notice me right away because her head is down. "Geez, Mom. You scared me half to death. What are you doing home this early?" She doesn't answer nor does she look up. On a second glance, she seems...off. Her hair is a tangled mess, blouse wrinkled and hanging out of her skirt. "Mom?"

Her head whips up as if she didn't hear me, or expect to see me for that matter. Her normally bright gaze is hollow. Dried tears stain her cheeks while black smudges line her skin. She still won't meet my eyes, averting her focus to something beyond my shoulder.

"Mom?" Why won't she answer me? My voice rises to a higher pitch. "What happened to you?" Still no answer. She walks past me, her shoulders sagging. "Mom!" I shout this time, and she stops mid-way up the stairs.

"I can't believe this is happening," she mumbles.

"Mom, you're scaring me. Did something happen to Avery or Dad?"

She raises her chin a fraction, fresh tears dripping down her cheeks. "I swear I didn't mean for this to happen," she mumbles again like I'm not in the room. Then her gaze finally connects with mine and her voice cracks. "We didn't mean to hurt anyone." Bringing a hand to the side of her head, she whispers, "We were both in pain...and lonely...we didn't want to hurt anyone...least of all our kids."

"Mom, *what* are you talking about?"

She continues climbing the stairs as my mind struggles to put the pieces together. None of this makes any sense—until it does. It can't be, though. How can it be? *No, no, no. Please, don't let it be true.* But deep down, I feel it.

The glass tumbles from my hand and shatters into tiny pieces, water splattering onto the tile floor. I hear my mother shouting, asking me what's wrong. But my only thought is of Vance. I sprint to the door and jam my feet in my sneakers then tear out of the house, practically tripping down the front steps. I'm gasping for breaths that won't come. Pressure builds behind my eyes before the tears arrive and I curse them for falling. It's almost like my heart knows. The walls around it already caving in, the beat slowing to a halt. And when I round the corner I close my eyes in silent prayer. But I already know. Even before I open my eyes—I know.

And I was right about my heart. It doesn't break.

I just can't feel it anymore.

part two

Three years later

chapter thirty-two
Vance

A CHILL HANGS in the air, a welcome burn to my skin. The sky is pitched in darkness, the moon clouded over—a perfect representation of my mood. I take a drag of the cigarette I've promised myself is my last one, not exactly giving a fuck tonight. Come to think of it, I don't give a fuck about much these days. Smoke scrapes the back of my throat before I blow it out in a wintery puff.

"Davenport, you're up in ten. It's a big crowd tonight." Paul's voice bellows from inside and I try to muster the enthusiasm I know he wants to see from me, but never manage to live up to. I can't remember the last time I had that much enthusiasm for anything. Actually I can. And that's the fucking problem.

"Hurry up." A girl laughs, rushing her friend inside. "I want to get a good seat. Hot musicians and all."

I roll my eyes. Every week chicks come in and fawn all over us. Little do they know, I don't want anything to do with them. Not that I haven't been lured in the past—I'm only human. But it's the follow-through I'm having the issue with lately. Mostly because I don't want the emptiness that a quick fuck carries with it. I want...well, it doesn't matter what I want. Any chance of me having what I really wanted, I fucked up a long time ago.

My mind kicks into high gear, reminding me of all the reasons we wouldn't have worked out. The cards that were stacked against us; our parents, my potential illness. As I go through the checklist in my brain, the same one that played repeatedly these past few years, it doesn't make me feel any better. It never does. My body sags against the rough brick and I expel a weary sigh.

"Hey, Vance. You okay?"

I angle my head to discover Chris peering out from the back entrance. Lucky for me, the absence of light out here cloaks the truth. "Yeah, yeah. I'm good."

"Yeaaaah. Okay. You can tell me l-later. You've got about five more minutes and then we're on."

Chris stares at me a second longer than necessary before he disappears. I should realize by now that I can't hide anything from him—he knows me too well. Three years ago when...well, when I didn't know where the hell to go, I showed up on his doorstep. He didn't fucking hesitate. He took me in as if nothing had changed, and I owe him big time.

It was Chris who stuck to my side when Mom passed away two years ago with complications from pneumonia. He helped me get through. Navigate the sea of devastation I found myself drowning in. Unable to get past my father's betrayal, he and I were in a tense stand-off and Julian was an emotional wreck. Our mother's death hit Julian harder than either of us expected. I found myself trying to lift him up, though I could barely keep my own spirits in check. Most of all, I missed Ember.

I still do.

Exhaling my regret into the frigid air, I flick my cigarette to the cement and stub it out with the heel of my boot. I head inside, making my way through the dimly lit hallway and out to the bar. Immediately, I'm assaulted by the scent of alcohol and too much perfume. Overly sweaty bodies are packed like sardines, dancing to music booming from the speakers as they wait for us to perform.

This gig isn't anything glamorous, nor is the dive bar we play in. But it keeps me going. It's something I feel passion for, and there is very little I can say that about these days.

BY THE TIME the set is over, I'm bone tired. Sweat drips from my neck, my t-shirt sticking to my skin. All I want is to crawl into bed and sleep for twenty-four hours straight. Not much different from what I'd like to do on most days. But I've been there, done that. And Chris won't let me get away with it anymore.

We stow our instruments in the back room and Chris gestures toward the bar. "Come on. L-let's get a drink. Of beer," he adds with a wink, knowing full well of my aversion to heavy alcohol.

It's almost two am and the place is still hopping, because it is New York City after all. It's true what they say—no one ever seems to sleep here.

We squeeze through a group of scantily dressed women and grab two stools at the bar. Chris taps the counter to signal the bartender over. "Two Coronas p-please."

"Corona?" I nudge his arm. "What are you, slumming it?"

"Nah." He leans forward, resting his elbows on the bar. "I just d-don't want to make you feel bad."

I smack him lightly on the back. "Thanks, man. You're a good friend."

"I know." He smirks. "Just don't f-forget it this time." The bartender brings over our beers and Chris slides a bowl of peanuts down, popping a few in his mouth. "Do you remember when we talked about opening up a bar together?"

"Yes." I take a long pull of my beer then set it down on the counter. "What a stupid fucking idea that was."

"I know, right?" Chris runs a hand through his dirty blond hair; longer in the front, shorter on the sides. "Of course, that was when you couldn't get a job to save your freaking life," he throws in, and I glare at him. "How the heck d-did we go from wanting to open a bar, to starting a consulting business?"

"Easy. We were always good at messing around with shit. Do you remember how many computers we took apart back in the day, just to see if we could actually put them back together?"

His mouth curves and he picks at the label of his beer. "I'll never forget that t-time when my father came home and saw us on the floor of the living room with his laptop." He laughs, giving me a sideways glance. "He nearly had a coronary."

"Eh, your father's a softie."

"Speaking of which," he turns fully on the stool to face me, "have you thought any more about c-calling your dad? You have to forgive him sooner or later."

Both my mood and my grin slip at the mention of my father. I stare down at my hand, now curled into a hard fist. "No, I fucking don't." I release a heavy breath. "He fucked everything up."

"No." Chris waits until I look at him. "You d-did that all by yourself."

"Thanks, dude." I grip his shoulder with a smirk. "I can always count on you for a reality check."

He flashes me his white teeth. "You're welcome."

The huge dose of reality he served causes me to suck into myself. I drop my head in my hands and we sit in silence as I stare blankly at my beer. The creaking sound of Chris's stool drags my gaze up.

"What are you staring at?"

"I know that g-girl. I just can't place where I know her from." I spin in my seat to check it out but there are too many heads blocking my view.

"So go talk to her," I urge, shifting back around. "Stop being shy for once in your life. Maybe you'll even get a date out of it."

His brown eyes narrow and he scowls. "I know how to get a date if I want one. I'm just n-not interested."

"Okay." I hold my hands up. "If you say so." I dig my fingers in the peanut bowl and shove a handful into my mouth.

"Look who's t-talking." He drags the bowl away from me. "Maybe you're the one who should get out there. You've had a bit of a dry spell, don't you think?"

"There were a few girls. But they meant nothing and I didn't mislead anyone."

"Yeah, b-but that was like, a while ago," he adds, pushing the issue. One I'm in no mood to discuss.

"Did I tell you your mom called me yesterday about your birthday shindig? I was confused because your birthday is three months away."

He smirks. "Nice d-diversionary tactic. And you know how my mom is. She's a planner—" He snaps his fingers in front of his face. "Now I know where I've seen that girl. She was at your mother's funeral."

"*What?*" It takes me a second before I stand up off the stool, scanning the crowd. "Who? Show me which one."

He pushes off his seat, surveying the faces of people huddled together near the stage and over by the makeshift dance floor. His gaze moves toward the entrance to the bar and he points a finger. "Th-that one."

Given that Chris has a two inch height advantage, I still can't see shit. I walk a few paces, pushing my way past the horde of inebriation. And then my eyes land on a face—her sweet, sweet face—and my heart begins to beat like a freaking drum inside my chest. Up until now, I didn't realize it was still there.

Ember.

Her name clings to my lips and my body stills, save for the erratic thumping of my heart and the slight tremble in my hands. After all this time, there she is. And here I am, unable to move or fucking breathe. All I can do is stare.

Her shoulder length hair is now mid-way down her back, her curves more pronounced. A dress cut above the knees accentuates her long, toned legs. Dresses never used to be her thing. It makes me wonder what else has changed, and how much I've missed.

Chris appears beside me. "Yeah, that's her."

I look over at him. "She was at the funeral?"

"Yeah. And the only reason I even remember her is because I actually b-bumped into her on my way out. She was upset and I gave her a tissue. I asked how she knew your mom but she was vague." His eyes travel my face. "You all right? Your skin is pale."

My glance returns to Ember. "That's her."

"Who?"

Of course he wouldn't recognize her. I never had a picture and she doesn't have a Facebook profile for fuck's sake. I would know, because I spent countless hours trying to locate one. Then again, I could have easily found her if guilt and anger hadn't stood in the way.

I choke down a swell of emotion to utter her name. "Ember."

"Holy crap. Well, what are you waiting f-for?" He gives my arm a shove. "Go talk to her."

My feet are frozen, regret keeping them rooted to the sticky floor. "I can't." I swallow hard and watch as a big hand comes around to engulf her shoulder, bringing her in close.

And I see just how much has changed.

She looks...happy and my stomach pinches tight. I can't lie. I wish he wasn't the one making her smile like that. But she deserves to be with someone who can make her happy. "She's not mine anymore." My gaze jumps to Chris's face and he frowns, the pain scrawled on my skin obvious only to him. "Let's get out of here."

The ride back to our apartment in the East Village is quiet, but my brain is filled with static. Seeing Ember again solidified how real my feelings were, and unfortunately for me, still are. But she's clearly moved on and I only have myself to blame. I didn't give her a choice. *I'm* the one who left. *I'm* the one who threw us away.

Chris's voice cuts into my thoughts. "I always wondered when we were deciding between New York and California, why you always p-pushed so hard for New York. It was because of her, wasn't it? Maybe you were hoping she'd be here, too?"

Buildings zip by in a blur of memories as I stare out the window. "It's a big city, Chris."

"You didn't answer my question." He sighs, the air heavy between us. "You can't keep doing this, you know? I get it, you w-walked away. And I'm not going to judge you and say whether it was right or wrong. It was all you could handle at the time." He grips my shoulder and I'm forced to turn around. "But your father has paid for what he did with your silence, and well, so have you. Ember's gone on with her life. You're the only one who hasn't. You've been punishing yourself for freaking everything. You don't even have symptoms anymore for f-fuck's sake. You may *never* have any more symptoms. Jesus, Vance. Let it go. Just let it all go."

Deep down, I know Chris is right. Yet somewhere below the surface, where everything isn't as clear and Ember's face is all I see—I can't let her go.

chapter thirty-three
Ember

"I WANT TO marry you," Grant breathes into my neck, peppering kisses along my skin.

"We're in a taxi," I laugh, "and that's the most unromantic wedding proposal I've ever heard."

He whips his head back and glares at me, hope springing to life in his eyes. "Are you saying if I change venues you'll consider it?"

"Grant." I sigh, frustrated more with myself than with him. He's a great guy and I'm an idiot. "We're too young."

"Wait a minute." The cab pulls to a stop in front of my building and he reaches over to pay the fare. He doesn't miss a beat though. As soon as we step out onto the sidewalk, he continues his tirade. "Let me get this straight. First it's the location, and now it's our ages. Which is it?" A frown tugs on one side of his mouth as he holds the glass door open. "Or, is it just that you don't want to marry me?"

"Look, Grant." I pause in the center of the lobby, inspecting the floor for an answer that won't make him feel bad. "I'm just really tired. Can we talk about this tomorrow?"

"Okay." My gaze lifts and he cups my cheek with a soft smile. "I don't mean to push, I just love you, you know." His eyes search mine and I know he's waiting for me to say the words, but I'm not ready. I can't admit to something that I don't feel. It's not who I am. The silence lengthens and he exhales a deep sigh. "Come on then. I'll walk you up."

We step off the elevator, his fierce attention making me want to climb the walls. With any luck, Avery will be home. All I want right now is to hang out with my sister and eat ice cream straight out of the carton.

The door clicks open and I let out an easy breath the moment I cross the threshold. I love our apartment. Avery and I wanted it to be simple, yet comfortable. And it is. With a little help from Mom, we chose to paint the walls in a light sage green and picked out two oversized buttery leather sofas, the focal point of the living room. An old, refurbished trunk sits between them that Avery discovered at this great vintage furniture shop in Midtown.

The scent of my favorite cinnamon apple candles slides under my nose and I inhale with a smile. From the looks of things, Avery must have felt guilty about our earlier argument regarding her messiness. Clothes that were hanging over chairs and shopping bags left on the carpet are gone. The faint sound of music flows out from her room and I breathe a muffled sigh of relief.

"Would you mind if I have a nightcap before I go?" Grant asks, and I direct my irritation toward the ceiling.

"Sure." I drop my coat on the sofa, then breeze past my favorite Mickey Mouse painting I bought from a street vendor last year. "Is wine okay? We don't have much else," I mention as Grant follows me to the kitchen. The space is not small by any stretch, with two walls of cabinets and a miniature farm-style table, but his six foot two frame suddenly makes me feel claustrophobic.

"It's great." He hovers over me as I pour the wine into a glass. "Thanks, babe."

I sneak around him, failing to understand what my problem is. I'm...antsy, and want to run around and throw open the windows to breathe in the outside air. "I'll be right back. Just want to use the bathroom."

"Okay, babe."

Behind the safety of the closed door, I draw in a breath then let it out. Then I head straight for the sink, turning on the faucet to splash cold water on my face. I'm not sure what's gotten into me tonight, but I don't feel like myself. Maybe it's Grant's insistence on the whole marriage thing, I don't know. How can you want to marry someone who hasn't even told you they love you? I don't get it. Beyond that, I realize we've been friends for almost a year and a half, and dating several months. Maybe that should be enough.

Patting my face dry with a nearby towel, I glance at my reflection in the mirror. The green eyes that stare back at me are dull, my cheeks paler than usual. Regardless, I steady myself with a big breath and traipse back out to the living room. I'm planning to ask Grant if we can call it a night when I freeze, my legs nearly buckling beneath me.

"Put that down." The words come out much harsher than I intended. Grant flinches, immediately setting my book on the table. I can't believe I forgot to put it away.

"I'm sorry," he starts. "I was just—"

"It's okay." I cross the room until I'm standing in front of him, then take his hand and hope my expression conveys my apology. "I'm sorry, Grant." My shoulders dip right along with the rest of my spirits. "Listen, I'm just...tired. It's been a long day and I'd like to get some sleep."

"Sure, babe. No worries." He hesitates before giving me a quick kiss on the cheek. I can't blame him for being apprehensive. I've been all over the place tonight. With one last glance, he grabs his jacket and heads out the door. As soon as it shuts, I sag against the wall, my gaze wandering to the book. After staring at it for far too long, I walk over to pick it up then drop down on the sofa. My hand is unsteady as I open it to the first page.

"He stepped down, trying not to look long at her, as if she were the sun, yet he saw her, like the sun, even without looking."
I thought Tolstoy said it better than I ever could.
xoxo Vance

I close my eyes, desperately trying to push it all away. But the hurt is still there. Sometimes it hides behind other things. Like a smile that's a little too bright, or a laugh that's much too loud. But I'm trying to move on. I *have* to move on. After all, it's been three years. Vance didn't even attempt to search for me. It was pretty easy for him to toss me aside, and that's what makes my heart resent him—or want to, anyway.

Still, he continues to invade my mind. He won't leave me alone. Those blue eyes and that crooked grin. That damn earring he used to tug on all the time. I miss our talks and the way he used to hold my hand, my face, my heart. And I wonder if he's okay, if he's healthy. The thought of him not being well makes my stomach clench. I slam the book down on the couch, slouching deeper into the leather.

"Whoa, whoa. Does someone need anger management classes?" Avery jumps on the sofa and I lunge for the book, shifting it to my other side. "Protective much?"

"*No.* It's just that the book—"

"Means a lot to you." She lowers her body until her head rests on my shoulder. "I know."

"It's just a book," I pout, heaving my feet onto the trunk. "Any chance we still have that half-gallon of cookies & cream in the freezer?"

"We do."

"Two spoons. No bowls."

Before the words are out of my mouth, she's sprinting to the kitchen. "Oh," she calls back. "Dad sent us a package and there was a puzzle in there for you." A drawer slams closed. "He misses us."

"I miss him too," I mumble.

"Just what the doctor ordered." She settles next to me and digs her spoon into the ice cream, scooping out a chunk of Oreo. "So tell me. How was your night with the even-keeled one?" she asks dryly, and I glare at her.

"It was fine. We went out for Thai food and then a movie. He wanted to go back to that bar we went to a few months ago to see that band he likes. But I wasn't in the mood for anything loud."

"I just want you to know," she taps her spoon against her mouth, "that every time I ask how your night was with Grant, you say *fine.*"

Swirls of vanilla suddenly capture my interest. "He still wants me to marry him, practically asked me again tonight."

"Again? First of all, you haven't been dating that long and second, you haven't even had sex with him." She lets out a dramatic groan. "You certainly can't marry someone until you know if you're sexually compatible."

I frown. "Yes, but we've known each other for a while. I feel bad. He's such a nice guy...and I'm an idiot."

"You're not an idiot, Em." She bangs her spoon against mine to get my attention and I look up at her. "He just may not be the right guy for you. When the right guy comes along, you'll be ready."

"Yeah. Given that I'm such an expert on relationships." I laugh, and she joins in. "I have too many other things to focus on anyway. Work, school, my sculpting...."

"Kickboxing classes at the gym with your sister."

"I didn't agree to that," I retort, shoveling a heap of ice cream into my mouth.

"You did," she counters with a not-so-innocent grin.

Since I know my sister, I crack a suspicious smile. "It must have been under duress because I don't remember."

"You remember...," she drops her spoon into the ice cream and pats her stomach, "everything." Her expression turns somber. "Seriously, though. I think you're doing really well. I honestly can't remember the last time you had a 'no bowls' kind of night."

"Yeah." I huff out a long, uneven breath. "I'm getting there."

Maybe if I keep telling myself that, I'll finally believe it.

chapter thirty-four
Vance

DARK CLOUDS INVADE the sky, various shades of gray reflective of my state of mind as we arrive at Chris's house. The threat of an impending storm chases us. My brain following the same pattern—flooded with chaotic thoughts that all lead to one person.

We pull up to the saltbox colonial, the home that Chris's mom and dad have owned for the past two years since moving from Oregon to New York. Wanting to be closer to their son but not being city people, they found a compromise in a suburban area of Westchester.

"Am I going to have to d-deal with this the entire day? It is my birthday, you know." Chris exits the car, and I slide the yellow tulips from the seat and slam the door.

"Deal with what?" I ask, caught in his rigid stare.

He stops short of the front door, hands plastered on his hips. "Really? You're going to p-play innocent with me? You forget how well I know you." He sighs, glancing over at the bushes then back to me. "Listen, Vance. I honestly thought your days of brooding were over. But ever since you saw Ember a few months ago in the bar, you've gotten worse. You could've gone up to talk to her and you chose not to. You could've looked for her after. I just...don't get it. But three months of your moping is my limit. I'm tapped out." The dirty look I throw his way doesn't faze him. "Remember what I said. Either do something about it or let it go." His eyebrow shoots up. "It's not like you don't have choices. Girls crawl all over you. It's disgusting, really."

That night in the bar plays on repeat like a fucking movie reel in my mind. I'm still trying to grasp the fact that Ember was at my mother's funeral and never came over to me. Even Julian didn't know she was there. Then again, she probably thought I wanted nothing to do with her. I guess my walking away made that pretty clear. Though it was the furthest thing from the truth. There didn't seem to be any other way.

"Do we have to talk about this shit? How about we go celebrate your birthday?" I grin, and he glares at me before knocking twice.

The door swings open and pint-sized Riley greets us with a toothy grin. "Unca Vance, Unca Vance. Unca Vaaaaaaaance is hewe!"

"Nice," Chris mumbles. "My own b-brother cares more about you than he does me."

I clap him on the back, wearing a proud smile. "Oh relax, birthday boy. He fucking sees you all the time." I smirk. "I'm a novelty." Then I wink, passing him the flowers. "Hold these, will ya?"

We barely make it into the house before Riley tackles me, almost knocking me over. I pretend to fall back and he giggles. Lifting him in the air, I let him hang there. "Hey, shortstuff. How ya been?"

"Gooooooood."

"I see you still have your exaggerated vowel tendency." His button nose scrunches as I blow a giant raspberry against his stomach, complete with sound effects. He squeals before I swing him around then gently set him down on his feet.

"Agaaaaaaaain," he shouts as he spins in dizzying circles and falls on his tiny behind.

Chris's mom emerges from the kitchen with a bright smile, wearing the frayed apron Chris made for her in middle school. Her blunt cut bangs highlight her big brown eyes, mouth covered in the same pink lipstick she's worn for years.

"Happy Birthday, sweetie." She makes a smacking sound and blows Chris a kiss. "You two are just in time. I made a fresh batch of Chris's favorite cookies. Would you like some cookies and milk to tide you over?"

Chris leans over and whispers to me. "She still thinks b-because I stutter I'm ten years old."

"I heard that, Christopher James."

"Well, Jesus, Mom. C-come on. Milk and cookies? Don't you have any hair of the dog? It was a long night."

Little Riley scratches his mop of dark hair and those big blue eyes turn inward. "We don't have a haiwy dog, Chwissy." He yanks on Mrs. Raven's skirt. "Mommy, can we get a haiwy dog?"

"Come here, you." I waggle my finger and Riley edges closer with big, excited eyes.

"Do you have a secwet Unca?"

I squat down, lowering myself to his level. "I was thinking maybe this week I could take you into the city. We can go to the toy store and you can pick out a new superhero for your collection."

The giant smile on his face tugs at my heart. "Yes!"

"Okay." I muss his floppy hair. "I'll talk to your mom and we'll pick a day."

"Yipeeeeeeeee."

As I push to my feet, Chris gestures to the flowers in his hand. I take them, and catch a faint sigh drifting over from his mom. Given that I used to bring flowers to my own mother, this is as much for me as it is for her. "These are for you, Mrs. Raven."

She closes her fingers around the crinkled tissue paper, her round cheeks glowing. "So formal, Vance. You know we don't do formal here." She opens her arms wide. "Get over here and give me a hug this instant."

The sweet smell of vanilla bombards me as I walk into her embrace. It takes me back to those days after school, when Julian and I would blast into the house to find Mom in the kitchen baking her all-natural cakes. Her arms are suddenly too tight around me, squeezing the spot inside my chest that is still raw. But whether I want to admit it or not, I need this. So I relax into her and let her carry me for a few precious seconds.

"Okay." She grips my shoulders and steps back. "Now let me see these flowers." She brings them to her nose and inhales. "These are beauties. Thank you, Vance. I'm going to put them in water." Her gaze roams to the flight of stairs. "Dan, pry yourself away from those video games," she calls out. "The boys are here."

"We're m-men, aren't we?" Chris snickers and I laugh, while his mom glances over with a hint of amusement on her face.

"Why don't you *men* take a load off," she tosses back over her shoulder. "And I'll bring out something to keep you until we have dinner. Dad should be down in a minute. Riley, why don't you come help me with the cookies." He flaps his arms like a bird and zooms into the kitchen. I can't resist the smile that breaks out on my face. Riley was adopted as a baby four years ago after his fucked-up parents abandoned him to focus on their drug habit. To see him this happy and cared for is remarkable.

"It's great what your mom and dad did for Riley."

"Yeah, I m-mean, the adoption took a long time to finally go through and they practically had to jump through hoops. But it was totally worth it. Besides, since I was gone, my mom needed someone else to fawn over. And...I love that little guy." He settles onto the couch and grabs a pillow, tucking it under his chin. "You're really good with him, Vance. Someday you'll be a great dad. Of course," he chuckles, "you need to be having sex to make that happen."

My lips form a snarl and I lob a pillow at his head. "You're a real comedian today. And just for the record, smartass, I'm having plenty of sex."

"With what, your hand?"

"What's this about hands?" Chris's dad walks over, extending his arm in my direction. As I stand, he pulls me in for a hug. "Good to see you, son."

"You too, Mr. Raven."

He releases me and takes a seat next to Chris, playfully punching him on the shoulder. "Happy Birthday, kiddo." Slinging an arm over the back of the couch, he gestures toward Chris with his thumb. "I just saw this one the other day. Did he tell you I whipped his behind in chess?"

"Is that so?" I settle back against the sofa and glare at Chris. "It must have slipped his mind."

"Remember all those chess competitions you two used to have when you were young? Such a great game to know how to play." He taps the side of his head. "A real thinking game, keeps your mind going." He opens his mouth, but then he frowns. "I'm sorry, Vance. I didn't mean—"

"It's okay." I shoot him a genuine smile. "Don't even think twice about it." He sends me an empathetic nod before changing the subject.

"So what's new with the consulting business?" He gives Chris's knee a squeeze. "You monkeys still considering hiring someone?"

"Yeah, Dad. We're d-definitely going to get someone else on board. We've recently gotten some new clients, and we're really busy setting up networks, doing administration—"

"That reminds me," I chime in. "I'm heading over near Rockefeller Center tomorrow to set up a cloud server for that new marketing company we met with last week. I'll probably be there most of the day. Were you planning on coming with me?"

"Actually, I'll—"

Chris's words are cut off by a loud crack of thunder. Riley bolts into the room and jumps onto my lap. He burrows his head under my arm, his small body racked with tears.

"Hey, it's okay, buddy." I pat his back with my hand. "It's just a little thunder," I whisper, but his tears keep coming.

"It's scawy...it makes me think a monstew is coming aftew me," he muffles through a stuffy nose, something hard digging into my ribs.

I stroke the top of his head, my thoughts straying to Ember and her fear of thunderstorms. I wonder if a storm blankets the city now. And if someone is holding her, too. Ignoring the thickness in my throat, I focus on Riley. "You know what, little guy. Someone special once told me that when you hear thunder, it's because the angels are bowling in the sky."

His head lifts, eyes brimming with that childlike curiosity. "Weally?" Red, puffy cheeks fill up with air and he looks down at my lap as if he's thinking hard. "You mean, they pway games up thewe?"

"They do." I smile, tweaking his nose.

He rubs a tear from his cheek with his pudgy hand. "So it's not some big monstew getting weal angwy?"

"Nope."

"Okay." He wriggles around and flings his arms around my neck. "Thanks Unca Vance." I wrap him up in a hug as he sniffles, wiping his nose on my shirt. In less than a minute, his arms drop and he hops over my legs to leap off the couch. The culprit of my side pain, his plastic Superman, held tight in his hand as he climbs the stairs with purpose. "Come on, Supewman. We're going bowwing."

"I guess my work is done here," I tease, prompting a chuckle from Chris and his dad.

As I watch Riley's small feet disappear, my mind veers off in its usual direction, that familiar ache rattling around in my stomach. Seeing Ember was unexpected, but now I can't get her out of my head—not that I ever could. If only I could go back. Get a do-over. But life has this odd way of moving forward. Even when you don't want it to.

Like a heavy rock sinking to the bottom of the river, my lungs are weighted down. My breaths don't come easy these days. But I need to man the fuck up and deal with a situation that I created. Ember has moved on. That much is apparent. I only hope he's taking better care of her heart than I did.

She doesn't need any more cracks.

chapter thirty-five
Ember

"RISE AND SHINE!" I pull the bright blue curtains open, letting the sunshine pour into Avery's room. She grumbles and hikes the covers over her head. "Up." I whip the blanket off and she squints at me. "I'm on my way to the gallery and you need to be at work in a little over an hour. So hurry up and we can head in together."

"I dislike immensely that you're such a morning person now," she grumbles again. "I should've picked a different roommate." Lifting herself to a sitting position, she hangs her legs over the side of the bed, her shoulders slumped. "You're in such a good mood today."

My stare goes to the window and the hustle and bustle of the city streets. "Actually, I feel better. I decided that I'm going to make more of an effort with Grant. He really is a good guy and I want it to work." A sigh bubbles up from my chest. "I need to start focusing on all the good. I guess I realized I've been focusing on the wrong things." I throw a towel at her and she catches it with a groan. "Anyway, we're going out to a club tonight. I need to make up for snapping at him the other night. He didn't deserve that. And, I think you should come with us." I reach for her hand to tug her off the bed. "Now hurry up and shower so we can get out of here."

"I'm wondering how many more words you can say before you take a breath," she muses, and I pierce her with a glare as she drags her feet to the bathroom. "Okay, Miss Happy. I'm going, I'm going."

From the other room, a sound alerts me of a text message. I stroll to the kitchen and retrieve my phone from the counter, sliding open the screen.

Mom: *Hi sweetie, just checking in. Wanted to let you know I got my airline tickets for next month. Can't wait to see you and Avery*

Me: *Hey, Mom. Can't wait, too! Avery is already mapping out your visit so get ready. Be sure to bring sneakers*

Mom: *You know I don't own any*

Me: *LOL. Yes you do. The ones you wore last time*

Mom: *Oh, right. Memory refreshed. Okay, sweetie. Have to run. Talk to you soon. Love you*

Me: *Love you too*

Not more than five minutes pass when Avery emerges with a towel wrapped around her body, blonde hair dripping onto the carpet. "Now I remember why I always shower first. I barely had any hot water."

"You snooze, you lose," I tease, my hands draped around a cup of steaming hot coffee. "I made you some, so you can use that to get warm."

"I don't like your attitude today." Avery groans, stomping off down the hall. She pauses just short of her room. "Can you make me a container of that lemon chicken from the other night? I'm going to take some for lunch."

"Sure."

By the time Avery finishes her morning beauty routine, the streets are crowded with people hurrying to various destinations. As they rush around us, I'm reminded of why we love living in Manhattan. Energy that you can feel in your fingertips. The waft of boiled hot dogs and the essence of warm, salted pretzels that greet us on almost every street corner. The fashion, and of course the wonder of the fashionably absurd. Every day is a surprise. Like reaching into a box of cereal for a prize. You never know what you're going to get.

"How do you like your new boss?" I ask as we weave our way through swarms of people talking on their cell phones and drinking their morning lattes.

"She's good. We've butted heads a few times because we both have strong personalities, but we talked and I think we've come to a new understanding."

"What's that?" We sidestep an attendant waiting to valet park. "Not to mess with you or you'll poison her coffee?" She laughs, reaching into her purse to yank out a pack of gum.

"Want some?" she offers, and I shake my head. "My breath could knock over about fifty rhinos right now, and as a Senior Executive Assistant that's unacceptable. I'm setting up a big meeting this morning with some new hotshot CEO." Folding the stick of gum, she pushes it into her mouth. "I must impress."

I toss her a sideways glance. "You always impress."

"Awww...." Avery grabs my elbow, sliding her arm through mine. "I knew there was a reason I kept you around." Her smile is warm. "You know, I'm really happy we moved here."

"Yeah, me too." And I mean it. I'm glad we didn't stay in Oregon. Too many glaring memories that I didn't necessarily want to forget, but didn't want to be faced with every day. The aroma of cinnamon drifts under our noses then and I look over at Avery as she licks her lips. "Do you have time?"

She checks her watch then glances up at me. "Not to sit down. But we could get one to go," she adds, and that's all it takes. Neither of us hesitates before pulling open the door to Bellaricci's Pastry Shop, the place we fortunately have to pass every day on our route to the subway. As always, it's packed with people. Avery stares at her watch again. "This might be pushing it." I can see the deliberation going on in her mind until she finally succumbs. "Shit. I can't. I'm going to be late.

Grab me one for home, will you?"

"Sure, Ave."

"Thanks. I'll see you tonight." She blows me a kiss then disappears out the door, the crowd quickly swallowing her up.

Twenty minutes and three cinnamon rolls later, I'm out the door and heading to the subway. I tell myself I can refrain from eating one now, but the longer the smell floats under my nostrils, the more difficult it is to resist. Giving in, I dig my hand inside the bag and remove a sticky chunk, sliding it into my mouth. A blast of sweetness coats my tongue and while it is definitely delicious, nothing compares to Anna's back home.

Anna's. My mind floods with memories of Vance strutting behind the register that day at the shop. Long hair hanging over determined blue eyes that wouldn't take no for an answer. That cocky swagger filling a space in a way that only he could. He was impossible not to notice. A heavy sigh pushes it all away. None of that matters because I'm happy with Grant.

One more big bite of pastry lands in my mouth as I casually make my way toward the subway. This is the great thing about working part-time at the gallery and going back to school. I never feel like I have to be in a hurry. Especially on days like this, when the sun is beaming over Manhattan and the air is crisp.

That all changes as I travel down the stairs leading to the subway platform. The foul odor of urine surrounds me and I wince, scrunching my face up as if that can somehow fight the disgusting smell. Taking the train on a regular basis, you would think I'd be used to it by now. But I'm not.

Fear of my sweets getting infected by the rancid climate, I seal up the bag and shove it into my purse. But all that is counteracted as I glance to my left. A young guy wearing a baseball hat and ripped jeans leans against the wall strumming a guitar. In front of him sits a beat up case, odd pieces of change scattered along the inner lining. I stare for a minute too long before crossing over to him and dropping a few dollars onto the red fabric.

When the train arrives, I follow the pack into the car and scan the long aisle for a seat. Being so crowded, I have to wedge myself between two people who don't look happy. But I've learned on the subway that it's every man for himself. Or in my case, woman.

A muffled announcement about a delay elicits subsequent groans all around me. I ignore them and pull out my notebook and a pen to review my checklist for the gallery. Most of what I do there is administrative in nature; checking on orders, paying bills, communicating with clients and buyers. But it doesn't matter to me. What matters is that I'm surrounded by what I love and one step closer to my dream.

My cell rings and I fish it out of my purse, smiling wide as Troy's number appears on the screen. I unlock it, pressing the phone to my ear. "Hey, you!"

"Hey, love. How are you?" His voice is broken up by sounds of screaming in the background.

I tuck my notebook and pen back into my purse. "I'm good. What are you doing up this early? You at the gym?"

"No, I'm over at the Griswold's. I'm helping Mr. Griswold build a shed in the back. His kids don't start school for a few hours so they're *trying* to help."

"You should really call my dad," I suggest, and more screaming ensues. "I know he's been missing us and you guys could hang out and build, I don't know...things."

Troy laughs and the sound makes my chest ache. I really miss having him close by. "Okay, maybe I will. So he and I can," he chuckles, "build *all* the things." The noise of a drill temporarily halts our conversation. "So nothing new since we talked the other day? How are things at the gallery?"

"They're fantastic. I'm actually on my way there now."

"Awesome." A pause and then, "And...how's Grant?"

"Good, good. He's good."

"Now that I know everything is *good*. I can breathe easy."

"Ha, ha. Listen, I have to run," I tell him as the train begins to move. "The train's going and I'll lose you in a sec, but I'll call you later. Love you."

"Love you too, Ems."

A bunch of people pile in front of me, anxious to reach doors that are not ready to open. Nonetheless, I push myself up from the bench and merge into line. Someone knocks into me and my cell phone drops to the ground. Bending down and hoping not to get trampled, I scramble to pick it up then sigh in relief once the group in front of me exits at the next stop. As the train starts running again, I curl my fingers around the metal pole and find myself wishing for a car. Although the idea of driving in Manhattan terrifies me. I'm certain I'd get crushed between two taxis. Unless Avery was driving. That last thought makes me smile.

The car has cleared out a bit, and I'm standing there humming to myself when I notice someone in the back. His head is down, face buried in a book. Long fringe hangs over his eyes. My mind automatically goes where it shouldn't and I turn away, rolling my own eyes. *Grant, remember*, I say to my brain. I laugh a little too loud at how ridiculous I am, glancing around the car. The guy with the hair looks up then and my breath catches in my chest. Spots form in front of my eyes. I blink. Then blink again. *It can't be*. My head is telling me.

But I know what I see.

I could never mistake that face or the way my heart is beating like crazy—wild, out of control, dangerous almost. My fingers clutch tighter to the pole for fear that I'm going to collapse. Our eyes lock and my lips part, mouthing his name. "*Vance.*"

Vance stands up, looking as stunned as I feel. His blue eyes are wide, feet molded to the floor. The subway doors open then and I don't know what I'm supposed to do. The decision is made for me though, because a man bumps into me hard and I practically fall out of the car. By some miracle, I manage to regain my footing and reach the platform. Suddenly I can't get enough air and I'm struggling to breathe. My legs won't move, and somehow I'm right back on our street, that very night I had to say goodbye to him—all those feelings that had nowhere to go—and now they are all pouring out when I had them boxed up so nicely. Or at least I thought I did. Time hasn't made a damn bit of difference. How can three years seem like a day? Because that pull is still there, as if some invisible string draws me toward him. And when I turn to find the train running again, his hand is pressed to the window while my own hand is pressed to my heart. His gaze pleading with mine, a piece of white paper etched with large numbers pushed against the glass.

I watch the train pull away, the numbers and his face getting further and further until I can no longer see them. My legs buckle and I wrench my hand out to latch onto a filthy column, thankful for it because it's the only thing holding me up right now. I don't understand what's happening. Yet my only clear thought is making sure I don't forget that number. Unzipping my purse, I scrounge for a pen and with trembling fingers scrawl out the numbers on a scrap of paper. Tears are falling faster than I can write. But the urgency to get the numbers down tells me that my internal talk this morning and everything I said to Avery was not the truth. Because the truth is—I've never gotten over Vance Davenport.

How do you ever get over your heart?

THE REST OF the day went by in a blur of numbers and silvery blue eyes I've tried hard to forget. The look I saw in them today, raw and vulnerable. A myriad of emotions passing over his face that I couldn't understand—that I had no right to, really. And still, they yanked on my heart.

So many questions flitting through my mind as I sit on the bed, staring blankly at those ten numbers. What is he doing in New York? How long has he been here? Why didn't he try to get in touch with me?

I fall back on the mattress, grabbing a pillow and tucking it under my chin. It's been three years. Three years of working hard to erase Vance from my heart. But the only thing seeing him did was make it start beating again.

"Hey, Em, I'm home," Avery calls out, and I groan an unintelligible response that she can't hear. I listen to her keys clank when they drop on the table, heels clicking until she's at my door. She analyzes my position on the bed with a frown. "What's going on? Aren't you supposed to be getting ready for tonight? I just bought the most amazing dress at Bloomingdale's." The bag crinkles in her hand. "Wanna see?" I grunt and push myself up to a slouched sitting position, continuing to squeeze the pillow. I'm not sure what will happen if I let it go.

"Ember." She snaps her fingers in front of my face. It's only then that I become aware she's standing beside the bed.

My gaze remains on the wall. "I'm not going tonight. I told Grant I wasn't feeling well."

"Actually, you don't look that good." She leans over and presses her palm to my forehead. "You don't feel hot but you're pale as a ghost."

What a perfect choice of words. Because I saw a ghost. The one that haunts my dreams, strokes my cheek and threads his fingers through my hair, whose touch I can still feel on my skin.

"I saw one," I admit, still dazed but finally able to look at her. "I saw Vance."

Her brows lift high on her forehead. "What?"

"I said—"

"I heard what you said, Em." She drops down on the bed. "But how, where?"

"He was on the subway. I saw him as I was getting off. We didn't talk because I almost fell and...the shock of it all...and then the train left." I blow out a weighted breath. "And now I'm a mess. I've tried so hard to forget him and move on. But the minute I saw him, it was like nothing had changed. All those intense feelings came back." Her glance roams to the paper on the bed. "He wrote his phone number down and held it against the glass."

"Wow." A soft smile forms on her lips. "Thank goodness for little things like a photographic memory."

"Yeah." I bring a hand to my head to stave off the impending ache. "Do you know what I thought about all day?" I don't wait for an answer because I need to keep talking. I need to get this out. "That if I hadn't turned around right then, I never would've seen him."

Avery closes her hand around mine and gives me a gentle squeeze. "And how did that make you feel?"

My mouth tugs down as my chin begins to wobble. "Awful. Because as startled as I was to see him, I realized how much I needed it...to know that he's okay."

"You need to call him. You know that, right?" She lets go of my hand and reaches behind her to retrieve the wrinkled square of paper. "You two have so much left unsaid."

Tears that have hovered all day like a dark cloud break free. "I'm afraid to see him. I...I'm good now, happy...and I can't go back."

"Oh, Ember." She slides a tissue from the box on the nightstand and hands it to me. "One of the many things I love about you is that you're always honest. Don't start lying to yourself now. It doesn't become you. Besides," she adds, patting my hand, "you don't have to go back. But maybe you can get some closure so you can move forward." She leaps off the bed, the Bloomingdale's bag swinging from her fingers. "Now. I'm going to put on this dress, find a movie, two spoons, and a half-gallon of ice cream," she grins, "because I refuse to let a good dress go to waste."

She's almost to the door when I call her back. "Hey, Ave," I say faintly, and she glances over her shoulder. "Thank you." She nods on a soft smile then saunters off.

My mind wanders to Vance again. I don't know that much about love, except what he taught me. That it's a quiet voice, a short distance between two hearts. Or maybe it's a flame that flickers then dies out.

chapter thirty-six
Vance

MY EYES DART between my phone and the subway car, the back and forth motion making me dizzy. I've been riding this fucking train every day for a week, hoping to see Ember again. I stare at my cell, wanting to throw the damn thing out the window because it's not doing what I need it to.

"Vance. That thing is going to explode if you stare at it any longer." Chris shoves a piece of doughnut in his mouth, grinning. "Seriously, you n-need to chill out. You're driving yourself insane over this girl."

I frown at the package of Twinkies Chris bought me. Even *they* don't hold any appeal. "She's worth a bit of insanity." My gaze travels to the window. "It's been a whole week and, I don't know. I guess...I thought she would at least call me. I just want a chance to explain. To apologize...to—"

"Grovel," he chimes in, and somehow I manage a laugh.

"Yeah, that too."

He brushes a sugar-coated hand on his pants. "Listen. You push people away. I know because you did it to m-me. But it wasn't done out of malice. You're not a selfish person Vance, and you didn't do it to hurt me. You were just scared and angry. And in this case you had just witnessed...." Chris's voice tapers off. "She'll understand that." His skinny hand latches onto my shoulder and he pulls me in close. "I forgave you, didn't I?"

I lean away from him, gripping the ends of my hair. "I didn't break your fucking heart."

He slaps a hand over his chest. "Oh yeah, who s-says?"

I laugh at his expression and his lame attempt at being serious. "Shut the fuck up." He snickers, his grin returning as he finishes off the doughnut. Powdered sugar settles on the fabric of his dress pants. "You shouldn't eat those before we see a client," I scold, and he glares at the package on my lap.

"Says the Twinkie King. Hey," he nudges me with his elbow, "remember that t-time in fifth grade when your mom found three packs of Twinkie's hidden under your mattress?"

I snort, my mother's wide blue eyes and pursed lips still in the forefront of my mind. "Yes, I remember. The smashed Twinkies."

"She was so mad," he recalls, and a sigh gets trapped in my throat. "Especially because one of the packages was open, and the cream filling leaked onto the c-carpet." We both crack up, our conversation interrupted by the sign indicating our stop as we hurry to exit the train.

The ring of my cell phone cuts off all laughter. Startled and anxious, I nearly drop the darn thing on the ground once we reach street level. Ignoring Chris's chuckles of amusement, I unlock the screen and hold the phone tightly to my ear. "Hello?"

"Greetings from California!" Julian sings, and disappointment festers in my stomach.

"Oh. Hey, Julian."

"Geez, don't sound so excited to hear from your brother." He cackles, the sound of waves crashing against the shore in the distance.

"Let me guess. You're at the beach?"

"Have I shared with you how much I miss your sarcasm, little brother? And yes, as a matter of fact, I am. I've finally mastered the whole surfing thing." He sighs into the phone. "I know I keep saying this. But you should've chosen Cali, Vance. It's really awesome out here."

"Charming your way through Southern California, are you?" Chris smirks next to me and I add, "Speaking of charming, we're on the streets of New York as we speak."

"Oh yeah? And how are things in The Big Apple?"

My chest constricts but I shrug it off. "Good. Busy." Chris mutters Ember's name in the background and I put a finger to my lips to shush him. "Technology never sleeps."

"So...anything else new?"

"Julian," I reply, unable to hide my frustration. "I just spoke to you last week. Not much has changed." Chris tilts his head, tossing me a look I disregard. "I've been too busy, anyway."

"Okay. Cut the crap, Vance. What's going on? And don't say nothing because I can hear it in your voice." I huff out a loud breath. "See, I knew it. Are you feeling okay? What is it?"

"I...ran into Ember on the subway," I confess, and he's quiet for so long I almost think he hung up. "Julian?"

"Please tell me that you got down on your hands and knees and begged for her forgiveness. Because you are insane if you let her go again."

I picture the dude in the bar and my throat tenses. I clear it and go on. "She's with someone now, Julian."

"Is she married?" he probes, and I should have kept my mouth closed. I already know his opinion on my actions three years ago and the fact that I didn't want contact with anyone, including him at the time.

"I don't know."

"Well, I suggest—"

"Julian," I interrupt, because I can't talk about this right now, given that she hasn't called me. "Thanks, okay. I appreciate what you're trying to do. It's just that...the ball is kind of in her court now so I have to wait it out."

"In other words, get off your back," he jibes.

"Basically."

"All right, bro, I'm off to catch some prime morning waves. But call me later in the week, otherwise I'm going to hunt you down." Someone shouts his name and his voice becomes muffled. "I'll talk to you soon."

"Later." I hit end and come face-to-face with Chris's smug grin.

"You've got it barreling at you from all s-sides. Don't you feel loved?" I frown at his choice of words and he grasps my shoulder, shooting me an empathetic smile. "Okay, wrong thing to say. But she'll call. Just give her some time."

Time is all I have.

"ALL RIGHT, LARRY. The Cisco firewall is up and running and all the Windows workstations are networked to the new server we installed. Chris handled setting up the network for the space on the first floor so you should be all set."

Larry extends his hand to shake mine. "You two are like the dream team. Which reminds me." He removes the wallet from his pocket and hands me a business card. "One of my old colleagues has a start-up and needs some advice with respect to network security and clouds," he scratches his head, "I think, anyway. I don't know all the details, but I did tell him that you'd be a fantastic resource."

"Great. Thanks, Larry. I appreciate it."

"Don't mention it." He slides his wallet back into the pocket of his suit jacket then checks his watch. "I'd like to buy you two some dinner." He glances at the time again and shakes his head. "But considering I've missed dinner every day this week, the wife isn't going to be too happy if I add another night to my list of travesties. I might be endangering my credit card limit."

"No worries." I laugh. "I get it."

My phone rings and I excuse myself from our conversation to scoop it up from a nearby cubicle. "Hello?" Silence greets me at the other end of the line, but I vaguely hear soft breathing. My heart skyrockets in my chest and I say a silent prayer. "Ember?"

A heavy sigh and then, "Yeah. Hi."

"Hey...I...I'm glad you called." I take a seat on the swivel chair in front of the desk. "I wasn't sure if you would," I admit, blowing out a nervous breath. Fuck, this is hard. "I need to see you." She gives me nothing but more silence and my jaw clenches. I roll a pencil back and forth over the desk, waiting for her to respond.

"I don't know...if that's a good idea." The uncertainty in her voice is stifling and I know I'm the cause of it, which only makes me more determined to remedy the situation. "Can't we just talk now?"

"No. I want to do this in person. Please, Ember. Can we meet up?" My tone reeks of desperation, but I don't really give a shit because that's exactly how I feel. "I promise it won't take long."

A lingering pause and then a sigh. "Okay. Where do you want to meet?"

Relief and anticipation fill my lungs and I smile. "How about The Comfort Diner at East Forty-Fifth Street. Do you know it?"

"Yeah, I think so."

"Okay." I glance at the time on the desktop. "How about we meet at six? Would that work?"

She squeaks her response. "Tonight?"

I want to tell her I think I've waited long enough. But instead I reply with a firm "Yes."

"Okay, I guess so."

"Great. I'll see you then." She hangs up without saying goodbye, but I try not to read into it too much. It's been a whole lot of time without any explanation—and I have a *lot* of fucking explaining to do.

Chris shows up carrying a stack of computer equipment. "Hey, I'm all set d-downstairs. You want to head out and grab a bite to eat?" He stops when he sees my expression. I must be grinning like a fucking idiot. "She called."

"She did."

He throws the Cat5 cables, an old Buffalo file server, and a few SSD drives into a box. "So should I gather I'm going it alone for d-dinner?"

"You don't have to. You could ask someone out." I slide my laptop in the bag and pick up the last of my tools off the desk.

Chris leans against the wall of the cubicle, arms crossed over his chest. "I could, but I won't."

Setting my bag on the carpet, I turn to face him. "Why the fuck not?"

He answers me with a shrug, staring at the floor. "B-because, you know I get nervous, and then I end up stuttering more. What girl wants that?"

His words incite a riot in my chest. "The right girl. That's who. You just have to find her. Now come on," I smack his arm, "let's get the hell out of here. Because I'm going to find mine."

chapter thirty-seven

Ember

TAXIS SKID TO a screeching halt as shoes click against the pavement. The sharp whistle of trucks making deliveries, the shouts of street vendors trying to sell everything from portraits to purses. All of it fades into the background, overpowered by the thoughts swamping my brain. The concentration it takes to will my feet to keep moving—to remind myself to breathe.

Street signs indicate only two more blocks separate me from my past. My heart picks up speed and I tell it to slow down, but it's a stupid heart and it doesn't listen.

Troy's words from our conversation last night stick in my head—*'give him a chance, love.'* His tone that always puts me at ease and then, *'you know you want to.'* I wish the people close to me didn't know me so well.

My thoughts find their way to Grant and his kindness, his quirky sense of humor—but he's not Vance. While I know I shouldn't be comparing, it seems that Vance has become my benchmark. And a ghost should never be a benchmark.

Except—he's no longer a ghost.

My brain doesn't stop until I'm standing outside the diner. I wring out my hands and exhale a few big breaths to try to calm my runaway nerves, but they won't be deterred. A woman exits the diner and holds the door open when she seems me there, but I shake my head and back up against the wall of the building. I need another minute...or fifty.

This is absurd, I tell myself. Just because my heart wants something, doesn't mean I have to listen to it. Fool me once, fool me twice, and all that. I'm going to hear what Vance has to say and then I'm going to leave and go on with my life. Easy.

With that last thought, I straighten my dress and smooth down my hair then head inside. *I can do this. I can do this.* I keep repeating this mantra in my head as I walk through the door. The jingle announces my presence and when Vance spots me, and our eyes meet across the room, all my confidence goes right out the window. Even the slightest curl of his lips from this distance make the flutters start up in my belly. My nerve endings practically melt as his gaze skates over me on the way to the table. Nonetheless, I keep my expression blank as I slip into the booth.

"Hi."

"Ember...." He breathes my name and relief seems to spill from his lips, almost as if he didn't expect me to show up.

I gaze at his long hair, the strong line of his jaw, those gray-blue eyes. God, I've missed staring into them. But then a mask slides down over my face—my only protection against my feelings and the desire to touch him, to make sure he's real. He looks exactly like I remember save for the additional lines around his eyes. I wonder how hard his life has been for the past few years.

"I'm really happy you called." His fingers are busy flicking the edge of the menu. "I wasn't positive you would."

This is a different Vance. An unsure Vance, and I'm not used to seeing him like this. It instantly chisels away a piece of the wall I've built around my heart, the one marked with several cracks.

I fold and unfold my hands in front of me on the table. "I wasn't sure I should, to be honest."

His cheeks lift on a half-smile. "But you did."

"Yes."

"Why?" He leans his entire body forward and rests his weight on his elbows, fingers steepled beneath his chin. He suddenly feels too close and I plaster my back against the booth.

"I guess I thought about something Avery said." I spit the sentence out quickly. "About needing closure."

"Closure," he repeats, as if testing it out on his lips. The partial smile gone.

"Yes. A lot has happened and I'd...like to understand so I can move on." The words taste sour but I feel the need to say them, if only to protect my heart.

"I better get to it then," he snaps. "So you can *move on*." The irritation in his tone and the formality of our interaction gives me a stomach ache. This isn't Vance and Ember. These are two strangers.

"Vance, I—"

"No. Let me just say what I need to say. Look...." He brings a hand to his head and closes his eyes. "*Fuck*," he mutters, and when he opens them they are brimming with apology. "I'm sorry. I fucked up. I panicked, got scared. You name it, I felt it. I didn't want to leave, Ember. I swear to you." He pins me with a sincere gaze, and I believe him. "But when I caught my father and," he winces, looking toward the window, "your mother, everything felt, I don't know. For lack of a better word, fucked."

"She didn't know," I whisper, fighting back tears as his gaze returns to mine. "She said she met your dad at her grief counseling group. I know it's crazy and it makes no sense, but she didn't know we were together that way. She'd been working so much and I hadn't talked to her about it. But I blamed her anyway...at first. I was so mad and hurt. I couldn't even stand the sight of her, and didn't speak to her for weeks. But, then I realized she wasn't the one I was angry with. It was you. She didn't *make* you leave. You did that all on your own." He nods in understanding, and I see now that his edge has lessened in some way—and my heart breaks for him and all he's had to endure. Still, it doesn't take away the hurt. "I was devastated when you left. I didn't understand it. I thought what we had," I swallow, willing myself not to cry, "mattered."

"It did—"

I raise my hand to stop him, staring at a spot on the table. "Let me finish." Inhaling an uneven breath, I finally let it all out. "After I had time for things to sink in, I actually understood why you reacted the way you did, why you left even." I blink the wetness from my lashes before my eyes lock with his. "But I thought you'd come back. I thought what we were beginning together was worth more to you." His hand moves toward mine and I pull away. "Don't." Removing a tissue from my purse, I dab it against my cheeks as we sit in silence. I try to gather my thoughts. But they are everywhere and nowhere all at once.

I tip my head up and breathe deep, making another attempt. "My mother was devastated. Because she loves me. And she would never intentionally hurt me like that, or my dad for that matter given how close they still are." I grab another tissue. "She broke things off with your dad a few days later. She told me she didn't love him, but she did enjoy spending time with him and she was lonely. And you know what? I can't fault her for that. I also wasn't, nor have I ever been in a position to judge anyone, including your dad."

Vance's gaze is unfocused as he scrubs a hand over his face, cheeks growing pale. "I won't make excuses, you know. It was all...too much for me. I thought they were together. Seeing my dad with someone other than my mom, when she was sitting in that...that place, day after day, I thought being forgotten by him. It was...I can't describe it."

"I'm so sorry about your Mom, Vance."

His eyes fly to mine. "You were there," he says so softly I almost don't hear him. "Why didn't you let me know?"

"Because I wanted to be there for you. But...I wasn't going to push myself on you, especially then." I try to hold it together but my chin quivers. "And you didn't want me anyway."

"That's not true." The words rush out, his hand inching closer. "I always wanted you." His fingertips brush mine and that barely there touch sends shockwaves up my arm. Even though every instinct tells me to pull away again, I don't. I need the connection as much as he does right now. "It felt like everything was stacked against us...seeing our parents together, my potential illness. It felt like a losing battle."

"But you're okay, right?"

"For now," he supplies, a wariness in his words. "The initial tests came back negative, but every so often I still have to go in for a CAT scan and an MRI. I had a tremble in my hands, off and on, and periodic headaches, but they've gone away and the doctors couldn't find a reason for it."

Relief sputters from my mouth and I give him a soft smile. "I'm so glad." Then I speak the truth. Because in the end, that's all we have. "I worried about you. A lot."

He smiles then. That crooked, one-sided lift of his lips that was somehow always clear in my mind. "I thought about you all the time," he admits, and I press my thumb along the underside of my wrist, hoping to slow down the heavy beat of my pulse.

The waitress finally comes over to take our drink orders, a much needed break to our weighted conversation. When she leaves, I ask one of the many questions circling my brain. "So what brought you to New York, anyway?"

His eyes swivel back to mine. "I...." He stops, then starts again. "My friend Chris, I told you about him briefly. We ended up working things out and moved here together. We got a place in the East Village."

"How long have you lived here?"

"We moved here shortly after my mom passed away." The waitress returns with our drinks and sets them on the table. Vance keeps talking and I shove a hand under my thigh, too fidgety now to sit still. I can't believe we've been in the same city for two years. "Before that, I stayed with Chris because I was short on money. But with Chris's dad's help, we took the plunge and started a technology consulting business."

"I guess all that tinkering paid off, huh?"

His mouth curves into a genuine smile and my chest inflates. "Yeah. It's actually going really well. It was slow at first and we had our doubts, but we've built up repeat clients and are getting new ones via word of mouth. What about you?"

"Me?" I roll a finger over the condensation building on the glass. "I'm two classes short of getting my Master of Arts Degree at Parson's, and I also work as the Office Manager for The Dubois Gallery in Midtown. Mostly doing administrative stuff, but I love it."

"So you went for it, after all. That's awesome." Genuine excitement for me fills his eyes. A sign that maybe he still cares. My heart does a tiny skip but my brain shuts it down.

"I'm getting there." A nonchalant smile covers my exhilaration as his gaze wanders over me.

"You wear dresses now." The way he says it sounds off. I can't figure out if I hear disapproval or something else.

I shrug and take a swig of water before placing it down. "Sometimes."

He scratches the light coating of stubble on his chin, and I try not to recall the way it felt scraping against my bare skin. "I thought you didn't like them."

"I don't, really," I admit, shrugging again. "But I need to look nice for work. Plus, I just wanted to be different."

"Why?" He delves, his focused gaze holding me hostage and making me squirm in the seat. "There was nothing wrong with the way you were before. You were beautiful then, and you're even more beautiful now. The dress can't change that," he adds, and my head buzzes in time with my heart. "I actually preferred the t-shirts."

My cheeks tingle with warmth and I clear my throat. "I need...to get going now." I slide out of the booth to stand up, but his hand finds my wrist. That simple brush of fingers against skin is too much. This time I back away, pulling out of his grasp. Air—I need air. "I really have to go, Vance," I emphasize with urgency and head toward any door that will lead me out of here.

"Ember, wait," he shouts, drawing the attention of other customers in the diner. I stop with my back to him, breath bursting in and out of my chest. I don't know if I can do this. My gaze drifts to the ceiling for strength before turning around. What I don't expect is for Vance to be standing there, and I nearly bump into his chest. He looks down at me, his blue eyes agonizing and true.

"Listen. I know I fucked up...and I know I can't turn back time. But...maybe we can be friends. I'm not going to lie. I want you in my life and I'll do anything to make it right." He chews on the corner of his lip then lets it go. "I also have a confession to make. I saw you at Blue

Monday a while back. Chris and I, and a couple of guys play there twice a week. You were with someone." He glances down at my ring finger then back up to me. "Are you in love with him?"

"I think it's my question," I counter. "That was months ago." I shake my head, disbelieving. "How come you didn't approach me?"

His shoulders lift and fall on a heavy sigh. "For the same reason you didn't come up to me a few years ago. I didn't think you'd want to see me. Not to mention, you weren't alone." His eyes zero in on mine again. "So are you...in love with him?"

Not enough space exists for me to take a breath without inhaling every inch of him. I feel like a balloon about to pop. "Vance...I need to go."

"Okay." He lowers his head, hands sliding into the pockets of his jeans. "Can I...call you sometime? Maybe we can hang out or something?"

Exhaustion wears me down and I let out a halfhearted response. "Maybe."

"Maybe, I'll take." More words start to form on his lips but then he seems to change his mind. His eyes dart to a spot past my shoulder. "Can I walk you somewhere?"

I hike my purse higher on my arm. "No, I'm good. Thanks." Awkwardness eats up the moment and I fill it. I don't know what else to do. "I'll see ya, okay."

"Yeah," he whispers now. "See ya."

Only a few steps away, I pause. Then I turn around and walk back to where Vance is still standing. Unable to look at him, I stare at his chest. "It really hurt me when you left without a word. I thought...well, it doesn't matter what I thought, because it's in the past." My gaze climbs to his face. "But...I can't let you hurt me again."

"Ember, I'm—"

"You don't have to say anything," I interject, and he nods in defeat. "I just needed you to know that."

I race out of the diner, not wanting to break down in front of Vance. But it starts anyway. A messy onslaught of tears forging a path down my skin. I can't seem to control it. Nor can I control the way my heart beats out of my chest being anywhere near him. Unfortunately, I also can't control the fear coiling tight around me until I'm dizzy with it, making my feelings take a back seat.

Still, I don't know what to do with all this emotion. I'm drowning in thoughts of Vance and me. Of what we had. Of what we could have. But the apprehension steps in and crushes that to little bits. And then there's Grant. None of this is fair to him. I've tried so hard, and the reality is that Vance stepping back into my life, regardless of what happens between us, makes me realize that Grant is not my future.

The only thing my future holds now, is a spoon and a half-gallon of ice cream—and I'm not sure even that can cure what ails me.

chapter thirty-eight
Vance

I HATE THE number four. Four fucking days. Four fucking long nights filled with shitty sleep. An endless barrage of the pain on Ember's face, the hurt in her eyes. It was like a living, breathing thing filling the space between us.

The damage I inflicted has become a physical ache. It starts in the pit of my stomach and travels up through my chest. And yet, something else overpowers that. The way my heart grew too big for my insides when I laid eyes on her. How seeing her smile calmed me. It made me feel like myself again. I don't know how she does that—how everything can be so dark and then she comes along and opens up the sky—as if it's effortless.

She is the most beautiful girl in this whole fucking city. Shit, in this world. And as much as she tried to keep me at bay, she also gave me a flicker of hope. It was there in the way she responded to my touch. It was in her gaze, the way her eyes roamed my face. I know, because I felt it too.

"Rise and shine, c-cupcake." Chris flings open the door, grinning a little too happy for my liking.

"I'd have to have slept to rise." I groan. "What's going on?"

"What's going on," he chuckles, "is that you promised a certain someone that you would take him to a toy store, and my mom just c-called and said he's ready to collect."

I squint against the bright sunshine, rubbing the lack of sleep from my eyes. "Today?"

"Yep. Today's your lucky day. He doesn't have preschool and you have the day off. What could be better than Riley and Toys 'R' Us? Besides, you have to do it s-soon anyway, because that Times Square store is closing."

I push myself up to a sitting position and glance around the room. "Actually," I grin, "that sounds like a fantastic idea. Wanna come with?"

He takes one look at my face and narrows his dark brown eyes. "What are you planning?"

"Don't worry about it."

"Yeah," he huffs. "And why does that worry me?"

I toss him a wink. "Hand me my cell, will ya?" Chris throws my phone on the bed and walks out of the room, his back shaking with silent laughter.

With a quick swipe across the screen, I unlock it and search for Ember in my contacts before typing her a message.

Me: *Hi*

Ember: *Hi back*

I didn't expect such a fast reply, but fuck if it doesn't make me smile big.

Me: *Happy Sometime Day*

Ember: *Huh?*

Me: *Do you want to hang out with me and a friend today?*

Ember: *Sounds mysterious*

I crack another smile.

Me: *I thought women liked mystery*

Ember: *LOL. Don't lump me into a category*

Me: *You defy all categories*

No response. Maybe that was pushing it. My finger hovers over the keypad until a message pings.

Ember: *I have to work at the gallery today*

Me: *Oh*

Since I didn't plan for that, I take a second to plot my next move when she responds.

Ember: *But I'm done at 1:00*

Me: *Okay. Can you meet me somewhere?*

Ember: *Somewhere as in??*

Me: *Times Square Toys R Us*

Ember: *Um...Okay*

Me: *See you there then?*

Ember: *I can get there by 2:30. Want to run home and change*

Me: *Okay. I'll meet you right out front*

Ember: *K*

Unable to tone down my grin, I drop the phone on the bed and lean back, lacing my hands behind my head. "Yo, Chris."

He shows up in my doorway, wet from a shower. "Yeah?"

"You sure you don't want to come with us? Ember is gonna be there and you can officially meet her."

"I knew you had s-something up your sleeve. And no," he rubs the towel back and forth over his hair, "I don't want to be in the middle of Toys 'R' Us with a million screaming kids. But good luck with that."

"Good point. Okay." He disappears down the hall and I heave my tired legs over the edge of the bed. "Oh, hey Chris," I yell out. "Does Guiseppe work on Fridays?"

"I think so. Why?" He calls from his room.

"I want to run down there and get my hair trimmed." In two seconds he's back, curiosity in his gaze. "Hey, my eyes are my best feature and I need to pull out the big guns."

"You w-want her back." He smirks. A statement not a question, but I answer it anyway.

"Fuck, yes."

He makes a noise in his throat as if he knew it all along. "You still love her."

My heart trips over itself thinking about how much. "Never stopped."

CHRIS WAS RIGHT. Times Square is fucking insane this time of day—music blaring, neon signs flickering, and little kids...everywhere. As we stand in front of Toys 'R' Us waiting for Ember, I watch wide-eyed Riley seek out his next target. I might as well have the word 'sucker' painted across my forehead as I pay for the fifth picture of him with someone else dressed up like a Disney character. This time Woody from Toy Story.

"This is the last one, little guy," I tell him, and he nods, eyes gleaming with excitement as he stares at all the costumes. I miss that element of being a kid, where the lines of fantasy and reality are blurred.

"I can't wait to show Chwissy evewyone I met today." His face is alight with wonder and awe, making me happy I could do this for him. I'm also somewhat distracted, casually glancing at my watch every few minutes. Riley peers inside the store, getting restless as he swings my arm and spins on the sidewalk.

"She's gonna be here soon," I mumble, more for my own benefit than his. When he knocks on the glass, I know a distraction is in order. "Okay, let's do this buddy. Make a fist." He doesn't hesitate because this is our thing. He curls his tiny fingers into a ball and I do the same, then he presses his fist against mine. "Wonder twin powers activate, form of...operation get Ember back," I whisper, and his cheeks puff up as he makes a fish face.

"Opewation what?" he asks, at the same moment I glance up to see Ember walking toward us. Already, the corner of my lips kick up into a smile and I have to tell my heart to slow the fuck down. She looks amazing, wearing faded blue jeans that hug her hips and a tight black t-shirt that says *Art is my Life*. Familiar worn red Chucks sit on her feet, her hair gathered in a ponytail highlighting the sweet curve of her neck. Even Riley seems to notice when she finally reaches us, squinting up at me like a one-eyed pirate, his toothy smile glowing. He cups a hand sideways over his mouth. "She's pwetty."

My eyes do a slow climb and fasten to hers, the sun making them appear greener in the light. "She is." We stare at each other and I fall into this peaceful void, forgetting we're in the middle of Times Square. She finally breaks our connection, something off in her smile.

"Hi." Her glance flickers between me and Riley, as if trying to figure out a puzzle. "You have a...son?" Shock renders me quiet, prompting her mouth to open again. "He's...beautiful."

"Ember," I start, wanting to set her straight immediately. "This is—"

Riley doesn't let me finish. He points a finger up at me, his smile crooked. Giggling, he tugs on my jeans. "This is Unca Vance."

"This is Chris's little brother, Riley. Riley, this is my friend, Ember."

Ember exhales a muffled breath that seems a lot like relief to me. "Hi there, Riley." She squats down until she's eye level with him and extends her hand. He takes it with a bashful smile then lets it go. "It's very nice to meet you." She squeezes his nose and makes a honking sound, giving Riley another fit of the giggles. It is by far the cutest thing I've ever seen. She stands back up, her lips twisted into a grin. "So toys, huh?"

"Yup." I nod, motioning toward the store. "Thought it might be fun."

"You just secretly wanted to ride the Ferris wheel." Her tone is light, and my chest loosens at her playfulness. Given the heaviness between us the other day, I wasn't sure what to expect.

I smile back, relieved. Playful I can handle. "You might be right."

Riley yanks on my hand. I've obviously made him wait long enough to enter utopia. He leads the way, pulling me along as the three of us weave through the craziness. Inside, my eyes bulge while my mouth hangs open. I glance down at Riley and his expression matches mine.

"Holy shit!" Ember hits my arm and glares at me. "I mean shoot. Shoot, Riles. Look at all these toys."

"First time here?" she asks, and I can barely drag my eyes away from the giant minions. I'm as bad as Riley.

"Uh, yeah. I would've loved to have had a store like this as a kid. We didn't have anything like it where I grew up."

"We didn't either." She flashes me a grin, a twinkle in her eyes. "Avery and I went to FAO Schwartz before they closed. We danced on the big piano. It was a lot of fun."

"*You* danced on the piano?"

"Don't look so surprised." She rocks on her feet. "Okay. Actually, it was more like Avery coerced me. But once I was on there, I was so glad she did."

"I want to wide the Fewwis wheeeeeeel!" Riley's squeaky voice cuts into our conversation. His head bobs from left to right, unable to take in everything all at once. Ember laughs, staring at the bright circle of color in front of us. "Can I get a toy, too, Unca?" He gazes up at me with those big blue eyes and I couldn't refuse him anything. "Pwease?"

"Of course, buddy." I pat him on the head. "I already told you I'd buy you a superhero. And you can get something else, too. Anything you want."

Ember clears her throat, blatantly trying to get my attention. I turn and she leans close, her hair brushing my cheek. She smells just like I remember. "You might want to narrow that down," she whispers. "There are some crazy expensive things here."

Her proximity and her scent makes me lose my train of thought. "Huh? Oh, right. Thanks." I smile, then shift toward Riley. "Let's see what you want first. Okay, buddy? Then I'll see if we can get it."

"Okaaaaaaaay." Riley hops over to Ember and bypasses me completely. I understand, because she has that same effect on me. He tilts his head back as he watches the ride. "Embew, will you come on the Fewwis wheel with me?"

"Of course I will." Ember glances up at me, teasing in her eyes. "But I think Uncle Vance should come too. Don't you?"

"Yes," he calls out, his excitement contagious as we both laugh. And fuck, it feels good to laugh with her again.

We brave the long line and several impatient children to finally make it onto the ride. Riley picks The Toy Story car and insists he sit in the middle. Ember steps in first and we file in right behind her.

"This is so fun!" Riley stomps his feet. "The best day evew!"

I point a finger toward the second level of the store. "Look, Riley, there's a big dinosaur over there."

"Ooooooooooh, can we go see that next?" he asks, bouncing up and down in the seat.

"You got it, buddy." I ruffle his hair and Ember looks over at me. The sweetness of her smile makes warmth spark in my chest and spread to my limbs.

The car surges upward, stopping every other minute or so to let people on. As we sit suspended in mid-air, the continual rocking motion brings on this weird dizziness. Blood rushes to my head and a loud buzzing noise fills my ears. As if I'm being sucked under by a giant wave, dark spots cloud my vision and I can't seem to catch my breath. I vaguely hear Ember saying my name but she sounds far away. Caught in a fog, my pulse pounds too loud and I'm afraid I'm going to pass out when soft fingers wrap around mine.

"Easy breaths, Vance." Ember coaxes in a gentle voice. "Breathe in through your nose, out through your mouth. That's it. In through your nose, out through your mouth." As I follow her direction, my breathing begins to level out, my heartbeat slows. The sounds around me gradually register again and I blink, staring at our joined hands. She starts to pull away but I latch onto her fingers, leaning back against the car.

"Don't let go."

"You okay, Unca Vance?" Riley asks, and I force a smile for his benefit.

"I'm better now, little guy." Then I glance at Ember and mouth, "Thank you."

MY UNUSUAL EPISODE on the Ferris wheel didn't deter Riley in the least. Since then, he's tested out one plane, two remote control helicopters, and a crazy light-up toy whose name I can't recall. After being wowed by the dinosaur from Jurassic Park, he's finally found his heaven in the superhero section. Ember and I follow behind as he browses up and down the aisle.

"That was so weird, what happened earlier."

Ember gives me a sideways glance. "I think you had a panic attack." She digs her hands in the pockets of her jeans. "I used to get them a lot after Zack died."

I pick up a model of Superman to examine it before tucking it back on the shelf. "It's never happened before though. I don't have a fear of heights or anything."

"It could've just been the swaying of the car." She reaches up to tighten the band around her ponytail. "Kind of like motion sickness."

"Unca Vance, Unca Vance!" Riley lets out a high-pitched squeal, his little feet scurrying along the floor. "Wook, it's Mickey Mouse!" I glance up to find a massive display of Mickey Mouse in every size, shape, and variation. "I love Mickeeeeeeeey," he sings, and my gaze swings to Ember, throat working on a soft swallow.

"Me too, buddy. Me too."

Ember's breath catches and her cheeks bloom pink. She turns away, making it impossible to get a handle on her feelings. Meanwhile, I jam my thumbs in my back pockets, struggling to control the urge to take her in my arms. To hold her until she tells me what I want to hear. Except that won't get me anywhere. Besides, that other guy is in the picture and I don't know where that leaves me. But I do know I have to go slow with her. I'm just having some difficulty with the execution.

She escapes behind the stuffed animals, eyes lingering on the Mickey Mouse key rings. Her finger rolls over each one, clinking metal against metal. Unable to keep my distance, I shuffle over to her until my front almost touches her back. She still smells like fresh peaches and I steal a moment to breathe her in. I haven't been this close to her in *so* long, but it's not close enough. Leaning in, I sweep her ponytail to the side, my fingers brushing her neck. "You should get one," I whisper into her ear. "You know you want it." She swallows, a slight shiver vibrating through her body.

"I don't really need it," she answers too quickly, stepping away from me and securing a safer spot next to Riley. "What do you think, Riley?" She rubs his head. "Which Mickey is calling you?"

"This one!" His voice bursts through the tension, making me chuckle.

"You had to pick the biggest one. Didn't you, Riles? That thing is bigger than you."

He peers up at me, hopeful, that big smile pushing all reason from my head. "Can I get it?"

I look to Ember and she shrugs, her lips bending as she tries not to laugh. "Okay, Riles. You can get that one." He immediately pulls it down and twenty other Mickey's fall in the process. "But you have to carry it," I tease, as we bend down to pick up the stray stuffed animals and place them back on the shelf. "Okay," I nudge Ember's arm, "I'm thinking three and a half hours is good, right? I mean, we did our time here." Riley is already off drooling at another display of toys and I've pretty much had my fill.

"I've got an idea." She perches the last Mickey Mouse on the display. "You want to hear it?"

"If it helps us get out of here." I wink. "Absolutely."

She nods toward the escalator. "There's ice cream downstairs, on the way out."

"Ah, the lady knows a good bribe." I call out for Riley and he spins around, disappearing behind giant black ears. "I'm going to pay for that and Ember will take you for ice cream. I'll meet you guys down there, okay?"

"Ice cweeeeeeeeam," Riley squeaks, his tongue dashing across his lips. He reluctantly lets go of Mickey, something I can relate to well, and takes Ember's hand as the two of them ride the escalator to the first floor. I stare after them, trying not to read too much into how fucking well this day has gone.

By the time I navigate the crowd and detour to the ice cream shop, Riley is running around, dark globs of chocolate smeared on his cheeks. "Chocowaaaaaaaate." He giggles, sailing across the floor with his arms in the air.

A laugh bubbles up from Ember's throat. I plop down next to her, giving Mickey Mouse his own chair. "Riley has this thing about exaggerated vowels."

She glances over to Riley then back to me. "He's adorable."

"He's a sweet kid." My phone pings a text and I slide it from my pocket.

Chris: *I've been roaming around this Godforsaken place for a half hour. Where ARE you?*

I chuckle and type back.

Me: *First floor, ice cream*

Chris: *Be there in a minute...hopefully*

As I look up, I catch Ember peeking at my phone. "Chris is here. He's been trying to find us and I don't know why he didn't text me when he got here."

"Because he figured he could spot your big head a mile away." Chris taunts from behind me, and Ember laughs. "Hi." He strides to the table, offering her his hand. "You m-must be Ember. I'm Chris. I've heard a lot about you." Her lips tilt into an apprehensive smile. "Don't worry. I never believe anything he says," he throws in. I glare at him with a fucking retort on the tip of my tongue when Riley hightails it over. He yanks Mickey Mouse's hand to drag him off the chair.

"Chwissy! Wook what I got."

"Wow, Riles, that's awesome." He kneels down and shakes Mickey's hand. "Listen, we need to get going. Mom is making dinner and your friend Lenny is coming over."

Riley licks a circle around his mouth, chocolate sticking to his tongue. "Okay, hewe." He shoves Mickey Mouse at Chris. "Howd this." Then he turns around, slinging his arms around Ember and squeezing until he practically cuts off her circulation. She smiles through it because she's a trooper. "Bye, Embew. See you soon?"

"Absolutely, sweet boy."

Riley backs away, kissing her cheek and my heart blows up. He moves on to me and gives me a big hug. "Bye, Unca Vance. Thank you fow bwinging me and fow the stuffed animal."

"You got it, little guy. I'll see you soon, okay?" I make a fist and he mimics me, pressing his curled fingers against mine. "Oh." I pry the small plastic bag from my pocket with the Superman action figure. "This is for you, too. A little surprise for when you get home."

His smile grows. "Thanks, Unca Vance."

"Sure." I grin. "Now scram."

"All right, we're outta here. Nice m-meeting you, Ember." Chris's gaze flashes to me with the discretion of a fly. "Hope to see you around."

"Nice meeting you, too." Ember waves once as Chris and Riley disappear into the crowd. She scuffs the toe of her sneaker against the floor, her gaze following the motion. "So...."

"So...." I wait until she raises her head then hold out my arm. She stares at it, hesitating for a split second before folding her fingers around my elbow. Small victories, I remind myself. "Shall we blow this joint, or what?"

"Let's."

We make it back out into the sunshine, prodded by a sea of people as anxious as we are to exit the store and breathe fresh air. Directly in front of the entrance, a group gathers around a man in a top hat and tails singing acapella. Not unusual for Manhattan and his voice is pretty damn good. Ember glances up at me, curiosity embedded in her smile.

"You said you play at that bar, Blue Monday, right?"

"Yeah. Every Tuesday and Thursday night. It's no big deal." I brush it off because when it comes down to it, the bar is a dive and the gig is solely something we do for fun. But I still fucking love it.

"I always thought you should do something with that voice." Her tone doesn't jibe with her expression. It's too soft somehow, and my jaw stiffens. She slips her arm out from under mine and shifts away, staring at everything except me. "I should get going."

"Do you want to grab a bite?"

"I can't. I...have plans." Her words are vague, but her message is crystal fucking clear. I know it's with that guy.

"Ember." I blow out a rough breath. "I don't want to talk to your head. Could you look at me?" She turns, her face blank of emotion. "Go out with me tomorrow night."

She sighs. "I can't."

I tug on my earring, suddenly wanting to rip it from my skin. "Why not?"

"I have plans with Avery."

I shove my frustration into my pocket. "The night after that, then?"

Another lengthy sigh. "Vance—"

"Ember." I tilt my head, searching her face. "I know you still care about me. I can see it in your eyes." Reaching out, I tip her chin up with my finger. "What happened to the girl who always told the truth?"

She blinks slowly, breath rattling as it leaves her mouth. "She's still here...she's just terrified of it now."

My eyes drift back and forth between hers, hoping she can see the sincerity in my gaze, feel it from my heart. "I won't hurt you again."

"You don't know that."

One thing I do know—words are fucking useless at this point. I need to prove it to her.

"Okay," I submit, dropping my hand. And for someone who claims to be terrified, her forehead creases in what looks a whole hell of a lot like disappointment.

"Thank you for today. I had a great time," her mouth slants, "and I love little Riley."

Without waiting another fucking second, I lean down and let my lips graze her cheek before stepping back. "Thanks for coming."

She walks away from me, and my stomach lurches. I can't help thinking how the roles are reversed now, and how I deserve this—because I never should have walked away from her. I damn sure won't make that same mistake twice. And since I can't manage to take things slow, before she gets too far away I yell out. "Admit it. You missed me."

Her movement halts and she spins around, throwing her hands up in the air. Even from here I can tell she's smiling. "Okay! I fucking missed you! *Happy*?"

Not entirely—but it's a start.

chapter thirty-nine
Ember

IT'S AMAZING HOW slow a weekend can go by, even when you fill every second. To make sure you have no free moments to think. I can't say it was all that successful. Hanging out with Avery, sculpting, and studying, definitely passed the time. But my mind strayed to Vance on more than one occasion. I blow out a ruffled sigh and lean back in my chair. Friday was great—more than great. While I can't bring myself to admit anything else to Vance at the moment, I can own up to the fact that I missed him—like crazy.

It's the simple things that I missed the most. His know-it-all grin, the way he tugs on that stupid earring when he's nervous. I missed our talks—about anything, about everything. I missed the comfort of our silences. And I missed his eyes—and how I can see a whole world in them.

"Daydreaming again, are we?" My boss, Monica strolls into the back office, her perfect black bob swishing from side to side. Under one arm, she carries a painting wrapped in brown paper. With her available hand, she smoothes her blue Armani pencil skirt, careful not to damage those brightly polished nails.

"Who, me?" I smile. "Never. Who does such things?"

She stops in front of my desk, surveying me with a subtle lift of her

261

head. "You've gotten feistier since you started here. I'm quite enjoying it." Setting the painting against the wall behind her, she adds, "The last girl who worked for me didn't know the definition of the word humor." In a blink, her smile straightens out, focus changing, and she's back to business. She plucks the proof for the new logo from my inbox. "How are we doing on timing for the updated business cards and postcards?"

I roll the chair to my computer and click the mouse to open up the calendar on my desktop. "I called the printer yesterday but realized they're closed on Mondays, so I spoke with them this morning and the cards will be here on Thursday. Also, that reminds me. Mrs. Lipman called about that painting she was interested in, and she wants you to give her a call. She has a new cell phone number and address. I sent you an e-mail with her details."

"Excellent. Thank you, Ember." She takes a peppermint candy from the bowl on my desk, crinkling the wrapper and popping it in her mouth. A hum leaves her red-stained lips and she smiles. "I've always loved these things." Designer heels click on the polished wood as she winks then saunters off. "I'll leave you to your daydreaming."

My mind refocuses on work as I make adjustments to a customer spreadsheet when a knock sounds on the door. Looking up from my paperwork, I notice a young kid standing there in a baseball hat, chewing gum like a cow grazing in a field. In his hand is a bouquet of pink roses. The color alone gives me pause.

"You Ember Bennett?" he asks in a thick New York accent, blowing a deep green bubble.

"Yes, that's me."

He struts over and lays the flowers along with a small card on my desk. "These are for you." Holding out a clipboard, he taps his thumbnail on the signature line. "Sign here, please." Then he stares up at the ceiling and continues to chomp on his gum as if I'm boring him.

Eyes glued to the card, I sign quickly and give him a hasty thanks and a tip before he disappears. I slide my thumb under the flap of the miniature envelope to pry it open. Inside sits a simple white card with a handwritten message.

Ember,
I MISSED YOU TOO.
xo Vance

Four words—and I'm breathless. How is that possible?

With the card pressed to my chest, I let his words seep into me. They burrow under my skin, filling me with him as if he never left. I guess in many ways he didn't. He was always there, tucked away in a corner of my heart I had to ignore—because I had no choice.

But now it seems that I do. Except fear haunts me, following me around like a shadow—never letting me forget that the two people I've loved most, I've lost. First Zack, and then Vance. I'm not sure if I'm strong enough to handle it happening again.

A silvery glint catches my eye. I pick up the flowers and unwrap the foil, setting their powerful fragrance free. In between one of the roses, hanging off a green stem is the Mickey Mouse key ring from the toy store. The one I said I didn't want—which I did—and of course Vance knew that.

My lips twitch and this peculiar fullness engulfs my chest, bigger than I can handle. My eyes swell and I close them, wanting to keep all the feelings inside. Even then, they sneak out. Fear and longing roll down my cheeks, until I'm crying about nothing, about everything. Overwhelmed by the past, trying to keep myself afloat in the present. It's funny. I'm so good at expressing myself with words and sculpting. But when it comes to the hard stuff, I'm lost. I'm afraid.

It's not good enough anymore. I'm twenty-five years old and I need to get it together. I sit up straighter in my chair and brush the tears away from my cheeks. My brain wanders for a minute until I realize I'm doing too much thinking and not enough acting. So I stop the madness in my head and open my desk drawer, reaching into my purse for my cell phone.

Me: *Thank you for the beautiful flowers and the key ring*

Vance: *You're welcome*

Me: *That was really thoughtful*

Vance: *I can be thoughtful when I want to be*

I laugh.

Me: *I love them and you were right, I did want the key ring*

Vance: *I know. And I'm also wise. You should listen to me more often*

Unsure of what I want to say next, I pause with my fingers over the keypad. When I don't respond, I wait to see if Vance types something else. But he doesn't and that's okay. There's something more important I need to do anyway.

"I'M NOT USED to seeing you in a t-shirt and jeans." Grant stares down at his black pants and crisp white shirt. "I feel a bit overdressed."

"You look great," I counter, fiddling with the napkin in my lap. But then something kicks in. I can't pinpoint exactly what, but it spurs me on. "I actually don't like dresses at all," I admit. "I never did."

"Oh." Grant's face is a blank slate, save for the tiny slash across his forehead. He plays it off, almost as if he wants to avoid what's really going on here. "So, should we order?"

"I'm not very hungry." I push the menu away, clasping my hands in front of me on the white linen tablecloth. "Do you remember that night when you were in my apartment and you were looking at that sculpture book?"

"Of course." He laughs anxiously before it peters out. "You practically bit my head off."

"Yes, and I'm sorry again about that." I gather my nerves on a big breath. "But...that was a gift from someone very special."

"Vance."

"How did you...."

He scrapes a hand through his hair and sighs. "I read the inscription Ember, while you were in the bathroom."

My eyes lower to the table then back to him. "Oh."

His brows pinch together, an expression forming around his mouth I've never seen before. "Yeah, *Oh*. How come you didn't tell me there was someone else?"

"Wait, no." I jump in. "Remember before we started dating I mentioned there was a guy? That was years ago, but...." I pause, trying to arrange my thoughts into something that will make sense. That will hurt less. "I found out recently that he's here in New York, and I've...I've never gotten over him," I confess, and he flinches. It's so subtle I nearly miss it. "You're a wonderful guy, Grant. Really you are. It's just that...I'm not one for playing games. Certainly not with your heart."

He reaches across the table, his hand covering mine. "I know you're not. That's one of the reasons I lo—admire you so much. Your straightforwardness and how you care." His eyes bounce around in thought before returning to me. "And if he hadn't come back?" I shake my head to give him my answer. Because the truth is, Vance coming back only brought things to light sooner. Grant gets up from his chair to stand beside me at the table, leaning down to kiss my cheek. "If he ever hurts you though, I'll have to...," he glances around the restaurant then back to me, "...kick his ass or something. You know that, right?"

I laugh and take his other hand in mine. "If he ever hurts me, *I'm* going to kick his ass."

He chuckles and squeezes my hand before returning to his side of the table, surprising me when he sits down. "Can we still have dinner together? I'd like to. Above all else, we're friends, right?"

His sincerity overwhelms me. It makes this that much harder, even though it feels right. I nod, my voice cracking. "Yes, absolutely."

We both pick up our menus, my mind and heart lighter than before. As I browse the vast selection of food, I can sense Grant's stare back on me.

"But if you ever change your mind?" I glance up to sadness I'm the cause of, and my stomach hardens. I give him a soft smile. "Okay," he shrugs, "I had to take a shot. Because you never know when you might get another one."

Truer words have never been spoken.

As I FUMBLE with my keys, attempting to juggle my briefcase, purse, and of course the roses, the door opens.

"Hi, love." A familiar voice greets me and I look up to discover my best friend, here, in the flesh. I squeal, dropping everything except for the flowers and throw my arms around his neck.

"If I had known I was going to get this kind of reception, I would've come a lot sooner." I pull back just enough to smack a big kiss on Troy's cheek and he grins. "Wait. That sounded weird."

"Do you have any idea how happy I am to see you?"

His lips slant upward and he brings a hand from around my waist, pinching his thumb and forefinger together. "This much?" He backs out of my grip, waving me in. "How 'bout I let you inside so we can catch up from last week." He eyes my expression. "Because it looks like we have a *lot* of catching up to do."

"Here." I press the flowers against his chest. "Hold these and follow me while I find a vase, and you can tell me what you're doing here."

"I'm off for a few days and wanted to surprise my best friend. Done. Your turn," he volleys back. "Grant usually sends you orchids, right?"

I lean against the counter. "Right. But Grant didn't buy these for me. Vance did."

"Told ya," Avery chimes in. She struts into the kitchen decked out in a low-cut black dress with matching boots, her blonde hair pulled tight into a sleek ponytail.

"You look like Catwoman," I tease, and she growls, curling her fingers into a claw.

"I'm on the prowl, what can I say?" She slides a chair out from the table, making herself comfortable in our discussion. "So what were we talking about?"

"*We*," Troy points a finger between us, "were talking about Vance and—"

"I've already filled Troy in on the latest with you," she interjects and I glare at her. "What? He's your best friend and he asked," she shrugs, "I had to answer."

Troy grabs a chair and joins Avery in their not-so-subtle interrogation. "First of all, what's the deal with Grant? You're dating both of them?"

I remove the vase from a cabinet underneath the sink, turning on the tap to fill it with water before facing them again. "You know I can't date two guys at once."

"Sign me up for that," Avery counters as she reclines back, stretching her long legs under the table.

Troy folds his hands on top of his head. "If I wanted to be confused, I could've stayed in Oregon. Someone tell me what's going on."

Not wanting to drag this out, I grab a pair of scissors from the drawer then set the vase on the table. "I broke up with Grant," I admit, casually trimming the ends of the roses before placing them in water. Talk about opposite ends of the spectrum. Troy frowns, while Avery's lips stretch into a pleased grin as if she's been waiting for this to happen.

"But he's so nice," Troy remarks. Now I'm frowning, guilt swirling around my stomach though I know it was the right decision.

"He is nice."

"He's too nice." Avery throws her opinion into the ring. "He doesn't challenge her. He's, you know, boring?" She glances up at me with a knowing smile. "Nail meet head. No need to say anything more."

I snort. "You. Need. Help."

"How did he take it, Ems?" Troy asks. "I know it's only been months. But still, you guys were friends before, and he told you he wanted to spend the rest of his life with you."

Mixed emotion stirs, drawing out a sigh. "I know." I twist to the side, resting my hip against the table. "He was great about it actually. Very gracious...very Grant."

"Of course. Because he's so...*nice*," Avery emphasizes with a smirk.

Troy lets his hand fall to the table and picks up a broken stem, twirling it between his fingers. "And Vance?"

Just like that, my heart races. "He wants another chance and I'm thinking maybe we both deserve one. But there's this whole other part of me that says, what am I supposed to do? Fall into his arms like he didn't hurt me and it hasn't been three years?" Avery kicks her chair back and stands, rising on tiptoe as she darts a glance over my shoulder. "What are you looking for?"

"The rules. I didn't realize there were any when it came to the heart." She holds out her hands in a sweeping gesture. "Please, do enlighten me." I scowl, but all it does is make her grin. As usual, she has a strong point.

"Yeah, what *she* said," Troy seconds, and the three of us laugh until my stomach hurts.

Avery swipes a finger across her cheek. "I'll be right back. I need to fix my makeup." She sashays out of the room and I stare at Troy.

He slides off the seat. "What?"

My eyes scan his body then return to his face. "Something is different. You've been spending more time than usual at the gym?"

His mouth edges up at the corner. "No."

"What then?"

He leans his weight on the chair, arms resting over the back. "My parents came over yesterday."

"*What?*"

"Believe me. I'm just as surprised as you are." He flips the chair around and sits backwards, exhaling a sigh. "We talked. Actually, they talked and I listened."

"And?"

"They apologized and my mother cried a lot. She said things."

I move closer, placing a hand on his forearm. "Like?"

"Like they don't care what my sexual orientation is, or who I date, or what I decide to do with my life. She said, '*In your heart, you're our son, and that's the only thing that matters. That's the only thing that should've mattered.'"* Emotion gathers in my chest and I touch my fingertips to my throat. "You're not going to cry on me now, are you? I don't think I can handle any more tears."

I shake my head. "No. I'm just...happy. Everything is changing."

"It is." Troy smiles at me with a lightness I haven't seen in him for years. "And we can change with it, Ems. We can choose forgiveness."

Avery comes back then, my mind stuck on his last few words. She pauses, inspecting my face. "*Now* what?"

My eyes briefly land on Troy before wandering to the calendar on the wall. The word Tuesday in big block letters glares at me. "What, is that we're going out." Troy and Avery's gaze burns up the side of my cheek as I position the flowers in the center of the table.

"Care to tell us where we're going exactly?" Avery latches onto Troy's arm and hauls him to his feet.

"We're going to Blue Monday." My stomach flutters and I glance down at my clothing, thankful I changed out of my dress before I met up with Grant. I don't want to waste any more time.

"What's Blue Monday?" Troy asks as I shuffle them out the door.

Where I'll find my heart.

THE CAB DRIVER speeds through the streets of New York, weaving and bobbing around cars and buses, nearly hitting a few pedestrians. Normally, my heart would be in my throat. But not tonight. Tonight the clouds carry me. Anticipation, not fear, fills me, reminding me of something Zack used to say before he'd go off on one of his crazy adventures. '*Em, it's always the three A's—Anticipation, Adrenaline, Adventure.*'" I feel like that right now. As if I'm about to embark on a new adventure, setting my life on a different course—one that certainly wouldn't be the same without Vance Davenport in it. I know that now. I think I've always known that.

"Jesus," Troy mutters as we exit the taxi. "Every time I visit you, I remember how you seriously take your life into your hands in those things. I'd prefer to walk next time and keep my balls intact."

"Ha." Avery barks out a laugh, glancing up at the neon blue sign. "So are you going to tell us what we're doing at Blue Monday on a Tuesday?"

"Ba da bum," Troy adds in and Avery pokes him.

We link elbows, making our way into the bar. We're barely in the door when I hear Vance's voice. It floats around us and a rush of goose bumps cascade down my arms. My eyes drift toward the sound, pulse picking up when I catch my first glimpse of him on stage. His eyes are closed, lips parted, deft fingers that left a mark on my skin strumming the guitar. He sends the lyrics into the air and I have to steady myself with a deep breath. He looks beautiful like that, as if he is one with the music.

"And I didn't know about this, why?" Avery stares me down, clearly as affected by his performance as I am. Well, not quite.

"Ditto, and holy shit." Troy echoes my sister as they gang up against me...again. Round aqua lights hanging overhead drape the bar and their smug faces in a shadowy blue haze.

"It's not like I've been holding back. I just found out myself."

Mesmerized, our attention travels to the band. Next to Vance, Chris plays a pretty impressive bass guitar. Toward the back, another guy plays keyboard and someone else is on drums.

Mainly though, my gaze is glued to Vance. The way his upper body sways to the music, his soul on display. My spine tingles with tiny jolts of electricity. As if he knows, he opens his eyes. Somehow in the near darkness, I sense he spotted me—because a grin sweeps clear across his face, spreading warmth over my skin like a blanket. I smile right back, my lips not leaving me any other choice. That's the only thing they want to do when he's around.

"We're gonna go get some drinks," Avery shouts. "What do you want?"

"Huh?" I snap out of my daze. "Oh, just a glass of wine."

She grimaces like I didn't quite understand her question. "This isn't a wine kind of a place, Em. I'll get you something else."

As soon as they walk away, my attention goes back to the stage. I might not read books, but I've watched enough movies to know this feels a lot like one of those scenes—where two people catch each other's eyes across the room—where everything around them disappears and all that exists is a crazy, out of control heartbeat that makes you want to run into their arms.

Fortunately, the song comes to a close. Vance sets his guitar down, stepping off the stage and stalking toward me. People clap him on the back and utter various praises but his eyes never leave mine. My cheeks feel flush, body overheating from the attention.

I want him to move faster.

When he finally reaches me, I lick my dry lips and try to swallow. Sweat clings to his t-shirt, his face, his neck—but I'm the one who might melt. Thoughts of tasting the salt from his skin make my knees weak.

He searches my face. "You're here."

"I am."

He lifts his hand as if to reach for me, but then lets it drop. "I'm surprised. I didn't expect to see you."

I shrug. All the words I planned to say disappear and I'm left with the wrong ones. "I wanted to hear you sing."

He glances around the bar then back to me. "Are you alone?"

"No." His expression falls and I'm quick to clarify. "I'm here with Avery and Troy. Troy surprised me by coming in tonight."

His smile returns and he exhales, warm breath feathering across my cheek. A body comes out of nowhere and crashes into me, nearly spilling a drink all over my shirt. Vance grips my shoulders and pulls me close. Blue eyes full of everything I've missed blaze into mine. "I'm really glad you're here."

My mouth is unable to form an immediate response. The way he's looking at me traps the words in my throat. "You...were...amazing out there." I try not to stare at the wisps of hair wet against his forehead, his feverish skin, damp lips.

"Thanks. I—"

"Well, well." Avery comes up behind him. "If it isn't Vance

Davenport." He turns and Avery throws her arms around his neck, winking at me over his shoulder. She draws back after a minute. "You were hot shit up there."

"Thanks." Vance offers his hand to Troy. "Good to see you again, man."

"Likewise." Troy shakes it then lifts his drink. "You want to head to the bar? I'll buy you a beer."

Vance flicks his gaze to me, eyes roaming my face. "No thanks. I'm good right here." Controlling my grin isn't an option, so I don't bother trying. Nor do I bother covering up the blush spreading over my cheeks like wildfire.

"Hey, Ember." Chris appears beside Vance and slaps him on the shoulder. "N-nice to see you again."

"You too." I point a finger toward my partners in crime. "This is my sister, Avery, and my best friend, Troy. This is Chris."

The rest of the band follows behind and after all the introductions are made, we head to a table. Vance sticks close to me as if he's afraid I might disappear. Little does he know, I'm not going anywhere.

Conversation flows and laughter ensues, but I can barely concentrate on anything except Vance's proximity. He's dragged his chair closer, our shoulders practically touching now. The smell of sweat and soap, and everything I've missed about him bleeds into my space, and I find myself breathing him in until it makes me dizzy. Every now and then I can feel him watching me, his gaze warming the side of my cheek. It makes me want to lean into him, bury my head in that spot between his neck and his shoulder.

"Dance with me," he murmurs against my ear, making me shiver. The reality that we're here together sinking in.

"But you don't dance," I whisper back, teasing.

"For you, I'll fucking dance." He growls words that are full of fire, disarming me until I'm a puddle at his feet. Three years of hidden longing surfaces and I get up from the chair, taking his hand. I stare at the way our palms slide together, fingers entwined, remembering the first time he took my hand and held it. A smile explodes on my face as he leads me to the almost nonexistent dance floor. *We're Forgiven* by

The Calling plays through the speakers.

Our gazes collide and he has that same smile in his eyes that I'm wearing on my lips. Strong arms slip around my waist, my hands gliding up the rigid planes of his stomach to drape around his neck. My head rests against his firm chest, his heart beating steadily under my cheek. His scent and the warmth of his body engulfs me. I close my eyes and try to breathe, keenly aware of all the places we're touching, of how connected we are. Even after all these years, we still fit like two pieces of a puzzle. Nothing feels forced about the way our bodies move together—the sway of our hips, the pace of our feet—and I'm floating.

"Ember," he whispers against my ear. I'm afraid to look up at him, scared he'll see everything—how much my heart has missed him, how much I want him. "Ember. Look at me," he whispers again, and I blink my eyes open and lift my chin. His gaze is searing, cutting through all the things we haven't said, all the time that's passed. I can see it clearly in those eyes that captivated me from the moment I first stared into them—that nothing has changed for him either. He cups my cheek in the warmth of his palm. "Go out with me."

"We are out," I counter, my pulse racing too fast.

"On a date." His mouth curves. "Go out on a date with me. You know you want to." His grin widens and my fingers flex against his shirt with the desire to touch him; his hair, his jaw, his lips.

"Still so cocky."

"Always." His whole face brightens. "Is that a yes?"

My eyes map the soft lines of his face and I nod. "Yes."

"When?" he asks without hesitation, and I let out a breathless laugh because even anxious, he's adorable.

"Whenever you want."

"Tomorrow night," he suggests right away, as if he can't wait a minute longer. I nod again, my head finding his chest once more. "Tomorrow," he breathes into my ear, and my toes curl inside my sneakers.

I didn't want to sleep tonight anyway.

chapter forty
Vance

Tomorrow.

A concept I never gave a shit about until I met Ember. Now I want to fill all my tomorrows with her, and the spaces in between too.

My mother's stone sits heavy in my hand, the weight of missing her bears down on me. Still, I'm uplifted. Maybe it's knowing I'm going to see Ember tonight. Or maybe it's because I know how much my mother would have loved her, evidenced by that one day they met. I picture them sitting down over coffee, talking about art, laughing together. The thought brings a smile to my face and settles me somehow. It dawns on me how Ember is like the river—how she calms me and brings me a sense of peace. One I haven't had for quite some time.

The stone finds its way to the familiar spot at the bottom of my pocket. I grab my wallet off the dresser and tuck it inside the lining of my leather jacket. As I run a hand through my hair, I take one last glance in the mirror, unable to recognize the guy staring back at me. But for once, I actually think that's a good thing.

Chris pokes his head in. "Where are you t-taking Ember tonight?"

"Not sure, still. I was thinking about either The Moth StorySLAM or the Village Vanguard." Sweat gathers under the neck of my shirt and I look over at Chris. "I'm fucking nervous."

"Why?"

I shrug, working my jaw back and forth. "I've never cared about another girl the way I care about her. It's pretty fucking scary, actually."

"I imagine love is." Chris grips the doorframe, eyes full of intent. "I d-don't know. She seems like she feels the same. I saw the way she was looking at you last night. Speaking of which," he smirks, "that sister of hers is a real character. Don't you think?"

I'm too focused on the first thing he said. My brain taking more time than usual to process. "What? Oh yeah, she's a character all right. She might be available too."

"*Anyway.*" He taps a finger against the wood. "I hope it goes the way you want it to. You d-deserve it."

"So do you." I snag my keys from the bedside table then walk over to him. We've known each other long enough that I know what's coming next.

His voice lowers, eyes avoiding my stare. "Deserving it and being able to g-get it are two different things."

"Bullshit," I snap, and his head lifts. "Stop using your speech impediment as a reason to bail out of life." He opens his mouth, but I don't give him a chance to speak. "Because I know all about that, remember? So you stutter, big fucking deal. You had years of speech therapy and it's hardly even noticeable anymore. Plus, it's not who you are. This conversation is getting old and you better get your shit together and ask out that cute chick from the diner who likes you," I grin, "or else I'll do it for you."

His eyes narrow into fine slits and he lets out an annoyed growl. "You w-wouldn't."

"Oh, I would." I hike up the collar of my jacket. "On that note, I'm outta here." I brush past him and he chuckles.

"Good luck."

THE ELEVATOR RIDE up to Ember's apartment takes too fucking long. I tap my foot against the floor, checking my appearance on the mirrored wall for the tenth time. The numbers ding by at a slow crawl and I tell them to hurry the fuck up under my breath. Even twenty-four hours is too long to be away from her now. Eventually, the doors open and I dart out of the car, scanning the hallway for apartment 88B.

As the number comes into view, my steps falter. I give myself a minute, rolling my shoulders and craning my neck from side to side. Then I take those last few strides and knock on the door—and wait. After too much time and when I'm beginning to think maybe she changed her mind, the door opens—and my jaw hits the ground.

My gaze sweeps over her, a slow drag starting at knee-high black boots and leading to jeans in the same shade, up to a green top cut low to the dip of her breasts. Dark silky hair spills in loose waves over smooth, creamy shoulders. Her beautiful face—free of makeup except for a little sparkle on her eyes, lips painted in a soft red gloss.

I brace my arm against the doorframe. "Wow. You look...*wow*."

Shiny lips that make me want to be covered in gloss tilt at the corners as she surveys me from head to toe. My standard jeans and black shirt are not that impressive, but she seems to think differently. "You look wow, too." She opens the door wider. "Come in."

"Nice place." I dig around for any other signs of life. "Where are Troy and Avery?"

"They went out to grab something to eat. Come on." She walks ahead of me and I blatantly stare at her ass because I can't help myself. "I'll give you the quick tour." She gestures with her hand. "Living room."

My eyes travel the space, zeroing in on family pictures lining the walls, evidence of her sculpting talent covering tables and spanning shelves. Various pieces of nostalgia sit on top of a television cabinet. A brightly colored painting of Mickey Mouse hangs in the corner and makes me smile. While the apartment is filled with many things, in no way does it look cluttered. "I'm not sure I've ever seen an apartment this clean." I chuckle. "Certainly not mine."

She flicks me a grin over her shoulder. "That's all me. If it were up to Avery, all the furniture would be draped with dirty clothes. This," she waves her hand like a wand, "is the kitchen."

"Nice roses."

"Thanks." She glances up at me with a soft smile. "Some guy gave them to me," she says in a quiet voice as we make our way out of the kitchen. "You've already seen the living room." She points to the right as I follow her down the hall. "Bathroom. And that door," her chin lifts, "leads to Avery's room. I'm a bit scared to walk in there so you'll just have to use your imagination." Crossing over to the opposite side, she reaches in to flick the light switch on the wall. "And this is my room."

All at once, her scent attacks me. It's everywhere, wrapping me up in so much fucking sweetness my chest fills with it. Distracted, I struggle to absorb everything that is Ember— sculptures on colorful shelves, picture frames full of memories, blown-up prints of sunsets, and another small poster of Mickey Mouse. A short distance away I spot the snow globe I bought for her and my heart jumps in my chest. "You kept it," I murmur, walking over to pick it up from her dresser. As I shake it, Ember comes over too, and together we watch the tiny white particles fly around inside the cheap plastic.

"Of course I kept it. It means something to me."

Means.

I set the globe down then turn to Ember, trying like hell not to focus on the present tense of her words. Vulnerability flashes in her eyes and all the questions I want to ask die on my lips. I don't know how I fit into her life now, and for me to push doesn't seem fair. "I'm kind of ready to start our date. Are you?"

"Yup. Let me just grab a jacket." My tentative expression makes her hesitate. She looks down at herself then up to me. "What?"

I brush back a few strands of her hair. "You fucking stun me. That's...that's all." A pink flush spreads over her cheeks and along her neck. I let my fingers slide down the soft skin of her arm to entwine our hands. "Let's go before I find reasons for us to stay."

We step off the elevator and weave our way through the lobby to street level. My mind still races with questions, but also with possibility. I release a breath and tell myself to have patience. It's obvious Ember is preoccupied too—but with what, or who, I couldn't say.

"Where are we going?" she asks, her warm palm in mine making me realize how much I missed this—fucking hand holding is underrated. "Vance?"

"Huh?"

She laughs, bending her head to catch my eyes. "I asked where we're going."

"You'll see when we get there," I retort. Her cheeks fill up and she looks like a pufferfish. "You trust me, right?"

Her hesitation makes me think maybe that was the wrong thing to say. Until she surprises me with her answer. "I do." Relief leaves my chest in a rush as we walk for a while, blanketed by conversation and periods of comfortable silence.

"How do you like living here?"

She breathes out a sigh. "I like it a lot. But at first it was hard for me to adjust. Everything was so big and in your face, and I found myself missing Oregon. But not Avery." She laughs. "I swear the moment we got here she got down and kissed the ground. It's like she knew she belonged here or something." She glances up at the lights of a plane flying overhead. "I love it here now, though. The energy became addictive." Her gaze travels down to mine. "What about you?"

"I like it. It definitely took a while for me and Chris to get our bearings and figure things out. But everything is going well for us. Plus there's the band which I love and...." I stop myself from what I really want to say—that being with her makes it feel like home. "Yeah, it's good."

"How's Julian? You know after you left I went to him, hoping he knew where you were." Her voice lowers. "But he didn't." The topic makes me cringe, but I'm not going to shy away from it. I'm willing to take full responsibility for being an asshole. "Anyway," she goes on, her tone more upbeat. "Shortly after that I popped by to see him and your dad said he left for California." I shrug off the guilt of leaving Julian behind, too. Although he told me there was nothing to forgive and we've moved past it.

"He's great. And yeah, he's in Southern California. He works at a sports marketing firm there and he's a real surfer boy now." I shake my head and toss in an eye roll. "I've been out to visit him a few times since he moved."

"What's the look for?"

I smirk. "California was definitely made for him. The girls follow him around like he's some kind of Greek God."

"I can totally see that." She chews on her bottom lip. "What about you?"

"What about me, what?"

When she senses my confusion, she spells it out. "Any...girls?"

"Nah." I stare straight ahead now. "There's only ever been one girl for me."

"Really?" she challenges, her voice teetering on the edge of a smile.

"Yup." I pop the P for emphasis. "Not sure if she's interested, though. Too soon to tell."

"Hmph" is all she offers, her eyes like flames on the side of my face. "She's pretty stupid if she's not," she adds, looking away from me as I glance over, trying to hide the grin bursting from the corner of her lips.

"She doesn't strike me as the stupid type," I throw in for good measure and she laughs. Tugging on her hand, I pull her closer then come to a stop. "Here we are."

Bright eyes climb to a sign that says SPIN New York. To the left is the word *Ping* in white block lettering. I hold the glass door open and Ember walks in, her face contorting in amusement as she reads the billboard: "I got 99 problems but ping-pong ain't one," and then, "If you're having pong problems I feel bad for you son." She turns to me. "Ping-pong?"

"Yup."

A contented sound leaves her throat and she smiles. "Cool."

A hostess greets us as Ember takes in the vast space and the first of two floors, more reminiscent of a night club than a sports club. However, as we head down to the basement, the atmosphere shifts. Twenty ping-pong courts are set up strategically in what looks like a large gym flanked by a bar and comfortable seating. Lights hang above us in frosted blues and whites, a variety of pinks, giving it a glow-in-the-dark appearance.

I put our name in for a table. Given it's not as crowded on a weeknight, we don't have to wait long. Another hostess leads us to a dimly lit corner where muted red couches surround a black ping-pong table. Tiny bulbs above colorful paintings on the wall provide the only source of light.

"I can't wait to whip your ass," Ember declares out of the blue, startling me. The way she says ass turns me the fuck on.

My brow rises a notch. "Taken to swearing, have we? Must be feeling pretty confident."

She cocks her hip against the side of the table, a smirk forming on her lips. "I am."

"I wouldn't get too confident there, sweetheart. If I remember correctly, your pool skills left a lot to be desired." I remind her with a smug grin. "Come to think of it. They sucked."

Ember's eyes are saucer wide, that pretty mouth hanging open. "You're in so much trouble," she counters, picking up the racket like she wants to take all her aggression out on me.

God, I fucking hope so.

"Okay, let's do this." Determined, she holds the wooden paddle tight in her hand and glares at me. "Ready?"

The bar in the back glows blue and I jerk my chin in that general direction. "Do you want a drink first? Or if you're hungry, we can eat."

Her tongue darts out in a slow swipe across her lips and I swallow hard. "Scared, are you? Trying to prolong your defeat?"

"All right, smartass." I shrug off my jacket and toss it on the couch before we both move to our respective sides of the table. As we volley, one game turns into more and I'm surprised to discover she's really good, beating me two out of three games. I drop my paddle on the table and scoop up my coat. "You weren't shitting me."

"Nope." She places hers down and crosses to my side. "And I have five years of camp to thank for that. Horseback riding and swimming weren't the only things we did there."

"You thirsty, hungry now?"

"Just thirsty," she answers, shouts of encouragement and groans of defeat loud in our ears as we stroll through the lounge. Ping-pong games at various stages being played all over the room. "This place is so cool."

"I'm glad you like it." A few guys leer at her as we pass by and I tug on her belt loop. I want them to know she's mine. Or I hope she will be. "Come closer, you're too far away."

The whole time we're at the bar I keep her near. While waiting for our drinks, she fans a hand in front of her face. "It's really hot in here. Are you hot?" She slides her arms from her jacket and lays it over the back of the chair. Tiny beads of sweat dot her forehead and as my eyes drift lower, the curve between her breasts. My tongue fights to stay inside my mouth. Her question pries my gaze away. "Are you still reading a lot?"

"I am." The bartender places a beer and a glass of wine down in front of us. "Last night for example, I couldn't sleep so I read into the morning." I sip my beer, eyeing her over the rim. "I've been getting into paranormal dark fantasy lately, and I was halfway through with a book so I finished it." Her stare is hard, disconcerting. It settles on my face like a heavy weight and my hand goes to my earring, rolling it between my fingers. "Ember, what is it?"

She moves her head back and forth, a vacant expression on her face. "I don't want to make small talk right now, I...." Her voice trails off and she looks away for a few beats. When she comes back to me her cheeks are flushed, breathing rapid. "It's really...hot. Can we get some air?"

"Of course." I retrieve my wallet and toss a few bills on the counter. As she grabs her jacket from the chair, I reach for her hand to entwine our fingers together then lead us outside. Once we reach the sidewalk, Ember lets out a visible breath. "Are you feeling all right? Do you want me to take you home?"

"No," she replies a little too quickly. "I don't want to go home. I just need air is all."

"Okay." The mood hovers thick as we walk the city streets. Ember is almost too quiet and I'm starting to think the worst. The longer the silence, the more the worry eats away at me. "Ember, are you sure you're all right?" I ask again. She nods, only it doesn't match up with the stiffness in her shoulders, the rigid set of her jaw. Unease continues to take root in my stomach until I'm ready to erupt. We turn a corner and Ember ducks into an alleyway between two shops, as I wait for whatever it is to come pouring out.

The heels of her boots slap against the pavement as she paces. With my fingers in a fist, I squeeze tight and brace myself for whatever I have coming—that I most certainly fucking deserve.

"After you left…." She takes a slow breath in then lets it out. "I told you that I blamed my mother. And I did. And then I blamed you. But when all was said and done, and the anger subsided, I blamed myself. I became one of those girls who thought that," she stops pacing and looks up at me, the pain of regret abundant in her eyes, "that maybe if I had only told you sooner how I felt or," she lets go of a sharp swallow, "did something differently. That you wouldn't have left."

"Oh, Ember—"

"No. Let me just get this out," she presses. Another breath falls in the air between us. I'm not sure if it's hers or mine. "Avery used to tell me that for someone who was so outspoken, and didn't care what others thought, I have such a hard time saying what I want for myself. And she was right. But I don't want to do that anymore. Especially not with you. I don't want to be afraid anymore." Her gaze shifts, eyes softening. "You asked me a question, and I'd like to answer it now." I nod, my breath held tight in my throat.

"You asked me if I was in love with Grant." The mention of his name makes something wilt in my chest, makes him real—makes me realize all that time she was with him, she could have been with me. Ember exhales a ragged sigh then slays me with her eyes. "I tried to return his feelings, I did. He's a great guy, but…," a single tear sneaks out and cascades down her skin, "I couldn't be with him, not when my heart belonged to someone else." Her voice goes quiet, too quiet, as if her words might drift away. "When you left, you took it with you, and I didn't feel it again until I saw you on the train." She shakes her head as more tears roll down her cheeks. "The love, it just wouldn't go away. It still won't."

Closing the distance between us, I cradle her face in my hands, thumbing away her tears. "*God*, Ember. I love you. From the moment you walked into my house," I smile, "into my life...with that damn Mickey Mouse shirt and those red sneakers, it's been you. It will always be you...for me," I murmur, gliding my fingers across her cheek. "I couldn't stop loving you. You never left my heart." I don't get any more words out because she flings her arms around my neck, sobbing messy, uncontrollable tears—but life is messy, and somehow I've learned that the hard way. And holding her now, it's like...like holding life in my arms, embracing it, in all its unpredictability and craziness.

"I love you," she whispers between soft cries, and something inside me gives way and my heart cracks open—and I come spilling out—all of me; the real me, the flawed me. Just me I guess. My whole body gives in, sagging against her, finally setting *me* free. Because this is where I belong.

When her limbs stop shaking, she draws back and presses her forehead to mine. "We've lost so much time. I already knew what was in my heart. I wasn't about to make you jump through hoops to get to it," she says softly, the tears still falling.

"I would have." Kissing the tip of her nose, I brush my fingers across her cheek. "For you, I would have." I pull away just enough for her to see my eyes. "*God*, I missed you so much." My thumb wanders over her brow, the curve of her jaw, the outline of her smile. "You're my sweetheart, you know."

"Yeah?"

"Yeah," I nod, cupping a hand around her neck and dragging her lips to mine, kissing her slow and deep—with all the tenderness she deserves, and all the love that's in my heart. The slide of our lips. The tangle of our tongues. The taste of her releases a hunger and I urge her body closer, one hand slipping through her hair, guiding her mouth. She moans and I think I do, too. I'm not sure because I'm lost in her taste, her scent, the feel of her soft skin beneath my fingers. Her hands roam my back, grazing the waistband of my jeans and I arch against her, needing her to touch me. Gradually, I become aware of the sound of voices nearby and the smell of rotten garbage, and think to myself, *not here. I don't want to do this here.*

"Ember," I pant against her lips. "Come home with me?" She gifts me with a silent nod that completes a scenario I've imagined in my head a million times in the last three years—and I'm high as a fucking kite. My hand finds its way to hers. "Let's go, Mickey."

chapter forty-one
Ember

THE CAB SWERVES through traffic but Vance's hand remains tightly wrapped around mine. My head rests on his shoulder, his fingers tracing patterns on my arm. Every now and then, I glance up at him. His profile is relaxed, mouth curled into a smile. Me, I'm smiling so big my face hurts. I haven't felt this happy in...over three years to be exact. As these thoughts dominate my mind, I snuggle closer. I want to make sure he's real, that I'm not dreaming.

"Are you trying to burrow under my skin?" he teases, and I laugh, hooking my leg over his thigh.

"I might be. Is that a problem for you?"

He slips a finger under my chin, bringing my eyes up to his. All playfulness dissipates as his gaze sears mine. "No, Mickey. It's not. Considering you've been under my skin since the moment I met you." He kisses me once and I sigh, laying my head back on his shoulder.

The taxi pulls up to his apartment building and Vance whips out a fifty dollar bill, paying the cabbie without bothering to wait for change.

"You gave him a forty dollar tip," I marvel as he leads me inside and up to his floor. "He looked like he just won the lottery."

"Good. Now he knows how I fucking feel." He unlocks the door, grinning as we step over the threshold. "This is it." My eyes wander the room consisting of a long black sofa and matching chair, both covered with clothes and remote controls. A rectangular table in the corner is crammed with computer equipment. Framed photographs and paintings I assume were created by his mom fill a second wall.

"Wow." I look back at him. "It's...it's...sparse."

He chuckles softly. "There you are." He smiles, eyes glittering. "God, I missed that. The way you cut right to the chase." We stare at each other for the space of several breaths before I turn toward the wall filled with paintings. I edge closer, wanting to examine their finer detail. "Those are some of my mom's pieces."

"I could tell right away. They're reminiscent of the style I saw when we visited her." The soft palette of a beach landscape draws my focus. "You must really miss her."

"I do." Vance crosses the room to stand beside me, his gaze on the picture. "It was really hard for her in the end. Her muscles had weakened to the point where she couldn't even feed herself. It was...painful...to see her like that." His breathing changes and I let my hand find his, interlocking our fingers. "After a while everything became too much for her. Her immune system had weakened and she ended up contracting pneumonia." His eyes drift to mine, a flash of sadness amidst the calm blue. "The mom that I knew and loved was long gone. Her spirit was already somewhere else, you know? And...I'm glad she's not suffering anymore." He clears his throat and gestures toward the sofa. "Sit down for a sec."

"Okay." I push aside clothes and wipe the wetness gathering in the corner of my eye.

Vance returns carrying the painting from his house that I admired all those years ago. Setting it against the couch, he smiles. "This is for you."

"What? No. I couldn't—"

"Yes, you can. I want you to have it." He takes my hand in both of his and gazes down at me. The unshed emotion in his expression makes my heart want to climb out of my chest. "You and my mom, you would've really liked each other. I can picture the two of you talking about art for hours at a time. I think it would make her happy for you to have this." He stares at his thumb trailing back and forth over my knuckles. "She may not have known who you were that day. But she took to you." His eyes find mine. "It's kind of hard not to." He pulls his hand away to bring it to my cheek. "You have this way of breaking down walls, Ember. You fucking took a sledgehammer to mine." Vance shakes his head on a quiet laugh. "All those days of not living caught up to me when I met you. But you...you opened my eyes and forced me to look. You made me want to live. You saved me, Ember."

A loud breath shuffles between us as he exhales. "I'm through letting fear and worry consume me. I'm done with it. I want my story to be different. I mean, I still have to get those tests done periodically and that won't change. But...if everything goes to hell, I want you by my side...until you can't be anymore. And I know that's selfish. But I want you, Ember." His voice softens, eyes fixated on mine. "There's nothing in my life I want more than I want you."

"Show me," I whisper.

Vance hauls me to my feet, gripping my cheeks as his lips crash against mine. Dizzy with bottled-up emotion, we're like two meteors colliding. My hands on his forearms, his biceps, his shoulders. His tongue in my mouth, licking across my jaw, sliding down my neck. My fingers wander higher, slipping into his long hair and tugging gently. He groans, spurring me to do it again before some other force takes over me—driven by his clean shaven smell, the taste of him, by how much I've missed him. I spin us around and push him down on the couch, straddling his legs and feeling the hardness between them. His tongue plunges deep into my mouth as if he's trying to crawl inside of me. And God, do I want him inside of me—I want him everywhere. I rub against him to show him how much and he growls, the sound vibrating between us as our kiss grows more urgent. My hands drift under his t-shirt. The solid planes of muscle move beneath my fingers and I'm itching to touch him, to put my lips all over his skin.

"Vance." I break the kiss, panting, and yank on the edge of his shirt. "Take this off."

"Anything for you, Mickey." His lips curve into the sexiest grin and my heart gallops in my chest. I can hardly fathom it—the want I feel for him—the love I have for him. I touch a finger to my swollen lips as he grasps the seam of his shirt, lifting it up and over his head. My eyes drop, drinking in the ripples and dips of his chest, the light trail of hair disappearing into the waistband of his jeans. But then I stop. My gaze flashing wide on a small tattoo of Mickey Mouse under his ribs, my name in script wrapped around him as if in orbit. My mouth opens on a gasp. I reach out with a shaky hand to gently trace the outline of the curled letters.

"What...when...did you get that?"

"The day after I left you." He brushes a strand of hair from my face, his touch soft. "I wanted a reminder of the girl I loved...and what I gave up—"

"No one has ever done anything like this for me before." I don't wait for a response before I grab onto the material of my top, sliding it up and over my shoulders. I'm not wearing a bra and Vance's eyes fall to my chest, my nipples drawing tight under his gaze. He reaches out, gliding the backs of his fingers over the hard tip and I shiver.

"Fucking stunning," he murmurs, leaning up and dragging his tongue across the firm peak, making me tremble. His wet lips cling first to one nipple, then the other, until I'm writhing against him.

"Vance...bedroom," I moan, arching my breast into his mouth, my head lolling back. "I want...." My words trail off as his warm breath gusts over my skin.

"What do you want, Ember?"

I let my brain float down to earth and peer at his face, alight with anticipation. "I want you to do dirty things to me."

He tucks his lip between his teeth then lets it go. "How dirty?" He grins.

"Filthy." He tries to lift me up then, but the position we're in is awkward and we end up tipping over onto the carpet, laughing. I grab for the button on his jeans, wanting to rip it from the hole.

"Hey," he reaches between us to latch onto my wrist, "I want to take it slow. We have a lot of time to make up for."

But then I surprise myself, and I think him. "We can go slow later. Right now I can't wait." I swing my leg out from underneath his and roll over, pushing myself to a standing position. "I don't know my way around this place, so you'll have to show me where your bedroom is. And make it fast."

Thrusting himself up from the floor, he catches me off guard by scooping me under my knees and into his arms. His breath hovers an inch from my mouth. "I want to do everything imaginable to you tonight. Are you ready for that?" Fevered eyes dart to my lips, staring at them until I'm about to combust.

"*Vance.*" I'm practically begging now. "Are you going to kiss me or what?"

He smirks, setting me down. "I'm going to do a lot more than kiss you, Mickey."

"Well?"

"Wait a minute." He draws back, teasing. "You're not using me are you? Because I don't do one-night stands."

I lift my chin, an uncontrollable smile tipping my lips. "That's good. Because I'm not a one-night stand kind of a girl."

"Oh yeah?" He matches the challenge in my eyes. "What kind of a girl are you?"

My fingertips drift over the hair at his temple, brushing it aside. "I'm a forever kind of girl."

"Well, you're in luck then." He catches my hand, bringing it to his lips for a kiss. "It just so happens I'm in the market for one of those."

epilogue
Vance
One year after...

"I CAN'T BELIEVE you're really doing this," Julian whispers so only I can hear. "And I can't believe I'm actually going to witness it." Glancing about the living room of Chris's house, we watch our dad and Ember's mom milling around each other in a pattern of subtle avoidance. "This is kind of like an intervention, isn't it?" he whispers again, cupping a hand over my ear.

"Yeah, complete with Twinkies," I add, grinning at the arrangement of pastries Ember bought at the bakery. The platter at the end of the table she stacked high with golden Twinkies just for me. I fucking love her.

Julian looks over at Ember, smiling at us as she carries another tray from the kitchen. "God that girl loves you. I can practically feel it seeping from her pores. And I don't get it," he muses. "I'm the charming one." I shoot him a mock glare. "Kidding, kidding."

Our father rounds the corner and runs right smack into Ember's mom. He clears his throat and stares at her sweater, muttering, "Dolores."

"Charles," she responds, finding a spot on his shoe that needs polishing.

"Well, *that* was awkward," Julian remarks, and I chuckle.

"Nothing wrong with a little awkward. Anyhow, Dad mentioned things were fine. They're cordial now, and he's dating that woman from work so everything is cool." I glance up to Dad heading in our direction, his stare determined and focused entirely on me. "Maybe I spoke too fucking soon."

"Vance, can I talk to you upstairs for a minute?"

"Uh, sure Dad." I glare back at a smug Julian as I follow Dad upstairs, wondering what this is all about. He makes a right into the guest room at the end of the hall and gestures to a winged-back chair in the corner.

"Sit down, son." With a smile that doesn't look quite right on his mouth, he leans against a nearby dresser, biting at the corner of his lip. In a span of about ten seconds, he crosses and uncrosses his arms four times.

"Dad, what is it? Just...spit it out already. You're making me uncomfortable."

Lifting a hand to drag it through his thick hair, he moves to the other side of the dresser to retrieve a package wrapped in brown paper. He holds it up and places it on my lap, coughing into his closed fist. A white envelope is taped to the top with my name.

My eyes flick to the handwriting then back to him. "What is this?"

"Well...when I was cleaning out the basement last week, there was a big box in the back that somehow I'd missed when I was packing your mother's things up." He swallows anxiously, his voice unsteady. "I found this inside. Initially, I was going to ship it to you in New York. But then figured since I was seeing you, I'd just bring it.

"Okaaaay."

"Right." He shoves his hands in the pockets of his suit pants. "I'll leave you to it, then." His eyes dart around the room before he edges toward the door.

"Dad, wait," I call out. He turns around, hesitance spreading across his face. "Stay." Then I clarify. "If you want to, I mean."

"Thank you," he utters on an exhale of breath. He takes a seat on the bed, watching me as I rip apart the paper. When all the wrapping has fallen to the carpet, I stare at the painting of my mother and me, and my throat burns.

"This is that picture," I say softly. "The one that—"

"I took of you and your mother right after you came back from the karate tournament. You were about twelve then, I think. You were both all smiles, and she was so proud of you. I guess she decided to paint it."

I trace over the colors and lines with my fingertip, the oval shape of my mother's face, her steel blue eyes that resembled mine. "I don't get how she always captured so much feeling in her paintings. She looks so—"

"In love with everything about her son," he interjects and my head snaps up, meeting his determined gaze. "She loved you so much, Vance. The boy that you were, the man she knew you would become. And you did her proud, son." He takes two steps to reach me, clasping a hand on my shoulder. "You did us both proud." Clearing what I gather is emotion from his throat, he ambles toward the door.

"Hey, Dad?"

One foot in the hallway, he stops at the sound of my voice. "Yeah?"

"Thanks." I catch his smile in the air before he disappears.

Laying the painting against the closet door, I tear off the white envelope addressed in my mother's perfect script. I thumb it open and lean back against the chair.

Dear Vance,

I wanted to write this letter to you before my hand got too shaky and my memory decided to leave me again. Because as much as it scares me, I know that it will. I just don't know when.

But I needed you to know that while my mind will eventually fail me, my heart will carry you in it wherever I go. It will remember for me the things that I no longer can—like that freckle under your eye that you used to try to rub off when you were little because you thought it was dirt, or your affinity for hiding Twinkies where you thought I'd never find them. The pride in your smile when you got your black belt, and the absolute delight on your face when your father bought you your first guitar.

What will stick with me most though, I think, is the way you always looked at me with wonder and interest as I read to you for hours at a time. Even when my throat was hoarse and I thought I couldn't go on, the moment the word 'more' left your mouth, I somehow found the strength to keep going. I hope someday you'll pass that gift on to your own children.

I want that same strength for you now…to keep going. Don't live your life worrying. Keep looking forward my sweet boy because tomorrow will always come. And I wish you a million of those tomorrows filled with all of the happiness that you brought into my life. Being your mother brought me more joy than you will ever know.

I love you,

Mom

P.S. Go easy on your Dad, okay? He's going to slip up and make mistakes. Help him learn from them. Oh, and eat a carrot every now and then. I promise it won't hurt you.

Tears soaking the paper, I stare at my mother's words. Grateful for the time I did have with her—for everything she taught me—for her love that is so much a part of who I am. My eyes fall closed as I press the letter to my chest, letting go of the past and embracing my future. Ready to move forward. Done wishing I could live my life in reverse.

"Vance?" At the sound of Ember's voice, I open my eyes. "You okay?"

"Yeah." A smile appears out of nowhere, surprising even me. "I think I am." As I hold out my arms, Ember walks over and falls into my lap, gazing at the letter. "From my mom," I point out, and she kisses away the tears from my cheek.

"Your dad told me to come up. He thought you might need me."

"Did he now?" I snake my arms around her waist, wanting nothing more than to feel her body against mine.

"Yes. He loves you, you know." Ember says this as if she's known it all along and I'm just catching up. Maybe I am. It takes a while to catch up to life sometimes.

"I do know," I admit, caressing the small of her back. "Even though it took me a while to figure it out because I can be fucking pigheaded when I want to be."

Her lips tuck into a smirk. "You? *Nooooo*." She brings a hand around to cradle my head and draws me closer. "So are you ready for this?"

"I am," I reply, peppering kisses to the corner of her soft, pliable mouth. "Thinking of backing out?"

"Nope, I'm good." She nods her head toward the door. "But I think we should go eat and get some fortification. We're going to need it."

I grin, giving her ass a squeeze. "I'm sorry, all I heard was fornication."

"Oh God." She laughs. "There will be plenty of that...after."

I sneak under her shirt, my fingertips grazing her smooth skin. "Is that a promise?"

"That," she kisses me hard on the lips then slides off my lap, "is a guarantee. Now come on, let's go. Time's a wastin'.'"

She's right, and I no longer want to waste another minute of it.

Ember holds out her hand to help me stand, closing her fingers around mine. I place the letter next to the painting and together we head off to join everyone in the living room. As we reach the bottom step, the front door bursts open and Riley runs inside. Red and orange leaves stick to his hair and shoes. That rosy-cheeked face scanning the room until his big blue eyes zero in on Ember and me.

"You're here!" Riley makes a beeline for Ember, bowling her over with a hug.

"Hey, Riles." She bends down to greet him, his tiny face buried in her long hair.

"Well...I guess I've been replaced," I mutter dejectedly. Ember and Riley glance up at me.

"Never." Ember reassures me with a bright smile before looking to Riley. "Right, little guy?"

"Never," he repeats, trying to replicate her expression with his slanted grin.

"Hey, you lost a tooth." His smile grows as he taps one finger against the empty space between his teeth.

"I did. And the tooth fairy came. I got ten dollars!"

"Holy cow." I gape at Chris and his dad. "Talk about inflation." Everyone laughs as the screen door flies open again. This time, Ember's dad walks in with Avery. His hair sticks up in a million directions, the buttons on his shirt off by one.

"I'm sorry we're late," he mumbles, wiping sweat from his brow. "The convention ran over." Avery turns around with a hand on her hip, piercing her father with a pointed glare.

"*Dad.*" She starts out angry, but then shakes her head and smiles. "I just spent three hours at a woodworking convention in Manhattan. I need alcohol." Avery's mom throws her a stern glance and purses her lips. "Don't look at me like that, Mom. You know what I'm talking about."

All is quiet until Riley climbs out of Ember's arms and shrieks. "When is it time? When is it time?"

Avery blows her blonde bangs away from her eyes as she stalks toward her sister, a question in her gaze. "Are you really still doing this?"

Ember reaches out for my hand and squeezes. "We are."

Her smile softens and she touches Ember's arm. "You know Zack is smiling big right now. Happy Birthday, Em."

"Happy Birthday, Ave."

epilogue
Ember

EVERYONE IS GATHERED around the trailer, and what a fabulous group they are. My mother, dressed to the nines in her Donna Karan suit bites a single manicured fingernail, while my dad fiddles with a button on his plaid shirt. Still, I know somewhere deep down their happiness overshadows the nerves they might be feeling—because I think this is as important for them as it is for me.

My gaze wanders to Julian and Avery who are goofing off, her flirty eyes captivating him just like old times. Next to them, Chris has an arm slung around his new girlfriend, Erika, his expression bright under the October sun. I catch a glimpse of Chris's parents gawking at the two of them with happy smiles bursting from their lips. Then there's Riley, jumping up and down like a pogo stick in front of Troy and his boyfriend, Quinn, as they all make silly faces at one another.

To the right of the crowd stands Vance's dad, finishing up a conversation with his son—the absolute love of my life. As I watch them, my vision clouds but I can't help it. Seeing them together and close again makes my heart fill up with joy. I'm not sure either one of them realized how much they needed each other.

Vance glances over and catches me mid-stare. His dad looks up and smiles, giving him a nudge in my direction. "We've got a pretty big audience over there," he comments on his way, gesturing toward our big family. "It feels like we're getting married or something." One of his eyebrows shifts ever so slightly but I don't miss it.

"Don't get any ideas, Davenport. I'm not ready to get married."

"Yet," he mumbles loud enough for me to hear, and my heart beams. "By the way," he adds, "if you're holding out for me to climb up a fire escape with flowers and an umbrella, don't think I won't fucking do it." He grins. "If that's what it takes."

Have I mentioned I love him? *I love him.*

Once all the harnesses and parachutes are checked and they give us the okay, we wave to everyone and follow the guides over to the plane. My feet slow, my stomach suddenly a ripple of nerves. I take a few deep breaths then turn to Vance. As if he senses my apprehension, he grabs my hand and tightens his fingers around mine. "We're really doing this. Aren't we?"

A smile that somehow calms me and settles my belly forms on his lips. "We are indeed, Mickey. And...." He stops walking and lifts his other hand to caress my cheek. "I want you to know that being with you makes me happy. A happiness I wasn't sure was real or even possible for me."

My skin warms to his touch and his words. "Why does that sound like something you say to someone before you never see them again?"

"Fuck no," he retorts, and I grin at his choice language. "We're jumping together and we're landing together. Just remember two things. One...breathe. And two...." He looks at me then, *really* looks at me, so much love shining in his eyes that my heart nearly explodes from it. "I'll catch you if you fall. I promise."

And I know he will.

acknowledgements

First and foremost, to my husband, Richard, and my kids, Isabella and Richie for putting up with me while I was writing this book. For the days I was glued to my computer for hours at a time, when I needed to type just one more sentence. To my daughter for bringing me paper and a pen when inspiration hit in the shower, which it often did. Thank you for being so incredibly patient with me. Here's to believing in signs, and thank you for believing in me. I love you.

To Nikki Groom for your friendship. I can hardly believe it's only been three years. It seems like an eternity, and I mean that in the best way. Two crazy souls that were meant to be friends. I cherish you.

To Cheryl McIntyre and Dawn McIntyre for just about everything. For dropping whatever you're doing to help, for responding to my gazillion emails, for all of your support and feedback with my novel. But most of all for your friendship. Lots of love.

To AJ Warner. You're the biscuit to my raisin. I love you to the moon and back.

To Cristin Ebright, Rachel Cressin, and Kimberley Barrois (TBM). Thank you ladies for making me smile and laugh every day. Smitty would be proud. Love you lots!

To all of my author pals, and I'm talking to you Cheryl McIntyre, Sunniva Dee, Monica James, Vi Keeland, Liv Morris, Kasia Bacon-Buczkowska, and Isobel Starling. Thank you for being a constant source of inspiration, and for your friendship, support and encouragement. I love you guys!

To Isobel Starling for coming up with the fabulous bar name, Blue Monday. It was absolutely perfect for this story.

To Natalie and the ladies at Love Between the Sheets for sticking by my side along this path, for your friendship, and for always helping me manage my book life.

To Sommer Stein, for designing a cover that is so perfect for my story. While it took a while to get to it, I think the end result was worth all the aggravation I put you through. I appreciate your talent and your patience.

To Angela McLaurin, this is number seven, baby! You always know the way to make my novel sparkle and shine, and I thank you. Love you!

To Lea Burn, for all your helpful comments and suggestions, for being available when I have a million questions and need to talk something out. I'm thankful that we're on the same page and that we both strive for perfection. I appreciate you so much.

To all of the bloggers, the ones who have been with me since I started this amazing journey, and the ones who have joined along the way. Thank you for your willingness to read, review, and share my work. For taking time out of your hectic lives to support me in my endeavors. I do not take that for granted and I know you are an integral part of the world learning about my books.

To Erika Gutermuth, Andromeda Jewls, Cheri Grand Anderman, Caroline Hattrich, Heather Reddy Andres, Barb Johnson, Cristina Arpin, Kizzy Williams, Emily Proffitt Plice, and Colleen Albert. Thank you for your passion about my books, for standing by me as I navigate this journey of writing, and for your love of the written word that rivals mine. I'm very grateful for your friendship and send you lots of love.

Finally, to my readers. I hope you enjoy this novel and these characters, and that in some way this story resonates with you. I am incredibly grateful for all of your support and enthusiasm about my work. Thank you for allowing me to live out my dream.

about the author

Beth Michele is the author of *Love Love, Lovely, Scarred Beautiful, Finding Autumn, Rex, For the Love of Raindrops,* and *Life in Reverse.* She is a Connecticut native who loves spending time with her husband and two children. If you can't find her, though, she's probably hiding out with her laptop or her kindle somewhere quiet, preferably a spot overlooking the ocean. She has an affinity for Twizzlers, is a hopeless romantic, and a happily ever after fanatic.

I would LOVE to hear from you,
so please feel free to reach out to Me:

Email: beth@bethmichele.com
Website: www.bethmichele.com
Twitter: www.twitter.com/bethmichele8
Bookbub: www.bookbub.com/authors/beth-michele
Goodreads: www.goodreads.com/author/show/6915179.Beth_Michele
Facebook: www.facebook.com/pages/Beth-Michele-Author
Booktropolous Social: https://goo.gl/E287rQ

Want to hear about new books, giveaways, receive teasers and excerpts? Sign up for my mailing list! http://eepurl.com/Q1Ky1

also by beth michele

Love, Love

Lovely

Scarred Beautiful

Finding Autumn

Rex

For the Love of Raindrops

Life in Reverse

Made in the USA
Monee, IL
20 March 2020

23641291R00182